Khu:
A Tale of Ancient Egypt

By Jocelyn Murray

ISBN: 1497524156

ISBN 13: 9781497524156

Library of Congress Control Number: 2014906497

CreateSpace Independent Publishing Platform
North Charleston, South Carolina

FOR MONICA
memoria in aeterna

Last night I crossed the desert sand
Where ruins lay upon the land
Where moon-glossed relics looked dismayed
Their stony grandeur now decayed
Where myths and monsters lay in a heap
Their fallen kings long gone to sleep

Jocelyn Murray, "The Desert Sand"

*Save me from those who deal wounds, the slayers whose
fingers are sharp,
Who deal out pain, who decapitate those who follow after
Osiris;
They shall not have power over me,
And I will not fall into their cauldrons*

Excerpt of Spell 17
R. O. Faulkner, trans. *The Ancient Egyptian Book of the Dead*

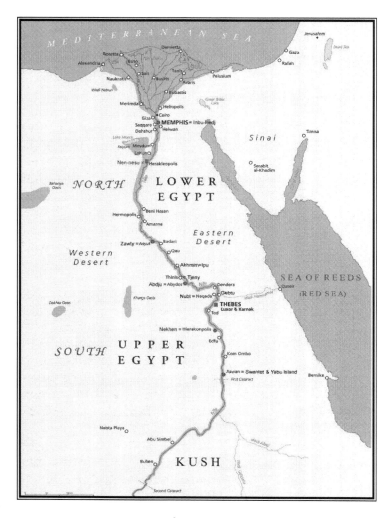

Map of Ancient Egypt

© Peter Hermes Furian / Fotolia

PLACES

Most of the names of the places in this novel are ancient equivalents of known sites based on the major cult centers and provinces of ancient Egypt. For other places, the author has used their commonly known or widely recognizable names, in an effort to reduce confusion and based on simple personal preference. While many of the names have evolved throughout the millennia, it is what lies beneath the shifting sands of time that is most intriguing: the histories, myths and legends hidden or buried within the artifacts and ruins themselves.

Abdju—now known as Abydos. It was one of the oldest sacred cities of the ancients, and the cult center of the god Osiris, as well as an important site of many temples.

Abu Simbel—located on the west bank of the Nile in the land of Kush. Abu Simbel was a sacred place where Ramesses II built two temples directly into the sandstone cliffs by the river, during the 19th Dynasty of the New Kingdom.

Deir el-Bahari—the mortuary-temple complex on the western bank of the Nile that includes the temple-tomb of King Nebhepetre Mentuhotep II.

Gebtu—now known as Qift. Its Greek name was Coptos, also spelled Koptos. Gebtu was the main cult center of the god Min. It also marked the beginning of the ancient caravan trade route that leads to the western coast of the Red Sea at Quseer. The caravan route follows a dry river bed known as Wadi Hammamat. Gebtu is the shortest point from the Nile to the Red Sea.

Inbu-Hedj—known by its Greek name Memphis; also known in ancient times as Inebou-Hedjou, Aneb-Hetch, Djed-Sut, Ankh-Tawy and Men-nefer. Inbu-Hedj is located by the modern-day town of Mit Rahina. It was the cult center of the god Ptah. It was also the seat of power during the time of Egypt's Old Kingdom.

Ipu—now known as Akhmim. The ancient Greeks called it Khemmis (also Chemmis and Panopolis). Ipu was the site of an ancient necropolis on the east bank of the Nile. It was also one of the cult centers of the god Min.

Kush—later known as Nubia. Kush (Kingdom of Kush, land of Kush) included territories in what is now known as Southern Egypt, Sudan, and part of Ethiopia.

Nekhen—known by its Greek name Hierakonpolis, it was the cult center of the god Horus. Located in Upper Egypt, Nekhen was called "City of Falcons," and sometimes interchangeably called "City of Hawks."

Nen-nesu—the site that is near the modern day city of Beni Suef (also spelled Bani Suwayf) in Lower Egypt. In ancient times it was also known as Henen-nesut or Hwt-nen-nesu (Greek names Heracleopolis, Herakleopolis, or Herakleopolis Magna). It was the cult center of the ram-god Heryshef. Nen-nesu was Lower Egypt's seat of power during part of the First Intermediate Period.

Nile—Nile River and River Nile are used interchangeably in this novel. The Nile was simply called *Iteru* meaning "river" by the ancient Egyptians.

Nubt—known as Naqada, it was also known by its Greek name Ombos. Nubt was the cult center of the god Seth.

Quseer—the site of a remote outpost and an important port on the western shores of the Red Sea in ancient Egypt. It is also written as Al-Quseir and Al-Qusayr.

Sea of Reeds—now known as the Red Sea.

Sopdet—now known as the star Sirius (Greek name Sothis). It is the brightest of all the stars in the sky. The ancient Egyptians based their calendar on the heliacal rising of Sirius which always occurred just before the Nile's annual flooding. Sopdet was personified as a goddess who was known as "Bringer of the New Year and Nile Flood." Her annual appearance in the sky was welcomed with great joy and anticipation.

Swentet—now known as Aswan, previously written as Assuan. It was the cult center of Anqet, goddess of fertility and the Nile at Aswan.

Thebes—the ancient province that includes modern day Luxor and Karnak in Upper Egypt. Thebes was the Greek name for the ancient Egyptian city of Waset. It was the cult center of the god Amun, and the Theban Triad which included Amun, Mut and Khonsu. Thebes was Upper Egypt's seat of power during the First Intermediate Period, and continued to be Egypt's capital during part of the Middle Kingdom and New Kingdom, thus earning it the title "City of the Scepter."

Tjeny—now known as Thinis, also written as This. Tjeny was the capital seat of power in the early dynasties of ancient Egypt.

Wadi Hammamat—the dry riverbed that served as an important trade and caravan route, being the shortest path from the Nile at Gebtu (Qift) to the Red Sea at Quseer. The Wadi Hammamat cuts through quarries and mines that were used in ancient times.

Yabu—now known as Elephantine Island. Its ancient name is also written as Abu and Yebu, both of which also mean "elephant." The island is located in the Nile River within the Aswan area. It was the cult center of the ram-headed god Khnum who was worshipped as part of the triad that included his wife Satis and their daughter Anqet.

Zawty—now known as Asyut, also spelled Assiut; also known as Səyáwt during ancient times. Its Greek names were Lycopolis, Lykopolis, Lycon or Lyco. It was the cult center of the funerary gods Anubis and Wepwawet.

GODS OF ANCIENT EGYPT
MENTIONED IN THIS BOOK

Ammit—crocodile-headed, soul-eating female demon with the upper body of a lion and the lower body of a hippopotamus. Ammit devoured the hearts of the dead who were deemed unworthy of eternal life. Her name means "Devourer."

Amun—king of the gods and one of the creator gods. Amun was the patron god of Thebes. His name means "Hidden" or "Invisible One" because his spirit was believed to be present everywhere, like the wind which symbolized him. Amun was often represented in human form wearing the tall double-plumed headdress—Two Feathers Crown. Together with his wife Mut and son Khonsu, he forms the Triad of Thebes. Amun was later merged with the sun-god Re and came to be known as Amun-Re when he was worshiped as principal god of all Egypt.

Anubis—god of the dead and patron of embalmers. The jackal-headed god Anubis weighed the hearts of the dead against a feather symbolizing truth, during their final judgment before the throne of Osiris. Anubis was also depicted in the full-animal form of a jackal. He was revered as a guardian of tombs, and oversaw funerary rites, embalming and mummification. His cult center was in Zawty, or modern day Asyut.

Apep—demon/god of all evil, and embodiment of all that was wicked. Apep was depicted as a very large water serpent. He was the evil brother of the sun-god Re. He lived in the darkness of the Underworld where he ruled over an army of demons, and was known as "Destroyer," as well as "Eater of Souls."

Bastet—cat goddess who was the patron of Lower Egypt. She was the daughter of the god Re, and the wife of Ptah. Bastet was depicted as a woman with the head of a cat, or in the full-animal form of a cat. She was the goddess of the home, cats, protection, love, joy, music and dance, and was also believed to aid in the growth of crops.

Hapi—god of the Nile inundation who oversaw the river's annual flooding.

Hathor—one of the fertility gods, Hathor was a mother goddess of love, joy, music and childbirth, and patron of women. She was depicted as a woman wearing the headdress of cow horns with a moon-disk between them, or in the full-animal form of a cow. Hathor's main cult center was in Dendera.

Heryshef—ram-god who was the ruler of the riverbanks. Heryshef was the patron of Nen-nesu in Lower Egypt.

Horus—falcon-headed god of the sky, son of Osiris and Isis. His name means "Distant One" also "He Who is High." Horus was the god of war and protection, and represented world order. He was the patron god of Nekhen in Upper Egypt. The Eye of Horus emblem was ubiquitous in ancient Egypt, and symbolized strength and protection.

Isis—goddess of motherhood, fertility and healing. Isis was the wife of Osiris, and mother of Horus. She was revered for her protection and magical powers.

Khonsu—moon god, and son of Amun and Mut. He was worshiped in Thebes as part of the Theban Triad.

Min—one of the male fertility gods. He was also the god of the eastern desert, and was believed to be the protector of gold mines, quarries and caravan routes that ran through the eastern desert region. Min was the son of Osiris and Isis, and brother of Horus.

Mut—wife of Amun, mother goddess, and queen of goddesses. Mut was usually depicted in human form wearing the vulture headdress. Along with Amun and Khonsu, she was worshipped as part of the Theban Triad.

Osiris—god of the dead and the Underworld. Osiris was the patron of Abdju (Abydos), and was revered for his life-giving contribution to the land's vegetation. He was represented in mummified human form, holding the crook and flail, and wearing the *Atef* feathered crown on his head.

Ptah—god of craftsmen and principle god of Inbu-Hedj (Memphis). Ptah was also revered as a patron of royalty. He was depicted in human mummified form holding a staff.

Re—sun-god who sailed across the sky each day in his golden Barque of a Million Years, then on through the Underworld in his night barque. Re is one of the creator gods who was often depicted in human form with the head of a falcon wearing a sun-disc headdress. Re was later called Amun-Re when he was merged with the god Amun to become lord of the gods. His main cult center was in the city of Heliopolis in Lower Egypt.

Sekhmet—lion-headed goddess of war, battle and vengeance, whose name means "Powerful One." Sekhmet was the wife of Ptah and daughter of Re. She was believed to have caused and cured epidemics as well.

Seth—god of the desert and storms, and evil brother and murderer of Osiris. Seth and Horus were eternal rivals.

Thoth—god of wisdom and patron of scribes. He was depicted as a man with the head of an ibis, as well as in the full-animal form of an ibis or baboon. Thoth recorded the verdict of Osiris during the judgment of the dead after the Weighing of the Heart proceeding.

Thoueris—one of the fertility mother goddesses depicted as a pregnant hippopotamus. She was closely associated with Isis and Hathor. It was believed that Thoueris ensured safe childbirth.

Wepwawet—one of the funerary gods, he was also the god of war. Wepwawet was the brother of Anubis, and usually depicted in full-animal form of a wolf or other canine.

ONE

On the east bank of the River Nile, where the papyrus reeds grow in abundance and the lotus flowers bloom, a boy was hiding. He had made the long journey south to Thebes from his village in the north, first on a small papyrus raft that had fallen apart after a few days, and then on foot. He walked for days on bare feet, keeping to the riverbank, pausing only to rest when his legs could no longer carry him, or to eat whatever fish he was able to spear with a makeshift lance, or to nibble on the ripened fruit that had fallen from the doum palms growing beyond the reeds in the lush floodplains. And deeply fatigued, he had fallen ill with a high fever after he had finally crawled into a small space between the tall papyrus reeds that would shade him from the sun's early morning rays, and keep him safely hidden.

Only the night herons spotted the bedraggled child with their red eyes, their light gray and white plumage softly luminous in the pale moonlight. The birds moved away from the boy, stepping closer to the river on short yellow legs where they came to stand still at the edge of the water. They waited quietly, hunched and brooding as they ambushed their prey with sharp black beaks, catching the silvery fish as they swam just beneath the water's surface. But the boy noticed nothing except for his own racking pain, for the fever had left him delirious and shivering long past the darkest hours of the night until he had at last succumbed to a fitful sleep.

Early the next morning three servant women who worked at the nearby palace were gathering some of the reeds and lotus flowers that grew by the water when they came upon the sleeping boy.

"What is it Mesi?" one of the three asked when she saw the first woman stop suddenly and turn to them, raising a finger to her lips in a gesture of silence.

Mesi did not reply. She only shook her head and motioned the other two over.

The sun's early morning rays were slanting through the scattered trees and over the reeds by the riverbank, setting everything aglow. The servant women would never even have suspected that the boy lay asleep nearby if Mesi had not almost stepped on his small frame. The women crept closer around thick clusters of flowering plants and tall grasses, eager to see what had startled Mesi. Then all three stared down at the sleeping boy who lay curled in a fetal position in the center of a bunch of reeds. He had fashioned a kind of nest for himself, away from the water, and away from prying eyes, until now. Perspiration beaded his forehead, and his skin took on a sallow pallor. His breathing was shallow and labored. He looked small and weak.

"He is ill," Mesi whispered as the boy began to stir.

The boy sensed himself being watched, much like a gazelle senses the presence of a lion. And fluttering his eyelids, he then opened them and fixed his feeble gaze on the women servants.

All three of them gasped.

Never before in their lives had they seen eyes like his. They were like the eyes of a cat, gold with speckles of green. The women stared in wonder at the boy, captivated by him. His almond-shaped eyes had a pale, translucent and luminous quality to them. They were a piercing shade of golden quartz with bits of malachite like the gemstones used to make precious amulets and jewelry treasured by the people. He was beautiful.

"He is the *One*," one of them uttered in astonishment. "The one in the prophesies... he must be," she said, unable to tear her gaze from the boy's eyes.

"He is beautiful," another one whispered.

The boy stirred again and mumbled something incoherent. He was still in the clutches of the fever, although it had subsided a bit with the night's retreat. His body ached, and his eyes burned with the effort of opening them. All his strength had long since drained away, and he lay helpless as a newborn lamb.

"It is alright, child," Mesi told him soothingly as she bent down closer to his side. "You are safe here."

The boy calmed down and relaxed his thin frame, exhaling quietly and closing his eyes once again. The three women took note of his blood-stained, dirt-encrusted clothing. He wore a linen shirt in the style of a short tunic over a loin cloth. Both had been white at some point, but had changed to a filthy-brown. The blood staining his clothing had long since dried to a thick crust, which also soiled much of his body. His head was shaved except for one long plaited lock that hung to one side, as was the custom for children who had not yet reached puberty.

The women exchanged worried glances, wondering what possibly could have happened to the boy. A red-tailed hawk screeched above as it glided under the cloudless sky, and one of the women shuddered. Dragonflies and butterflies fluttered their iridescent wings by the shoreline where rocks jutted out from the Nile's murky depths.

"Let us carry him to the palace," Mesi suggested, and the others agreed.

Together the three women cleared away some of the reeds and took the boy to the palace that was set farther back from the floodplain. Mesi—the strongest of the three—lifted his small frame while the other two carried the baskets with the lotus flowers and reeds.

"Khu..."

The boy heard a sweet voice whisper to him. It seemed to float from someplace far above where he slept. He dreamed of fields of wheat and barley stretching as far as the eye could see. They rippled softly in a breeze, like golden waves in a sea that caught the light of the midday sun.

"Khu..."

The voice again. Beautiful, melodic and sweet like a juicy ripened fig. He walked in those amber fields searching for the voice that called to him, wading through the lush crop that was ready for the harvest. The sun warmed his skin as he ran his hands over the tall stalks whose bearded spikes tickled his belly like fur.

"Khu..."

The boy stirred, leaving the amber fields behind. He moaned softly in his sleep as he sought the voice that beckoned him once again. Then slowly he opened his eyes with the effort of one who had lain ill for days. At first his vision was blurred with sleep. But the figure sitting by his side came into focus as he blinked and sighed from the low reed mat serving as his bed. The mat was stretched over a wood frame, and covered with a thin woolen mattress and linen sheet. His head was supported by a wooden headrest and cushioned by a small pillow.

"Khu..." the woman smiled when the boy finally fixed his gaze upon her. "You are Khu," she stated with a proud upward tilt of her chin. "Protected One," she continued. "*My* protected one."

The boy did not reply at first. He believed himself to be dreaming still. He did not recognize the beautiful woman with the melodic voice. Nor was he familiar with his opulent surroundings. He had been born to a simple peasant family who lived in one of the many mud-brick dwellings that were clustered together by the fields where they toiled. His village had been attacked by raiders who wreaked havoc throughout the northern region under one of the pretenders who had claimed the throne of Lower Egypt. All of the villagers had been slaughtered including his family. Only he had escaped.

But he remembered none of this.

All memory of his family and village had been swept from his mind, including his name. The traumatic events had left him without any recollection of his identity or past. All that remained were bits and pieces of elusive information, vague situations or feelings that were triggered by unrelated occurrences.

"You are Khu, child. That is your name now. Khu," the woman repeated. "And you are *my* son now," she said in a softer tone as she stroked the long plaited sidelock of hair that lay on the small cushion by his shoulder. "Son of Tem. Tem Salih-et, She Who is Righteous, King's Beloved, and Queen of Upper Egypt."

The boy only nodded. He did not know what to say to the woman sitting before him. He had never seen a noble, let alone a queen. Her title did not really mean much to him at all. He felt strangely removed from everything as though nothing were real.

Tem had a serene expression on her lovely face, making her natural beauty radiate from within her. Her dark straight hair was cut to frame her oval face, and just brushed the tops of her shoulders as was the custom for women at that time. A thin gold band encircled the top of her head, from which hung an amulet carved of lapis lazuli that rested on her forehead. She wore a long white belted linen tunic dress that was wrapped about her slender body and gathered over one shoulder.

Tem was queen and principle wife of King Nebhepetre Mentuhotep II—Lord of the White Crown and Ruler of Upper Egypt. Her royal blood had descended from a long line of kings, just like her husband Mentuhotep. Like most noble marriages, theirs had been a dynastic alliance to secure their bloodlines and continue the royal succession. Tem was already related to the king. She was his half-sister. But she had never born him any children.

Tem had tried to conceive a child but had failed again and again. She had tried all the prescribed herbs and potions that were believed to help increase fertility. She had also consulted with the priests of several temples and made many offerings to the gods on behalf of this special intention, especially to Hathor and Thoueris who oversaw fertility and childbirth, as well as to Amun who was patron of Thebes. Hathor was the ancient cow-goddess whose nurturing character imbued the milk of life into all things worthy. Tem had prayed most fervently to her—patron of all women—pleading before the statue that bore the headdress of cow horns with a moon-disk between them. But none of the gods had listened, and the herbs had only made Tem's skin break out in an unsightly rash. Nothing had helped. And feeling defeated, she had finally given up on the dream of ever becoming a mother. Her womb was as barren and dry as the desert surrounding Egypt, east and west of the Nile.

But that did not matter anymore.

"Mesi," Tem called her servant over.

The boy did not even recognize the young woman who had first found him in the reeds seven days before, shortly after the fever had started. He had been desperately ill, and the trauma of his ordeal, and the shock of his torment had left him feeble and teetering on the edge of a great precipice overlooking an abyss.

"Lady," Mesi replied as she handed a small copper cup to the woman sitting by the boy's side. The dark liquid released a small wisp of steam that melted away into the air. Mesi bowed her head as she withdrew to one side of the room. She was pleased to see Khu awake.

"Drink," Tem instructed the boy as she placed one hand behind his head in support. "Small sips, child."

Khu put his lips to the cup and drank. The warm liquid made him cough at first, and he pulled away. But Tem encouraged him again to sip the diluted wine concoction mixed with coriander, garlic and willow. It had been sweetened with a little honey but it still tasted bad. He drank it obediently nevertheless. He rested his head again and watched Tem as she handed the cup back to Mesi.

Then their eyes met. Khu recognized the look of wonder in Tem's eyes as she stared at him. Many others had regarded him the same way, before averting their gazes and touching an amulet that hung around their necks or rested inside a pocket. They were the eyes of a cat, at least in color, but far more intriguing. There was something strangely riveting about his gaze. It was as if he could see right through a person. Right into the very soul. But what made it most unsettling was that he seemed to know what lay hidden within the heart. Something about the way he stared, left no doubt that he could truly see what was there.

And he did.

Khu had been born with a special gift, not unlike his jewel-toned eyes that held people spellbound. He had the gift of discernment. With a simple glance he knew if someone were telling the truth when they spoke. He might not know what they were thinking, but he could tell if they were being honest or if they were lying. It was his purity of heart that allowed him to see into the soul and know if that person were true or false.

Tem regarded the boy quietly with a tilt of her head. She knew that he was special. Like Mesi, Tem also believed him to be the one described in the Prophecy of Neferti.

The ancient prophesy had predicted a time of chaos where Egypt's unification would disintegrate under a succession of ephemeral dynasties, then be restored once again in unity and prosperity. A new kingdom would be established after a series of war campaigns were mounted to defeat enemies of Egypt. It was believed that one especially righteous warrior who was pure of heart and unwavering in loyalty, would rise to lead these campaigns to victory under the guidance of the king. This warrior was described as having eyes of gold, just like Khu. Tem narrowed her eyes a little in thoughtful consideration as she looked into those eyes now. They were like warm limpid pools where one could easily get lost.

The sound of children running and playing could be heard from somewhere else in the palace. They were the happy sounds of innocence, delightful squeals full of the energetic joy of life. The smell of fresh baked bread wafted through the air, mingling with the fragrance of the lotus flowers that floated in a deep earthen dish resting on a small table in the corner of the room. The walls were painted in flower motifs of scrolling vines and bindweed creeping about bunches of irises, chrysanthemums and jasmine. A rectangular window was cut high into the wall, over which hung a reed mat to keep out the dust, heat and flies. Sunlight pierced the mat in long thin shafts that made crisscross patterns on the floor which was inlaid with large blocks of colorful stone cut into geometric shapes.

A gray cat wandered into the room, momentarily distracting the queen from her musings, and she motioned to the animal with her hand. It was one of the many pets living with the nobles in the sprawling palace compound. The cat rubbed itself along Tem's leg, and then offered the queen his head. She scratched his silky fur, running her hand over his smooth back, and he purred loudly. Khu shifted in his bed to glance at the animal that sniffed at the boy curiously, before eliciting more caresses and then wandering out of the room.

Tem's attention turned back to Khu, and she placed one of her own hands over the boy's, marveling at his perfection. She had surmised what had happened to the boy after her servants had brought him to her with his bloodied clothing. It was not uncommon for robbers to attack villages, both in the northern and southern areas that lay beyond the present jurisdiction of Mentuhotep II. Asiatic nomads had attacked Lower Egypt sporadically, entering through the Delta's intricate waterways and causing much unrest. People from Kush had also plagued Egypt from the southern lands when they were not maintaining a grudging peace. The Kushites sometimes posed a troublesome threat to the many mines and resources that enriched Egypt from the south. But it was the lawless bands of domestic renegades whose contemptible ways betrayed a seditiousness and disloyalty to everything in sight, that caused the most problems. They preyed most heavily upon the smaller settlements and townships in the Nile Valley that lacked the protection and backing of a king and his administration. Those bands were like the hyena that ran in bloodthirsty clans, stealing, ravaging and snatching spoils after laying waste to those places they visited.

Thebes had been much safer than its northern neighbors. King Mentuhotep II had done a fine job at protecting his own people from such vile atrocities, and had thus enjoyed a more peaceful reign so far. But it was still in the early years of his rule, and nothing was guaranteed, especially while Egypt remained a divided kingdom.

"Rest now, child," Tem whispered as she began stroking his head and plaited sidelock of hair once again. "Close your eyes and rest Khu, my son. My beautiful boy."

Khu closed his sleepy eyes as the drink he had finished sipping coursed through his blood and relaxed him, his thick dark lashes grazing the tops of his cheeks. His features were perfectly proportioned and Tem marveled at his beauty once again.

She wondered about the family he left behind, and a profound sadness filled her soul for the mother who must have loved him deeply. He would never see her again. But he would know a mother's love—her love. And despite the sadness of his circumstances, Tem could not help feeling secretly relieved that Khu did not remember any of his past. She did not want him to suffer from it, nor did she want anyone trying to claim him and take him away from her.

Tem smiled and exhaled a small sigh of satisfaction when she saw that Khu had fallen asleep once again. Gone was the ashen pallor in his complexion from those first few days when he appeared to teeter precariously on the edge of death. His smooth skin was regaining some of its natural healthy color as he improved.

Tem had been by his bedside constantly from the moment her servants had brought him to her. With Mesi's help, she herself had taken upon the task of carefully washing the blood and filth from his body, then anointing his skin with perfumed oils which were delicately scented with flowers, to protect him from Egypt's arid climate. She had watched and waited anxiously as he struggled under the fever's terrible power which left him very weak, and had placed cool herbal compresses made with willow leaves over his forehead and on the sides of his neck below his ears. She loved him already as her own son—as the child she could never bear. And she wanted to keep him for herself.

Yes, Tem thought to herself with a mother's conviction as she watched Khu lying on the linen sheet. Khu belonged to *her* now. It did not matter anymore that she had not been able to conceive a child of her own, because she had him now. He was her son now. And he would be raised and educated right alongside with the other noble children of the palace. Perhaps even her husband Mentuhotep II would claim him as a son as well. He already had an infant heir by Neferu, who was his second major wife. It had been determined that Neferu's son would succeed Mentuhotep to the throne as ruler someday after Tem had failed to conceive a child herself. This had been decreed before Mentuhotep's third wife, Henhenet, had died in childbirth.

Henhenet's death and that of her unborn child, had occurred recently just before Khu had been found in the reeds. She had been expecting her first child with Mentuhotep when the double tragedy struck, casting a mournful pall over the palace. Although the pregnancy had been relatively easy, the birth had been a nightmare. Her labor had lasted days on end, while she was attended by women and nurses who were skilled in the birthing process. She had spent her final days in a special confinement pavilion within the palace, which was reserved for the baby's birth, and dedicated to the goddesses Hathor, Thoueris and Isis in hopes that they would oversee the birth and protect both mother and child. Numerous amulets carved from jasper, lapis lazuli, malachite, and carnelian encircled the cushioned reed mat where she lay. A curved ivory wand engraved with deities had been placed on her swollen belly for protection, while statues and effigies of gods stared out from their platforms around the room, ready to ward off any evil spirits that might be lurking within.

Every so often Henhenet would be assisted into a squatting position so that she could push through the contractions. But try as she might, the baby did not budge. She was also given special potions to drink that were believed to aid in the birth of a child, while scented unctions had been massaged liberally onto her belly. But nothing had helped. The baby was blocked by the placenta within her womb. After days of struggling, with the women chanting every known prayer and incantation, and burning incense and scattering flowers over the floor, Henhenet had finally died.

A terrible sadness befell the palace. All joyful anticipation for the birth of a new baby was replaced by a bitter mourning for the loss of both mother and child. Funeral preparations for the deceased were undertaken immediately, and the king ceased shaving his head and face in order to grow hair as an outward display of his grief during the embalming period until the funeral ceremony would be held.

Tem was sad for the loss of Henhenet and her unborn child. The woman had been like a younger sister to her. Mentuhotep was also distraught. Although he had children by a number of lesser wives, the loss was heartbreaking, for the heart's capacity to love is infinite. Death was a constant risk when it came to new life, especially in a time when the mortality rate for infants and mothers in childbirth was high. Their deaths were a grim reminder of the transience of this world, and the importance of readying for the Afterlife.

The finding of Khu could not have come at a better time, thought Tem, as she bent down to gently kiss the sleeping boy on the forehead. For a few seconds she watched his chest rise and fall with the quiet rhythm of his breathing. Then she got up from his bedside and walked over to the room's entryway, pausing to turn and glance at Khu once more before leaving.

The children of the palace were deeply loved and cherished, she acknowledged to herself. How could Mentuhotep not accept Khu as his own son? Particularly after the painful loss of Henhenet and her child. Khu would be a balm on the king's wounded heart. Yes, she nodded to herself, one more child would be a blessing.

Especially *this* child.

TWO

Morning dawned bright over the funeral procession snaking its way across the shimmering Nile on a barge. Unlike some parts of the great far-reaching river whose murky waters were a dirty brown, the water here shone blue as the vast blue sea lying north of the Nile Delta, and into which the great river disgorged its branched veins. It mirrored the brilliant sky above, a placid reflection of the heavens. Its smooth glassy surface belied a current which made the barge seem to glide effortlessly across.

From stem to stern, the graceful boat stretched long and slender with chiseled beast heads mounted on the ends which rose high above the deck, facing inwards to the vessel's occupants. A black stone representation of Anubis carved entirely of jet, sat on top of the canopy shading the coffins of the deceased. The jackal-headed god was depicted in full animal form. His lithe reclining body supported a long-snouted head with perked ears alert to any possible danger as he protected the spirits of the dead, while leading them safely to the Afterlife.

Once crossing to the river's west bank, the procession continued past the verdant floodplains, and on to the dry sandy desert waiting beyond, where an ox-drawn sledge hauled the mummified remains of Henhenet and her infant child. The baby had been a girl. More than seventy days had passed since their deaths, during which the priests had washed, anointed and preserved their individual bodies with mixtures of spices, salts and resins, before wrapping them in the finest linen.

The great ox lumbered steadily forward, harnessed to the heavy cargo it pulled under a warming sun. Loud wailing from professional mourners mingled with the noble family's cries as they followed the shaven-headed priests leading the group in somber dignity—their

27

leopard-skin cloaks draped over a single shoulder, and their long staffs in hand as they chanted solemn ritual intonations and wafted sweet incense through the air. The perfumed wisps of smoke mingled with the cloud of dust rising in the wake of the mourners, so that the long procession was enveloped in an aromatic haze.

Tem took her place beside Mentuhotep with Khu by her side. Neferu walked on the king's other side with her infant heir to the throne. The king's second major wife held her baby close, as the child's nursemaid walked a pace behind, ready to take the babe from her mistress at a moment's notice. But Neferu did not relinquish the infant. She held him closely to her chest, wrapped in a long linen cloth which had been fashioned into a sling. It was tied across one shoulder and around her back. The movement of the procession had lulled the child to sleep.

Neferu kept looking at the sleeping babe worriedly, and casting surreptitious glances Khu's way. She distrusted Khu. As mother of the heir to Upper Egypt's throne, Neferu took her place in the royal palace quite seriously. And in a time when infant mortality was high, she cared for the child with all the protectiveness of a whole pride of lions guarding their young. Small amulets were tied to the infant's limbs, and spells were chanted daily for his protection.

Khu felt Neferu looking at him, but every time he glanced back she would turn away. And although she was physically attractive, her brows were often drawn, and her mouth taut with pride, which lent her features a hardened and brittle edge.

Neferu feared Khu. It was not just his strange eyes that unnerved her either. Now that Tem had claimed Khu as her son, Neferu was afraid that Khu might usurp her own son's position as heir to the throne. This was ridiculous, of course, for nothing could take the child's future crown from him but death. Although her fears were unfounded, her jealousy and ambition clouded her judgment and good sense. She did not want anyone or anything to

28

thwart her child's future as king. And for all her motherly instincts, she could not help seeing Khu as a constant threat since his arrival to the palace compound.

The rest of the royal family, nobility, officials and palace servants followed behind the king and his main wives, their heads bowed with grief. They were headed to the rock-carved royal tombs that waited in the desert by the side of a cliff on the western bank of the Nile across from Thebes.

The mortuary temple shone almost white under the desert sun. Though still under construction, its pillared halls and columned hypostyle rose like a palace for the dead, where it was believed that the sun would carry the deceased to the Underworld. The walls would later bear hieroglyphic texts and high relief images of the king in various scenes of his life, along with the principle gods of Thebes, including the god Amun. Once completed, artisans would also paint the inscriptions in vivid pigments befitting of the monarch's eminence.

Khu watched the paid mourners weeping and throwing dust over their heads in a flamboyant display of sorrow. Some flung themselves onto the ground, waving their arms miserably through the sand, while others threw their heads back toward the sky, wailing loudly in various tones of violent and distressing cries and exclamations that filled the air with their lamentations. But the sadness was palpable, especially as Henhenet had been young, and her death unexpected. There is nothing more painful than the untimely death of someone young and dear to the heart. The harrowing grief surges from a bottomless well of sorrow, drowning the mourner in a torrent of agonizing pain; an exquisite pain that continues to afflict the mourner with heartache and loneliness long after the deceased is buried and gone.

Khu glanced up at Mentuhotep who remained stoic at his side. The king had shaved off his beard and head once again, now that the prescribed seventy days of mourning before the funeral ceremony had passed. On top of his smooth scalp he wore the formal conical-shaped *Hedjet* White Crown of Upper Egypt. He did not carry the crook and flail at this funeral—scepters symbolizing his power as shepherd and protector of his people, and his position as leader and inflictor of justice, respectively. But he did have his ritual golden *sekhem*—another scepter symbolic of his authority, and he held it in front of him as he walked. Black *kohl* lined his lids in the traditional fashion, elongating his brown eyes, and lending his face an intriguing aspect.

The king was not a handsome man. But he had a jovial sense of humor and a quick wit that enlivened his otherwise plain features into something attractive. Mentuhotep was a deep and complex man with a great love for his children and Egypt. He was highly respected by his officers, advisors, and others in his court. And he was known to be fair, kind and honest throughout his dominion. He was a warrior with the heart of a lion who stopped at nothing to protect his kingdom. And his greatest ambition was to reunify the lands of Upper and Lower Egypt under his rule.

Mentuhotep glanced down at Khu. He could feel the boy's jeweled eyes studying him. The child's piercing gaze distracted the king momentarily from the funeral, and his thoughts turned to the day when he first met the boy. His chief wife Tem had brought the child before him shortly after the death of Henhenet and her unborn child.

"Lord King," Tem had bowed to Mentuhotep as she held Khu's small hand possessively within her own.

They were in the main pavilion of the palace where the king conducted most of the kingdom's official matters. The bright pillared hall was pierced by several rectangular windows running along the tops of the walls, and light flooded the airy space which was kept cool from the sun by several rooms surrounding the pavilion on all sides, buffering it from Egypt's heat. The high ceiling also allowed the room's warmth to rise above and exit through the windows which were presently unshuttered by the reed mats used to close them. The king was seated on a bronze carved armchair resting atop a dais in the center of the room. Two advisors stood at either of his sides, their impassive faces avoiding Khu's gaze.

"Arise, She Who is Righteous," the king had addressed Tem by her formal title. This had been a good and promising sign, and it had bolstered Tem's confidence. It was a sign of respect, and meant that the king was open and willing to listen to what she had to say.

Tem had already approached the king informally about Khu a few days before, telling him how the child had been discovered hiding in the reeds, and how she strongly suspected he had escaped death at the hands of raiders in one of the northern territories. She had also told him about the boy's eyes, and how she believed him to be the one mentioned in the prophesies.

Mentuhotep observed the child standing patiently by Tem's side. He knew that his wife had already bonded with the boy, and that she would do anything in her power to keep him for herself. He saw the anxiety in his wife's face. Her darting eyes kept blinking, and her thin frame was tense and drawn.

He thought of all the things Tem had told him about Khu. And then he thought about that which she had not said—about how much she wanted to be Khu's mother; about how long she had suffered the curse of a barren womb; about how she desperately longed to care for a child of her very own, and now that the opportunity presented itself, she wished to grab hold of it with every fiber of her being.

Tem did not believe in coincidences. She believed Khu's arrival had somehow been ordained by the gods, and she had said so to her husband. Whatever happened to the boy, whatever violence he had witnessed or atrocities he endured, it was not for naught. Something good would come from this. After all, new life is birthed in the anguish of blood. The gods would take that spilled blood, and fashion something better and stronger from the puddle that soaked the ground. And nourished by the fertile fluid of life, the little sapling would grow larger and stronger until a grove spread over the plains, and a new unified land emerged from the darkness.

Mentuhotep's heart went out to his wife. Her anxiety made her look small and young. But the boy stood calmly by Tem's side, unruffled by the proceedings. Something about the child moved the king, stirring the fatherly instincts deep within his core. And although Tem had begun to speak on behalf of Khu, humbly asking for the king's protection and guardianship, her voice seemed to grow distant as Mentuhotep lost himself in the boy's crystalline gaze.

Slowly the king stood from his throne and stepped down from the dais on which it rested, coming to stand before the child. He had moved carefully so as not to frighten the boy. But Khu was not afraid. He could see inside the soul of the ruler. Compassion, kindness and curiosity emanated from deep within the sorrowful heart of the king, who was grieving for Henhenet and his infant child's deaths.

"Son," Mentuhotep had stated clearly so that the scribes in the room would carefully record these proceedings with accuracy, "whose given name is Khu Salih—He Who is Protected and Righteous—and who from this day forth will be known as Khu Salih Nebhepetre—Pleased is the Lord Re with He Who is Protected and Righteous. And who will also be known as flesh of my flesh, and blood of my blood."

The scribes were scribbling frantically, bent over the table where they worked, jotting down every word exiting the king's mouth.

The advisors stood with their backs unnaturally straight in an awkward attempt to hide their surprise. Their wide eyes finally landed on Khu and they could not seem to move from there. They were riveted to their spots as they watched the king officially accept the boy as his own son. Once the formalities had been inscribed on the papyrus scrolls, nothing but death itself could undo or break the bonds made on that auspicious day.

Tem beamed as she lifted Khu's small hand and placed it within the hand of Mentuhotep, his father. She finally felt complete. The yearning that had claimed her soul for years had finally been fulfilled. And closing her eyes she exhaled all the anxiety which had left her tense and afraid up until this moment. *It is done*, she thought with relief as she nodded and bowed low before the king with tremendous gratitude before the formal blessings were bestowed upon the boy.

It is done.

Mentuhotep was well aware of the Prophesy of Neferti, and could not help believing Khu was indeed truly the One. Perhaps this belief was due to the superstitions to which Mentuhotep clung. Perhaps it was due to his long-reaching ambitions to reunify the broken lands. Or perhaps it was the king's own painful grief which made him want to believe this. His heartache left him a little vulnerable, and he felt a deep longing to reach out and grasp at hope. And the boy—Khu—embodied the hope he craved in the days following the loss that distressed him.

But things had not been so easy for Khu, despite the king's formal acceptance. In the very beginning—when he was first claimed by Tem—most people had regarded the boy with tremendous distrust. People often cast suspicious glances his way, then whispered behind his back, their narrowed eyes watchful as they touched a talisman or invoked one of their gods in an effort to ward off any possible curse or evil from befalling them. Besides Neferu, Mentuhotep's other wives had also stared at the boy with wariness. Many of the noble women in the palace had also warned their young children against Khu.

"Do not look him in the eyes," they cautioned. "Avert your gaze and touch the pendant," they instructed uneasily, referring to the *Wedjat* Eye of Horus, or the *kheper* scarab beetle amulets hanging around their necks for protection. "And may Isis protect you from all harm," they prayed, breathing three times over the heads of their children in an effort to ward away evil.

People had no way of knowing they were wrong to fear him. They had never seen a child—or any person for that matter—with eyes like Khu's. Yet despite their unwarranted suspicions, there had been something calming about his demeanor. Even at such a tender age—he had only been alive for almost seven seasons of the Inundation—his character emanated a strength and wisdom well beyond his years. And his strange and penetrating eyes seemed to heighten the gifts within him. Like the great Sphinx reclining near the pyramid-tombs of Lower Egypt on the western bank of the Nile, Khu was an enigma.

Khu, Mentuhotep mouthed silently to the boy holding his gaze as they continued with the funeral. Mentuhotep blinked in a deliberate manner with the slightest nod in the child's direction.

Khu acknowledged the king's kindly gesture and the corners of his small mouth upturned into a faint smile. It was then that the boy slipped his hand into that of the king's.

Mentuhotep grasped it firmly within his own warm hand, before turning his attention back to the procession.

Tem was consoled by their burgeoning affection and she smiled to herself, while Neferu's eyes widened, and she clenched her jaw, tamping down a surge of jealousy which burned at the sight of their new bond.

Servants followed the ox-drawn sledge, carrying some of the smaller items that would be buried with the mother and child, along with the larger things resting in crates behind the two sarcophagi. They were things believed to be necessary in the Afterlife such as food and drink, toiletry items, clothing, musical instruments, furniture and jewelry. Small carved human figurines called *ushabti* were included to serve them faithfully in the

Afterlife, so that Henhenet could continue living in the luxurious and pampered lifestyle to which she had been accustomed here. There were even toys for the tiny child who lay in her own little sarcophagus. They would be buried together within the king's own temple-tomb, so they could all meet once again in the Afterlife.

The procession entered a courtyard and proceeded up a ramp to a terrace, then up a second ramp leading to the inner chambers of the beautiful temple, finally arriving to Henhenet's tomb. All work on the sprawling tomb-temple complex had been redirected to Henhenet's tomb so it could be completed within a timely manner. The construction of her burial chamber had only recently been finished. It was a small room adjoining what would eventually become the king's larger burial chambers.

The priests took their places before the entrance of the tomb as musicians plucked the haunting notes of a dirge on an arched harp. A single melancholic voice rose from the poignant melody, prompting fresh tears from the mourners, as it invoked the aid of Anubis in judging Henhenet and her daughter with mercy so they might be regarded as worthy of Eternal Life, and granted admission to the Hereafter:

Come, O Anubis, Leader of Souls, Tester of Faith
Come, Guardian of the Scales, Weigher of Hearts
Come to our beloved sister Henhenet Latif-et,
She of the Gracious Heart
And to her innocent child, as yet unborn to the
earthly realm
Judge them worthy and commend them to the gods
Guide them in their journey
Admit them to the Field of Reeds
Protect them in the Hereafter, in the Eternal Dominion
of the Just
For they are pure in heart
Blameless and without reproach
Their souls do rise as a sweet perfume, pleasing
to the gods
Rebuffing all malevolence and evil

Come, Mighty Anubis, Protector of the Deceased
As we commend our beloved ones to Thee

Khu bowed his head as the heavy weight of the mourners' collective grief pressed upon him, and hot tears fell from his eyes. The last rites were held, more prayers were chanted, more incense was burned, and the symbolic Opening of the Mouth ritual took place to reanimate the senses so the deceased could eat, speak, hear and see again in the Afterlife. A forked blade carved of black agate was touched to the mouth, eyes and ears of their coffins to also allow the immortal soul *Ka* to come and go freely. Then the ceremony was concluded with a formal burial dance and followed by a feast.

And the tomb, which now housed the remains of Henhenet and her child, as well as all those things deemed necessary to their comfort and well-being in the next life, was shut and sealed tightly against the robbers, reprobates and rogues who dwelt in the shadows of the land of the living.

THREE

In the darkest hour of night, a boat glided stealthily over the Nile. A band of thieves pulled their oars through the cool waters that shone like obsidian under the gibbous moon. The dark water sluiced and swirled as the men slowly plowed their oars into the river. They passed a float of crocodiles submerged by the marshes where they were hunting for waterfowl sleeping in nests by the reeds. The beasts watched the boat moving through the night, their yellow reptilian eyes glittering fiercely in the moonlight.

The men were scouting the banks of the river in Thebes, their dark eyes wide and watchful as they hunkered warily within the vessel whose sail was tightly furled. They rounded a bend in the river and drew in their oars as they neared the rocky shore. One of the men stood at the stern and poled the boat forward through the shallow waters.

A pair of great white pelicans flapped their wings in the dense reed beds where their nests were hidden, but then settled back down quietly. A soft chorus of chirping crickets and croaking frogs lent their voices to the night. Then a splash sounded, momentarily startling the men, as an osprey swooped down from the air and plunged feet first into the water where it caught a small fish, gripping the scaled prey with its long dagger-like talons.

"There," one of the men whispered with a tilt of his head. "The storage houses." They had arrived close to the village which lay just northeast of Mentuhotep's palace compound.

"Wait," another stood up in the boat, his hand raised for them to stop. A rustling among the reeds caught his eye and he pointed to a man stepping out from a cluster of branches. Then he whistled very softly and the man returned his signal with a wave. "Stop here," he told the rest of the men in the boat. "We have arrived."

Among the many mud-brick homes sheltering the people and serving as their workshops, were the granaries where wheat and barley were stored. They were set back from the river within the walled village sitting higher above the floodplain, to protect them from the rising waters of the annual inundation.

The other men turned to look at the silos which housed grain from the fields. More precious than gold was the food that nourished the people. Bread was one of the things crossing all social boundaries. It was a staple in the diets of peasants, priests and princes alike. All the people—from those in the nobility, to the ones toiling at the bottom of the pyramid-structured socio-economy—relied on its sustenance.

The men swallowed against the greed that made them salivate. They were hungry, but not to fill their stomachs. They hoped to steal some of the grain and trade it elsewhere for a profit.

Times had been hard on many of the settlements which eked out a living on the Nile Valley's floodplains. Although the settlements and villages under Mentuhotep's authority had not suffered during his reign, many others had. Famine and hunger afflicted the people who toiled in vain under a hot sun which scorched the crops in the fields. Those harvests that had not withered were drowned in the waters which flooded the plains like the hungry tide of the sea washing over the shoreline. Without the carefully constructed canals, ditches and dykes lying useless from disrepair and hardship, the life-giving water of the ancient river could be transformed into a ravenous and unappeasable glutton, destroying all laying in its path during the river's annual inundation, including the storage houses where the harvested grains were kept.

Over the centuries, flooding sometimes destroyed entire villages whose homes and workshops were built of mud-bricks. New villages were then built right on top of the remaining debris from the previous structures, so that with time, the newer villages rose higher on a kind of artificial mesa. But if the natural elements were not conspiring against those villages which managed to survive, raiders and disease often took whatever had been left.

Somewhere inside the palace Khu stirred in his sleep. He tossed and turned in his bed as he sensed the danger lurking nearby. Then he awoke and sat up at once to seek out his mother Tem.

"Are you certain?" Tem eyed Khu with doubt.

She had been sleeping in the women's quarters of the palace when the boy woke her. She had opened her eyes to find him standing quietly by her bedside. He was barefoot with nothing but a white linen loincloth wrapped about his bottom. His plaited sidelock of hair hung by his shoulder. The feeble light of the moon drifted in through the window cut high into the wall, but only seemed to accentuate the shadows draping the room. A ceramic oil lamp sat on a low table in a corner of the room, its reed wick unlit. No sounds echoed through the palace. No dogs barked in the night. It was deathly quiet.

"Yes, Mother," he nodded, "I am sure."

He was fidgeting. Tem had not seen him do this before. His usual calm demeanor was tense, and he picked at his fingers with a restlessness that unnerved her.

Tem did not feel like moving. Hazy remnants of sleep numbed her senses with a thick sluggishness, and her limbs felt weighted by the resulting inertia. Her eyes were the first to move as they darted about the room, roaming over the wooden cabinet against the wall where her clothes were kept, then to a small table where an elegantly carved cosmetics box stored the miniature alabaster pot of *kohl* eyeliner she applied with a stick applicator to her eyelids each day, along with the green *udju* eye shadow made from ground malachite. Next to the box was an alabaster jar covered with a strip of leather to keep the oil-based perfume within from evaporating into the dry air. The cosmetics and perfumes were prized by the people for their mystical and healing powers. But even they could not stop evil from entering the hearts of men.

Tem's eyes finally came to rest on the window. Its reed shade lay rolled up on the ground below to allow the night air to circulate through the room. She took a deep breath, got out of bed, and lit the lamp's wick before turning back to face her son.

The lamp's light reflected golden pools in Khu's eyes. He looked upset, worried.

Tem thought of what Khu had just told her while she slipped on a pair of leather sandals. She did not bother to change out of the simple linen dress she wore to sleep. Perhaps Khu was being plagued by frightening dreams, she thought to herself. Such things were common after traumatic events. Maybe his mind was reliving the horrors he had suffered before arriving here. Some dreams were a way of attempting to process certain things which could not be faced in the waking hours; a repository deep within the mind that would fracture when obstructed by repressed fears and memories too frightening to contain.

"You do not believe me," Khu shifted from one foot to the other. He closed his eyes a moment, lowering his head and swallowing hard. Then he drew himself up and opened his eyes again to look at Tem.

Tem was watching him, her mind working. She was trying to decide whether to send the boy back to bed, or go and warn the king. But there was an urgency in Khu's eyes that finally persuaded her into action.

"I believe something is troubling you," she admitted.

"But you don't know if it is just in my head."

Tem nodded.

"And you aren't sure what to tell the king."

She nodded again, and Khu looked away frustrated. He studied the small yellow flame of the oil lamp throwing large shapeless shadows on the wall. Then he turned back to her.

"Tell him, Mother." His voice was low and insistent. "Tell him."

Tem watched him with a curious expression, pursing her lips in indecision. "Very well," she said after a short while.

But she looked unsure. And as they left to tell the king, she hoped she had not made a mistake by believing Khu.

Mentuhotep wasted no time in sending guards to investigate. He did not wish to take any chances, especially given the circumstances in the northern territories. He grabbed his dagger and tucked it in the strap tied about his kilt. But he paused before leaving the room, and turned around to face Tem and Khu once again.

"Come with me, Khu," he told the boy. "I want to know where the sounds came from."

Tem had told the king that it was Khu who informed her of the danger. Mentuhotep then simply assumed that the boy might have heard a noise. He was not yet aware of Khu's heightened perception. Besides, if Tem had said so, the king might not have been convinced enough to believe them. He would have brushed them both away and sent them back to their quarters. People are far quicker to believe that which is experienced through the senses.

Tem looked frightened when Mentuhotep told Khu to join him. She did not want any harm to befall her son. Khu looked up at Tem before moving toward his father. He could feel the anxiety within her, and he squeezed her hand reassuringly before stepping away.

"I will keep him safe," the king said, as he ran a hand over his smooth-shaven head in an anxious gesture. "Do not worry."

Tem was biting her lip behind her folded hands which she pressed against her mouth as though in prayer. But she said nothing. She simply nodded her head in a perfunctory bow before her child left with the king. Then she closed her eyes, touched the amulet hanging from her neck on a golden chain, and said a silent prayer to the gods for their protection.

Mentuhotep was well aware of the dangers that had beset many of the settlements. Lower Egypt was not only divided from the kingdom of Upper Egypt, it was divided against itself. There had been as many pretenders ruling as there were scattered communities spreading out like the branches of the Nile Delta. And the thrones of those territory-kingdoms rested on foundations that were not unlike the soft silt and marshlands saturating the land. It was unstable and chaotic.

The stability Egypt had once enjoyed, had disintegrated into a number of *sepats*—local territory divisions—at least in the north. And without political stability there had been much pillaging throughout those lands which had also been plagued by drought.

The collapse of the unified kingdom had trickled down to all levels of the land. Tombs, temples and monuments had been pillaged and plundered. Canals lay broken, water-storage basins were in disrepair, dykes and ditches abandoned. The complex irrigation system which harnessed the floodwaters of the life-giving Nile had fallen into ruin, leaving the unruly northern territories impoverished.

Bands of robbers and lawless tribes crawled throughout the region like the grain beetles and cockroaches which destroyed the stored cereals. They took whatever they pleased from whomever they chose, with little consequences. And Mentuhotep had no intention of letting the darkness that shrouded his northern neighbors creep over his own dominion.

The men pulled their boat through the tall reeds of the riverbank and tied it to a stake. Somewhere in the distance a jackal howled and the men shivered as they touched the amulets hanging from their necks, in hopes that it was not an ill omen. The stars were a blanket of bright pin pricks pulled across the night sky. Frogs and crickets grew silent as the men pushed through the tall reeds growing in thick clusters by the water's edge. One man stayed behind to guard the boat as the others followed the man who had been anxiously awaiting them on the shore. They moved slowly through the darkness, their daggers in hand.

"How far?" one man asked.

"Just follow me," the leader instructed as he headed toward the village in front of the others. "But keep your distance. If any one of us should be caught, we do not know each other." He glanced back at the others, pausing to make sure they understood. "I will deny everything," he continued. "I will deny ever seeing you, and deny having any knowledge of these acts," he wiped his forehead with the back of his hand, then over his shaved head in a nervous gesture. His was the only shaved head in the group. The other men wore their hair cropped just above their shoulders, as most of the laborers, peasants and skilled workers did. "And if you know what is good for you, you had better do the same."

"We know the plan," the first man retorted, wanting to silence the leader.

"We swore by blood," another reminded him.

But the leader only grumbled and dismissed their replies with a wave of his hand. He trusted no one, blood or no blood. Relying on others was an unavoidable nuisance that sometimes proved necessary.

The land rose muddy above the marshes, then dipped beneath an outcrop of wild grasses before smoothing out before them. The thatched vegetation carpeted a plain where sycamore, mimosas and doum palms dotted the expanse. The goats, sheep and cattle which normally grazed here during the day, had been safely corralled for the night. Flame trees were in full bloom, though their fiery red flowers were lost to the darkness, while the low hanging branches of willow trees caressed the ground like long feathered strands in the soft breeze. An owl hooted its forlorn call, and somewhere another owl responded, prompting some of the men to touch their amulets again.

The men walked past several plowed fields and onto a road leading through one of the entrances in the walled village. Houses and workshops of every kind spread out in large orderly blocks divided by narrow streets which were deserted at this late hour. The palace lay farther south, and was separated from the village by a short road that led to an entrance in the wall enclosing the great compound and its private gardens.

Somewhere a dog barked but then fell silent again. A cat darted out from the shadows, crossing their path before it disappeared into the darkness. The men continued until the first of them arrived to one of the structures housing the grain. They were planning to use the large coarsely woven linen sacks kept inside by the vats to transport the precious cereals back to the boat. There were no windows cut into the wall facing this side of the street. And keeping by the building, they crept farther into the village like serpents through the deep shadows hiding the moon's wan light.

The king's guards were roaming outside the palace walls with torches to illuminate their path. They had first combed the private gardens where vines and fruit trees grew in manicured splendor around the ponds stocked with fish, before stepping beyond the gate. The gatekeeper was not at his post, and Mentuhotep assumed he had left to join the guards searching for the interlopers.

"Where is Odji?" the king inquired of the missing gatekeeper, when they stepped away from the abandoned post.

"Searching the grounds perhaps, Lord King," a guard said.

Khu just kept close to the king's side as they followed the guards.

"Which way, son?" the king asked the boy. Khu simply lifted his chin northwards toward the adjacent village.

A few of the guards had gone ahead when one shouted a warning. "Over here! Stop! Stop in the name of Amun who sees all in darkness and light. Stop!"

But the man he called out to didn't stop. He scurried away in the darkness like a nocturnal thing living in the realm of the shadows.

"Go, go, run!" one of the thieves shouted when they saw they had been discovered.

"Split up!" another ordered.

The thieves dispersed to take cover within the village. They sprinted down the streets, cutting through narrow alleyways, and running between some of the tightly packed workshops and homes arranged in ordered blocks, all the while puzzling over how anyone could have seen or heard them when no sound had been made. They had been as quiet as the dead lying in their tombs.

But not anymore.

Some of the villagers heard the commotion and woke up to the sounds of screams and chases. A dog began to howl, others barked, and somewhere a baby cried.

"Wait here!" a man warned his wife as she held a small child to her bosom. The man peeked out of the mud-brick home adjacent to the blacksmith shop where he worked, when he saw a guard running down the street.

"Stay back!" the guard shouted to the man before turning a corner.

A few of the villagers hurried up to the roofs of their homes, climbing the side staircases built against the exterior walls of their houses. It was where they slept during those times when the heat proved too stifling to stay inside. They gathered their families safely above where they also hoped to get a better view of the commotion on the streets below.

One of the guards saw a man crouching in the darkness by a date palm before scrambling up a wall and disappearing through a window. The man had entered inside a bakery's storage room which sat across the road from the grain storage houses. His heart pounded as he waved his hands blindly before him so as not to bump into anything in the dark. The nutty aroma of emmer, barley and yeast clung to the room where bread was stored after being baked outside over a fire in the ceramic *bedja*—large, bell-shaped bread pots. The man was perspiring. He felt like a rat trapped in a large clay pot, with a cat circling by. He tripped, knocking the back of his head against something hard, and a ceramic pot crashed to the ground.

"Don't move!" the guard yelled as he climbed through the window after the man.

The thief was still on the ground, feeling around for something he could use as a weapon. He lifted one of the bedja with both hands. It was heavy. Then he threw it toward the guard, but missed, and it fell with a loud clatter and broke. He used the momentary distraction to find his way to a doorway, before he slipped out of the room and escaped.

Two other thieves were running across the rooftops, jumping from one to another of the closely spaced buildings. They were heading west, back towards the river that waited under the pale moonlight. They crouched low and kept away from the side of the block bordering the street so no one would see them.

Someone lunged at them from the shadows, but they were too fast, fueled by the adrenaline of fright. It was one of the villagers—a craftsman—who had gone up to the roof to sleep in the open air where it was cooler than inside. His wife remained asleep below with their young son.

The thieves kept going, running across three more rooftops before one of them tripped over a clay pot, nearly falling over the side of the building. The other man almost left him in his haste, but then turned to help him up. They continued on, taking better care to watch their footing, especially around the center of the roofs which opened up

46

in a kind of atrium from the floor below, for much-needed ventilation.

Most of the houses were simple structures with two or three rooms. The main living area was in the front, while the kitchen lay at the back where grain was ground into flour, the flour was sifted, and food was prepared. No cooking was done inside due to the heat, but rather outside over an open fire, or in the case of the larger upper-class homes, on top of the roof in clay ovens before it was brought back downstairs. The different classes of people were mixed together in the towns so that the larger white-washed upper-class houses stood two or three stories next to the simpler laborers' homes.

The two thieves finally made it to the edge of the village, and paused to look down over the side of one of the single-story structures over which they had fled. No guards were in sight, and they were anxious to get away.

"Jump down!" one whispered urgently. "Hurry, we are almost there."

"You jump," the other said. His ankle was hurting from having tripped and fallen over the clay pot recently. "I'll take the stairs."

The first man leaped over the side after a moment of hesitation. He landed safely on his feet like a cat, and pressed his back against a wall in the shadows to avoid being seen. He ran a hand across his forehead, wiping away the dirt-streaked sweat from dripping into his eyes. When his accomplice caught up to him, they took off toward the wall surrounding the village. Its exit waited just beyond a row of date palms casting monstrous shadows in the murky light of the moon.

"To the boat!" one said as they left the trouble behind them.

His partner hesitated, looking back toward the village. "What about the others?"

"That is their problem. We must go! Remember the plan," and they took off toward the river waiting beyond the fields.

Inside the village, the chase was still on as the remaining thieves sought cover from the guards.

"Over there!" a guard pointed when he caught sight of one man. "Stop! You are surrounded!"

The thief was sneaking up a ladder propped against a wall, which led to the rooftop of one of the mud-brick workshops when he slipped and fell on his own knife, cutting himself badly in the lower belly. The guard caught up to the injured man and thrust the tip of his spear at his throat. He kicked the injured man's knife out of reach, and it skittered several paces away on the ground.

"I'm hurt," the helpless man mumbled in pain.

"Don't move," hissed the guard, "unless you wish to die, and you want your remains thrown in the desert for the jackals to feast upon."

The thief swallowed hard against the pain from his injury. Blood trickled down his neck from the prick of the guard's spear point. He lay on the ground, sprawled on his back, his arms up by his head in surrender. He closed his eyes and exhaled in defeat.

The king caught up to the guard and injured thief, with Khu following closely behind.

"Take him to the pavilion," Mentuhotep instructed, referring to a court near the Temple of Mut.

The Temple of Mut was a shrine built in honor of the goddess Mut—wife of the god Amun, and daughter of the sun-god Re. Mut was a mother goddess and queen of goddesses, portrayed wearing the double crowns of Lower and Upper Egypt to symbolize her authority over all of the lands. She was also depicted wearing the royal vulture headdress symbolizing her protective and loving bond with her husband Amun, and their son, the moon-god Khonsu. Together with Amun and Khonsu, the three gods formed the Theban Triad, and were worshiped and revered for their protection and patronage of Thebes.

Mut's temple was situated next to the Temple of Khonsu, and by several smaller shrines and public buildings spreading out behind the village near the palace compound, including the pavilion used by the king for official public proceedings and judicial matters. The temple faced an open square ringed by shops catering to those visiting the temples. In the bustling daylight hours, and especially during the great festivals throughout the year, one could find stands laden with crates of vegetables and colorful fruit, heaps of freshly baked bread, clay pitchers brimming with brewed *heqet*, baskets of dried fish, pottery hanging on hooks or sitting on the ground, bolts of finely woven linen, carved amulets from semi-precious stones, and other items used in daily life. The temple complex paved the way leading to the larger Temple of Amun which honored the patron god of Thebes.

But now the square in front of the temple was deserted under a sullen moon, as two guards dragged away the injured man toward the pavilion where he would be tied to a pillar to await the serving of justice.

"There are more of them," Khu told Mentuhotep in a soft voice, his golden eyes fixed on the trail of blood left by the injured thief.

Mentuhotep looked at Khu, the lines between his brows deepening, as he narrowed his gaze dubiously, wondering how the boy could know this. He ran a hand slowly over his smooth scalp before finally giving the boy a hesitating nod. Khu's large eyes were completely without guile, and betrayed nothing but sincerity. The king then turned to his other guards. "Hurry," he ordered them, "do not let the others escape!"

The boat waiting on the riverbank slipped quietly away in the darkness, whose tranquility had been disturbed by the commotion inland. Its four occupants dug their oars into the muddy shore and pushed with all their might. They bent low over the sides of the boat as they turned the vessel around and steered it north, away from Thebes.

Only three of the five men who had disembarked earlier had returned.

The man who had stayed behind and waited with the boat was frustrated with the night's outcome. He vented his anger with every heave and push of the oar grasped tightly in his hands. He tried to tamp down his disappointment by forcing his thoughts back to the successes he had met recently. But that did not help.

It had not been his idea to come to Thebes. One of the men in his band had convinced the others that it was a good plan. He had told them how Thebes had enjoyed a greater prosperity than its northern neighbors. It had not fallen into the state of disorder which had left chaos and famine in its wake. And although its good fortune had made it a worthy target, it had also made it more challenging to infiltrate than the scattered territories spread throughout Egypt.

"They have not been touched by famine," one of the men had said. "Their fields have yielded immeasurable *heqats* of grain."

"How do you know this?" the boatman asked doubtfully, his eyes narrowed and distrustful. "You are not among them, but here with us." It was *his* boat they wished to use. It was always his boat. The others did not have two pieces of silver to call their own.

"Because I know someone there," the man replied sourly, setting his jaw.

"Really," was the flat response.

"Yes, and he happens to work for the king himself."

The boatman's eyes had widened at that, but he tried to hide his interest. He was the only one with something to lose in this bargain, after all. None of the others had any property of their own. Whatever loot they acquired had always been spent far quicker than the time it took to obtain it in the first place. It had disappeared like water evaporating from the hot desert sand. And after arranging further details, the man convinced all of them—including the boatman—of the plan. His promise

of abundant grain spilling over the huge stone vats barely containing it within the storage houses, had been too
much to resist.

And so they came.

They had planned to steal the grain, which was
highly valued in the northern settlements that were afflicted by drought, and trade it for a profit. It had all
sounded so easy. Too easy, in fact. And then everything
that could have gone wrong, did go wrong.

"Cursed," the boatman spat under his breath, his
mood sulky and resentful.

But no one dared reply. They kept their eyes fixed
on the river as they rowed.

"The night was cursed," he grumbled louder as they
moved farther away from Thebes. "We were cursed!"

The men continued to row, putting more and more
distance between them and the scene of the foiled crime.
What had gone wrong? What had caused them to fail?
Their plans had been meticulously calculated. They had
gone over the details countless times before this night.
They had even studied a crudely drawn map, sketched
by one of the men on a scroll. They had not made any
noise, nor had anyone seen them when they arrived. And
their spy who worked for the king—the same man who
had been waiting for them by the riverbank—had assured
them of their safety, and of the soundness of their plan.

"We were betrayed," another man said. But by
whom? None of them suspected anyone; certainly not
each other.

"It was bad luck," a third said as he touched his
amulet.

"Cursed," the boatman repeated again, nodding to
himself with a frown. "We were cursed."

A breeze picked up, stirring through the reeds, over
the water, and drying the perspiration from the men's
bodies. The boatman dug harder with his oar, making
the vessel lurch suddenly in the darkness. The other men
adjusted their oars in time to the boatman's lead, so that

they kept moving in unison. A chorus of frogs sounded from the shore, and a nighthawk called out as it flew across the water.

The boatman exhaled his disappointment in a long and noisy breath, shaking his head in frustration as he rowed ahead. Nothing was guaranteed. He had known this—had known all the risks involved—but he had grown confident and brash after their previous successes. None of them had ever been caught before. No one had ever been hurt, and no one had been the wiser. But now their band had lost two men. Their streak of luck had broken, shattered under a Theban sky.

The gods watched, even in darkness. The gods always watched.

The moon had drifted west, glossing the lush valley and the desert hills rising in the distance. Its wan light left a pale glimmer on the water's surface. The boatman touched a hand to the amulet encircling his wiry neck, and felt nothing but bitterness in the pit of his stomach. He stopped rowing to glance behind them once more, but saw that they were alone. No one was following.

Even the moon had lost interest and abandoned them in the dark.

Khu stared at the gatekeeper who hurried over with one of the guards. The man was perspiring heavily. His eyes darted around in the darkness, and he shifted from one foot to the other with a nervous energy. Even his shaved head glistened with sweat. But it was not that hot. The guards who had been running about were not perspiring as much as he.

"Odji," Mentuhotep spoke to the gatekeeper as the man bowed before him, "did you find any others?"

"No, Lord King," Odji uttered as he tried to compose himself.

"But you followed them?" the king frowned. "Is that not why you were away from your post?"

"Yes Sire. I heard a noise. But... but I did not see anyone," he stuttered.

Two of the would-be thieves had been caught and were now tied to a pillar, awaiting justice. They would be flogged in the morning for trespassing and attempting to steal that which did not belong to them. They had denied it, of course, but their guilt was obvious. They would not have run if they had been innocent. Tomorrow they would pay the price for their transgression and admit the guilt of their deeds. They were fortunate they had not been caught with any stolen property. The punishment would have been more severe.

"I do not think there are any more robbers, Lord King," one of the guards said. "We have checked all the streets." He seemed confident in his opinion, and the king believed him.

Mentuhotep glanced down at Khu. He saw the boy staring intently at the gatekeeper. "Khu," the king touched the boy's shoulder and Khu startled, but the boy kept his eyes fixed on Odji. Perhaps Khu was still afraid, thought the king. Maybe the events of the night triggered frightful memories of his past. The king gave the boy's shoulder a reassuring squeeze, but Khu kept staring.

Odji felt the boy's eyes on him. He tried to collect himself and steady the pace of his beating heart. How could things have gone so wrong this night? He frowned at Khu, wondering why the boy kept staring at him, and wondering what the boy was doing out here in the dead of night. He should be asleep with the rest of the children inside the palace.

What a strange night, Odji thought disappointedly. It had all been so carefully premeditated. It was supposed to have been an easy theft. There was no way anyone could have heard and discovered them. It was not possible. Especially someone from the palace, for they had not made any noise, nor been seen by anyone. Even if they had made noise, they had been far enough away from the palace for anyone there to hear them. And the villagers had been fast asleep.

The gatekeeper returned to his post where he guarded the entrance in the great wall surrounding the palace compound, along with two other subordinates who were away for the night. Odji had planned their shifts accordingly, purposely waiting until his assistants were away in order to avoid the possibility of having any witnesses. He shook his head in confusion as Mentuhotep, Khu and the rest of the group walked away and headed back to the palace grounds. Then he rubbed the back of his smooth-shaven scalp. It hurt from having knocked it against something hard. He had hit his head when he tripped and fell after trying to get away from one of the guards by scrambling up through a window into the bakery storage room. That had been a perilously close call, he thought with relief, as he remembered how the guard had nearly caught him. He felt something slick and brought his hand around to inspect it. Blood. He closed his eyes against the adrenaline giving him palpitations. It had been a narrow escape—a very narrow escape—at least for him.

Odji hoped that the two thieves who were caught would remember their bargain and keep their mouths shut. But that did not really matter now. They had only just met that night when he waited for them on the bank of the Nile. The only man who really knew him had gotten away on the boat, and was probably heading back north at that moment. And the apprehended men did not even know his name, he thought optimistically. His identity had been partly cloaked in the night's darkness, and in the ignorance of the other men. He would make sure to stay far away from the prisoners tomorrow, in case they should recognize him and point their fingers in accusation.

Odji exhaled loudly against the anxiety churning in his stomach and making him drip with perspiration. So much for all their meticulous planning, he thought bitterly with a heavy sigh. It was all wasted. A chance like this would not come again, especially now that the king was alert to the danger. Odji braced himself against the disappointment carving a deep line between his brows, and he rubbed the back of his bleeding head once again. And closing his eyes in an effort to calm himself after the night's precarious events, he brought his hand around and licked the blood clean off his fingers.

FOUR

K ing Mentuhotep II watched with pride as his sons Khu and Nakhti fought in the mock-battle exercises in a clearing which backed into the high palisade lying beyond the palace and deeper within the desert. The sun blazed over the reddish rock that climbed in a steep and jagged line toward the sky. A hawk was soaring through the air, climbing a thermal updraft with its broad wings and wide fanned tail, then gliding effortlessly as it rode the current against the vast blue sky. The bird screeched a high-pitched and haunting call as it eyed the parched landscape below, which lay east of the lush floodplains by the river. It was late in *Shemu*—the Season of Harvest— long after the crops had been picked, and the fields were cleared and left bare. The ensuing drought was warm and dry.

This year marked Khu's fourteenth Season of Inundation, just as it did for Nakhti. The boys were the same age. Seven flood cycles of the Nile had passed since the time Khu was first discovered along the river's bank. He was fourteen years old.

Khu had just parried a thrust of Nakhti's spear. He ducked, leaping back in an easy motion before stepping forward with a succession of quick cuts with his dagger. Nakhti deflected the blows with the shaft of his spear, then withdrew his own dagger. He feigned a left while moving to the right, swinging the blade toward Khu's belly. Without breaking his rhythm, Khu sidestepped out of Nakhti's reach before driving his dagger in a smooth and unex- pected lunge of his own. He stopped just short of Nakhti's neck, resting the tip of the blade along his sun-darkened skin glistening with perspiration. Some of the other boys watching from the sidelines were calling out and cheering. Their trainer—a man by the name of Qeb—frowned. The battle exercise was over, the outcome clearly favoring Khu.

Mentuhotep smiled. He had watched his sons grow strong and upright over time. Although Nakhti was his firstborn, he was not heir to the throne. Nakhti was born of one of Mentuhotep's lessor consorts, as were some of the younger children participating in the training exercises here. But there was no rivalry in Nakhti's heart for his siblings. He had earned a place of respect within the hierarchy of his family, and he also knew he was one of his father's favorites.

Yet of all of Mentuhotep's children, it was Khu who had developed most in the years since the ruler had first claimed him as his own son. The king remembered when Tem first introduced him to the frail boy—a mere slip of a child who reminded him more of the slender papyrus reeds than anything else. The memory was a sharp contrast to the young man he had grown into since that time.

Mentuhotep thought of these things as he observed Khu and Nakhti drinking the thickly brewed *heqet* directly from an earthen jug handed to them by an attending servant. Made of barley and sweetened with honey, the herbed liquid ran down their chins, spilling onto their bare chests, and cooling their skin as it refreshed them. Nakhti wiped his mouth with the back of his hand as Khu grabbed the jug from him and drank his own fill of the nutritious beverage that was a staple in the people's diet.

Khu was the tallest of the king's children. Whereas Nakhti was built stocky, Khu's muscular frame was lean and sinewy. He also possessed a natural grace and confidence, moving and speaking with the ease of one comfortable in his own skin.

Nakhti's confidence had a cocky edge to it. He was the more impulsive and boisterous of the two brothers, who had been best friends since childhood. Nakhti was also always the first to throw down a challenge or jump into a fight. He was the kind who acted before thinking, while Khu proceeded more cautiously.

Like most of the women in the palace, Nakhti's own mother had warned him to keep his distance from Khu when the strange boy had first come to live under their roof. Her fears were based on age-old superstitions passed from one generation to another, and there was little to change them now. But unlike Neferu who was jealous of Khu and the king's affection for him, Nakhti's mother did not feel threatened by the child. She just felt uncomfortable by those catlike eyes of his which almost seemed to look *through* people.

Despite the superstitions, fears and jealousies following the innocent child like the dust clouds kicked up by the beasts of burden on the dirt roads, it had not been long before Nakhti and Khu became fast friends. Like most children whose natural curiosity gets the better of them and trumps their initial reserve, Nakhti's own curiosity and interest in Khu drew them together. And their personalities—though opposite—suited and complimented each other well. They became inseparable.

Before long, the rest of the palace occupants and others who came into contact with the boy, let go of their doubts and suspicions when they saw no evil befall the young Nakhti, who could always be found playing with Khu. No strange illness claimed his body, no madness overtook his mind, and no injury of any kind incapacitated Nakhti. This was enough proof of the young Khu's harmlessness, leading the others to accept Khu as one of their own.

Except for Neferu.

Although Neferu's own infant son Sankhkare had grown into a healthy and inquisitive toddler in the first few years after Khu's arrival, she still regarded Khu with tremendous jealousy. It most certainly must have been due at least in part to the great affection held for him by the king. Mentuhotep loved Khu.

Whenever the ruler's gaze came to rest on the boy, it was as though someone had kindled a light within his eyes. His whole face seemed to glow with the warmth that filled him. Perhaps it was the timing of their introduction that played a significant role in their bond. It was like all the warmth and tenderness that Mentuhotep had felt for his third wife Henhenet and their unborn daughter had been transferred to Khu upon their deaths. And once that favor had been bestowed on the child, nothing could shake it. It was as strong and steadfast as the pyramids of Lower Egypt which dated back to the Old Kingdom.

It was this bond that Neferu envied. The rational part of her knew that nothing but death could take the kingdom's future throne from her son. Sankhkare's heirdom had been decided from the womb, conditional to his being born male. But another part of her feared for her son's future, and wished to guard it jealously against any would-be usurpers. Although she despised the uncertainties that hardened her heart and filled her veins with poison, she could not stop the tension from gripping her whenever she saw the easy father-son relationship shared by Khu and the king.

She hated Khu. She hated him because she feared and envied him. She wanted the same bond for Sankhkare and the king. And although she would not admit it to herself, she also hated him because he was everything that she wanted her own son to be. Her hatred possessed a depth and complexity that would take nothing short of a feat of supernatural proportions to dispel.

And that is precisely what finally happened.

It was during the festival of *Heb Nefer en Inet*—the Beautiful Feast of the Valley—that Neferu experienced a dramatic change of heart. Khu was nine years old at that time. The annual celebration took place during the second month of *Shemu*—the Season of Harvest—and saw much feasting and rejoicing throughout the kingdom of Thebes.

A shrine bearing the statue of the god Amun was transported with great pomp and circumstance in a procession led by the temple priests out of the Temple of Amun. The golden shrine was covered in finely woven linen dyed in brilliant hues of turquoise and purple, to hide it from the public's eyes. It was carried on a sacred barque by a procession of priests draped in animal skins, who followed after a slew of fan-bearers, singers and musicians.

The great Temple of Amun dominated the temple complex in Thebes, for the god Amun was king of the gods and creation, and one of the chief deities in all Egypt, especially in the Upper Lands where he was honored with his wife Mut and their son Khonsu as part of the Theban Triad. The temple's limestone architecture reflected white under a dazzling sun. Two obelisks stood like sentinels before the grand pylon which rose formidably toward the blue sky.

The procession of priests stepped out of the towering entrance and walked down the Avenue of Sphinxes in the presence of the many people who had been granted time off from work in order to participate in the important festivities. The priests made their way beyond the temple complex, through the village streets, and onto a gilded barge floating over the Nile. This was followed by a flotilla of smaller boats carrying people and a profusion of flowers and choice offerings of food and drink including bread, meat, spiced honey cakes, dates, figs, melons, wine and *heqet* that had been brewed especially strong for the joyous occasion.

People throughout the region cheerfully greeted the god with incense, music and dancing. They saluted him with joyful hymns, prostrating themselves in adoration and gratitude as the sacred icon of Amun passed before them. Amun's statue was transported to the various mortuary temples and tomb chapels housing the remains of their beloved dead on the Nile's west bank, before returning back on the barge and over the land as the sun crossed the sky on its daily voyage over the earth. It was a time of rejuvenation, jubilation, and thanksgiving for the bounty bestowed upon the land and the people. It was also a time of remembrance when people honored and paid tribute to the dead.

"Amun! Amun!" many called out as they flung themselves on the ground to bow low before the passing shrine.

"Adoration to thee! Ruler of gods, life-giver to the lands!"

"Amun! Beloved sovereign of sovereigns!" others cried in the grip of ecstasy intensified by the sweet incense and potent heqet inebriating the people.

Khu and Nakhti were among the large group of children that cheered, clapped and danced in tune to the music filling the perfumed air.

By this time, the late afternoon's setting sun blazed with a crimson fire over the revelers who had been celebrating since the early morning, and its warmth heightened the effects of the heqet that flowed freely among the people. The long day's festivities had continued on the east bank of the Nile after all the religious ceremonies had been completed. People rejoiced throughout the village, by the riverbank, and in front of the temple complex long after the golden shrine had been returned to its home within the great temple's sanctuary.

A crowd of wealthier revelers including the high officials and their families, the nobility, and the royal family and their friends had withdrawn from the streets and temple complex to celebrate on the lavish palace grounds whose pillared halls and lush courtyards spread out like an oasis of earthly delights. Everything had been decorated for the feast, so that garlands of fresh flowers and vines encircled the columns and hung from the buildings in colorful displays. There were tables laden with platters of food, earthen jars brimming with heqet, and clay amphoras filled with red wine that was kept for special feast days.

People bedecked themselves in their finest garments, makeup, and jewelry made of gold with precious gems including garnets, carnelian and lapis lazuli. Women wore perfumed wax cones over their festival wigs so that

61

the sweet oil ran over their shoulders as it melted, enveloping them in its fragrance. Even the beasts in the private palace stables were adorned with wreaths for the special occasion, and given extra helpings of fodder.

People were laughing and swaying by the musicians, their heads spinning as they gave themselves over to the elation suffusing the air. Professional musicians played an assortment of instruments including harps, flutes and lyres, while nimble dancers performed acrobatics as part of the festival amusements.

It was then that Khu noticed little Sankhkare toddling over by a pond.

The pond was one of the many pools kept in the lush palace gardens that grew with an abundance of date palms, fruit trees, and flowering plants surrounding the spacious living quarters. It was strewn with lotus flowers and miniature floating oil lamps whose flames imbued the murky water with an emerald glow. Sankhkare was alone, and had somehow escaped the watchful eyes of his mother and nursemaid. And free of their restrictive attentions, he scuttled happily away before anyone could notice.

The two-year-old heir to the throne was holding a date in his chubby little hand. He had been gnawing at it while creeping closer to the pond's edge which was fringed with purple fountain grass, foxtail, flowering rushes, and bur reeds. Getting down on his hands and knees, he stuffed the date into his mouth, leaned forward, and stretched out his arm over the water. The spiked bluish petals of the lotus blossoms had not yet closed for the night, and their fragrance was intoxicating. Sankhkare tried to reach one of these delicate beauties when he slipped and disappeared beneath the dark water without a sound.

A bolt of anguish shot through Khu in that instant.

Khu was standing about twelve paces away from the pond. He had been clapping his hands in time to the rhythm of a tune along with a large group of children when he flinched suddenly, forcing him to turn and look for the little boy he had just seen wandering toward the pond moments before. He knew something was terribly wrong. His heart was beating like the wings of a scattering of heron who had been startled while wading through the river marshes.

Sankhkare was gone.

A rippling in the water's surface was all that remained after the pond swallowed him up without so much as a splash. But Khu knew he was in trouble. He felt the child's distress as strongly as though it had been *he* who had been engulfed by the turbid water.

"Sankhkare!" Neferu cried out, scanning the area about her.

Her son had simply vanished. He had been sitting on the ground nearby a moment ago, playing with a wooden toy cat, and the clay pieces of a stone board game. Neferu saw the circular playing pieces strewn haphazardly about, while the toy cat lay abandoned on its side. But the little boy was nowhere in sight.

Neferu thrust her cup of wine into the hand of a servant, and got up to leave the group of women with whom she had been chatting. She searched wide-eyed for the little boy who meant the world to her.

"Where is Sankhkare?" she asked in a panicked pitch of the nursemaid who was looking bewildered herself. "WHERE IS HE?" she yelled as she grasped the nurse by the shoulders and shook her hard.

"I... I-I don't know, my lady," the woman stuttered, her eyes filled with fear. "He was just here."

Khu ran over to the pond, catching Neferu's eye. She stopped to stare at him in confusion as he jumped into the water without hesitation.

"Khu!" someone yelled from the crowd after he leaped into the water.

The musicians stopped playing their instruments, and people everywhere turned to see what was happening.

Khu ducked under the pond's surface and grabbed Sankhkare by an arm, pulling him up out of its depths. By now everyone had stopped dancing to gather round the pond and watch as Khu lifted the small boy out of the water, and lay him down on the dry ground next to the grasses.

Sankhkare was not breathing.

The little boy's face was ashen as he lay unconscious on his back, eliciting a loud gasp from the crowd whose eyes were now riveted to the scene. And climbing rapidly out of the water, Khu turned the boy on his side and struck him firmly on the back. Then he shoved his finger in the boy's mouth and pulled out the partially eaten date that had gotten lodged in Sankhkare's throat when he fell into the pond.

"Sankhkare!" Neferu ran to her son, crouching down on the ground beside him, her eyes wide with the panic that drove her to the edge of madness as the realization of what had just happened dawned on her with a jarring impact.

The little prince began to cough, gasping as he gulped for air. Then he cried inconsolably as the shock of the accident wore off, and the seriousness of the events struck him with dread.

"Sankhkare... Sankhkare..." Neferu whispered as she held her son closely, rocking him back and forth to sooth the frightened child and calm her own frayed nerves. "It is alright now, my child... my sweet child," she cooed lovingly to her boy.

"He will be fine," Khu said in a low voice.

Neferu looked up suddenly as though she had forgotten Khu was there. She said nothing at first, but stared at him with wide eyes filled with emotion. "Thank you," she mouthed to Khu as hot tears streamed down her face. For a moment she just closed her eyes tightly and buried her head in her son's chest, as a tumult of emotions assailed her. Then she lifted her head. "Thank you, Khu... thank you, thank you, thank you," she repeated again and again as she locked eyes with Khu while scooping Sankhkare up closer to embrace him.

Khu blinked his eyes with a slow nod to Neferu in acknowledgment. He reached out to caress the little boy's shaven head, and the plaited sidelock of hair that was dripping water from the pond. That was when Neferu placed her own hand on top of Khu's. She squeezed it with all the emotions overwhelming her for the tragedy that had so nearly happened, and for what Khu had done to avert it.

Khu turned his golden gaze on Neferu, looking her in the eyes with gratitude for the kindness she was showing him for the very first time. And from that day on, the ice that had previously clogged her veins and frozen her heart, melted away.

And all the hate, fear and envy were replaced by a reverential blend of wonder and admiration for the boy who saved her son's life.

Mentuhotep regarded Khu and Nakhti with a faraway look in his eyes, as a servant handed each of the boys clean linen cloths to wipe away the sweat and dirt from their faces.

The boys had spent the first part of their day in their schooling lessons as was customary for male children of the nobility and wealthier classes. Temple priests and scribes tutored boys in reading, writing, mathematics and medicine, along with a limited amount of geography, history and foreign phrases where applicable, so that they were well acquainted with governmental and temple procedures. While all pupils were taught to read and write, the other subjects were only reserved for those who would require them in their future careers, be it as government officials, priests, doctors or scribes, among the various occupations.

The daily lessons lasted several hours from the early morning, and could be long and tedious with much memorization and endless copying of hieroglyphic scripts. The tutors were hard taskmasters, and were quick to correct wayward students with a lash of a rod. By the time the lessons were finished for the day, the boys had a great deal of pent-up energy which they were eager to exhaust in their combative training exercises, under the guidance of Qeb. It was a strict and vigorous routine, both mentally and physically, but one which helped to mold the boys into men.

The king was pleased with his sons' training and all the progress they had shown over the years. Both of them were intelligent, strong and capable. Khu's natural aptitude was especially impressive, though one would never guess from his pragmatic and unassuming nature.

Mentuhotep was remembering the time when he first discovered Khu's special gift.

The king had been attempting to settle a quarrel between two villagers who had come to the palace with some officials. Both of the men were skilled craftsmen, and worked in the village workshops. One of them was a carpenter while the other a metalworker. They lived on the same block and had enjoyed a comfortable living from the talents which had made their skills profitable.

The two men waited quietly before the king. The proceedings took place in a shaded courtyard where the king usually managed the local affairs of his lands and people. The men standing before him had been foes for a long time. The years had engendered a spirit of competition which had degenerated into jealousy and envy. They tried to outdo each other in wealth and status, and the flames of that rivalry were fanned by their family's petty conflicts, so that their mutual enmity extended between their wives, children, and other relatives.

One of the men had begun stealing from the other several years before. At first it was an act of malice done to spite the other, but as time passed, it deepened into something more wicked. The guilty man sought to disparage the other's good name. He would sometimes plant evidence to falsely accuse his rival of stealing, and to defame his good character. But nothing had come of it until recently, when the innocent man was found in possession of an amulet hidden in his shop. That amulet belonged to a temple priest. This was a serious crime, for while thieves were not tolerated, and their crimes were met with harsh consequences, stealing from the temple or from one of the temple priests was especially disdained as an egregious offence.

Both men stood with their faces tight and jaws set. It was impossible to tell who was guilty or innocent by looking at them, as both pointed their fingers to each other in accusation.

"For years he has been stealing from my family, Lord King," the first spoke with his head bowed in humility as he stood before the king who was seated on a throne on top of a raised platform.

Two advisors waited at either side of Mentuhotep, watching the events with the corners of their mouths turned down. Four temple priests were also in attendance, including the man from whom the amulet had been stolen. This case had been tried by priests earlier, but they had not been able to reach a decision on their own, even after praying to the gods for help in their deliberations. And so the villagers had petitioned to take their case before the king, where Mentuhotep would have the final say and judgment on the matter. But no one knew what to make of the testimony. It was one man's word against another.

"Years?" the king asked.

"Yes, Lord King."

"That is not true!" the second man spoke emphatically. "He lies!"

"Quiet!" one of the advisors yelled. "Do not speak unless spoken to."

"You will have your turn to speak," the other advisor said.

Mentuhotep frowned. He leaned back in his chair and raised an arm to rest his chin on the back of his fisted hand as he thought. "And why have you not complained before this?" he asked the first man.

"I have, Sire, but I did not have proof."

The second man scowled at that. He shook his head and closed his eyes in a grave attempt to keep silent and wait his turn. He tried to steady the beating of his heart.

The first man was perspiring noticeably, and kept wiping his beaded brow, and then his clammy hands on his kilt, yet it was not that warm. A pleasant breeze carried the scent of roses, narcissus and myrtle flowers blooming in the surrounding gardens beyond the courtyard.

Tem had been watching in silence from the back of the room with Khu by her side. She had already known of Khu's gift of discernment from comments he would make, or simply from the way he would look at someone. And although she had tried to convince Mentuhotep before of Khu's gift, the king had not believed her. He had dutifully listened with the measured tolerance of a lion putting up with the annoying antics of a cub.

The young Khu stood by his mother's side and observed both men enter the courtyard and present their testimony. But even before either had spoken, he knew who was guilty. He could see into their hearts as clearly as if they had been carrying them in the palms of their hands and presenting them to the king for all to see.

Khu tugged at his mother's arm and she looked at him. Without saying anything, Khu lifted his chin in the slightest gesture toward the first man presenting his testimony. He was the guilty one.

Tem nodded to her child, and then whispered something to a nearby guard who went to Mentuhotep's side and relayed the message.

Mentuhotep frowned, and the corners of his mouth fell. How could the child possibly know who was guilty? The king wanted evidence of some kind before passing judgment. He prided himself on being a good and just ruler, following the ethical principles of *maat* which sought truth, morality, justice and order. He could not simply take the word of a child. Grave consequences would follow, and he had to make sure that the man who was truly guilty got what he deserved. It was how the gods had ordained things, and Mentuhotep was one who believed in living in accordance with divine will. It was the only way to ensure harmony in the world.

"Have them come here," the king whispered to the guard, referring to Tem and Khu.

Both walked over to the dais, and bowed respectfully before the king.

"Come closer, child," Mentuhotep waved Khu closer, and the boy stepped up on the dais by the throne. The king draped an arm about Khu's waist, drawing him closer so that they could speak out of earshot from the men standing trial. "Now tell me why you think this man is guilty," he said in a low voice. "I cannot just condemn him. What if you are wrong? It is shameful to wrongly accuse the innocent," he explained. "We will all be judged upon our deaths, and our hearts weighed against the feather of *maat*."

Khu listened patiently to the king's advice, his expression unreadable. He knew that Mentuhotep sought to do the right thing, and he loved and respected his father for this. He was well aware of the arduous journey that the spirit went through as it traveled through the Underworld on its way to the Afterlife. It was a path rife with danger and monsters ready to consume wicked souls. After crossing a wide river and passing through narrow beast-guarded gates, the spirit would stand trial before Osiris in the Hall of Two Truths. Once there, Anubis would weigh the heart of the spirit against a feather of *maat* on the scales of justice, the verdict of which would be recorded by the ibis-headed god Thoth. If they weighed the same, the spirit would pass on to the glorious Field of Reeds. But if the heart out-weighed the feather, it would be devoured by the crocodile-headed, soul-eating demon Ammit, after which it would be forever condemned to a second and eternal death and damnation.

The two village men glanced at Khu and Tem. They wondered why they were here, and what the king was telling the boy with the strange eyes. They were both very nervous, knowing that the outcome of this trial would forever change their lives.

"Khu?" Mentuhotep prompted. He was waiting for the boy's response.

Khu looked into the king's eyes and simply said, "If you go into the first man's house, you will find something of value hidden there that does not belong to him; something he had stolen from the other man's family, and then hidden in his own home. It will be the evidence you seek."

And that is exactly what had happened.

A stolen carnelian charm carved into a *kheper* scarab beetle was discovered after Mentuhotep had the guilty man's home searched. The king questioned the innocent man and found that the charm did indeed belong to his family. It had been stolen the previous year, and hidden within a jewelry box belonging to the first man's wife.

The first man was found guilty and publically beaten by the guards. He and his entire family were immediately exiled from the village, and made to leave without taking their things. Their home and belongings were given to the innocent man in recompense for all the damages he had suffered.

After that, Mentuhotep learned to trust Khu's instincts, and began to rely more and more on Khu's gift to help him as he presided over important matters.

Shouting distracted the king from his reverie as he turned to see his younger sons wrestling on the sandy ground. They had been pole sparring when one of them hit another a bit too hard. A fight ensued, drawing the rest of the boys into a tangle of striking limbs and insults mingling with the dust.

"Coward!" shouted one of the boys as he punched another in the chest.

"You are the coward! another yelled back. "And you smell like a donkey!"

"Sniveling swine!" a third was kicking a boy on the ground.

"Diseased goat!" another shouted.

"You hit like a girl!" the first lashed out.

Then the sounds of their individual voices were lost in the general cacophony of the fight.

Mentuhotep's eyes widened and his eyebrows shot up. For a moment he wondered what unholy world the squabbling and shrieking mass had come from. Only Khu and Nakhti watched in amusement. Then the king glanced at Qeb. The trainer shook his head slowly while muttering something under his breath. He looked like he had had enough for the day, as he stood with his muscled arms hanging limply by his sides. It had been a long day in the company of the rambunctious boys whose temperaments sometimes got the better of him.

"That is enough for today, Qeb," the king said with a wave of his hand. "Let them be."

The boys ceased their wrestling at the sound of their father's voice. And when they went to drink some of the heqet from the jugs waiting under the shade of a tent by their older brothers, Nakhti doused them with the drink, laughing as he poured it over their shaved heads.

"That is to cool your hot tempers," he told them with a grin.

They shrieked and giggled as the liquid soaked them and dripped down their single plaited sidelocks, forgetting their warrior's training as they reverted to their childish ways.

Servants collected the fighting accoutrements and other materials used for the day's training as the king took Qeb aside for a private word.

"I plan to take Khu and Nakhti with us on our next expedition south," he said.

Qeb looked away for a while, his expression guarded as he pondered the king's intentions. Perspiration beaded his smooth dark skin that gleamed like burnished bronze under the hot sun. He ran a hand over his smooth ebony scalp in an absent-minded gesture. His densely-coiled, wooly hair was kept shaved, so that it never grew beyond a stubble, and only when an expedition or other important matter kept him from shaving every day.

Qeb had been with Mentuhotep for many years, since before the king ascended to the throne. He had been captured in a raid when he was just a boy down in the land of Kush from where he had originated. Like many of the captured Kushites, Qeb had been assimilated into the Theban royal army where he had honed his fighting skills under the tutelage of other warriors. He had fought many times alongside Mentuhotep in the years since then, and had proven himself to be a formidable soldier of steadfast loyalty.

Qeb had earned the illustrious, hard-won title of Military Chancellor in Mentuhotep's army at the beginning of the king's reign, and was highly respected by all the king's soldiers. Although Qeb had men working for him who assisted with all the boys' training, there were some things he preferred to oversee himself. It was this hands-on approach that earned him great respect. He was never one to dictate to others what he would not do himself, whatever the circumstances might entail.

Qeb watched Khu and Nakhti as they led the smaller boys back to the palace. The two boys had lost their long plaited sidelocks when they had reached adolescence, and their shaved heads shone golden under the sun. Qeb worked his jaw a little, crossing his long arms over his broad chest as he thought of the boys he had been training for years. He knew they were talented and that they would prove themselves fine warriors someday. He just did not wish to see that day come too soon.

This would not be the first expedition in which the two boys had accompanied their father. But previous missions were mainly administrative in purpose, where the king visited the various settlements in his kingdom in order to meet with the officials overseeing them, discuss local matters and concerns, and to collect the taxes that he was owed as their regent.

It was important for Khu and Nakhti to accompany their father since one day they too would be given the responsibility of governmental positions, overseeing settlements or perhaps even becoming commanders in Mentuhotep's elite army. Whatever they ended up doing required training. These responsibilities had to be earned in accordance to their abilities. The king was not one to grant favors lightly. He wanted people he could trust and depend on in positions of power. Those positions required a great deal of diplomacy—a skill which was learned and subsequently honed into a fine art.

But this mission was a little different.

The king was planning to go to the land of Kush. All his expeditions to Kush were handled with great care because of the threat of encountering conflict. Mentuhotep never knew how a journey to Kush would result, and Qeb felt a little apprehensive about letting the boys go. Perhaps it was his own foolish sentimentality. He loved them as sons.

"The Kushites…" Qeb began uncertainly in his deep, accented voice. It was strange to be talking of his own people this way. Yet they were not his people anymore. He barely even remembered his parents. He considered himself a Theban and an Egyptian. Many former Kushites were Egyptians now. They did not see themselves as anything else.

"Yes," Mentuhotep nodded, "I know." The king could see Qeb's doubts on his face, almost reading his mind.

"They cannot be trusted," Qeb said.

"And how long has it been since we've encountered any conflict with them?"

"Several years."

Mentuhotep turned to watch a hoopoe-lark land on a spiny shrub. It perched there for a moment before turning its head and jumping to the ground, where it ran a few paces on long legs. Then it stopped to probe its curved bill and dig for an insect in the ground. The dark markings on its pretty face resembled the *kohl*-drawn lines adorning the people's eyes.

"No, they cannot be trusted," Mentuhotep agreed as he looked back at his military chancellor, "but they are also predictable. Gold makes men predictable."

"Hmm..." Qeb intoned dubiously, his mouth set into a hard line.

The king could see Qeb's concern and hesitation carved into the handsome line of his brow. "I was not much older than they when I became king," he said, glancing at the boys while standing alongside his loyal soldier who was also his friend. "Battle makes men of boys," the king continued. "You yourself know that more than anyone."

"I was younger than they, by a few seasons I think," Qeb stared unblinkingly ahead, his face grave.

"You were," the king nodded, "and that is why you turned out the way you did."

Qeb looked at Mentuhotep, his face unreadable. He was going to say something but then thought better of it and held his tongue. He would never disrespect his ruler, regardless of their years together and the casual air of their friendship. Mentuhotep was still his sovereign.

"They are ready," Qeb finally admitted with a resolute face. He worried for them.

"Good," Mentuhotep looked satisfied. It was time to involve his eldest sons more considerably in his business and military affairs.

The peace that had reigned in the early part of Mentuhotep's rule was fading fast. He had squelched several small uprisings over the past years, but more were expected. It had been a tumultuous time in Egypt with the kingdoms divided. Skirmishes, political unrest, disorder and hardship stemmed from the power struggles in the North, where various would-be kings had fought to claim the throne of Lower Egypt, which stood on a foundation riddled with uncertainty, treachery and greed. Those power struggles left the region of the Nile Delta weak and open to invasion from the Sea Peoples and the Hyksos, as well as the many thieves that preyed on the Nile Valley's weaker settlements like fleas on a dog.

The king glanced in Khu's direction as his son walked away with the rest of his boys in the group. Mentuhotep recalled being told that when Khu was first found hiding in the reeds, his clothing had been bloodied. He had been covered in blood and filth—blood that was not his own. Khu had been protected by the gods, or he too would have died in the terrible massacre he had escaped. He *was* the chosen one from the prophesies. Mentuhotep believed that now. But the king had to plan his moves in accordance with the gods. After all, he himself was a god-king—son of many gods in one physical form that was a simple extension of his divinity. He was Horus, Ptah, and son of Re, to name a few.

Mentuhotep planned to make special offerings in the temple of the god Amun, as he often did. As patron of Thebes and king of the gods, Amun was especially honored throughout the upper lands of Egypt. All of creation was attributed to him, and his hidden spirit manifested itself in all living things. Amun was also believed to guide imperial fighting expeditions. And with a resurgent of uprisings, every prayer and blessing would be needed to lead the king's army to a triumph he had wanted since first acceding to the throne.

FIVE

Odji the gatekeeper waited until long after the king had departed before allowing himself a sly and sinister grin. He had watched Mentuhotep and his retinue of officials, advisors and delegates prepare for their journey, and he was waiting until Mentuhotep left so he could have a clandestine meeting.

Mentuhotep had boarded a ship on the Nile that would take him to the mines waiting in the southern territories of Egypt in Kush. A fleet of smaller boats followed the monarch's vessel with supplies including grain, linen and papyrus that would be traded with the Kushites, along with a number of weapons to arm the king's men in case things did not go as planned.

These trading expeditions could take a dangerous turn without warning. People of Kush had long proved to be capricious neighbors who could easily turn antagonistic. And yet the ranks of Mentuhotep's army and those of his predecessors had swelled with Kushite mercenaries over the years. The Kushites were highly skilled archers and had passed their expertise on to the Egyptian warriors. Their skills were so renowned that the Egyptians referred to Kush as *Ta-Seti*—"Land of the Bow."

Odji was glad that the king had taken his eldest sons along with him, especially Khu. He distrusted Khu. The rumors he had heard about Khu's gift made him nervous. Odji was certain that *that* had been the reason why the robbery he had planned years earlier had failed. Why else would it have turned out badly when it had been practically foolproof? The rumors had to be true.

The two men who had been caught had indeed kept their mouths shut, luckily. Odji had kept his distance so that they would not accuse him of being an accomplice. It would have meant his death if they had indicted and convicted him, since treason was punishable by death. The men had less to lose because they were not in the king's service. They had been flogged at the pillar as the punishment decreed, and then let go. They were fortunate they had not yet stolen anything when they were apprehended, or their punishment would have been more severe. Trespassing with the intent to steal was more than enough to earn them the penalty they received.

Odji remembered how Khu had been staring at him after the night's foiled events. It was as if the boy had *known*. Odji exhaled in disgust as the memory sent a wave of repugnance through him. But how could he have known? He was just a child, and one of unknown origins. He had also been asleep in the palace, tucked away in a room behind several walls, gardens and spaces that kept him safe, secure and sequestered, far from the scene of the attempted crime.

Khu's eerie catlike eyes had been fixed on Odji with a piercing force. It had made Odji feel like a despicable cockroach hiding in the rich grain he had planned to steal. But the boy never said a word—not to him, and not to anyone else. Whatever knowledge he might have possessed had remained locked away behind his peculiar gaze. And thankfully, Mentuhotep was none the wiser.

"Bothersome boy," Odji mumbled aloud as he shook his head disdainfully in irritation. It was hard enough to arrange the details required for such an undertaking, without the boy thwarting his schemes.

But not this time.

Khu was gone. They were not due back for the course of a moon. It all depended on how things would go for them in Kush, naturally. But having the boy gone gave Odji a greater sense of freedom. At least for what he had been planning this time.

Odji had lived comfortably in his position as gatekeeper of the wall surrounding the palace grounds. He had two subordinate assistants with whom he alternated shifts in guarding the gated entrance to the sprawling compound. It was an easy job, and a respected position that afforded him a pleasant life. But it was not enough. He wanted a position of greater power, and he wanted control over his own domain.

Odji had risen from humble beginnings due to his father's natural gardening ability to coax almost anything from the ground. His father had worked as a peasant in the fields before transferring to the palace gardens. His talents had been noticed by the palace officials who subsequently sent their own gardeners to him for advice before finally employing him to work in the royal compound. The nobles there took great pleasure in the gardens flourishing on the edge of the fertile floodplains. Fruit groves, vegetable gardens, herbs and spices, ponds surrounded by abundant grasses and colorful flower beds, and many varieties of shade trees thrived among the rows of columns hung with grapevines. They were lush and life-giving, especially given their proximity to the merciless dry desert lying east of the floodplain.

Nevertheless, Odji had felt nothing but shame for his father who would come home each evening covered in dirt. And rather than admiring the man who worked hard to carve out a living for himself and his family, Odji despised him. His father reminded him of the swine covered in mud. They were filthy creatures, and were banned from religious ceremonies because they were regarded as unclean.

"Father, you are dirty," Odji once complained when he was a child.

His father's fingernails were always encrusted with soil, no matter how much time he spent washing his hands. Odji did not wish for anyone to see his father this way. It was disgraceful and embarrassing, especially in a society that valued purity and cleanliness. But Odji's father just laughed at his son's repugnance.

"Better to be dirty and blameless, than clean with a filthy heart," his father replied wisely. "There is no shame in work, Odji. Even those who spend their days cleaning the dung from the animal pens are doing honorable work," his father spoke around a mouthful of bread, and paused to wash it down with a long gulp of heqet. "And this soil that you detest is what grows the food we eat. It is the fertile black land of life."

"But I detest it on *you*, Father. You smell bad! And everything you touch gets dirty!" Odji raised his voice to his father before running outside and up the narrow staircase leading to the rooftop.

They lived in a caretaker's lodge next to the servants' quarters on the palace grounds. Although Odji was the son of a gardener, he had been granted special permission to attend school with the children of the upper classes, where he was taught to read and write. He proved to be a bright child with talent, and his parents encouraged him in his lessons. They had wanted him to become a scribe because the work opportunities would be plentiful and lucrative. But Odji was lazy and found the work tedious. He did not want to invest the time and effort in learning something he did not like. He also felt inadequate. Every day that he studied with the other boys, he was reminded of his own humble position, not from anything they would do or say, but from his own inferiority complex. He was selfish, ungrateful and vain. And he blamed his own shortcomings on his father.

Odji swore that he would be different from the man who begot him. And he was. He was nothing like his father. While his father had been a humble man who was grateful for his place in the world, Odji wore his pride like a heavy cloak—a cloak reeking of arrogance. He felt entitled to a life he had not been born into.

"Odji!" His father said. And when the boy did not answer, he followed him up to the roof.

The sun had already set earlier, and all that remained of twilight was a thin band of silver glossing the edge of the horizon. No moon shone in the sky, and long shadows spread like black wine spilling over the land. The trees edging their home deepened the darkness, making it difficult to see.

"Odji?" his father called as he climbed the last few steps near the rooftop. "I know you are up here."

Odji did not answer. He was sulking behind a tall clay amphora on the opposite side of the roof.

His father reached the roof and paused. He was tired, and it had been a long day. "You have nothing to be ashamed of, son," he said. "There is nothing shameful about hard work. It is hard work that got us here, and it will get us into the Field of Reeds as long as we live a good and moral life."

Odji still said nothing. He kept sulking behind the amphora, as he listened to his father's footsteps.

"We could still be living in the village next to the other peasants. And you would never have had the opportunity to learn how to read and write. Instead, we'd all be doing back-breaking work in the crop fields all day long." He took small steps, trying to avoid tripping on anything. "But even that is honorable," he nodded to himself. "Yes, hard work is honorable, Odji. We must live by the principles of *maat*, for truth, order and integrity are everything."

Odji exhaled, slumping down further into his self-made misery. By now even the silver lining on the horizon was gone, having faded away into the night. Only the bright stars lit up the sky with their glittering splendor.

His father squinted as he peered into the darkness, hoping to find his sullen boy. "Come out, child," he said. "Come out and stop this foolishness. Do not be offended by a little dirt. It is the dirt within men's hearts that is most offensive; the filth you cannot see. Remember that always, son."

And those were his last words.

Something frightened Odji and he tumbled out from behind the amphora and into his father's legs. It might have been a spider crawling over his hand, or a cricket hopping in the darkness, or even just his own skittish imagination which made him screech in surprise as he tumbled into his father.

And startled by the commotion, his father lost his balance and tripped. He tried to avoid falling on the boy at his feet as he stepped away awkwardly, but he lost his footing as he came perilously close to the roof's edge.

It was not the fall that killed Odji's father, but rather the pile of mud-bricks sitting on the ground below. He lost his balance and fell off the roof, over the side of the house, landing awkwardly on that pile of bricks where he broke his neck. It had been swift. So swift, that his father did not even scream.

Odji stood, wide-eyed for a heart-stopping moment. He kept very still, staring into the darkness as he held his breath, suddenly aware of the sounds of the night. Crickets were chirping, and a dog whined in the distance. Hushed voices drifted from the servants' quarters in another part of the compound, and a light breeze ruffled the branches of the palm trees nearby. He heard an owl call, and he shivered involuntarily, touching the amulet hanging from his neck. Then he headed back slowly downstairs.

"Mother?" he called.

Odji was strangely calm. It was as though an invisible burden had been lifted from his shoulders. The load weighing him down was gone. He knew his father was dead. He knew it an instant after his father had fallen. And yet he felt nothing. No sadness, no remorse, no sorrow. Because he was dead inside.

Together he and his mother had gone outside to find his father's body.

At least his father had died with his eyes closed.

Mentuhotep's father, King Nakhtnebtepnefer Intef III, was king at the time when Odji's father died. He was a kind man who allowed Odji and his mother to continue living on the palace compound where his mother worked as a servant. They had moved out of the caretaker's lodge and into the smaller servants' quarters. Odji gladly abandoned his studies after that. A scribe was not something he aspired to.

Odji did odd jobs for several years until he commenced his guard training. When he was old enough, he began working as gatekeeper, where he remained through the rest of Intef's reign, and Mentuhotep after him. Yet his job as gatekeeper—though honorable—had never been good enough as far as he was concerned, for some people are born restless and can find no satisfaction in life. Odji was not going to sit around and wait for a change that would never come. He refused to accept things as they were.

So he began to plot something new to bring about that change for himself.

Odji had a friend named Mdjai who lived north of Thebes in the district of Abdju, which was an important religious site of many temples. Mdjai had boasted about his life as an official, and how he oversaw one of the district's smaller villages of craftsmen and laborers. Although he answered to a noble, the people of the village answered to him.

Odji wanted the same arrangement for himself. It would be far more exciting than what he did now. He was able to read and write, and believed that these skills made him worthy of a higher occupation.

Odji had never taken a wife, nor did he have any children. He did not care for those sentimental things, nor did he have time for the burdens accompanying such mundane and tedious bonds. All he wanted was power; a power to wield according to his own will.

"I am responsible for settling petty conflicts among the villagers," Mdjai had said.

"You are their judge?" Odji asked interestedly, when he had seen the man at one of the many festivals celebrated throughout Egypt.

"Yes. Their first judge. They bring their cases before me and I listen to their complaints. Then I arbitrate in their disputes."

"And if they are unhappy with the ruling?"

"They can petition to have their case heard by the temple priests."

Odji liked that very much. It would certainly be more interesting than what he did now. He wanted the respect and fear that would be shown him as an official overseeing a village of his own. He wanted the deference of a people subjected to his authority. He got a secret thrill from other people's fear. It made him feel powerful, and flooded his veins with a kind of decadent exhilaration. Just thinking of it made his skin prickle with anticipation.

He closed his eyes as he indulged in one of the fantasies which helped him get through the day-to-day routine in his dull existence. In his mind's eye he saw people begging for mercy before him. Their pathetic pleas gave him a titillating rush as he grabbed a whip to inflict a merciless punishment upon their backs. Odji swallowed and opened his eyes, tamping down the excitement that made his heart beat faster.

It would not be long now.

Odji had been biding his time and working out a new plan. He had made an arrangement with his friend Mdjai, where they would secretly exchange information so that Odji would keep him abreast of Mentuhotep's business affairs. Mdjai knew important officials who were interested in having inside knowledge about Mentuhotep. The Theban king had rivals who would pay well for this information.

After their agreement, Odji sent messages to Mdjai in Abdju every so often by way of the boatman who had come down the Nile on that blundered robbery attempt several years before. He was paid for this information according to its importance. Odji felt no allegiance to the Theban king, and did not hesitate to betray his ruler. He felt no loyalty to anyone except himself.

Odji had told Mdjai that King Mentuhotep often went down to Kush to see to his mines, trade resources, and to visit and collect taxes from some of the settlements along his route. He told his friend how the king was getting richer from the gold he often brought back. And in return, Mdjai also shared information about the political intrigues throughout the northern lands.

The boatman had recently informed Odji that a revolt was being planned in Abdju. It was being led by King Khety of Lower Egypt, who ruled from the seat of his throne in Nen-nesu, south of the Nile Delta. Khety had been conspiring with forces from the settlement of Nekhen—which was not too far south of Thebes. With the help of Ankhtifi, who was the governing chieftain of the province of Nekhen, Khety planned to capture Abdju and then continue on south in hopes of capturing Thebes as well.

Abdju had remained neutral in the political conflict dividing the once-unified powers of Egypt. It was an autonomous district, independent of the sovereignties of Lower and Upper Egypt. But some of its people wanted the protection and power that an alignment with Lower Egypt's throne would afford. Odji's friend Mdjai was one of them. Others, like many of the high priests in the temples, were more sympathetic to Mentuhotep and preferred to position themselves alongside the Theban ruler if neutrality were no longer possible.

King Khety had his sights set on overthrowing Mentuhotep, seizing the throne of Upper Egypt, and consolidating the two kingdoms under his own rule. Gaining control of Abdju would be a pivotal step in the direction that would empower him over the divided lands.

"Just try to distract your sovereign with local matters," the boatman told Odji, as though it were that easy. "Then everything will fall into place." He was relaying a message from Mdjai in Abdju.

Odji just stared at the boatman, the lines between his eyes deepening. His mind was trying to sift through and organize all the information the man had told him. He knew that Mentuhotep was wise. It would not be easy to distract him with anything. The king would see right through the weakness of that plan, and wonder what he was up to. But Mentuhotep's expedition to Kush could not have come at a better time. All Odji had to do was wait and hope that the king would be delayed by the Kushites. That would give King Khety the time he needed to capture Abdju.

"You will be compensated well. The Lord King Khety himself will see to it that you get your own village in one of the more prosperous districts in the north."

Odji swallowed at the lure dangling before him. His time had finally come. He would soon quit Thebes for good, and go north to live as a lord overseeing a village. If only his father could see him now. Everything looked promising on that sun-drenched afternoon which even made the dirt roads sparkle. Power was the elixir that made his head spin, not unlike the potent ceremonial heqet brewed very strongly during times of great feasting.

Odji pondered the boatman's message as images of a thriving village over which he ruled flitted through his mind. There was a cruelty to Odji's thin mouth that made the boatman nervous. The boatman kept glancing anxiously about him. He knew he was in danger here, and did not wish to be caught conspiring against the king. The punishment for high treason was death—death by decapitation. But that was not all. His filthy remains would be scattered in the desert, and left for the wild animals to devour. This terrible fate would leave him incapable of crossing the great divide to the Field of Reeds in the Afterlife. Without a body and proper burial, his immortal soul *ka* would forever be doomed to roam restlessly in the Netherworld.

"When will the revolt take place?" Odji asked, distracting the boatman from his dismal thoughts. Odji hoped it would happen soon before Mentuhotep returned from Kush.

"King Khety is probably on his way from Nen-nesu as we speak," the boatman said. "The annual Festival of Osiris will be celebrated in Abdju soon."

Odji frowned. "Why would he go then?" he wondered aloud.

"I think he wants to time the revolt to coincide with the festivities."

"With the Festival of Osiris?" Odji was confused. It did not make sense to him. For a moment he wondered if the boatman got his facts mixed up. The man was getting on in years.

"That is all I know," the boatman said, shrugging his thin shoulders. He shifted uncomfortably from one foot to another as he spoke. His sun-darkened skin was stretched tightly over his wiry frame, and the lines on his weathered face gave him a look of being perpetually worried.

A gray short-haired cat watched him with aloof eyes from the shade of a doorway lying beyond the main entrance to the palace compound, and the boatman touched a hand to the amulet hanging from his neck. He felt guilty and wondered if the gods were watching as well.

"Ankhtifi is there already, with a small army of his own," the boatman added. His eyes darted around nervously, making sure no one was in too close proximity to overhear their conversation. But no one even glanced their way.

"Ankhtifi?"

"Yes," the boatman said, "King Khety's supporter. The chieftain of Nekhen."

Odji nodded absentmindedly. He was imaging himself again as a lord. It was a far cry from the boy who was born to simple peasants.

An ox-drawn cart passed by on its way to the village. It hauled a crop of melons, cucumbers, leeks and onions. A man and his son led the beast of burden through the street, tugging on the animal's yoke. They did not even glance at the gatekeeper and the thin, older man with whom he was talking.

No one noticed the avarice gleaming in Odji's eyes. And as the boatman took his leave of Odji, hurrying to head back to his small vessel so he could get away from Thebes, Odji once again slipped into his reverie, dreaming of the day when he would oversee a small village of his own.

SIX

K ing Wakhare Khety III, Ruler of Lower Egypt, stood in the pavilion of his palace in Nen-nesu. He had just dismissed his advisors and needed a moment alone to think. A servant was clearing away two platters of food and several cups of heqet that had been set on a long side table standing between two columns. Khety exhaled as he stepped down from the dais where his throne sat. He walked over to the table where he had left his cup earlier. The servant paused from her work to refill his cup with heqet before bowing and leaving with the platters.

Today Khety received word that Ankhtifi had arrived in Abdju with a small army. This was good news. It was what he had wanted, and what he had been planning for several seasons now. Yet he felt a little ambivalent at how these long-awaited events were finally unfolding.

The king walked over to the edge of the pavilion with the cup in his hand. He took a sip of the heqet and stared out at the view. His palace sat on a piece of land which rose sharply from the Nile's western bank. It was set higher than the crop fields growing closer to the water's edge. A village lay south of the palace, and west of the fields. From its elevated ground, the palace commanded stunning views of the River Nile and the lush floodplains to the east, as well as of the desert ridges, sand plains, and rocky plateaus stretching interminably to the west.

There were no clouds in the vast blue sky, and the king interpreted that as an augury boding well for his plans. He needed the gods to smile upon him, for tomorrow he would depart for Abdju, where he would be joining Ankhtifi with his own army of men. The timing was perfect, for it happened to be the Festival of Osiris which was celebrated annually in Abdju. Hopefully no one would suspect anything untoward.

King Khety had descended from the Akhtoy lineage known as the House of Khety which rose to power from their seat in the district of Nen-nesu, after the disintegration of the Old Kingdom. His forefathers were buried near the great tombs of the sixth dynasty kings at Saqqara near Inebou-Hedjou. Over the last hundred years, Nen-nesu's dominance in the northern territories, and the power of the House of Khety had grown to extend over most of Lower and Middle Egypt as far south as Amarna and the province of Zawty. But that power was ridden with corruption and greed spreading out like fine fissures over the land, allowing the infiltration of all sorts of ills from thieving and bloody raids, to natural disasters including plagues and drought.

Nen-nesu was the cult center of the ram-god Heryshef, Ruler of the Riverbanks. But the ram-god's temple lay in ruin. Many of the temples of the north had been pillaged over the decades, and nothing had been done to rebuild them, so that their painted walls and pitted columns were crumbling in decay. Supplies were scarce as it was, and people were hungry.

Many of the royal necropolises had been plundered as well. Even in prosperous times the living robbed the dead. But with the breakdown of the centralized authority from the early dynasties, all within the fractured lands was vulnerable to robbers. Various rulers vied for power like wolves fighting for dominance over a pack whose alpha male had died. Thus the ancient tombs had been destroyed, and their relics left to decay under a careless sun. And Khety did not waste time, effort, or funds in rebuilding any of them—funds he did not possess and sorely needed.

King Khety was not overly concerned about the state of his dilapidated lands at the moment. He had more important things to keep him occupied. He wanted to keep hold of his throne in Nen-nesu and of Lower Egypt in general. He also wanted more power; a power extending to Upper Egypt, so that he could reunite the divided lands under his rule. Resources were scant, and he needed all of them spent on his efforts to capture Upper Egypt's throne. He had his sights set on Thebes where King Mentuhotep's throne was set firmly into the land of Upper Egypt. And King Khety was relying on Ankhtifi to help him take that throne from Mentuhotep.

Ankhtifi had been King Khety's ally for many years. Ankhtifi's own father had once served Khety's predecessor in the House of Khety that ruled Lower Egypt in Nennesu on the west bank of the Nile. Although Ankhtifi had outwardly remained neutral in the political schism between the thrones of Lower and Upper Egypt, his loyalty lay with Khety. Ankhtifi's neutral pretense was critical to the preservation of his township in Nekhen, especially given Nekhen's close proximity to Thebes. He did not wish to turn King Mentuhotep against him.

Khety pondered the news he received today as he stepped outside the pavilion to wander through the walled gardens of his palace. It was his favorite place to think. The jasmine was in full bloom, and it filled the air with its heady perfume from where it crept possessively over the thick limestone columns supporting the pergola above him. Grapevines wove through the overhead beams, shading the walkways that were framed by flower beds next to one of several ponds stocked with ornamental fish. An orchard grew beyond that.

Filled with a blend of anxiety and anticipation, Khety paused to pluck a sprig of the jasmine by one of the columns. He could not help wondering if he had made the right decision in summoning Ankhtifi to Abdju. But he knew that if he had not done so, nothing would ever change. And it was time to expand the House of Khety which had been left to him by his father, and by his father's father before him. It was time to push south and capture the throne of Upper Egypt from his nemesis Mentuhotep.

Khety thought of the Theban king as he twirled the stem of the jasmine sprig between his fingers. The milky sap left a sticky residue on his skin which he ignored as his thoughts turned to his rival in Upper Egypt. He envied Mentuhotep. He begrudged everything about him: his kingdom, his wives, his children, his gold mines in Kush... the list was endless. He knew Mentuhotep was wealthy— far wealthier than he certainly was. Khety's spies had told him so, and the prosperous state of the Upper Kingdom's lands was proof enough of this. But it was more than his wealth that Khety desired. Mentuhotep seemed happy. Khety's spies often mentioned the Theban king's contented and satisfied demeanor—something which came from having everything he had ever wanted. Yes, it was his happiness that Khety mostly envied.

Khety had no heirs of his own. His first two wives had died in childbirth many years before, when he was a young man. After a long period of mourning, he had finally taken another wife at the insistence of his advisors. Shani—his third wife—had proved strong and fertile, and had borne him four children in quick succession: two boys, followed by two girls.

Khety inhaled the fragrance of the sprig of jasmine as he braced himself against the painful memories that flooded his being like the Nile waters during the Season of Inundation. He could still remember the delighted squeals of his young children as they ran playing through the gardens; the very same gardens where he now stood. He could almost catch a glimpse of them hiding among the trees, or chasing each other through the shaded paths, or frolicking and tumbling on the soft velvety grasses. Those happy shrieks had ceased shortly after his eldest son had celebrated his seventh Season of Inundation.

His son's sudden illness had left the child immobile. It had begun with a sore throat accompanied by a high fever, which grew very painful so that he could no longer eat nor drink. Then all of his joints became painfully inflamed—his elbows, knees, wrists and ankles—so he could not walk. He was breathless and extremely fatigued. After that, he had quickly withered into a shrunken sack of bones in less than the course of a moon. Then his younger siblings fell ill just as suddenly, and all of them died of the same mysterious ailment which left them so weak, their hearts simply stopped beating.

Shani had been heavy with child at the time, expecting their fifth baby. Khety remembered the haunted look in her eyes as she struggled night and day by her children's bedsides, willing them to regain their health. Her beautiful eyes were sunken with dread, as she moved about in a harrowing daze of angst and disbelief. She refused to leave them, even after he had ordered her to get some rest in her own private quarters. She had stayed put in their room, trying to get them to sip warmly brewed infusions, placing compresses on their swollen throats and limbs, lighting incense in the room, and encircling their beds with amulets to ward off the evil ravaging their little bodies. Priests and doctors from near and far had come with every imaginable remedy, chanting endless spells and invocations known to bring healing. But nothing anyone did had made a difference. The tragedy had caused Shani to miscarry before her time, and she died along with the child she had been carrying.

Cursed. It was as though he had been cursed.

Khety shut his eyes tightly against the anguish that was always present, just beneath the surface of his forced composure. Why else would death come to smite all those whom he had dearly loved? It had been hard enough to lose his first two wives. He had not wanted to remarry after their deaths, and had closed himself off to any relationships for years. But with the passing of time, the scars of his wounds had faded from an angry red into something less caustic, so that he had allowed himself to be talked into taking another wife.

Shani had been a dream come true. In a time when marriages were formed as dynastic alliances, theirs had unexpectedly blossomed into love. They had been immensely happy together. And with the birth of each of their children, their love had only grown stronger.

Perhaps the gods had been jealous of him. All Khety knew was that when death ripped Shani and his children from his bosom, he had nearly lost his mind. Something within him died along with them; something loving and tender and kind. And when the doors to their tombs had been shut and sealed, echoing loudly through his ravaged soul, a door within his heart slammed shut like the bars of an iron cage.

The king was staring into the past with his brow furrowed, the jasmine still held under his nose. These gardens had become his private sanctuary after their deaths, and were strictly off-limits to anyone other than the servants who tended them.

But nothing had ever been the same again.

He no longer celebrated any festivals other than making a perfunctory appearance to the holiest high feasts. He no longer ate, drank or socialized with others, outside of those diplomatic meetings demanding his presence. Khety had grown very bitter. All the anguish he had tried to repress, twisted inside him, infected his soul, and hardened his heart into a kind of imposing granite obelisk which struck fear into those who stood before him.

He was a very handsome man before the tragedy; strikingly handsome with kind gray eyes, a high forehead, straight nose, sensual mouth, and a tall, sculpted physique which drew appreciative stares from those around him. But the grief had imbued his masculine beauty with a glacial edge. It had contorted his handsome face into something harsh and almost feral, thinning his mouth into a dour and rigid line, and replacing the warmth of his eyes with an icy glare. And from the depths of the misery which had destroyed all that was kind and compassionate within him, emerged a cold and ruthless ruler driven by ambition, by conquest, and by a senseless retribution that could never be avenged in a thousand lifetimes.

The capital of Nen-nesu had grown stronger under Khety's rule. It was largely due to his ability to swiftly crush the sporadic rebellions of the would-be kings from other districts who had tried to overthrow him. Khety was well aware of the many divisions within his realm. Each of the cult centers subsisting along the banks of the Nile between Upper and Lower Egypt had been largely independent since the unified powers of old had split. But their independence had left them vulnerable to raiders, turmoil, and subsequent famine due to the breakdown of the political and economic infrastructure which had fallen into decay. And like the ruins buried by the shifting sands rippling under a searing desert sun, their ephemeral rulers would rise and fall with the fickleness of time.

But not the House of Khety.

The king was determined to soar above them all. But he had to continue growing his empire for it to remain strong. Otherwise one of his opponents would swoop in like a falcon over a nest of fledglings to usurp the throne from him. Nevertheless, Khety did not worry about that now. He felt confident because he had well-placed emissaries in the most important townships, testing the waters and garnering support for his cause. He had promised them wealth and power in return for their allegiance; riches which he planned to take from the kingdom of Thebes. He wanted Mentuhotep's gold mines to fill his own coffers. But he had to first get rid of the king of Upper Egypt. And Abdju was one of the important townships which would help him achieve his ambition. So tomorrow morning he would set out for Abdju to join Ankhtifi in preparation for realizing his long-awaited dream of placing all of Egypt under the House of Khety's rule.

Ankhtifi had taken a small fleet with him to Abdju from his settlement in Nekhen under the pretense of trade. It was a believable ruse because Nekhen was a thriving trade center with access to mineral resources in the eastern desert, and was known for its skilled craftsmen which included potters, masons, weavers and bronzesmiths. It was also a major cult center for the falcon-god Horus.

Ankhtifi's fleet carried many craft items aboard its ships to prevent any suspicions from arising. But beneath the bolts of cloth, crates of pottery and exotic goods, a cache of weapons remained hidden. And the men aboard the vessels were trained warriors disguised as craftsmen.

Ankhtifi handed a scroll to an official who had boarded his lead ship when they arrived at Abdju—the main cult center of Osiris, who was god of the dead and the Afterlife. The portly man took the scroll with the casual authority of one used to being in command. He slid off the thin strip of leather binding, and then unrolled it with a show of boredom and patience, as though he had nothing better to do and all the time in which do it. The bill of lading enumerated the details of the goods on board.

Ankhtifi held his breath and tightened his grip around the handle of a weapon hanging discreetly at his side, as the official lifted a linen cloth to cast a cursory glance over the merchandise packed in one of several large crates. The only sign betraying Ankhtifi's tension was a slight involuntary twitching of his clenched jaw—a tic he had had since childhood. He regarded the official quietly with deeply set hooded eyes, before forcing himself to breathe.

"Thirty cubits?" the official questioned casually, reading from the scroll as he prodded one of the bolts of cloth with a stick.

"Yes," Ankhtifi said, "each bolt is thirty cubits long."

The official looked impressed but said nothing for a moment. He was not a rich man, but knew from Ankhtifi's fleet and position as chieftain of Nekhen that Ankhtifi was wealthy. But chieftain or not, Ankhtifi had to answer to him now. The official obviously enjoyed this part of his job, and how people stood aside to wait on his every word. He strutted about with his head held high, flaunting his power.

"Life must be good in Nekhen," he told Ankhtifi as he ran his beady eyes over the crates on the ship. There was an envious note to his tone. "But it could take a long time to make a thorough check of everything," he said without looking at the chieftain. "Procedures are procedures, after all."

Ankhtifi just watched him silently with narrowed eyes, the tic in his jaw twitching of its own accord. The official took his time, seemingly oblivious to everything going on around him.

The port at Abdju was bustling with activity, and there were people everywhere. It was far busier than usual due to the preparations for the annual festival that took place here. Boats and ships of all sizes were arriving to the major cult center of Osiris. They brought pilgrims coming to honor the god of the Afterlife, and all sorts of food and other goods that would be bought, sold and consumed during the high feast celebrations.

Some people had come from as far north as the Nile Delta lying just beyond Inebou-Hedjou and the pyramids of old. A few had traveled from as far south as Abu Simbel in Kush where the great rocky mountainside would one day—centuries later in the nineteenth dynasty of Egypt's New Kingdom—be carved into two massive temple monuments honoring Ramesses the Great and his principle wife Queen Nefertari. But most people were arriving from settlements lying somewhere in between, the majority of which were near and north of Abdju. They were eager to abandon the tedium of their hard lives in order to lose themselves in the celebration of the festivities, if only for a few glorious days.

Oxen and donkeys pulled wooden carts or were laden with heavy burdens which were unpacked from the boats and transported into town. Some people balanced large baskets over their heads or on each shoulder as they trod carefully, weaving through the crowds. Others moved along with nothing but the simple linen clothes they wore, as they clutched the hands of their children and relatives, and headed toward the festival.

The port was accessible from a kind of inlet formed where the Nile branched off into a creek. It was protected from the rising floodwaters by a strip of land growing thick with date and doum palms, sycamore figs, and acacia trees. One side of the land strip was a dark earthen mass which had been carved out by the water over time. It rose high and muddy in parts before disappearing below the copse of trees, and then sloping back down beneath the reeds on the opposite side of the bank. Pelicans, grebes and wild geese waded by the reeds in search of fish, while others neared the port where they hoped to snag some of the discarded offal tossed into the water by the fishermen cleaning their catch. The port itself had long ago been cleared away of vegetation and paved with large blocks of stone where the boats were dragged ashore.

Abdju was largely a temple-town set deeper into the dry desert beyond the western bank of the River Nile, where stone shrines and chapels rose from the sedimentary rock out of which they were carved. It was also home to a large royal necropolis where past monarchs of the early dynasties were entombed. The ancient *mastaba* tombs were rectangular-based, flat-roofed stone structures, resembling a wide bench with sloping sides from far. Deep, hidden chambers housed the dead, while above-ground rooms kept items such as clothing, furniture and food, believed to be useful to the deceased in the Afterlife.

Beyond the sprawling temple complex was a town where the craftsmen and other workers lived. The streets hummed with visiting pilgrims and local workers readying for the great Festival of Osiris. Everywhere the excitement of the annual celebration was felt as musicians tuned their instruments, acrobats practiced their dances, merchants set up their stalls, and priests readied the temples.

But the man checking Ankhtifi's ships behaved as though nothing special were happening, and he took his time with his work. It was just a show of his power, for he had no real interest in the items Ankhtifi carried, which he checked with a passing glance of one with little curiosity for the things around him. He behaved as though they were beneath his concern, which was fine by Ankhtifi who was eager to get on with his work.

"You are staying for the festival, yes?" the official asked nonchalantly.

"We are."

"Things are busy as you can see for yourself," the man swept a hand over the port, indicating the crowds. "As I mentioned, it could take a long time to make a thorough inspection of everything," he shrugged and shook his head as though disappointed. "A *long* time," he repeated with emphasis. Then he stopped to look Ankhtifi in the eye as he lifted a single *kohl*-elongated eyebrow in an unspoken message.

Ankhtifi took the bait and stepped closer to the man, the urge to clobber him barely kept in check. "Perhaps this might speed things up a little," Ankhtifi said as he handed the man a gold piece.

The official's eyebrows shot up greedily, and he snatched the gold and tucked it away into a pocket. "Of course, of course. It most certainly will speed things along," he smiled to Ankhtifi, and scratched a mark on the scroll before handing it back to him. "In fact, we are finished here. Everything looks satisfactory and has passed inspection. Welcome to Abdju. You may proceed with your business. Enjoy the festival," he gave a curt bow and then left the ship.

"Thank you sir," Ankhtifi replied tightly. He forced a smile that did not reach his dark eyes. He was relieved that this part of his mission was complete.

This was not the first time Ankhtifi had been on a clandestine mission for Khety. He had built himself a fearsome reputation over the many years of his service to the king who wore Lower Egypt's *Deshret* Red Crown. Ankhtifi had come to be known as *He Who Wields Death*: an informal title bestowed upon him by enemies who uttered it behind his back. His favorite weapon was a copper-headed mace which he carried with him wherever he went. It hung from his sword belt by its elaborately carved wooden handle overlaid in bronze, and reinforced with interwoven strips of sinew.

Ankhtifi had been instrumental in helping Khety flush out many of the traitors conspiring to take Khety's throne in Nen-nesu. One of them had been a pretender who had claimed the defunct throne of Inebou-Hedjou, which had once been the old capital of the unified lands of Egypt during the Old Kingdom before its subsequent division. The would-be ruler was captured, questioned, and then put to a shameful death as a public example of the terrible consequences that would befall anyone who opposed Khety's rule.

Before the traitor was executed, Ankhtifi had coerced him into revealing all of his allies. One by one, each of his supporters was apprehended and brought before Ankhtifi. Some of them had broken into a fetid sweat at the intimidating sight of Khety's enforcer, as he towered above them by the length of a head. His implacable expression was made more menacing by dark hooded eyes whose irises were the same color as his pupils. He had a long skull with a wolfish face, high cheekbones, a long thin nose, and prominent elongated chin. And as he circled around each of the men with the deliberate grace of a leopard, the spiderlike fingers of his hand resting on the hilt of his mace, most of the men had broken down and confessed to their share in the conspiracy. But before being beaten and put to death, they had pleaded for a mercy they would never receive.

And none was shone them.

Ankhtifi had then gone to Khety's palace in Nen-nesu and presented the king with the severed right hands of his dead opponents.

"What has been done with the rest of their remains?" the king had asked Ankhtifi.

"Wrapped in goat skins, Lord King, and left in a shallow grave."

Khety regarded his enforcer with a look of apprehensive curiosity, narrowing his eyes as he tilted his head to one side. He was aware of Ankhtifi's reputation, especially as it had been earned under his service. He knew that the man was feared. He was even familiar with Ankhtifi's informal title and had once asked him about it.

"Are you aware that they refer to you as He Who Wields Death?" Khety had asked this with a smile, though he was not truly amused by it. He actually found it rather disturbing and ominous.

"Worse things have been said," Ankhtifi replied indifferently, his eyes gazing away at nothing.

He seldom made eye contact with Khety or anyone else for that matter; rarely held anyone's gaze. And when he did, there was something cold within his eyes. It was as though he felt nothing inside—was *incapable* of feeling anything—neither joy nor sorrow. He was stoic to the point of seeming inhuman at times.

Khety just stared at the chieftain and surreptitiously touched the amulet hanging from his neck, as he suppressed an inexplicable chill that left him uncomfortable. He distrusted the man. Yet Khety could not say why, or what it was about Ankhtifi that made him wary and watchful. It was more of an instinct cautioning him to be alert and on guard. It was as though he were standing in front of a wild and unpredictable animal which had been raised to do his bidding. But for all his training, the animal was still feral at heart. He was a savage in civilized guise.

Although Khety had known Ankhtifi for many years, he realized that he really did not truly *know* him. It was impossible to really know the man. There was something very guarded and enigmatic about him. Ankhtifi lacked the empathy to understand or relate to others' feelings. It was as though he were surrounded by a thick stone wall.

Ankhtifi was not one for conversation either. He didn't say very much, nor did he laugh. He did not find humor in anything, even when others were joking and laughing around him. All implied humor went right over his tall wolfish head.

Over the years Khety had learned to be very direct and explicit with Ankhtifi. He knew that the man seldom strayed from routines. He was highly functional and prosperous yet took little delight in his affluence. He was the kind who found satisfaction in the accumulation of wealth, rather than in its spending, as though it really did not mean any more to him than its intrinsic value. He was an intelligent man, and highly skilled at calculations so that he was aware of the precise values of all items imported and exported from his settlement, and he kept the many details of these calculations mysteriously stored in his mind.

Ankhtifi was also very independent; so independent that he had never married nor had any children. He showed no interest in relationships due to his inability to relate to others. But he was loyal to Khety, and that was all that mattered as far as Lower Egypt's monarch was concerned. He had been loyal to him since childhood.

As far as Khety knew.

Khety watched Ankhtifi as he stood quietly before him. He pondered the chieftain's response and how he had disposed of his enemies' remains. Ankhtifi's answer satisfied him. He had wanted his enemies dead. And he had wanted their immortal souls to be forever vanquished from the Afterlife. Burying them in goat skins was one of the worst things that could be done to the deceased, for it would prevent them from entering the Eternal Dominion of the Just, impure and unclean as they were. And severing their right hands would cripple them in the Hereafter, by taking their strength for eternity.

Khety subsequently rewarded Ankhtifi with more power and wealth, and asked him to move from his settlement in the north so that he could govern the land of Nekhen in the south as a neutral lord, replacing the former chieftain who had died from illness. But the move was mutually beneficial. Not only would Ankhtifi get the much-coveted land which had once been the ancient religious and political center of Upper Egypt, Khety would also have a spy planted within close proximity to his archnemesis in Thebes. Ankhtifi would be the eyes and ears of Lower Egypt's monarch. He would keep Khety abreast of the comings and goings of Mentuhotep.

Many seasons of the Inundation had passed since Ankhtifi first became Chieftain of Nekhen—the City of the Falcon, after the falcon-god Horus. It had been shortly after the tragic deaths of Khety's wife Shani and their children, when the bereaving ruler attempted to spend his dark and fathomless grief on a rampage of Lower Egypt. One by one, Khety had slaughtered his enemies, driven away threats, and cleansed the land of any potential adversaries with the help of Ankhtifi's iron fist. But the ensuing peace was transitory, for a peace wrought in blood is nothing short of tyranny.

Ankhtifi had claimed Nekhen about that time, moving to the settlement lying south of Thebes, under a pretext of neutrality in the great schism dividing Lower and Upper Egypt, all while helping Khety to purge the north of his enemies. But what Khety did not know, was that Ankhtifi had acted inexcusably beyond the duty of helping Khety to solidify his kingdom and rid him of his enemies. He had traitorously gone behind Khety's back, and secretly raided other settlements in the ensuing years as well—blameless, neutral settlements that had nothing to do with Khety's enemies; something Khety would have despised, had he known; despised enough to have even rightfully condemned Ankhtifi to death.

Khety loathed treachery of any kind, and he abhorred deceit and disloyalty, especially where his own warriors were concerned. But he had not been aware of his enforcer's clandestine raids. He had no knowledge whatsoever of Ankhtifi's heinous crimes, and the innocent blood staining the man's already-blackened soul. While Khety had sometimes felt a bit leery of Ankhtifi's peculiarities, he needed Ankhtifi to help keep hold of his kingdom, and he relied on his assistance in achieving his longtime ambitions.

Perhaps it was the influence of Ankhtifi's men that urged him to commit such vile atrocities. They were certainly motivated by greed and the promise of plunder—whatever meager loot they might find in those small villages they attacked. Perhaps it was the dark, perverted satisfaction Ankhtifi took from the raids that had become routine for him, which led him to continually pursue a blazing and violent path of destruction with death in its wake. Perhaps it was his inability to connect emotionally with others, or to feel anything but a twisted sense of accomplishment which he derived from the wickedness of his actions; or a compulsion to savagery and evil he embraced with a dead conscience.

Whatever the cause or reason, Ankhtifi had amassed a large band of loyal men over time, and he paid visits to several of the villages scattered along the edge of the Nile's floodplain, as he made his way back and forth on his innumerable journeys between his home in Nekhen and Khety's palace in Nen-nesu.

People whispered about the lawless barbarians that destroyed innocent lives and property. They spoke of the ruthless raiders in hushed tones as they touched a trembling hand to their amulets and invoked the protection of their gods so that it would not happen to them.

But the barbarism continued.

And keeping his identity hidden, Ankhtifi and his men laid waste to those smaller settlements. They descended upon the villages like a pestilence, killing their people, stealing their grain and livestock, and plundering their temples, tombs and treasures; leaving nothing but a bloody aftermath of death, defeat and devastation.

One of those villages had been Khu's.

SEVEN

It was Ankhtifi who had led the massacre on that fateful day that destroyed Khu's village, murdered his family, and forever changed the course of Khu's life. The sun-god Re had already made his twelve-hour journey across the sky in his *Mandjet* solar boat, Barque of a Million Years, then descended beyond the horizon where he embarked on his *Mesektet*—night barque—through the twelve hours of darkness in the Underworld where he would journey eastward in preparation for his daily rebirth. The moon-god Khonsu rose full in the night sky, gilding the sleeping village with his silvery light.

No one stirred as the vicious raiders glided along the Nile, drawing their oars soundlessly through the black shimmering water. Even the frogs and crickets that filled the night air with their chorus remained silent as they hid from sight. No breeze whispered through the doum palms, willows and sycamores bordering the plains, and their branches hung motionless in the night's stillness.

The men hopped out of their boats into the shallow water, and pulled their vessels through the dense reeds up onto the riverbank, leaving them with the oars inside. Their weapons gleamed in the moonlight as they stepped quietly on the soft grassy turf toward the sleeping village. No wild animals howled, no owls screeched, and no dogs barked in the stillness of the night as the invaders crept through the village and into each of the mud-brick homes to slit the throats of their sleeping occupants. The slayers moved with such calculated agility, that they managed to slaughter most of the village without a sound. No one but the moon-god Khonsu watched impassively from his sky throne as the pooling blood spilled in rivulets, and stained the ground. But even Khonsu had betrayed Khu's village when he illuminated a treacherous path for the killers to accomplish their grisly deeds.

It was a scream that had awoken young Khu and his family. He had been in the deepest stage of sleep and completely oblivious to the danger around him. He was in a room he shared with his parents and little sister when a woman's voice had broken through the night's silence. It was a short, startled cry that sent shivers up the spine of the young boy who sat up at once. But the sound was immediately cut off by the blade of an assassin.

"Stay here," Khu's father ordered as he grabbed a sickle from a large earthen vessel sitting on the floor in a corner of the minimally furnished room. It was the reaping tool he used to cut the flax and barley in the fields lying just beyond the dwellings. Then he ran out the door with the tool's wooden handle grasped firmly in his hand, its serrated flint blades poised to swipe at an unknown enemy.

He never returned.

Khu's father was ambushed from behind as he moved swiftly toward the sound that had woken his family. He was struck over the head with the heavy force of a blunt object before falling to the ground in a daze. And as the images of his wife and children crossed his mind for the last time, his own sickle was used to cut his throat.

Khu's mother was crouched over her children in the darkest corner of the room, away from the single window cut high into the wall. She was trying to shield them with her body and a linen sheet. Fear tightened her chest and she could feel her heart thumping against her ribs. The hairs on the back of her neck prickled as she strained to listen for clues of the danger sweeping through the village like a plague. She kept invoking the protection of Isis over her children, her eyes searching the darkness, as she called upon the goddess who was friend to the poor and prosperous alike.

"Sweet Isis, wife and sister of Osiris," she muttered softly, "be with us in this dark hour, protect us from harm. Protect my children especially, you who are a mother divine—mother of Horus. Use the true name of Re to banish those who seek to inflict a scourge upon us."

"Mother," Khu peeked from beneath the linen sheet hiding him and his sister.

"Shh," his mother whispered with a panicked shake of her head. "Shh... it's alright, it's alright. Just be very quiet and we'll be alright," she tried convincing herself more than anyone else.

"They have moved away, Mother. We must go."

"No," his mother's eyes were wide. "We are safest here." She gnawed at her lower lip anxiously, paralyzed by indecision. She was both too terrified to step outside, and too frightened to remain there.

"But—"

"Your father said to stay. We must stay. It's alright. We'll be alright."

For a few minutes they just waited in the gloom. The silence was oppressive. Each moment felt like an eternity. Their hearts fluttered like sparrows trying to break free from a tight cage, their wings beating against the bars trapping them.

Shadows stretched across the length of the bare walls, and hunkered down in corners like goblins.

"They will come back, Mother. They are not finished. They will come back and find us."

"No..." she shook her head rapidly in denial, "no, child... shh... it's alright... just be still and silent, and we'll be alright."

Khu could see the fear in his mother's eyes. She almost seemed dazed by it. "We must go while we can," he said. "This is our only chance."

Khu's mother just stared at him, her face full of uncertainty and dread, while her mind's eye probed the narrow alleys and obscured pathways running throughout the village.

During the day, the village radiated a comforting warmth with the familiar sounds of craftsmen and artisans hammering away in their shops, or bakers filling the air with the delicious aroma of freshly baked bread prepared in clay ovens. There were donkeys carrying baskets filled with vegetables, fish or grain. Oxen pulled carts laden with pottery or bricks, and goats were herded from one place to another. These were the reassuring sights, sounds and smells of daily life. But on this night, the darkness that usually cast a peaceful hush over the bustling village, had transformed it into a daunting labyrinth. It had been cloaked in menacing, inky shadows which hid the raiders who would ambush them like waterfowl ensnared by hunters.

"No. We must not leave. They will find us!"

"Let us go Mother," Khu urged.

"Your father will return soon. We must do as he said and stay here."

"Now Mother," Khu insisted, "before it's too late."

But his mother refused to go. She believed they were safely hidden.

Now that Khu was fully awake and alert, the magnitude of the terrible danger they were in hit him with full force.

He knew his father would not return. He knew this. He knew something had happened to him; something terrible. He was gripped by a sudden chill at the moment of his father's death, and had cringed from the force of it. But he did not say so to his mother. It would only make her panic. He knew death was sweeping over the village like a scorching sandstorm blown by the hot desert winds over the land, and all they could do was wait like mice burrowing in a shallow hole.

He wanted to flee. He wanted to run. He wanted to head over to the river before the predators returned to sniff them out and pounce on them. But his mother was too afraid to go anywhere. She did not want to expose her children to the danger outside.

And so they waited.

More screams pierced the darkness, shattering the tranquility that had reigned only hours before. Khu's mother clung tightly to her children and shut her eyes against the fear burning within her. She had heard rumors of other villages besieged by raiders. She had heard talk of how villains slayed entire settlements—men, women and children—before plundering whatever wealth could be found in their tombs, temples and granaries. But it never entered her mind that *this* village could be attacked as well. It was the kind of inconceivable atrocity that happened elsewhere, far from the safety of home.

Those were the unthinkable horrors that happened to *other* people.

And as she bent down on the floor, adjusting the sheet to shield her precious children from the danger looming nearby, a man entered the room. He was tall with a wolfish skull and elongated chin.

Khu's mother stood up at once with a startled gasp, stepping quickly in the opposite direction to draw the man's attention away from the corner where her children hid. A surge of adrenaline filled her with the courage of a lioness protecting her young from a clan of ravenous hyenas. She faced her attacker squarely with nothing but her clenched fists at her side.

Under the sheet, Khu's sister squirmed and began to cry. He tried to clamp his hand over her mouth, but she got away from his protective embrace.

Khu's mother shot a sidelong glance at the little girl who crawled toward her on the floor. His mother tensed her entire body, her jaw clenched tightly, and her eyes wide with terror as she held her breath, willing the child to back away with all the might of her being; willing her to disappear from view, out of danger's sight; willing her to remain safe and invisible; willing for the impossible, for a feat of godlike proportion that would never come.

But the girl did not go.

And with every inch of the child's movement, Khu's mother felt her heart beating harder and louder to nearly bursting point.

The man followed her gaze as he slowly lifted the dagger in his hand. He pushed Khu's mother out of the way before killing the girl in one swift strike.

His mother fell back against the wall, shrieking at the senseless and incomprehensible brutality of her child's murder, and her eyes filled with a wild hysteria. It was a savage, bloodcurdling sound that wrenched Khu's heart in two.

She lunged at the killer then. She leaped toward him full of anguish, desperation and madness, but her agony was snuffed out with another strike of the man's blade.

Khu did not move.

His mother's dead body crumpled over the sheet that partially covered him, saving his life as it shielded him from view.

The man stood there for a few moments searching the darkness with black sunken eyes, glittering with a feral glare. He did not see Khu watching him intently, absorbing every nuance of his lupine face—including the tic that made one side of the man's jaw twitch. And as the slayer turned to leave, Khu shuddered from the depravity seeping from the man's dead soul, like the blood pooling around him.

Khu went into shock after that.

He lost all track of time as a strange numbness crept over him. It might have been minutes or hours that he lay under the sheet drenched in the blood of his mother and sister. He was curled into a ball with his knees drawn up under his chin, and his arms wrapped tightly about them. He rocked back and forth in the darkness, bracing himself against the trembling that assailed his body. With every passing moment, his mind retreated further and further away from the terrible violence which threatened his life and sanity.

He remembered nothing after that.

Nothing of the massacre that changed his life in one cruel and merciless instant. Nothing of the way he crawled out from the sheet and stared, transfixed, at the lifeless bodies of his mother and sister, in whose blood he was soaked. Nothing of the way he crept soundlessly like a cat in the shadows through the village whose occupants now lay dead. Nothing of the way he climbed aboard a raft, and pushed away from the river's muddy bank with an oar, to glide silently along the still waters of the Nile. He floated on the river, putting more and more distance between him and the ravaged village, before finally falling asleep from exhaustion.

Only the traitorous moon watched from the black sky, along with a solitary jackal that paused from his feeding on a fish he had caught in the shallow water by the riverbank. The jackal froze with the fish in his mouth, blood dripping down his chin, to stare with glowing eyes at the boy who was drifting through the death-defiled night.

EIGHT

"Higher, aim HIGHER," Qeb enunciated the word in his deep, accented voice while gently lifting Nakhti's arm supporting the bow whose string was pulled taut. "Good, now watch your stances." He was circling both Khu and Nakhti as they practiced their archery skills from the ship's bow. "Balance, BALANCE. Straight, but not stiff," their trainer alternately raised and lowered his voice, his long muscled arms crossed over his chest as he watched the boys closely.

They were aiming the bronze-tipped points of their goose-fledged arrows toward a thicket in the marshes where wild geese were feeding by the egret and heron picking their way through the tall grasses on long spindly legs. A heron thrust its sharp dagger-like beak into the opaque water, plucking out a green frog wading nearby, and swallowed it whole in one gulp before disappearing behind the reeds.

No clouds marred the wide blue sky stretching as far as the eye could see. They had gotten up early to hone their archery skills and to hunt for the wild birds foraging in the cool morning before the midday sun burned too hot. The mist which had settled over the Nile's bank had thinned and pulled away like long tentacles drawn back into the dense wetlands bordering the river.

The boys pulled the bowstrings tighter until they were touching their noses and mouths, their elbows poised slightly above their shoulders. They anchored their drawing hands against their cheeks, brows drawn in concentration, as they aimed at the wild geese pecking at small insects and fish by the reeds along the riverbank. All the muscles in their backs were as taut as the bowstrings upon which the arrows were nocked. Then they released the strings, loosing the arrows as their bodies absorbed the recoil of the effort.

The arrows shot silently through the air, hitting their targets as the startled geese flailed wildly, trying in vain to escape certain death. The commotion alarmed the egret and heron, and flushed out some quail, snipe and other smaller birds hiding in the shrubbery. A bunch of feathers broke free of the wild flutter of wings, and rose softly through the air, as the birds flapped anxiously before settling back in the marshes that afforded them refuge.

The boys hooted, proud of their success, and clapped each other on the back.

Qeb looked satisfied but did not smile. It was enough to cheer the boys. He sent them off on a small reed boat to collect the birds which would be eaten that night, along with the fish caught that day.

Khu and Nakhti would often hunt with their bows and arrows to help feed the men on board. Mentuhotep sometimes participated in the hunt, which was a favorite pastime for him and other nobility, and something in which he indulged whenever he could at home. The boys practiced their fighting skills daily aboard the ship. They were at least as good as any of the best men in Mentuhotep's army.

But they had never fought in battle.

They had never killed a man. They had never sought cover from a barrage of arrows raining down a storm of fire and death from above. They had never seen the madness in a man's eyes as he charged with the rage of a ferocious wild boar with daggers poised to gouge like tusks. They had never smelled the rank fear of a man loosening his bowels in the face of death, or vomiting bile as he choked on terror and his own blood.

These were the things that tore jagged wounds into the soul. The deep and invisible lacerations which bled long after the fires were put out, and the cold ashes were scattered by the wind.

Nothing could undo the red, angry scars disfiguring a man's soul. Nothing could erase the suppressed images which bore painfully into the mind, and woke him shivering and panicked in a cold sweat during the night. Survival was more than the preservation of life. It was tenacity in the face of ruin, an unbroken resolve in the midst of defeat, a glimmer of hope in the maelstrom, and peace despite the wreckage.

No, the boys had not yet been tested.

But their time would come soon.

Ten days had passed since they left Thebes. Their ship's narrow prow and stern were painted in bright blue, green and gold, jutting proudly as they cut through the water. It was built long and lean, flaring gently at midship so it could float over shallower water. No keel projected from its flat bottom, whose acacia and tamarisk planks were fastened together and caulked with papyrus. Its wooden mast was tipped with a bronze finial to which the papyrus sail was tied when in use. Its oars were secured on deck when not slicing through the water like knives, from the ropes which served as a fulcrum to hold them in place.

They had sailed past small villages and settlements flourishing along the lush Nile Valley. Date palms grew in a thick expanse, and their branches looked like giant green feathers swaying gently under the sun. There were sycamore and tamarisk trees, and acacias with their large curved canopies bowing down like the protective arms of a mother gathering her children. Carob trees hung with long green and dark purple pods in varying stages of ripeness. And beyond the marshes flanked by the slender papyrus reeds, the land was speckled with flocks of goats, sheep and cattle feeding on the velvety grasses carpeting the smooth and fertile valley.

They had stopped in Swentet just north of the Nile's first cataract, where some of the best granite quarries were found. Mentuhotep had taken Khu and Nakhti with him and his entourage of officials when he checked on the mines supplying some of the finest stone in all of Egypt. It was these quarries that furnished the rock which was carved into monolithic shrines, statues, obelisks, columns and monuments, among other structures gracing the east and west banks of the life-giving Nile. The mines were also supplying some of the stone which would decorate Mentuhotep's partially constructed mortuary temple *Akh Sut Nebhepetre*—Splendid are the places of Nebhepetre—that was cut into the rock of the cliffs, where Henhenet and his infant daughter had been laid to rest. His tomb was the first in a complex of mortuary temple-tombs and shrines which would eventually become known as Deir el-Bahari in the subsequent millennia.

Swentet was also an important garrison town and served as a military training base for Mentuhotep's soldiers. Many of the men had been recruited from the peasant and laboring classes, and trained from their youth. Others had been captured as children in battles and foreign raids, and trained since boyhood, while others still were mercenaries or foreign prisoners who had been forced into the army to serve the king. Boys from the nobility and upper classes were also enlisted and trained. Mentuhotep's infantry was adept at fighting on both land and water, in the heat of hand-to-hand combat, or from the warships, galleys and skiffs equipped with brave fighters and a vast stock of weapons.

Tomorrow they would arrive in Lower Kush. It was there that the bulk of his gold mines waited. But it was not just gold that Mentuhotep wanted from Kush. He wanted more men.

Like his nemesis Khety in the north, Mentuhotep also had loyal spies and emissaries stationed in various parts of the land along the most important settlements and cult centers on the east and west banks of the Nile.

And he suspected trouble was brewing.

Every so often these things would arise. It was part of the bad blood which had poisoned the land since the great nation of Egypt had split. Part of the venom that had been the blight of both Lower and Upper Egypt, plunging the opposing kingdoms into a period of darkness. It was time to purge that darkness threatening not only Mentuhotep's throne, but the future of Egypt as a whole. That threat was far closer than the king would have liked. His suspicions had deepened after they visited the township of Nekhen, four days into their journey, where Ankhtifi was chieftain.

Mentuhotep often visited many settlements on his way to Kush. He liked to keep abreast of their activities himself, instead of relying solely on the reports of his viziers. Nekhen had a port that stretched along a section of the Nile which curved inward, forming a natural harbor. It had been paved with large blocks of stone to keep the river from muddying the banks during the Season of Inundation. A few of the barges used to lug the heavy limestone columns and sandstone blocks that were elaborately carved with hieroglyphs, or painted in vivid colors and used in the construction of temples and tombs, had been pulled ashore to keep them from rotting.

"Where is Lord Ankhtifi?" the king asked an administrator who greeted their arrival after they docked at the port.

The man helped manage Ankhtifi's affairs while the chieftain was away. Mentuhotep had disembarked the ship with Khu, Nakhti, Qeb, and a retinue of officials who usually accompanied Upper Egypt's monarch on all his administrative visits. The man bowed to the king in a show of subservience that attempted to mask the surprise he felt at Mentuhotep's question.

"Forgive me, Lord King, but we did not expect you," he replied after a moment as he gathered his wits about him, hoping to deflect any probing questions from the king. "Lord Ankhtifi is away."

"Away?" Mentuhotep asked as he stared at the man, before darting Khu a sidelong glance.

Khu was standing next to Nakhti and Qeb. He observed the man quietly, noting the nervousness flowing from him like the steady buzzing of cicadas perched on a tree.

"On some trade matter, Sire, and a pilgrimage," he hastily added, clearing his throat nervously.

"North or south?" the king asked with narrowed eyes.

The man's eyebrows shot up before he could reply, betraying his discomfort. He looked anxious. Khu wondered what the man was hiding, and how much he knew of Ankhtifi's affairs. Khu had heard of Nekhen's chieftain, though he had never heard of the rumors whispered about him by adversaries in the north. Neither had he ever met him before, at least he did not remember ever meeting him. Khu had no idea that it was Ankhtifi who had led the attack and slaughter on his village, a massacre he had buried far too deeply within the dark recesses of his mind to recall.

"Uh, n-north, Sire," the man stuttered, blinking rapidly.

He glanced over at Qeb with a frown, wondering about the tall Kushite who managed to look both impassive and intimidating at the same time, before he turned his gaze to Nakhti. But when his eyes arrived to Khu, he drew back involuntarily, touching an amulet as he shuddered from the catlike eyes that stared right back at him. The man was thin with stooped narrow shoulders, bulging eyes, and a long hooked nose whose tip hung by a mouth that reminded Khu of one of the catfish gliding along the bottom of the Nile.

"North," the king repeated with a nod, crossing his arms over his chest.

"Yes, Lord King. He took linen, pottery and other goods with him." The man pursed his lips and frowned, then squeezed his eyes shut momentarily, as though silently chastising himself for blurting out more information than necessary. He was fidgety, and kept scratching the skin on one of his elbows.

The king arched his brows, but he said nothing. He knew that linen and pottery were commonly made products in the north. Why would Ankhtifi trade them? It

116

did not make sense, but he did not say so aloud. Ankhtifi never struck him as the type to go on pilgrimages either.

Mentuhotep noted the nervous manner in which the official behaved. The man shifted his weight from one foot to the other, and worked his jaw before speaking again. He seemed to be hiding something.

"Where exactly was he headed?" The king asked with narrowed eyes. "I have some news for him, and wish to share it with him myself," he fibbed with a forced smile.

The man took the bait and smiled back, "Abdju, Sire. For the Festival of Osiris."

The last time Mentuhotep had seen Ankhtifi was several years before, and only briefly at that, when the king had sailed down on one of his visits to Swentet. He did not usually stop in Nekhen, but would send an emissary to conduct any official matters on his behalf. But this time he wanted to show Khu and Nakhti the settlement which was known for its crafts. Their jewelers were among the most talented in Upper Egypt, and the king wished to have a beautiful collar necklace made for Khu's mother Tem, so she could wear it at the next Festival of the Inundation. It would be a gift from Khu as a sign of respect and honor to his mother, and would be presented to her when Khu reached his fifteenth season of the Nile's flooding, as was the custom for boys who had made it into adulthood. In a time when infant and childhood mortality ran rampant, those children who had reached adulthood often bestowed a token of gratitude to their mothers who had nurtured them through the often hazardous period of youth.

Mentuhotep had never quite trusted Ankhtifi. He did not know if it was due to the predatory aspect of the man's canine face, or to the way the man's dark eyes took in all of his surroundings, or even to the way he spoke with a slow and deliberate articulation. There was something guarded about the chieftain; something both aloof and menacing at the same time which he could not quite identify.

The king was satisfied enough to conduct his affairs through an emissary who would trade goods with the neutral settlement. Because Nekhen was not under Mentuhotep's rule, the king did not collect any livestock, grain, crops, and finished goods as part of the yearly taxes owed him, as he did from other settlements in his kingdom. But he did exchange goods. Nevertheless, the king liked to keep a close watch on his enigmatic southern neighbor.

Mentuhotep had learned to trust his instincts over the years, even if there was nothing to substantiate the strange and eerie impression raising his hackles and putting him on guard. The chieftain's absence certainly unnerved him because it came at a time when rumors had begun to circulate about trouble making its way south like a sandstorm from the desert. And the Festival of Osiris would provide the chieftain with the perfect excuse for going to Abdju.

It could not be a coincidence that Ankhtifi was gone. Mentuhotep did not believe in coincidences. He reached up to touch the gold amulet hanging from his neck as he brooded silently for a moment. He was certain the chieftain's trade expedition had been a ruse, just as his own expedition to Kush was a ploy. He shook his head, relieved that he had decided to stop in Nekhen, yet mentally berating himself for not keeping closer watch over Ankhtifi.

Before they had departed Nekhen, Ankhtifi's administrator had personally escorted the king and his entourage on a tour of some of the settlement's finest workshops and most talented artisans. A private meeting had been arranged for Khu to choose the precious gems that would be made into the collar necklace for Tem, and he picked yellow topaz and malachite which had become his mother's favorite gemstones since she had claimed Khu as her own son. They were the stones that most nearly resembled his eyes.

"Go to Abdju, Sudi," Mentuhotep later instructed one of his most trusted men after they had spent part of the day in Nekhen, "and see what you can learn. Find out whatever you can about Ankhtifi's visit—the *true* purpose of his visit."

The king had been pacing back and forth on the deck of his ship as he spoke to the man who would leave later that night, under cover of darkness.

"He is afraid of something," Khu later told the king about Ankhtifi's administrator, when he, Nakhti and Qeb were alone with him, long after they had left Nekhen.

"Afraid of Ankhtifi perhaps," Qeb interjected.

But Khu knew there had to be more to his fear than that.

"Why would he be afraid of Ankhtifi?" Nakhti wondered aloud.

"Because he is hiding something," Khu replied as he turned his eyes on the king.

The effect of Khu's gaze had never lost its uncanny power, and Mentuhotep could not help feeling momentarily transfixed as he looked at his son. He stopped his pacing to stare with his lips slightly parted.

"Father," Khu distracted the king with a wave of his hand, "Ankhtifi must be planning something."

But Mentuhotep just turned away to stare out over the Nile as they made their way south to Swentet. It was what he had suspected as well.

"Ankhtifi is a bully," the king said, inhaling deeply through his nose, and exhaling though his mouth.

The night air was cool, and the breeze smelled of the river, tall grasses, reeds and the rich mud along the bank, with hints of something floral, but its fragrance was lost on the king whose thoughts were preoccupied elsewhere.

Mentuhotep pushed his shoulders back and pressed his lips together into a hard line. "It is not surprising that his administrators fear him," he nodded slowly. He was remembering the chieftain's bearing, and how there had been something aggressive in his stance. It was as though

Ankhtifi were primed and ready to pounce on anyone who opposed him. There had been something slippery about his administrator too, like an eel slithering through the dark river. "He may be intimidating to some, but he is not that smart. He relies more on his brute strength than his wits."

If Ankhtifi were indeed planning something, he would not be alone. Someone else would be coordinating it. Someone stronger and more powerful than the chieftain of Nekhen.

"So there is someone else involved," Khu said, almost reading the king's mind. "Someone smarter."

The king nodded to Khu before turning to stare again out over the water lapping the sides of the ship as they glided through the river.

A half-moon spilled its light from the sky onto the dark water, glossing its surface so it appeared like a thin layer of pewter floating on top. It was quiet, but Mentuhotep knew the stillness was deceptive. For a world of night creatures had awakened with the setting of the sun-god Re's fiery *Mandjet* solar boat. A world that crept out in the darkness after the day was done. A world whose beasts—great and small—breathed and hunted and killed and devoured their unwary prey.

The king was very much aware that he was part of that world, and he wanted to tread carefully through the realm whose thin line separating predator from prey was smudged in the darkness of men's false hearts.

Mentuhotep turned his thoughts to Sudi, who had left already. Part of him feared for the man's life. He might have been sending him into the den of a wolf, but he was sly, quick and cunning enough to slip away before being caught. At least that is what Mentuhotep hoped.

Sudi would be sailing on a skiff with two more men, posing as fishermen with nets, and floating along the muddy waters that would take them to Abdju, the cult center of Osiris. Once arriving, they would roam through the town, and among its inhabitants and many visiting pilgrims and merchants, discretely asking questions, prodding people to speak with the assistance of a subtle yet well-placed comment, and listening with every one of their senses to all that was said, and more importantly, to what was left unsaid.

They would wander through the town like the numerous cats living there, roaming inconspicuously among the tombs, temples and townspeople to wait, watch and witness anything they might report back to their king, whose hackles were now raised, and whose ears were now perked in suspicion like a fox on the prowl. The king smelled a hint of treachery on the breeze ruffling the branches, whispering through reeds, and moving over the Nile's surface as it flowed around a bend of trees whose trunks were gnarled and knotted as they bore the weight of their heavy branches and leaves.

Sometimes a fox's quarry requires some digging to unearth it from its shelter, perhaps even a trick or two to lure or flush it out of hiding. But once exposed, the king planned to trap and crush any traitors, much like the fox crushing the thin bones of his victim with teeth made sharper by a fierce and impassioned hunger.

NINE

Sudi watched from the shadow of a stone column in an arcade, as several priests carried the portable gilded barque holding the cult-statue of the god Osiris on their shoulders. The god of the dead and Afterlife was made of gold, and stood with his legs wrapped in mummified burial fashion as he held the crook and flail in arms crossing over his chest. His serene face had a long, slender, black-painted beard on a chin that jutted proudly, while his head was crowned by the tall, white conical-shaped *Atef* crown with two ostrich feathers on the sides. The feathers of his crown symbolized the *maat* concept of universal order, truth and justice against which the souls of the dead were weighed and subsequently judged.

But only the priests saw the magnificent god-statue, for he was shielded from the common people's eyes by a curtain woven from the finest linen. The priests bore the heavy weight of the god on the gilded barque, which was decorated with hieroglyphs carved in relief, as they exited the Temple of Osiris in Abdju.

It was the Festival of Osiris.

The annual feast drew many pilgrims from all over Egypt, as well as those people seeking to profit from the throngs and festivities filling the crowded streets with excitement. Today was the culmination of a celebration that had commenced eight days before with much prayer and chanting to the god who gave life to the floodplains through the fertile fields' vegetation. People craned their necks to get a glimpse of the venerated god as the reenactment of his burial took place. The procession would take Osiris from the inner sanctuary of the temple, beyond the sacrificial rooms, through the hypostyle hall, colonnaded courtyard, and out through the pylon's massive entrance guarded by two colossal stone figures of Osiris. All the civil servants and courtiers of Abdju waited in the Avenue of Sphinxes leading up to the temple's grand pylon, while the masses of people stood beyond the guarded walkway and its surrounding gardens, which were graced with fountains sparkling in the morning light.

Sudi thought he saw Ankhtifi standing among the officials. But his view was obscured by smoke rising in spiraling plumes from the burning incense, waved by a priest circling the barque carrying the golden god. A priest chanted in prayer as the fragrant incense wafted over the effigy of the god:

> *Glory to you, Osiris*
> *King of the Everlasting*
> *Homage to you whose names are Manifold*
> *Holy Protector and Guardian of Eternity*
> *Who dwells in the Land of the Just*
> *Mighty are your ways*
> *Clothed in the Light of Truth*

The procession made its way out of the temple and down the Avenue of Sphinxes. Priestesses shook hooped *sistra* ceremonial rattles as fan bearers waved their long wooden-handled ostrich-feather fans reverently over the barque. People prostrated themselves in adoration, welcoming the god with hymns of devotion and gratitude. The officials followed behind the priests in observance of the Going Forth of Osiris Ritual commemorating the burial of the god who would be accompanied by his wife Isis and son Horus, whose smaller statues waited at the ancient Tomb of Osiris that once belonged to King Djer from the First Dynasty of the Old Kingdom.

Sudi followed behind some pilgrims as the procession took them through several of the cemeteries lying west of the temple, where more ritual prayers and chanting brought blessings upon the dead who continued to pay homage to the great god from their otherworldly realm. Those who could afford it dedicated *stele* stone tablets bearing elaborately carved inscriptions and paintings of scenes in tribute to Osiris, while others placed small offerings of food and flowers they had bought from the village marketplace catering to pilgrims celebrating the special feast. The poorest pilgrims left a small lock of their hair in a symbolic gesture of their subservience before the god to whom they desired to give a part of themselves, and as a sign of their meekness and humility.

Sudi lost sight of his two companions who were somewhere in the vast crowd. More than ten days had passed since Mentuhotep's trusted emissary had left the ruler's side on the evening they had departed Nekhen, after the king had sent him off to spy on Ankhtifi. The three men had gone back to Thebes before setting off for Abdju.

Odji the gatekeeper had seen them arrive, and had wondered why they had returned so soon without the king. But Sudi had not even glanced his way when he and the other two men entered the royal compound, after leaving their boat in the care of a ferryman by the riverbank. They gathered fishing nets and other supplies, before changing out of their finer kilts to don the simple loin cloth of humble fishermen who worked along the Nile.

Odji grew instantly suspicious when he saw the three men disguise themselves before they left. He surreptitiously followed them as he tried to eavesdrop on their conversation in hopes of learning what they were up to. But Sudi had kept his mouth shut the entire time as he efficiently went about his work. Only one word had slipped out of the mouth of one of his partners: Abdju. But it had been enough.

Sudi and his partners had arrived in Abdju disguised as fishermen with a few baskets of fish they had caught in their nets along the way. They sold their catch in the open air market of the village where people traded all sorts of goods during the busy time of the festival.

Pilgrims flooded the streets excitedly, pausing to look here and there at the many stands laden with food, crafts and offerings made available during the ritual feasts. There were large sacks of wheat, barley and lentils sitting on the ground next to baskets of onions, garlic and leeks, as well as crates of melons, cabbages and cucumbers. Tables were piled with varieties of dates, figs, colorful grapes, and raisins, while others were stacked with cheese, dried and salted fish, fowl and other meats. Bunches of herbs and heaps of colorful spices including aniseed, coriander, cinnamon and fennel, filled the air with their enticing fragrance. Jars of oil pressed from flax, sesame and almonds waited on the ground. Pottery, copper goods and all sorts of craft items lured spectators over for a closer look.

A short distance away was an assortment of live animals corralled in a pen. They too were traded in the marketplace, or obtained for ritualistic slaughtering in sacrificial offerings.

The three men had spread out over the sacred city whose tombs, shrines and memorials drew pilgrims from far and wide, seeking to pay homage to the great Osiris who ruled the Underworld.

Ankhtifi had come ahead of King Khety so he could make good use of the time and opportunity to influence the many local officials and visiting chieftains gathered there from the surrounding smaller settlements. Since he had arrived, he had tried to persuade them to support Khety in his military quest to conquer Upper Egypt and reunite the kingdoms. With their backing, he would then convince the priests, and they in turn would prompt the people to follow along. But it had not gone so easy.

"What do we have to gain by supporting him?" one asked, crossing his arms over his chest

"Security, prosperity, wealth," Ankhtifi said.

"But we have been doing fine without him," another objected with a high chin.

"Speak for yourself," blurted another. "Times have been very difficult."

"And there have been raids too," another added. "I know of more than one village that was destroyed by raiders.

"So do I," the first nodded sternly.

Ankhtifi said nothing at first. He just let them speak. Many of them were venting their frustrations with the way things were. They wanted to better their lives and improve the status of their settlements. But they were not sure how to go about it, and were wary of supporting someone who might bring about a change for the worse. Change for mere change's sake could be a very foolish thing.

"And what about the droughts?" another shook his head, narrowing his eyes. "The river's flood has been low where we are. Does King Khety have the power to stop the droughts?" His tone was dubious.

"Can he make our fields yield more grain?" one man challenged derisively, pushing his shoulders back. "Or our cattle more fertile?"

"What about King Mentuhotep?" Another interrupted, jabbing a finger into the air. "What would he say to your machinations?"

"If you call a desire to better your lives 'machinations,'" Ankhtifi retorted coldly. He was making mental notes of those dissidents that might stand in the way of Khety's plans, and filing their names and faces away in his mind. His jaw started to twitch in frustration, and he began to open and close one of his hands at his side, trying hard to resist the urge to grab the handle of his mace hanging under the layers of his kilt.

Many of the officials were hesitant at first, but some managed to come around after assurances were made that their support would be repaid tenfold.

"You will be rewarded with positions of greater power in the reunited kingdoms of Lower and Upper Egypt under King Khety," Ankhtifi told them.

The procession had finally arrived at the Tomb of Osiris. Its columned façade rose above the high plateau of the desert, facing east. The lengthening shadows of the late afternoon, silhouetted the stony grandeur against the golden light of the sun, which kept ducking behind puffy clouds scattered in the heavens, like the frothy peaks of waves in the vast blue sea. People watched as the priests disappeared with the god into the tomb's heavily fortified entrance, where the Mysteries of the Divine Rites would be performed, enabling the spiritual essence *ka* of Osiris to join that of Isis and Horus, and in their joyous reunion, prosper and make fertile the land of the living.

The joyful and devout worshippers began chanting along with the priests as they gathered outside the tomb. Priestesses were shaking their *sistra* rattles along with the musicians who played tambourines, clappers and flutes as they encircled the barque. Other priests wafted incense in copper burners, while fan bearers waved the blessed smoke over the barque with their long wooden-handled ostrich-feather fans.

Some of the people in the crowd lifted the linen cloth draped on their shoulders and pulled it over their heads in reverence of the moment, joining their voices to the chanting which rose to the heavens like the smoky wisps of incense perfuming the air.

Arise Osiris, Life-giver to the Land
Arise god of the earth and Underworld
Make the river waters flow
Imbue life in the fields
Make fertile the black soil
And the hearts of men
Arise O Great One
Father of Horus
Faithful Husband of Isis
Arise and prosper in your kingdom of old

Sudi noticed the serious expression on Ankhtifi's face as he retreated with a few of the officials back to the town center of Abdju where the evening festivities had already begun. Ankhtifi had hung back and waited with the officials while the rest of the crowd had dispersed. At one point, Sudi could not find Ankhtifi and thought he might have already left. But then the chieftain mysteriously emerged from the tomb, whose entrance was barred from anyone but the high priests laying the god to rest.

A chill prickled Sudi's spine when he saw Ankhtifi's face, as he ducked out of the narrow, rectangular opening cut into the rock of the mastaba tomb. A streak of blood was smeared across his cheek. But the chieftain casually wiped it away with the back of his hand as though it were nothing more than perspiration beading his brow. It was not his own blood, Sudi realized, but that of someone else. Two other men followed Ankhtifi out of the tomb, and they joined several officials who had been waiting outside.

Sudi closed his eyes for a moment and drew a linen cloth about his head to hide his face. He had a very bad feeling about this, but could not risk getting caught by lingering behind. He knew that he would find out whatever had happened inside the tomb soon enough, whether he wanted to or not. So he left the tomb site with the last of the pilgrims so that no one would suspect anything of him.

Sudi realized that the men who had stayed behind at the tomb site with Ankhtifi, were those whose loyalty sided with King Khety. This included Odji's friend Mdjai, whose own small village was one of the several nearby settlements under the jurisdiction of Abdju. The rest of the officials had gone back to the town center soon after the chanting and incense had faded away, and the priests had entered the royal necropolis to complete the requisite prayers and ablutions which were part of the Mysteries of the Divine Rites, honoring Osiris in his tomb.

"Stay as close to Ankhtifi as you possibly can," Sudi told one of his partners after they had found each other. They had abandoned their fishing pretense days before, and had taken on the guise of simple pilgrims in order to mingle more freely through the crowd.

"They are planning a revolt," the other man said, leaning in closer so that no one would overhear them. "Everywhere people are whispering of it. Have you not seen Ankhtifi's men? Look for yourself." He angled his chin toward a group of men watching the crowd with somber expressions. "They are not pilgrims."

"Warriors," Sudi whispered with a growing unease. He had noticed them also.

"And over there," the other man indicated with his head. "And there... and more by the temple." Everywhere he looked, Sudi saw the men who had accompanied Ankhtifi to Abdju on his fleet. They were warriors disguised as pilgrims; but nothing could mask the hardness of their features, and proud bearing of their postures, that belied a false humility. Sudi also noticed the daggers strapped to the belts of their kilts, even though the weapons had been concealed under the linen cloth.

"But where is King Khety?" Sudi asked.

"Here already. He met with the priests yesterday, but they do not wish to support him. If they cannot remain neutral, they prefer to follow King Mentuhotep."

"Ah," Sudi replied with a slow nod as he began to realize how their enemies would stage the revolt. "I imagine King Khety was not pleased."

"Not at all," the man replied as he swiped at a fly. It was warm outside, and the throng of people and food attracted insects.

"I would not wish to be in their position right now," Sudi said of the priests. "I am certain that Khety will not stand for their refusal."

"True," his partner agreed, "he will take the town by force and manipulate the people to help him push south into Thebes. That is why Ankhtifi is here."

Both men brooded silently for a while as they stood watching some of the people eating and drinking on the streets by the Temple of Osiris. Tables were laden with free bread and heqet, provided by the officials governing the province in honor of the annual feast. Men, women and children were eagerly participating in the festivities following the long religious ceremonies. Many were laughing happily as the musicians began playing their instruments, and acrobats enlivened the feast with their tricks. Others were passing around jugs of the ceremonial heqet, consuming the bread, or enjoying some of the food they had gotten from the venders in the open market.

Sudi was studying the throngs of people, trying to locate their third partner whom he had not seen in a few days. He scanned the crowd with his eyes, wondering where the man named Pili had gone.

"Have you seen Pili?" he finally asked.

"Not for three days," his partner answered. He turned to help himself to a piece of the flat bread when they neared one of the tables set under the shade of the colonnaded gallery, next to the vast gardens by the Temple of Osiris.

Sudi glanced at the food but did not touch it. He was too preoccupied to eat anything.

"He was going to try to talk to one of the officials and get information for us," his partner said.

"But three days..." Sudi said, with a hint of fear. "Three days is a long time."

"It is. A lot can happen in three days. Good luck trying to find him in this crowd. It could take longer than that."

"Hmm..." Sudi mumbled uneasily, forming his mouth into a hard line. A current of apprehension surged through his blood as his mind turned to Ankhtifi.

If one of them should be caught by Ankhtifi's men... Sudi let the thought trail off unfinished. He had heard stories about Ankhtifi. The chieftain's reputation preceded him like the stench of death from a rotting carcass. He did not know how much of it was true and how much was simply rumor inflated over time. But he did not want to find out. The chieftain looked intimidating.

"Go back to Thebes," Sudi finally said. "Leave to-night and warn King Mentuhotep." He paused a moment to think as his eyes roamed to a group of children who were chasing each other through the gardens which had been readied for the annual feast. They were squealing delightedly without a care in the world, tagging each other and then running away. "Tell the king that there will be bloodshed if he does not hurry."

Sudi turned his thoughts back to Ankhtifi as his partner disappeared into the crowd. The people were eager to lose themselves in the revelry of the festivities. The strongly brewed ceremonial heqet was already flowing freely throughout the town, where musicians continued to play their instruments, by the people who sang and danced through the streets, and the lush gardens and parks surrounding the Temple of Osiris.

Some of the people had come a long way, abandoning their impoverished settlements, whose small shrines and temples had fallen into ruin after robbers had plundered their towns. Without the means to harness the Nile through dykes and canals, their fields had produced few crops, and now lay fallow under an unforgiving sun that had grown indifferent to their plight.

And so they made their way south to Abdju for the annual celebration, which promised free bread and drink during the festivities that would last for about six days, in honor of Osiris to whom they prayed for a new life of prosperity. They came bedraggled and beaten, with nothing but the flame of hope enkindled within their souls, as they sought work in more prosperous settlements. They came hungering to fill their stomachs, aching from emptiness. And they came in search of a god-king who would protect and provide for them as their lord and master, giving them light and salvation in a time of darkness and uncertainty.

Rumors spread from mouths to ears of a revolution that would transform their lives and their beloved Egypt—rumors skillfully planted by Ankhtifi and his men. And as those rumors swept throughout the town, which grew ever more rowdy with each passing hour of the setting sun's voyage through the cloud-speckled sky, a mob began to form.

The mob took on a life of its own under the control of King Khety who manipulated the crowd like a deft puppeteer. He had been biding his time over the last few days, staying away from the people, as he waited patiently in the hidden rooms of the lavish residence of an official who had sworn an oath in his support. He had purposely kept from public sight when the festivities commenced, and especially during the elaborate religious ceremonies which cast a reverential haze over the people. But his own men and those of Ankhtifi had been weaving through the crowd and garnering support from the masses, telling them that King Khety would be coming to save them from their abject poverty and restore Egypt to its former glory. All they had to do was pledge their allegiance to him.

Those same conniving men who had been filling the peoples' ears with promises of plenty, if they supported King Khety's expanded rule, had also been slandering King Mentuhotep with vicious, deceitful rumors meant to turn the people against the Theban king.

"He cares for no one but his own kingdom," one scowled with a frown.

"He grows fat while the rest of Egypt is starving," another claimed with a loud snort.

"He eats from alabaster plates, and sleeps on a bed of gold," another lied, nodding for emphasis.

And eyebrows were raised in surprise, and furrowed in anger, from the perceived injustice of it all, as the liars sought to divide and conquer by instilling class envy and spreading malicious lies.

But not everyone believed the rumors. Those pilgrims who had come from settlements closer to Thebes knew that the king of Upper Egypt was a good and generous ruler, and that he had protected them from the lawlessness plaguing the north.

"We have had no droughts," one spoke up in Mentuhotep's defense. "Our fields have yielded much grain and plentiful harvests," the man touched an amulet hanging from his neck to avert the evil eye.

"Our villages have been safer than those closer to King Khety," another said. "Why hasn't King Khety done a better job protecting his kingdom the way King Mentuhotep has done with his?" he shook his head.

"Yes," another piped in. "If the state of King Khety's lands are any indication of what we are to expect under his rule of all of Egypt, I will want none of it," the man set his jaw and crossed his arms over his chest before continuing. "That sort of change will lead to the destruction of all of Egypt. What hope will we have then?"

"King Mentuhotep is a good and just ruler," another stated proudly, with a high chin. "Son of the Great Osiris and Amun."

"Then why is he not here, honoring Osiris during these holy days?" Khety's man countered, as he continued trying to turn the people against Mentuhotep.

"But neither is King Khety here," responded the man.

"Oh, but he is. He is here and he is the true son of Osiris. You shall see him when he chooses to show himself."

And on it went.

The seeds of doubt had been sown among the people, whose hunger for change made a fertile breeding ground.

By now all the people returned to the main part of town after laying their god to rest in his ancient tomb, and they succumbed to the festive atmosphere by the temple. Musicians played their lutes, cymbals, sistrums, and *sheneb* trumpets, while people clapped and danced around the acrobats performing on the streets. It was a loud and joyful ruckus, swirling with an energy that quickly spread throughout the town.

King Khety had waited for the heqet to lull the crowd with its intoxicating effects so that their inhibitions would be lowered, their spirits raised, and their wills more pliant and amenable to the power of suggestion. He had gone to wait with a group of his advisors and several guards in the colonnaded courtyard of the Temple of Osiris after the crowds had followed the priests on their procession to the god's final resting place.

When Khety finally emerged from the temple's pylon, it was like one of the gods coming forth in the flesh, resplendent in all his dazzling regalia including a golden scepter, a ceremonial wig, the *Deshret* Red Crown of Lower Egypt, and the long, narrow, false beard of Osiris that he wore on special feasts. He made a magnificent sight as he dangled glittering promises before the pilgrims, who had fallen to their knees before him. They were transfixed by his *kohl*-lined gray eyes, gleaming with a fierce and glacial beauty from his handsome, chiseled face. Even the austere quality of his features that he had acquired over the years, imbued his face and bearing with a godlike dignity, not unlike the great sphinx inspiring reverence as it stared out over the desert.

A hush fell over the inebriated crowd as they drank his words like one parched from the desert heat. He spoke of sacrifice, and blood, and the intense labor required to give birth to a new nation—a new and unified nation of Egypt.

"And you will prosper once again," his voice rang out after the musicians had stopped playing so all could listen. "The gods will resurrect the dead and imbue new life throughout the land."

There was much murmuring of voices in assent. Even the children running about through the crowd, paused from their rambunctious activities to stare at the king who captivated the people's attention. Khety was radiant, regal and refined; all masculine grace and magnetism.

"This division must end for a new life to begin," he continued.

The king of Lower Egypt paced before the temple that rose above the gardens like a beacon. Each of his measured steps accompanied his words like the beating of a drum. His voice resonated deep and melodious above the susurrations of the crowd. The sun had just set, and the torches lining the Avenue of Sphinxes had all been lit. Their smoke rose to the heavens, toward the sky whose clouds had been ignited by the last rays of the sun, into tongues of fire which bled a passionate haze over the people, who were feeling the rapturous effects of their revelry.

"YES," the people shouted back, falling under his spell. They were pushing to get closer to the god-king who had bewitched them.

None of the people even remembered Egypt as it used to be before the breach which had left it crippled and vulnerable to corruption. The rise of the provincial powers in Lower, Middle and Upper Egypt had weakened the central authority, so that the Old Kingdom had greatly declined during the sixth dynasty under King Pepi II. By the end of Pepi II's long reign at that time, civil wars tore apart the last remnants of the unified kingdom, and the fractured lands were plagued by severe drought, famine and conflict.

But the people did not recall these details. All they knew were the stories they heard which had been passed down from their parents and their parents' parents: tales of prosperity and plenty under a succession of god-kings who had reigned from the Old Kingdom's throne in the great city of Inebou-Hedjou, north of Nen-nesu, at the base of the Nile Delta, where the creator god Ptah was revered as patron of craftsmen and giver of life to all things in the world springing into existence through the power of his word.

"Blood and sacrifice!" the king shouted as he thrust a clenched fist into the air with wrath in his eyes.

The crowd's energy spiked his adrenaline, and his radiating power sent a ripple back over the throng in return.

"YES," the people shouted back, lost in his allure. Many of them were rocking back and forth, entranced by his irresistible magnetism, their heads flung back toward the sky, and their eyes closed in ecstasy.

Sudi felt his heart beating faster as he watched the mesmerized crowd, whose hunger for change was stimulated by the words of Khety. And he could see why. The king's deep voice and aristocratic bearing were simply bewitching. He looked every inch the god-king he proclaimed himself to be. His perfect features, erect bearing and booming voice left people spellbound.

Sudi also felt himself almost swept away by Khety's stunning presence, and he had not had a single drop of the ceremonial heqet. He saw the people go down on their knees and bow low to worship the king, who seemed to grow larger than life in the elongating shadows cast by a fiery setting sun. Several cats wandered near the king, one of which went right up to him and rubbed itself along the king's muscled legs. And the crowd gasped, wide-eyed, as they took it as a sign that the goddess Bastet—protector of Lower Egypt—had shown favor over the king whom she would defend.

"Save us, Lord King!" some of them shouted as the crowd pressed closer to the temple.

"Deliver us!" others yelled.

"We shall restore the great nation of Egypt to her former glory!" Khety boomed.

"GLORY TO EGYPT," the crowd thundered.

"To the land of plenty that our ancestors knew!"

"LAND OF PLENTY," they echoed, as many of them held up the pottery jugs of heqet being passed around liberally. They stretched out their arms in elation with the jugs lifted up high in an offering, as though the gods themselves would partake of the copious libations that inflamed their euphoria.

"The great divide that has weakened the north, while fattening the south, will be eradicated so all may flourish!" the king continued.

"FLOURISH, LORD KING."

"Your children will thrive in a new and prosperous land!"

"YES, LORD KING.

"And we will vanquish our enemies—enemies who seek to oppress Egypt!"

"VANQUISH THEM."

"Enemies who prey on the weak while paying homage to the strong!"

"VANQUISH THEM."

"Enemies who wish to trod upon your bowed heads!"

"VANQUISH THEM."

"We will gather them round like cattle for the slaughter." Khety's piercing eyes shone like a man possessed, as he whipped the mob into a frenzy. And they hung on every word that came from his mouth.

"GATHER THEM, LORD KING."

"And we will slaughter them!"

"SLAUGHTER THEM. SLAUGHTER THEM. SLAUGHTER THEM," they chanted.

It was then that the king motioned to Ankhtifi with a stabbing glance. Ankhtifi had been waiting patiently to one side, watching the events with his dark fathomless eyes that absorbed every detail of the crowd. He had his hand clasped around the upper arm of a man whose hands were bound behind him, and whose head was completely covered by a linen hood.

"Blood and sacrifice!" Khety yelled as Ankhtifi pushed the hooded man toward the king, forcing him to his knees.

Two other bound and hooded men waited under the watchful eyes of a guard. They stood next to one of the sphinxes that stared out through the torch-lit shadows engulfing the temple in the growing darkness.

"BLOOD AND SACRIFICE," echoed the crowd as their hunger grew more savage.

Ankhtifi withdrew the hood which had been covering the kneeling man's head and upper chest, and the crowd gasped once again. It was one of the temple priests who had carried the gilded barque of Osiris.

Three of the priests had been secretly ambushed inside the tomb after refusing to swear their allegiance to Khety. Repeated efforts to coax and convince the priests to support Khety had been fruitless. Even the bribery attempts were unsuccessful in enticing them. The pressure had only made them hostile, so that they threatened to speak out against Khety publically. And when a more diplomatic approach had failed to sway them, they were bound and beaten for their resistance. Ankhtifi then brought them before the king so he could make an example of one of them—the ultimate sacrifice that would seal the pact between Khety and the people.

A blood sacrifice.

The bound priest managed to still look dignified in his long kilt, shaven head, and somber expression that belied the fear and outrage churning within him. But one of his eyes had been blackened, and blood ran down his scalp, as well as from a corner of his mouth. The ceremonial leopardskin cloak which was draped over a single shoulder across his body had been torn away, as had been the heavy collar necklace and carved staff that symbolized his authority. But his thick, gold arm bands set with carnelian and lapis lazuli, gleamed in the golden torch light.

Sudi tensed when he realized what Ankhtifi and Khety planned to do to the helpless priest. All at once he understood it had been the priest's blood which was streaked across Ankhtifi's face, when Ankhtifi had mysteriously emerged from the tomb of Osiris earlier. The ruthless chieftain must have been the one to beat and bloody him and the others who had stood against King Khety's plan.

Sudi watched with disgust as Ankhtifi placed his hand on the hilt of a dagger hanging openly at his side. The chieftain's favorite mace was no longer hidden, and also hung in plain sight from his hip.

Someone in the crowd began to chant, and other voices joined in the chorus.

"Blood."

"Blood."

"BLOOD."

"BLOOD."

They condensed all their hate, despair and desire for change into one murderous thought which they irrationally believed would deliver them from their plight.

The individuals in the crowd no longer acted alone, but melded together, transforming into an angry mob pulsating with a life of its own.

Sudi felt the dynamic change as a thrumming energy resonated through the people who freely forfeited their individuality to the collective force. He was transfixed as he watched this distinct entity charged with hate and need, demand a justice they felt they were owed, from a man who played upon their weaknesses like an accomplished musician plucking the strings of a harp.

"BLOOD."

"BLOOD."

"BLOOD."

The mob chanted louder this time, as it slithered and coiled more tightly around the temple, like a great serpent whose head was the king. Even the children who had been running around excitedly, had long abandoned their play and gone to stand by their parents' sides, clutching their hands nervously.

Khety climbed upon a platform that had been used earlier by the priests, so the pilgrims could more easily observe the performed rites before the gilded barque had visited the cemeteries. But Ankhtifi and his men kept the entranced mob from touching the king.

The mob pressed against itself, and all the constraints that had subverted it for so long, becoming a creature of violence which fed on hate. The downtrodden who had come to Abdju in search of a new life, had infected others who had simply come to pay homage to the ancient god Osiris who now lay impotent in his dusty tomb.

Just as Ankhtifi raised the dagger in his hand and poised it over the helpless priest, who now lay prostrate before the unyielding king, a scream pierced the night, momentarily distracting the mob and Ankhtifi. It was a shrill cry that caused King Khety's own confidence to waver. And as he turned his gray eyes upwards, he spotted a ball of fire flying through the air toward him.

"Osiris!" one of the hooded priests cried out in a desperate plea for divine help. He had not seen the fiery arrow barely miss the king. But he had heard the commotion which ensued as the lupine-faced Ankhtifi ran for cover with King Khety, whose fiercely regal expression had crumbled.

And just as quickly as it had formed, the mob disintegrated into chaos.

That single shriek and fiery arrow had broken the spell of the mob's madness. Its coiled body split apart, morphing into a kind of frantic herd of frightened wildebeest that ran, pushing and shoving in a frenzied stampede, whose only thought was escape. The stupefying effects of the heqet, the fast encroaching darkness which swallowed the sky whole, and the torch smoke wafting over the crowd by a parched easterly desert breeze, convinced the people that the gods had suddenly turned against them in anger. And in their madness, they perceived the fire as a sign of the gods' fury.

Several more arrows illuminated a fiery path as they whizzed above the dispersing crowd toward the temple, whose sphinxes overlooked the now-vacant avenue which had been hastily abandoned. People were screaming and shouting as they left the temple grounds and ran blindly through the narrow streets of the town—streets which were made more frightening by the erratic shadows cast by torches in the marketplace. Pottery crashed to the ground, sacks of grain and spices spilled, fruit and vegetables rolled in the streets as tables were upturned and people tripped and fell on one another, some of them getting crushed in the process.

"Stay here, Lord King," Ankhtifi told King Khety.

They had withdrawn into the colonnaded courtyard of the Temple of Osiris with an entourage of guards and officials, and their three captive priests. A silent rage was beginning to replace the shock of the sudden turning of events, and the king grit his teeth against it.

"Someone did this," Khety snarled through his clenched jaw. "This was not an act of the gods."

Khety was envisioning all his meticulous arrangements being swept away like the Nile waters over the floodplains. Over a year of scrupulous planning had gone into the details which had unfolded this night. Over a year of meetings, and training, and strategizing, and waiting. But it had been a lifetime of ambition.

"An enemy," Ankhtifi said.

"Find them," Khety growled at some of his guards, with fury in his eyes, as several of his men left the temple to see who was behind the disaster, "and burn the town. Burn and destroy everything, including the royal necropolis. Leave nothing untouched! Destroy it all!" The power he had wielded over the crowd had dissolved as soon as they had panicked and dispersed.

But the battle had not yet been lost—it was just beginning. He would just have to go about it differently than he had originally planned.

The king thought about his small kingdom that was barely held together by the blood of his enemies. He thought of the throne which had been left to him by his father, and his grandfather before him. That throne rested on a dream of reunifying the lands—a dream which had been stoked and nurtured over time.

The seat of Lower Egypt's throne in Nen-nesu had never been very large or stable to begin with. It had risen from the ashes of the Old Kingdom's disintegration in Inebou-Hedjou. But other thrones had risen as well, as the central authority over the land disintegrated, and the provincial powers grew stronger. And although they had ruled their own city-settlements effectively, their power did not extend beyond the short reach of their arms. One by one, Khety had crushed them and usurped their power, growing more gluttonous and greedy as a result. King Mentuhotep was the last obstacle to his dream of ultimate power over Egypt; but a formidable obstacle indeed.

"Leave me!" Khety shouted abruptly, as one of his attendants tried to calm him.

The startled man slunk away like a dog with his tail tucked beneath him, and stepped outside the courtyard.

Khety was pacing back and forth among the gigantic columns that safeguarded and adorned the temple's private covered courtyard. He felt like a caged beast. He wanted to destroy the temple whose pillars felt like the constricting bars of a colossal pen. He flung his scepter onto the stone floor instead. He took a jagged breath and rubbed the back of his neck, as his thoughts roamed south, to Thebes, where Mentuhotep ruled. He closed his eyes against the envy burning in his blood. He closed his eyes tightly and drew his brows together, so that a deep, vertical line appeared to cleave his high forehead in two.

He coveted the Theban throne. He coveted it with every fiber of his lonely being. And he coveted everything belonging to the Theban ruler—his wives, his children, his lands, his very life.

Khety wanted power over all of Egypt, and he wanted the respect and adoration the people showed the ruler of Upper Egypt.

All he saw in the eyes of his own subjects was fear. They feared him when they stepped into the same room with him. They feared him when they whispered his name. They feared him when they knelt on trembling knees before him. They feared him when they opened their mouths to speak, and then stammered as they did so.

This bothered Khety. He hated their fear because fear breeds contempt. And contempt leads to rebellion. And rebellion induces treason.

The king exhaled, bristling against the realization that he could never be like Mentuhotep. He would never be respected and revered as was the Theban king. Yet like Mentuhotep, Khety was not a vain man. He was even oblivious to his own good looks and the flustering effect they sometimes had over others. Khety had always attributed his power over others to their fear; and though this was true, it had not always been that way. There was a time when he was cherished and loved, even if those sentiments only extended to the edge of his dominion. Yes, there was a time when he was venerated for the integrity and honor within his heart. He had cared deeply for his people, and they had esteemed and treated him with loyalty and devotion in return.

But that was a long time ago. It had been long before the tragedies wreaked havoc in his wretched life. Long before he built thick walls around himself; walls hewn from grief, anger and an agonizing loneliness that hardened his heart.

None of those ephemeral things mattered anymore, anyway. Feelings come and go. They wax and wane like the moon's endless cycles throughout time. And if Khety could not have the people's devotion, he would at least have their obedience.

Yes, he thought to himself, as he clenched his jaw determinedly once again, he would have their obedience; an obedience wrought by force if necessary.

Obedience wrought in blood.

TEN

Mentuhotep had given the signal to Qeb to loose the fiery arrow that flew over the people toward the Temple of Osiris, like a portent of death. The Kushite warrior had the eyesight of a hawk, and had released the string of his bow with the intent of using the arrow to kill the northern king, and jolt the mob out of its trance.

"Aim for the pretender," the king told Qeb, as he eyed Khety and the people with a frown on his face. "It is time to disperse this maddened crowd."

Khu, Nakhti and one of the soldiers had their arrows poised to fly toward the temple as well. And just as they were ignited with fire, they too followed Qeb's arrow over the mob that was now screaming. The mob's bravura had swollen disproportionately large by Khety's incendiary speech, and then burst like new wine in an old goatskin.

"Seth! It is Seth!" Some of them shrieked in their delirium.

"He's come to murder us all!" others screamed of Seth, who was the god of chaos and storms, as well as the brother of Osiris and Isis.

"Run! Get away! Death is upon us!" they panicked, as their heqet-steeped imaginations exploded into hysteria.

According to the Legend of Osiris, the dark and moody Seth grudgingly lived in the shadow of his brother, whom he despised with all the bitterness of a sibling rivalry as vast as the unyielding desert stretching on either side of the Nile Valley. After much plotting, the jealous Seth killed Osiris by trapping him in a wooden chest, which he sealed with molten lead, before hurling it into the Nile. Isis secretly retrieved the chest which was eventually discovered by Seth who, consumed by an unquenchable fury, dismembered Osiris's dead body, and scattered his

144

remains throughout Egypt, before claiming the throne of the gods for himself.

With Seth on the throne, chaos prevailed over the land. It unleashed cruelty and injustice, provoking humanity's baser instincts, as well as hardship, famine and disease. But the actions of Seth did not go unavenged. Horus, son of Osiris and Isis, later hunted down and confronted his evil uncle Seth. He engaged him in an eternal battle of good versus evil, which is fated to end with the victory of Horus reinstating Osiris as king, who, until that day comes, remains god of the dead, ruling justly in the Afterlife.

Panic spread over the dispersing crowd like wildfire as their thoughts turned to the evil brother of Osiris. Upon seeing the fiery arrows, they believed that Seth had come to inflict a terrible destruction over the town, smiting them in a jealous rage for their devotion to Osiris. What the people did not know was that the battle for Egypt was being fought, not by gods, but by the two most powerful kings at the time.

The people ran for their lives, thinking Seth would release a pit of snakes, spitting fiery venom from the Netherworld to consume them. The jubilant mood following the grand ceremonial reenactment commemorating Osiris, which had been sullied by Khety's talk of blood and sacrifice, soured into a fear reeking of desperation.

It was every man for himself as the people sought cover from an impending doom.

Mentuhotep had arrived at Abdju only hours before. He had cut his trip to Kush short, where he had hired more mercenaries before returning to Swentet to assemble an army and head back north, not even bothering to stop in Thebes.

He traveled in a fleet of ten ships with about six-hundred men, most of whom were trained soldiers, armed with bows and arrows, spears, scimitars, battle axes and shields. They sailed north on the Nile and docked at a small farming settlement just south of Abdju, so their arrival would not be noticed. They uncoiled the thick papyrus ropes stored on deck, and used them to secure the ships to the shore, looping and tying them around some large boulders used for this purpose. A small crew stayed behind to guard the ships which would remain here, safely out of sight from the enemy. Only one of the ships would follow to dock in Abdju in the morning, along with a few smaller boats that would be at the king's disposal.

"We go on foot from here," the king instructed, as his men left the ships and took their weapons to head toward the city that was celebrating the Festival of Osiris.

Although the farming village south of Abdju appeared to be largely deserted, a few people stopped whatever they were doing to watch the armed men move in disciplined form after the king of Upper Egypt. A young, expectant mother grasped the hand of her little boy in alarm, as she cradled her swollen belly in a protective gesture. They stared, unblinkingly, with their mouths slightly agape, at the men who passed by in silence. An old man herding a small flock of sheep had also turned to face the men leaving the ships by the shore. Several of the sheep were bleating as the stillness of the aging day was broken. There were a few children wading in a shallow pond under the watchful eyes of two elderly women, who were weaving large reed baskets that would be used for storing fish caught from the river, after it had been cleaned, dried and salted.

Startled birds took to flight while others sought shelter in the dense reeds by the riverbank. The agricultural settlement had fields lying next to a small village with a heqet-brewing facility. Most of the laborers had taken time off to celebrate the annual festival in Abdju, where it was believed that the entrance to the Underworld waited in the mouth of a canyon.

Khu and Nakhti walked behind their father and Qeb on the dirt road that crept along the rocky vegetated

146

bank of the Nile. The land rose sharply away from the river, then continued into a gently sloping plain running westward, with slender palm trees rising against the sky whose colors deepened with every passing hour of the sun's ancient voyage.

A vulture circled above, catching Khu's eye.

"It is a good omen," Nakhti said as he too watched the bird. "Mut is watching over us."

Mut was the vulture goddess of the sky. She was Amun's wife and mother goddess of Thebes. It was believed that all life was conceived through her, and she was worshiped alongside Amun and the moon-god Khonsu who was her son. The three of them were revered as the Triad of Thebes.

The boys watched as the bird soared gracefully with its outstretched wings, whose dark flight feathers were tipped in white. Nakhti was in high spirits, feeling excited about the prospect of fighting alongside the soldiers in his father's army. He walked with his head held high, carrying himself as one who believed he could not be defeated.

But Khu felt a little apprehensive. He could not place the source of the strange feeling which grew stronger as they neared Abdju. All he knew was that something dark and evil waited for them there.

"They might be expecting us," the king said, as they kept close to the riverbank whose thick vegetation shielded them from view.

"Expecting a fleet on the river perhaps, Father," Nakhti answered confidently. "But they will not expect an army on foot."

"Even if they are, it does not matter," Khu spoke up.

Khu had been the one to persuade Mentuhotep to leave the mines for another time and go to Abdju. He had sensed the fear and deception in Ankhtifi's administrator. The fish-faced man was as slippery as an eel and just as dangerous. And as Khu had suspected, the man had indeed sent word to Ankhtifi about Mentuhotep's visit right after the Theban king had departed.

But Ankhtifi had not been overly concerned when he received the message from an envoy. So what if Mentuhotep had stopped by Nekhen on his way down to Kush? He did not see anything unusual in that. And the fact that Ankhtifi was in Abdju during the Festival of Osiris had been perfectly reasonable. Why would the Theban king suspect anything when Mentuhotep himself often attended many such festivals?

There was nothing suspicious in that. At least that is what Ankhtifi had convinced himself. And so he had kept this information from Khety, after the envoy had delivered his message, so as not to distract Lower Egypt's monarch from their scheme. They had purposely planned this revolt to coincide with the Festival of Osiris so it would not arouse suspicion, and so they could enlist the help of the several thousands of people who would be there. Khety had believed their plan to be foolproof.

It almost had been.

Ankhtifi was not aware that Mentuhotep had been told that he had gone to Abdju to trade goods which were commonly available in Abdju. It was that simple ruse that had made the Theban king suspicious of his southern neighbor. That, and Khu's own intuition which was as sharp as an owl's hearing.

Mentuhotep might not have suspected anything if Khu had not insisted that something more sinister was at work. But over the years he had come to rely on Khu's perceptiveness, and to trust his ability to see things in the light of truth, no matter how well it might be concealed beneath many slippery layers of deception. Strangely enough though, Khu had never mentioned anything about Odji the gatekeeper over the years since the botched robbery attempt. Perhaps that was due to Odji's own clever instincts to keep his thoughts well hidden behind a façade of honesty. He had always made it a point to stay far from Khu whenever the boy was entering or leaving the palace compound. Keeping his distance had helped to keep his thoughts well hidden from Khu's piercing gaze.

Mentuhotep's army passed by one of the hundreds of cemeteries bordering Abdju as they headed deeper into the western desert. Little more than the crumbled relics of the ancient stone structure survived of the Predynastic grave. The elaborate, brick-lined tomb showed the charred traces of fires which had once consumed the area. Thorny shrubs, weeds and wild grasses sprung from the dry ground, clinging to the broken walls of roofless chambers, which had long since been claimed by foxes, snakes and lizards. A few scattered bearded sheep cocked their heads to one side, eyeing the men as they grazed on the brush growing in clumps from the rocky terrain.

Some of the men touched the amulets hanging from their necks in protection against any evil spirits that might be lurking among the dead, whose graves had been disturbed over time. Khu closed his eyes momentarily as he grasped his own talisman hanging from a leather cord. It was a small, winged *kheper* scarab beetle carved from black onyx, holding a sun made of pure gold. His mother Tem had given it to him during their first celebration together of the Inundation of the Nile, when he was seven.

"Wear this always my son," Tem had told Khu, as she tied the cord around his neck. "It will protect you from harm."

Khu thought of his mother now as he touched the amulet. It was warm from the heat of his sun-drenched skin, and reminded him of her warm smile that was always touched with a hint of worry for the son who claimed her heart. He hoped she was well, and that she would not fret if she found out about what was going on in Abdju. Like most mothers, she often worried for him. And although she had been very supportive of Mentuhotep in his desire to take the boys with him to Kush, there was an underlying apprehension that made the corners of her smile waver ever so slightly. Only Khu knew of her true feelings and the depth of her love and need to protect the boy who had grown into a young man.

"Stop..." Qeb raised a hand to halt the procession of men as they marched past the derelict grave.

Qeb had been walking about fifty paces ahead of the king, to scout for possible danger lurking on the outskirts of Abdju, when he suddenly spoke up. He crouched down to examine something on the ground.

Khu saw a thick cloud of flies buzzing loudly around Qeb, and some buzzards perched on a scraggly tree with thorny branches, stripped of leaves. The dark-feathered birds were hunched and brooding as they observed the landscape below, with beady eyes feigning indifference. Their yellow, dagger-like beaks were stained with blood.

Qeb was still crouched on the ground when the king arrived by his side. All was quiet except for the angry flies that had been disturbed from their bloody feasting. Even the buzzards waited patiently, biding their time in the tree, which cast a fragmented shadow on the uneven ground strewn with sand, rocks and brush.

Mentuhotep said nothing as he approached the grisly scene with caution. Nakhti and Khu had followed, curious to see what was there. Khu heard his brother's sharp intake of breath as Nakhti stifled his shock. It was not the first time the boys had seen a mutilated body. They had witnessed prisoners punished, men whipped and caned, and others put to death for high crimes against the king that included treason and attempted grave robbing among other offenses. But they had never seen a body torn apart with such savagery, it almost seemed inhuman.

Khu cast a sidelong glance at his father. The king's face remained stoic. Only a barely discernible flexing of a muscle in his neck betrayed an implacable fury seething behind his eyes, which were fixed on what was left of the face of one of the men he had sent ahead to Abdju with Sudi, to spy on Ankhtifi.

"It is Pili," Qeb said in a low voice, mindful of the dead man's spirit which probably roamed restlessly nearby.

Mentuhotep just lowered his head, closing his eyes as he slowly exhaled. Then he turned away to stare at the horizon, waiting beyond the limestone bluffs, that shone pink in the glow of the dying day.

Pili had inadvertently discovered King Khety staying at the home of an official in Abdju, when he had split up from his other two partners to comb the town for information. He lingered near some of the more lavish residences of the town, in an attempt to find out more about the Nen-nesian ruler's plans. It had been three days before the Going Forth of Osiris commemoration that would culminate the religious proceedings of the annual festival, before the people lost themselves in the reveling.

Khety had been biding his time to make his appearance after the effigy of Osiris had been laid to rest in his mastaba tomb. He had been partaking in secret meetings to perfectly orchestrate the last touches of the events, which were unfolding just as he had planned for so long. The king of Lower Egypt was talking with someone in the courtyard, beyond the gardens near the official's residence where he was staying, when Pili happened by. Pili quickly ducked and hid behind one of the thick columns supporting a pergola, under which a small shrine dedicated to Isis stood. He thought he recognized King Khety from his striking presence, though he could not be sure since he had never actually seen him from up close before. It was the response of the king's companion, and how the man had addressed the king, that pricked Pili's ears and removed all doubt as to Khety's identity.

"Yes, Lord King," the man had said. "Everything is ready for you."

"Good," King Khety gave a curt nod. His *kohl*-lined eyes sparkled a pale shade of slate. It was hard to look into those eyes without feeling discomfited. He was not wearing his ceremonial wig, and his smooth-shaven head shone golden in the dappled light filtering through the leaves of a sycamore fig tree. The tree's wide-spreading branches bore thick clusters of fruit in varying stages of ripeness. It was the sacred tree of life connecting the two worlds of life and death. Khety picked a small cluster of the figs which had ripened into red succulent orbs. He blew the dust off one of them and popped the whole thing into his mouth, chewing thoughtfully for a while as his mind continued to work. "Have the priests agreed to support us then?"

"Some of them, Sire. We just need a little more time to convince the others." The man looked a bit nervous. He knew Khety would not be happy to hear this.

"Hmm," the king looked away as he thought of the stubborn priests who refused to pledge their loyalty to him. If he could not have their allegiance willingly, he would take it by force. "Tell Ankhtifi to join me when he is finished for today," he looked back at the man who was eager to leave.

But the man did not need to tell Ankhtifi anything. The chieftain of Nekhen had overheard them speaking as he made his way over from the town's center. He saw Pili listening in the shadow of a column, like a mongoose eyeing a snake. Ankhtifi gripped the handle of his mace and ducked behind another column. He moved without a sound, inching closer to the man he knew instinctively was an enemy. And as he moved from behind one column to another, Khety spotted him from across the courtyard.

"Ankhtifi!" he greeted approvingly, unaware that Pili was there.

Pili whipped his head around in time to see Ankhtifi bearing down on him like a wolf closing in for the kill. The dark, lupine eyes of the chieftain were fixed on the smaller man, who did not stand a chance. Pili backed into a column as his panicked eyes darted around frantically, but there was no place for him to go. He could not outrun him. A terrible fear and indecision immobilized his limbs.

The last thing Pili saw before dying, was the wolf-man's baleful glare, and the copper-headed mace shining in the light before crushing his skull.

"We cannot leave him here," Mentuhotep said of Pili.

Khu and Nakhti had stepped away from the gruesome scene after staring wide-eyed at the carnage. Blood stained the ground where the buzzards had been tearing at the flesh of the dead man. The boys glanced at each other, wondering what the king had in mind. They knew the buzzards and other wild animals would only finish what they had started, leaving nothing but his thin, brittle bones and a thatch of blood-matted hair, to bleach in the sun. The man's remains had to be buried in order to free his spirit.

"I could take him back to the ship, Lord King," one of the soldiers offered.

"Very well," Mentuhotep nodded as he touched his amulet. "At least take what is left. And go with someone else." He looked up at the tree where the buzzards waited patiently. A few of them were preening their dark feathers, some of which were stained with Pili's blood. "I wonder..." the king let the words trail off.

"Wonder what, Lord King?" Qeb asked. He had stepped out of the way of the two men who were gently wrapping Pili's remains in a plain linen cloth. It would have to do for now, at least until his body could be taken back to Thebes where it would be cleansed, purified, and receive all the necessary ablutions before a proper burial could take place, so that his spirit could be sent to the Afterlife to rest for all eternity.

But the king just shook his head and kept his thoughts to himself. He waved at the flies landing on the ground that was sticky with congealed blood.

"Cover this with sand," he pointed to the blood, "so the flies go away."

But nothing could mask the stench of death that had fouled the day, foreshadowing the battle lying ahead.

Mentuhotep divided his army so they could infiltrate Abdju in smaller groups without drawing much attention to themselves. Some had gone to wait close to the west bank of the Nile, so they could block the enemy from attempting to escape by way of the river. The king sent more men over to the temple complex dominating the town's center. They were barely able to get through the mass of people who were vying to get closer to King Khety, as he captivated the mob with his larger-than-life persona. Mentuhotep split up the rest of his men into smaller bands surrounding the town, while he, Qeb, Nakhti, Khu and several other men positioned themselves at a shrine which stood more than 150 paces from the Temple of Osiris.

Nobody thought it strange that soldiers moved among the crowd. The temple priests had their own soldiers positioned to keep over-zealous pilgrims from getting too close to the temple. Those men stood on bare, thickly calloused feet, watching the crowd impassively with their large ox-hide shields stretched over wooden frames, and their bronze-tipped spears glinting in the sun. With so many people flooding the town for the annual celebration, more soldiers had been employed to keep the peace, maintain harmony, and be on the lookout against the inevitable parasites which followed the pilgrims in hopes of profiting from the festival by less than honorable means.

Khu was not able to see Ankhtifi's face from this distance. All he saw was the group of men standing with their three hooded prisoners in front of the Temple of Osiris, where King Khety was speaking to the crowd.

The torch fires threw long, skulking shadows that undulated in the dry breeze. Khu narrowed his eyes at the king of Lower Egypt who was bewitching the mob with lies. He had never seen him before this night. And although he could not make out the features of Ankhtifi and the other men guarding the Nen-nesian king, he felt the malevolence seeping from Ankhtifi's soul like the foul secretion of an infected pustule. A strange tingling sensation spread through Khu's fingers and toes, and his heart beat faster. He watched, transfixed, as the captive priest was forced to his knees before the king. Qeb had already drawn the string of his bow, with the bronze arrow tip aiming at the northern king.

In the chaos unleashed by the fiery arrows, Mentuhotep's army infiltrated the crowd with a single purpose: to crush King Khety's supporters. People were running and screaming as the opposing armies withdrew their weapons and began slashing at each other in the maelstrom. But Mentuhotep wanted to face Khety on his own terms. Qeb's arrow had barely missed the northern king, who had quickly disappeared into the temple with his entourage.

This was not the first uprising staged by the House of Khety from Lower Egypt's Akhtoy lineage in Nen-nesu. After the last of the Inebou-Hedjou kings died childless, the provincial leader of Nen-nesu jumped on the opportunity to declare himself god-king of Egypt.

But he had not been the only one.

The Theban leaders also staked their claim, as did other governors in the ensuing chaos which led to civil war between all the opposing powers. Like a pack of wolves, they all competed for power after the alpha male god-king had deceased and left his supreme position open.

King Khety's father had attacked Mentuhotep's grandfather King Wah-ankh Intef II, in an attempt to crush his enemies and eliminate the rest of the competition that also vied for the *Pschent* Double Crown of Upper and Lower Egypt. Their bloody battle had occurred in the city of Tjeny—just north of Abdju. And just as Abdju would suffer much ruin from King Khety's revolt, the battle at Tjeny had also resulted in the desecration of its tombs and utter ruin of its city.

It was after a subsequent skirmish years later, that Mentuhotep saw Khety for the very first time in his life. Mentuhotep was about nine years old when Khety—a grown man about fourteen years his senior—had met with Mentuhotep's father briefly on a diplomatic mission. By that time Khety was already king of Lower Egypt, and Mentuhotep's father—King Nakhtnebtepnefer Intef III—occupied the Theban throne. The meeting took place shortly after Intef III successfully defended one of his territories north of Thebes, where he had quickly quashed the beginnings of a small rebellion, and in doing so, managed to keep the duration of his short reign peaceful.

Mentuhotep recalled seeing Khety step inside the room where his father waited with his advisors. Young Mentuhotep was standing off to one side with a tutor, from where he quietly observed the proceedings, as was required of the crown prince who would one day follow to take his father's place as king.

Neither of the kings had bowed to each other, but they had behaved courteously, treating each other with the respect and dignity their positions warranted. Mentuhotep was struck by King Khety's tall, regal bearing and handsome looks. There was a casual grace and confidence to the way he moved.

A hush claimed the room the moment Khety had stepped inside, and all eyes turned to him. He stood out from the crowd like something shining in the desert sand. From the way the two kings had spoken together, it almost seemed as though they might have been friends if their kingdoms had not opposed each other.

"It is a pity he occupies the northern throne," Intef had later said, long after their meeting was over.

"Why Father?" young Mentuhotep had asked.

"Because he is not a bad man," Intef replied with a nod.

That had been long before Khety's features were hardened by the tragedies that would come later in Khety's life. Even then, he was the kind of person with a strong presence and a magnetic aura which attracted attention. His sharp gray eyes sparkled with intelligence as he took in his surroundings. Wherever he went, people stopped what they were doing to turn and stare at him. They couldn't help it, for he had that effect on others.

What struck Mentuhotep most at the time was that Khety actually looked like a god—a god with perfectly proportioned features, exquisitely carved in granite, limestone and alabaster, with pale slate eyes. It was an impression that stayed with Mentuhotep all these years.

And it was intimidating.

The peace forged by Khety and Intef III on that day long ago had been transitory; for after Intef's death, Mentuhotep had to crush a few small skirmishes which erupted along the southern perimeter of Middle Egypt, though he did not come face-to-face with Khety again.

Mentuhotep wondered how much Khety had changed over the years. He wondered how much his father's opinion would have changed as well. He still imagined the Nen-nesian king to be the very same as he had last seen him so many years ago. But he knew that *that* had been the impression of a young child, and that Khety would have changed since then.

Mentuhotep had heard of the king's tragedies, and had also kept abreast of his activities over the years. But he could not help feeling apprehensive about meeting him in person. And for all his childhood impressions of the godlike man who claimed Lower Egypt's Deshret Red Crown in the north, Mentuhotep had to remind himself that Khety was just another pretender who had risen to power from a transitory lineage—a lineage he intended on crushing for good.

Mentuhotep hoped that would happen today.

Khu and Nakhti had jumped into the frantic churning mass along with the rest of Mentuhotep's men. They fought side by side, guarding each other's backs as they defended themselves against Ankhtifi and Khety's men, who showed no fear in their blazing eyes. Some of the enemy had been lulled by the festivities, which had been going on for many days, while Mentuhotep's army was still fresh, having arrived only a few hours before. And although Ankhtifi's men had been warned that the Theban king might be surprising them with a visit, their initial caution melted away during the long ceremonial processions, and with the heqet they drank to keep from dehydrating under the glaring sun.

Nakhti was eager to draw blood. All his natural impulsiveness gave him a courage he might otherwise not have felt. But Khu could not shake the malevolence he had sensed earlier. There was something disturbingly familiar about it. He tried burying those thoughts as he scanned the large public square in front of the temple. He saw people huddling under tables whose contents had spilled on the ground. Others were limping away, or trying to drag off loved ones into safer surroundings. Some people had been trampled to death in the havoc, while others lay unconscious from their wounds. All about the town, skirmishes had broken out between groups of his father's soldiers and the enemy.

Khety had long disappeared within the confines of the massive temple structure, along with his entourage. His guards had warned him of Mentuhotep's men scouring the streets. They had seen the Theban army rounding up or killing anyone involved in the revolt. They had seen the priest's guards also join in the battle, siding along with the Theban soldiers.

Regardless of Khety and Ankhtifi's combined forces, they were still outnumbered by Mentuhotep's troops. Without the support from the pilgrims and general public, Khety knew he did not stand a chance. He needed the people's support to help him push south and take the

Theban crown by force. He had counted on their sheer numbers to overcome resistance from Upper Egypt's ruler. And since the people had panicked, he had no choice but to flee.

If he wanted to get out of Abdju alive.

Khety and Ankhtifi's soldiers were a mismatched assortment of solitary, masterless men from all over Egypt and the foreign lands lying to the east. They were hungry for power and plunder. Especially Ankhtifi's men. Like the lean jackals hunting in the shadows, the men under Ankhtifi's command were opportunistic marauders and ruffians whose experience was largely drawn from raiding small settlements. Many of them were not battle-hardened warriors, but rather bullies whose strength lay in their penchant to trample innocent, unarmed men, women and children.

Mentuhotep's men were skilled soldiers, and Khu and Nakhti had the agility and speed of youth. The adrenaline coursing through their blood, flooded their veins with an indestructible mettle. All their years of training had led up to this point. So as they were weaving their way through the scattering crowd in search of the radical supporters of the northern king, one man stepped out from behind a column to lunge at Khu with a dagger meant to split him open.

Khu did not think twice before parrying and pivoting away. He slashed back at the man who had someone else's blood smeared across his broad chest, but the man sidestepped and hissed, baring his teeth in a growl.

Khu lost all his initial reserve. Any last traces of nervousness had evaporated like water from the scorching desert. He moved with the lethal grace of the blade, his face a taut mask of concentration, as he traded strikes with his opponent. Then he stepped to one side, tricking the man into thinking he was trying to catch his breath. And that was when Khu delivered the deadly strike to the man's neck. The man clutched his throat as blood poured down through his fingers. He sputtered and gargled a final protest as he slashed feebly at the air one last time before going down like a felled ox.

Khu darted a glance at Nakhti just in time to see two men approaching his brother. One was armed with a battle ax dripping with fresh blood, from someone he had killed moments before. The other held a dagger in each of this fisted hands. Seeing the young warriors made the men grin.

"This will be easy," one boasted to the other.

They sensed the boys' inexperience. But Nakhti leaped toward the first man, shrieking as he whipped his blade in the air, like a demon from the Netherworld. The man jumped backward and spread his arms wide as though welcoming the assault.

"Behind you!" Nakhti yelled, as another man ran toward Khu, roaring as he swung with a downward cut of his blade.

Khu sidestepped, but not quickly enough, and in the clangor of blades his own dagger broke in half. The man sneered, his yellow teeth gleaming in the fading light. Khu thought he smelled heqet on his sour breath as the man lunged for Khu's chest. But Khu dodged the blade and thrust his knee into the man's groin. He snatched the dagger out of his opponent's hand, and stabbed him in the throat as the man bent forward, grimacing from the pain. Khu kicked the dying man backward as he pulled the blade free, then turned to find Nakhti.

Nakhti was holding his own against two men. One of them slashed Nakhti's forearm and had drawn blood, but it was not deep. The man moved like a weasel, fast and slippery, as he came in with a succession of quick short swipes. His attacker then tossed both his daggers into the air, and for a moment time stood still as the blades caught the dazzling light of a torch fire burning from the wall of an abandoned shop, reflecting it back like liquid gold. The blades whirred in the air as they spiraled back down before the man caught them by their hilts. He was showing off. But his confidence made him careless.

"Kill the whelp," his partner spat.

Nakhti swung then. He ducked low and swept the blade of his dagger before him, slicing into the man's ankles, crippling him at once. The man shrieked as he fell, letting go of the daggers which fell to the ground. His partner immediately stepped forward, driving his battle ax down over Nakhti's prone head. But Khu rammed his blade into the man's belly, and he dropped the ax, stumbling back with a look of utter shock on his contorted face. The man gripped the hilt of the dagger embedded in his gut, ripping the blade free from his flesh, just before Nakhti finished the job with a death blow to his throat.

On went the fighting as smoke spread over the settlement like a gray cloud, deepening the darkness that reeked of death. Blood soaked the ground where colorful flowers had been strewn before. All the singing and dancing accompanying the religious ceremonies and festivities had turned into shrieks and wailing. Time passed in what seemed like an interminable stretch of violence, with screaming and shouting that told of pain and death. Black smoke choked the night air from scattered fires, whose flames danced red and gold like giant burnt offerings to the gods. The blaze scorched parts of the marketplace and public areas, smearing soot, burning the vegetation, and charring the structures throughout the cult settlement.

Mentuhotep's army drove the enemy back from the town's center. Those pilgrims who had joined in the fray were the first to be subdued, and were bound in reed ropes to await justice. Many of them pleaded for mercy, claiming to have been swayed by Khety's glittering promises and their own passionate desire for change, which was true. They professed their allegiance to the Theban ruler, but were still rounded up and herded away along with other prisoners to an open field lying adjacent to the town.

Khety's and Ankhtifi's men were shone no mercy. They were promptly beheaded and left in a clearing before being thrown into a shallow pit, which would be dug in the desert, far beyond the fertile plain. The temple priests who had not been ambushed in the tomb, and those clerics who had been elsewhere in the town, led their own guards against Khety's and Ankhtifi's men. They managed to seize some of the officials who had betrayed them by siding with the Nen-nesian king, including Mdjai—the friend of Odji—who had boasted about his position to the power-hungry gatekeeper. They too were shone no mercy, and they were put to death in a manner that would also banish their souls from the Field of Reeds, damning them for eternity.

After the mob had disintegrated into a state of panic, Mentuhotep had immediately embarked on a search for Khety.

"They have retreated into the temple," he told Qeb. "Do not let them get away. I want to confront Khety myself."

They left the shrine where they had been spying on Khety during his speech. Only Qeb and a few others had stayed behind to accompany Mentuhotep, who was wearing the blue-stained leather *Khepresh* royal war crown with a gold rearing cobra fastened on the front. The king and his men skirted around the southern part of the large public square leading to the Temple of Osiris. The colonnaded arcade, parks, gardens and open halls were mostly empty now, except for the fallen and injured whimpering in confusion or lying in a pool of blood.

Most of the fighting had moved farther away by the open marketplace of the village, and closer to the Nile where some of Khety's men were attempting to flee. People ran screaming on the narrow streets which were shrouded in darkness, like black *kohl* smeared in thick brushstrokes across the land. A few rogue fighters pounced from the shadows to lunge at the Theban king and his men like feral cats. But they were quickly subdued, mostly by Qeb's scimitar which the Kushite warrior wielded expertly as though it were a mere extension of his own hand.

The torch fires burned brightly along the deserted Avenue of Sphinxes. The human-headed monsters seemed to scowl at the night, daring man to rise above his baser instincts and join the immortal ranks of the gods. The regal heads rose imperiously from leonine bodies made tense by a barely checked urge to crush and devour the evil crawling throughout the earth. They symbolized the power of mind over matter, of spirit over flesh, the godlike human head controlling the bestial body, and the never ending battle of good versus evil.

Mentuhotep and his men approached the Temple of Osiris with great caution, touching their amulets in a silent plea for protection and aid from the gods. Shadows wrestled on the smooth, paved ground like battling beasts in the eternal struggle of mankind. Smoke writhed around them, and dogs barked in the distance, from the town which had been turned into a battlefield. The king kept his hand on the hilt of his dagger, while Qeb held his scimitar protectively before him, ready to strike at the enemy. With every tentative step, they neared the nest of vipers. Arriving to the pylon, they pressed their backs against the walled entrance rising intimidatingly toward the black sky. No sound emerged from within.

Qeb gestured to the others to wait as he moved slowly around the colossal sandstone statues of Osiris flanking the pylon, where the god stood guarding both sides of the entrance with the crook and flail in his arms which were crossed over his chest. The massive stone entrance was carved in heavy relief. Osiris watched them from the colorful painted walls, seated from his otherworldly throne, with the crook and flail also held in his crossed arms; and again from where he was standing with a spear in one hand, and a dagger in the other, as he was depicted in several carved poses, battle-ready and menacing, with the war crown on his head—the same blue *Khepresh* war crown that Mentuhotep wore. The others followed slowly behind Qeb, stepping soundlessly through the rectangular opening and into the empty hypostyle courtyard.

"No one is here," Qeb whispered.

"Look," Mentuhotep pointed to the scepter that Khety had flung to the floor earlier. It lay abandoned by a column. One of the guards picked up the scepter and handed it to Mentuhotep.

"Khety was holding this," Mentuhotep said, as he angrily recalled how the king of Lower Egypt had appeared when inciting the crowd from the platform in front of the Temple of Osiris. Mentuhotep grit his teeth as he thought of the man who wanted to take his throne from him.

From the distance where Mentuhotep had been watching, he didn't think that Khety had changed all that much over the years since he last saw him. But he had not been close enough to the northern king to really tell, and darkness had already been settling over the temple. Regardless, Khety still possessed an undeniable presence which left people spellbound. That much was obvious. The crowd's reaction was evidence enough of Khety's allure. He most certainly must still possess the striking features with which he had been blessed by the gods. And whatever creases he had acquired over time, and the hardened aspect from all he had suffered, would only have made him more fiercely handsome.

"Lower Egypt's crown will be yours one day, Lord King," Qeb said, as Mentuhotep was recalling how Khety had captivated the crowd. "You will wear the Double Crown, as you are meant to."

"When the Prophesy of Neferti is fulfilled," Mentuhotep said, as he left the scepter where it had been found on the floor, before continuing to look around the courtyard for any signs of the enemy.

The huge columns framing the courtyard shone translucent in the milky light of the full moon. The lunar god Khonsu had made his appearance in the night, where he took his regal place upon his sky throne. Mentuhotep peered into the thick shadows beyond the colonnaded galleries, but saw nothing.

Nothing sinister moved in the darkness that settled between the columns. Nothing scratched or scurried on the ground, which was kept immaculately clean by the priests who oversaw the temple rituals, and daily tended to the ancient god's human needs. Nothing but the sounds of their own movement and breathing disturbed the space around them.

The group moved deeper into the hypostyle hall waiting beyond the courtyard. Qeb grabbed two torches flanking the second pylon's entrance, passing them to two men whom he urged forward before following them inside the roofed structure. Three sets of double-rowed columns rose in what seemed like a petrified forest, appearing taller than the columns in the courtyard. The colossal pillars were topped with papyrus and lotus capitals, gently flaring toward a ceiling pierced by shafts of spectral light, that drifted through openings cut into the sides of its raised center aisle. Although the hypostyle hall was smaller than the courtyard, its limestone opulence dwarfed the men who touched their amulets in awe. They were overwhelmed by the surroundings meant to evoke the densely reeded marshes of the outside world, which screened the holy and secluded dwelling place of the god from unworthy eyes.

The hypostyle hall was used to perform religious rituals, and was forbidden to the general public. Only the high priests and king were permitted to enter, and only after obligatory purification rituals including meticulous bodily cleansing, and a strict adherence to dietary laws prohibiting the consumption of certain foods like fish and pork, which were considered unclean. But all protocol had been cast aside in order to rid the settlement of the wickedness that had taken refuge within its holiest temple.

Every step through the magnificent space filled the men with a sense of wonder and trepidation, and their grips on their weapons tightened with the need to feel something tangible in the elusive world of gods, which dazzled mortals. The men holding the torches, swept the flames over the walls surrounding the outer columns, where the darkness was most profound. The fire's light threw ominous shadows that imbued the paintings with a life of their own. Brightly painted, carved reliefs portrayed religious rituals and scenes of the life of Osiris, and were lavishly decorated with lush plant-life including lotus flowers and papyrus reeds.

In one of the painted scenes, Isis stood with her hands resting on the shoulders of Osiris, who was seated before her with the crook and flail in his hands. He wore the *Atef* feathered crown, while Isis wore the horned crown of Hathor, symbolizing healing and fertility.

In another painted scene, Osiris stood next to Isis, while their son Horus, who was wearing the *Pschent* Double Crown of Egypt on his falcon head, stood before them with one foot in front of the other. Horus was holding the *ankh* key of life in his right hand, and the canine-headed *Was* Scepter, symbolizing his divine authority, in his left hand.

The eerie play of shadow and light made the gods seem as though they were actually breathing. Even the columns were elaborately carved, depicting more scenes from the life of Osiris, including a painting of the god seated before an offering table heaped with food, drink, oil and incense. Everywhere in the hall, the paintings, reliefs and the architecture of the temple reminded one of the god whose mythos dominated the structure, and whose essence permeated the very air, which was redolent of smoke and incense.

The men grew tenser as they moved deeper into the temple, exploring its sacred surroundings for the evil lurking within. Mentuhotep wiped his forehead with the back of his hand. He was perspiring. Qeb just ignored the trickle of sweat running down the side of his face.

They entered the Sanctuary—the Holy of Holies—in the deepest part of the temple where Osiris lived. But his cult statue had not yet been returned. It was still at the tomb where it would remain for several more days, before once again reclaiming his throne upon the raised shrine enclosed within the monolithic syenite *naos*, which was topped with a decorative cornice and polished to a gleaming shine.

In front of the naos stood another platform in the room's center, where the gilded barque was usually stored. That too was missing, as it would be used to transport the god back to the temple from his tomb. The room's two bronze wall braziers, that were kept burning year-round in the presence of the god, remained unlit in his absence. Nothing but the men's torchlight illuminated the walls of the room, which were covered in images of gods and goddesses, and in intricate hieroglyphic texts.

From floor to ceiling, illustrations were carved into the walls, portraying Osiris in different stages of his life. There were images of priests making offerings of food and drink to the beloved god, while scenes of clerics and other ministers were paying homage before him, or serving him in a variety of manners as was befitting to the god.

For a moment no one moved. Even though Osiris was not there, they felt the god's omnipresent *Ka* watching them. They held their breaths in reverence, knowing that their presence here would never be warranted under normal circumstances.

Few ever had the chance to enter the temple-mansions of the gods. The priests who did enter had to undergo a ritual of purification rites before stepping within the hallowed structure. Cleanliness was indeed next to godliness, as they were required to wash and oil their clean-shaven bodies four times daily—twice in the morning and twice at night. They wore no leather or wool, abstained from all intimate relations, followed strict dietary laws, and rinsed their mouths out with a cleansing solution of natron. Even those lesser priests who did not have any contact with the divine cult image, were also required to partake of the ablutions so that they too would be considered ritually pure before stepping within the hallowed temple grounds.

"Blood!" one man gasped in alarm. He crouched down to examine the drops which thickened into a trail, smearing its way behind the platform.

Qeb took the torch from the man, his other hand never leaving the hilt of his scimitar, as he followed the bloody path. Every one of his senses was in a heightened state of alert. He could feel the tiny hairs on his body standing on end as his skin prickled with fear, anticipation, and anger.

The trail led them behind the shrine to an oval stone basin that was larger than the opening of a well, and set directly into the floor. It was filled with holy water from the Sacred Lake lying just outside the temple, behind its grand structure. The sanctified waters were used in the temple purification rites and offerings. But the once-crystalline water ran dark with the blood of a priest who was sprawled face-down in the basin. Two more priests lay on the floor nearby. Their dead eyes stared blankly ahead, the light of life extinguished and cold, as were the bronze braziers affixed to the walls.

Mentuhotep tore his gaze from the bloody scene, grabbed a torch from one of the men, and scanned every corner of the vacant room that lay at the very back of the temple.

But no one was there.

King Khety and Ankhtifi had vanished.

ELEVEN

K ing Khety and Ankhtifi were on a ship bound north to Nen-nesu. The oars bit into the Nile, spreading ripples across the dark water glinting in the moonlight. The ship's prow rose to a sharpened point on which a metal lion's head jutted out almost horizontally over the water. Its jaws gaped open in a menacing snarl meant to scare away any evil spirits lurking in the river.

The narrow elongated hull cut through the river, parting it evenly in two. A large steering oar used to navigate the ship was fastened to the stern, above which rose the bowsprit in a long and graceful curve, its end flaring out like the head of the papyrus reed—the symbol of Lower Egypt.

The ship moved soundlessly through the water with its cargo of defeated men. It slipped away from the dwindling battle in Abdju, which had been ignited by King Khety's uprising. Fires continued to burn all through the night, visible along the southern horizon where they destroyed and blackened much of the old necropolis and other parts of the settlement.

The ship moved steadily, looping around wide marshes and mudbanks where night heron and grebes stalked and foraged through the reeds. The haunting wail of a loon sounded a lonely call echoing in the darkness.

King Khety and Ankhtifi had escaped from Abdju shortly after the fighting had commenced. They had disguised themselves as pilgrims, and had stolen away through a secret passage hidden within the temple. They had tortured their captives into revealing the entrance to the passage before Ankhtifi killed them inside the sanctuary, and left their lifeless bodies on the defiled floor. It was a sacrilege of the worst kind, a blasphemous desecration of the holiest of holies in the murder of innocent men, whose blood violated the god's earthly domain.

No purification ritual could wash away the darkness staining a wicked soul, or the evil festering within an infected heart.

The narrow mouth of the secret passage had been concealed by a thin stone veneer etched in elaborate hieroglyphs, overlaying a thicker slab of limestone in one of the corner walls of the hypostyle hall. It had been difficult to find at first, and even more difficult to pry out. The priests had searched frantically, only pausing to argue amongst themselves as they sought the opening that had not ever been used in their lifetimes.

"Find it," Khety hissed at them. "And do it quickly!"

"Y-Yes Lord King," one replied in a shaky voice.

All three priests darted nervous glances at Ankhtifi who was shadowing their every move. His ominous presence rattled and frightened them, making it more difficult to think. They had been right to fear him. For after they finally found the ancient passage, Ankhtifi had killed the priests to silence them forever.

"Hide their bodies," Khety told him, "but not too well. Let their deaths serve as a warning to anyone who may come searching for us."

Once they were able to wrench the stone covering the hidden passage free, Ankhtifi had a hard time fitting through the hole that was slightly smaller than the width of his broad shoulders. But he finally squeezed inside, following after the king of Lower Egypt and three other guards who had also disguised themselves as pilgrims. The chieftain of Nekhen had then carefully replaced the slab and stone veneer after him, with the help of a thin reed rope and the edge of an ax which he used to fit them back over the lip of the opening to the passage, so that no one would be the wiser. Anyone searching for them would not even know where to begin looking. Their only hope for clues now lay dead in a pool of blood.

The fugitives had taken a torch with them to light the dismal path, which descended several feet beneath the ground. It was a dark tunnel, lined with large rough-hewn stone bricks that clung heavily with a silt-like dust, rising about them like a cloud of spirits from the Netherworld, reducing the visibility to almost nothing. The men moved slowly, having to stoop very low in the tight shaft as they stretched out their hands before them in an attempt to feel their way through the cramped space.

Doubts assailed King Khety's resolve as he peered ahead through the murky cloud that was a pale color of sand. He was carrying a linen sack with the Deshret Red Crown, and the ceremonial wig and beard he had been wearing earlier. With the other hand he pressed a strip of fabric over his mouth and nose, which he had wound about his head in a vain effort to protect himself from inhaling the thick dust. He wondered if he had done the right thing in escaping through the tunnel. What if they could not find a way out? Going back was not an option. But neither did he relish the thought of slowly suffocating to death in the entrails of the ancient city. Its bowels concealed a stale earthiness, much like the tombs whose lifeless air had not been disturbed in centuries.

The men perspired heavily with the strain of their efforts, as they followed the passage which cut beneath the city in what seemed like an interminable stretch to the ends of the earth. They forced themselves to take shallow breaths through the layers of linen, which made them look like living mummies creeping through the land of the dead. Their backs and legs ached from their half-crouched stances, and the dust burned their eyes and nasal passages. They were heading north to one of the royal chapels in the Terrace of the Great God, which lay along a processional route waiting at the edge of the town.

Centuries had passed since anyone had crept through these tunnels, which dated back to the first dynasty of the Old Kingdom. They had been constructed as a safety precaution against tomb raiders, and other thieving reprobates, who had a canine ability for sniffing out treasure like a fox in the desert sand. The last time anyone had been down here was well over five hundred years earlier, before the building of the pyramids of the great Giza necropolis that served as tombs and rose like citadels for the dead, in Lower Egypt's west bank of the Nile.

The channel-like passages were connected by small chambers cut into the bedrock upon which several tombs were built. But the entrances to those chambers were also hidden within the tunnels themselves, and even more difficult to find than the mouth of the passage within the Temple of Osiris. There were false passages and false doors leading to dead ends, all with the purpose of thwarting would-be robbers from desecrating the holy graves, temples and monuments. They would suffocate long before locating the chambers which remained sealed against all living things. Their only hope for escape was to remain on the path that would take them to one of the shrines belonging to the Terrace of the Great God. And so they continued feeling their way slowly, moving like moles burrowing through the earth, away from the fighting and chaos they had unleashed, which continued raging on the streets above them.

The men followed the directions of the priests who had assured them that this particular path of the tunnel would arrive to a dead end at the edge of the settlement, preventing them from getting lost. Since the priests had never been down in the tunnel themselves, the fugitives were relying on secondhand information they had gotten from the priests, which had in turn been passed on by a long line of Keepers of the Temple, whose guarded secrets had been relayed in the oral tradition of the Old Kingdom, as well as inscribed on papyrus scrolls which were promptly incinerated before their escape. Khety had verified their information by comparing it to the diagrams on the scrolls, before Ankhtifi had burned the ancient evidence over a torch flame.

They finally arrived to the end of the tunnel. But it took well over an hour just to find the trap door concealing the exit. Khety and the other men were bent on their knees, feeling blindly along the walls, running their palms over the rough surfaces as they searched for any telltale markings that would reveal the exit's hidden location. They tried to smother their coughs behind their linen masks as more of the fine, silt-like dust rose in a thick veil around them, and the flames of their single torch lapped greedily at the dwindling oxygen of the cramped space.

It was stifling.

But Khety refused to give up, believing the priests had told them the truth. No one could resist Ankhtifi's agonizing methods of extracting information. The priests had gladly revealed all they knew in hopes for a swift death at the hands of their tormentor, who inflicted pain with the calloused aggression of a crocodile.

"Hold this," Khety ordered from behind his linen mask, as he reached for the arm of a man next to him, and placed the handle of the torch in his hand. "I think I found the opening."

He brushed away the dirt outlining a crevice in the wall, keeping his eyes closed against the burning dust. The opening was about the same size as the one they had entered in the Temple of Osiris. With the help of another man, Khety carefully pried out the stone covering the hidden exit of the passage, and climbed out of the cramped space. The men stood up slowly, working out the kinks from their aching muscles as they stretched to their full heights. They wiped away the grimy sweat running down their faces like crocodile tears.

No one but the *Wedjat* Eye of Horus watched as the disheveled group of men finally exited the tunnel, and entered inside the shrine that was dedicated to the son of Osiris and Isis. The *Wedjat* stylized eye and eyebrow was carved into the stone walls of the shrine, covering much of the space which had been built to honor the brave young warrior-god Horus, who had sacrificed one of his own eyes so that his father Osiris could see again, after his murdered and dismembered body had been revived by the loving devotion of Isis. The *Wedjat's* symbol of protection matched the amulets worn by two of the guards, which they promptly touched upon entering the shrine.

But nothing could ward off the evil that ulcerated within the chieftain who wore no amulets himself. Ankhtifi held little regard for such fanatic zealotry, and had long dispensed with those tokens believed to provide divine aid to the people. The only talisman he believed in was the power of his mace. And he grasped its hilt warily after he replaced the stone covering over the exit on a lower section of the wall.

It was mostly dark inside the shrine. No braziers or torches burned in honor of the god. Only the flame of a small oil lamp sputtered a weak glow over the engraved and painted walls. The sounds of men fighting, and the frantic cries of people fleeing in panicked haste, sounded in the distance, far beyond the chapel as the men froze a moment to get their bearings. Their linen clothing was brown from the dust of the tunnel, which also clung to their skin in a thick dirty layer. Anyone spotting them might think they were one of the walking dead who had left their tombs to wander among the living.

"We should be safe here," Khety whispered as he withdrew the dagger hanging at his side.

A small war ship was waiting for them in the harbor lying just beyond a field bordering a dirt road. It had been a precautionary move, just in case things did not turn out as planned. Khety unwound the linen from his face and drew the cloth over his head to cloak his features. The other men did the same as they tried to pass for pilgrims fleeing from the city. The king motioned to the men to follow him as he left the enclosed pillared shrine and exited to a small courtyard facing the street. Other shrines and chapels lining the Terrace of the Great God stared out from their stone niches at the darkness that stank of smoke and death.

Khu stopped suddenly as he and Nakhti walked along the Terrace of the Great God. Pilgrims scurried away, keeping to the shadows as they sought cover from unfriendly eyes. Most of the fighting had receded to small pockets scattered throughout the settlement which continued to burn well into the darkest hours of the night.

"What is it?" Nakhti asked. Although he trusted Khu's instincts, he also believed his brother to be a little too sensitive at times. Sometimes being overly cautious can be just as deadly as lacking any caution whatsoever. It is in those moments of hesitation and uncertainty that trouble strikes.

"Wait," Khu lifted his palm as he froze for a moment on the narrow street where debris was strewn, and flowers had been trampled by the fleeing crowds. Khu turned his head slowly towards the shrine of Horus across from them. He drew his brows together, narrowing his eyes as he stared, unblinkingly, into the darkness. He seemed to sniff the air like a wary dog sensing trouble. A vague and inexplicable suspicion prickled the back of his neck, telling him danger was near.

"There is no one here," Nakhti lowered his voice instinctively.

But Khu shook his head and placed a hand on the hilt of his dagger. He felt the same tingling sensation he had felt earlier while staring at King Khety and his entourage, just before the Nen-nesian king would have had Ankhtifi slay the priest in a bloody sacrifice before the transfixed mob.

Khu suddenly pulled Nakhti aside, quickly stepping behind a wall as five men emerged from the darkened

175

courtyard waiting across the road, outside the shrine of Horus. Although they were dressed as common pilgrims, there was something clearly uncommon about the men. And they were armed. All of them held daggers with wicked tips glinting in the moonlight. Their proud and menacing postures were more fitting for battle-hardened warriors rather than humble supplicants seeking salvation. The tallest of the bunch also had a mace hanging by his hip. He seemed to prowl with the bearing of a predator on the lookout for prey. His broad shoulders swayed above a long, curved spine resembling the threatening pose of a cobra readying to inflict a deadly bite.

The boys watched the men from their hiding place. Even Nakhti could tell that these were no ordinary pilgrims, and he admired Khu's uncanny ability to sense danger, grateful for his brother's mysterious gift.

Khu was perspiring beside Nakhti. He felt an eerie chill shoot through his limbs, and yet he broke into a cold sweat despite the iciness flooding his veins. His eyes were locked on the largest of the men, who was cloaked in inky shadows smeared over the settlement.

There was something familiar about the man, and it filled Khu with dread.

"Let's follow them," Nakhti whispered, as he nudged Khu.

But Khu did not move.

"Khu," Nakhti urged quietly. And when Khu still said nothing, Nakhti turned to look at him. "What is it, brother?" he asked with a frown, the tone of his voice full of concern.

But Khu only shook his head. He could feel his heart race and his breath quicken. His eyes were riveted on the group of men as they stepped away from the shrine and headed cautiously down the street, darting leery glances about them.

Khu did not understand the terrible fear that gripped him. He had never felt so confused and afraid in his life. There was something about one of those men in particular that left him frozen and immobile. It was as though the pliant tissue in his muscles had been replaced by lead. And although anxiety addled his mind and slowed his movements, he managed to follow after Nakhti who led the way.

An owl hooted in the darkness, like a omen boding ill, and somewhere in the distance dogs were barking. A cat darted across the street and disappeared into a shrine, and a warm breeze blew the smoke from the fires across the settlement.

Then someone screamed.

It was a piercing sound that was immediately stifled as the largest of the men in the group ahead of them silenced the shrill cry of a woman with his dagger. She had run out in front of the men with her two children, thinking they were pilgrims like herself, and that they would help her to flee the burning city and all its havoc. But when Ankhtifi raised his dagger, teeth flashing as he snarled threateningly, the woman panicked when she realized that death, rather than deliverance, was at hand.

Nakhti and Khu had closed most of the distance between them and the men stalking the street ahead of them. The boys kept close to the shadows of the shrines they passed along the Terrace of the Great God. Most of the colonnaded façades stared out at the deserted street, with little more than an ashy light seeping from the darkness beyond their small courtyards, where forgotten oil lamps burned in solitary confinement, within the chapels paying homage to indifferent gods who had forsaken the major cult center of the ancients.

The moon's light shone full on Ankhtifi's face from this angle, throwing his lupine features into high relief. Khu saw Ankhtifi's face, and reached out a hand to steady himself from the jolting shock that nearly knocked him over. He grasped Nakhti's shoulder, who walked a pace ahead, stopping him at once. Nothing blocked Khu's view of the wolf-man's face, as Ankhtifi kicked the woman's lifeless body, and those of her two young children, away after they all fell to the ground.

Something twisted painfully inside Khu. Something within him was wrenched with a violent force, and he groaned softly in spite of himself. It was a low guttural sound, like that of an animal which had been mortally wounded. He stared, wide-eyed, catching his breath as the full force of the horrific memories that had long been repressed and deeply buried within the furthest recesses of his subconscious mind, came crashing over him like a tidal wave. He winced, shutting his eyes tightly, unable to thwart the violent sensations from wracking his being.

Time stood still then.

It came to a screeching halt before reversing backwards with a jarring force. For a few moments Khu stood riveted to the spot as images of his mother's and sister's deaths flashed in his mind. In that instant he was transported back to the bloody room in his old village, on the night of the terrible massacre that had annihilated the small agricultural settlement.

Every detail of that cursed night tore through his mind with the vivid clarity of lightning striking through a blackened sky, wrenching his heart in two.

One of the two children who were thought to be dead on the street next to their mother, made a mewing sound then. She twitched awkwardly as her little hand opened and closed next to her bloodied face. Ankhtifi grabbed his mace, swinging it over the child's head, delivering the final death blow that forever silenced the girl with a low crushing thud.

It was all that was needed to jolt Khu from his riveted trance. He leaped out of the shadows and ran towards the men, howling like a raging bull out of the darkness.

For a moment the men panicked and dispersed, wondering what wicked fiend had been unleashed from the bowels of the Netherworld. It was an inhuman, ghastly cry that struck a terrible fear into the men who touched their amulets for protection. Even Ankhtifi panicked and stepped away looking for cover.

Nakhti took full advantage of the element of surprise, catching up with two of the men as they were running away from Khu. The thugs staggered off balance in their haste, parrying as Nakhti lunged, but their efforts were weak and ineffectual against the adrenaline-induced fury that suffused Nakhti's blood with a godly strength. Nakhti screamed as he ran his blade into the belly of one opponent, gutting him open like a fish, then twisting the blade free before driving it into the second man's back, stabbing ferociously with a hulking strength, then pulling it from the bloodied flesh.

Khety had immediately taken cover in the shadows of another courtyard when he heard Khu scream. Nakhti ran after the third guard who had fled before the others. The man turned to face him, dagger in hand, as he swept the blade toward Nakhti's belly. Nakhti blocked the assault and lunged furiously at the man who sidestepped out of reach. Nakhti swung again, hacking at the air as the man ducked away each time. Then the man feigned a thrust, but Nakhti did not take the bait. He twisted to the right, bending low as he stepped forward with an uppercut of his dagger, catching the man below the jaw. Blood spurted out into the darkness as Nakhti drove the blade deeper. The man stumbled and fell, dropping his weapon. Nakhti kicked the fallen blade away, and then withdrew his dagger, pulling hard at the blade, as more blood drenched the night. He wiped its crimson edge on the dead man's cloak.

Khu was about twenty paces behind Nakhti, locked in battle with Ankhtifi. He had pounced on Ankhtifi's back, screaming like a demon, and startling the larger man into dropping his dagger as he reached up to grab Khu. Ankhtifi twisted around, ducked, and then rolled to the ground in an attempt to throw Khu off his back. It was only when Khety stepped out from the shadows that Khu got distracted and released Ankhtifi.

Nakhti caught up to his brother, lunging at Khety as the Nen-nesian king joined in the fray. But Khety kicked Nakhti with a powerful force, and Nakhti skidded away on his bare back. A small group of people passing nearby screamed when they saw the men fighting, and they took off in alarm, scattering like a flock of birds flushed from a thicket. Khety's eyes flashed as he glanced at the pilgrims running away. It was all the time Nakhti needed to jump back on his feet, his dagger in hand.

"Ankhtifi! Let's go!" Khety called out to Ankhtifi when he saw an opportunity to flee after Nakhti retreated. He wanted to rush to their ship before it was too late.

But Ankhtifi crouched low, growling as he faced Khu with the mace in his hand. He did not recognize the young man standing before him as being the same little boy who had been hiding under a blood-soaked sheet, in a shadow-shrouded room that stank of death. He had never seen him, nor had he even suspected that the boy had been hiding inside the room on that fateful night, when death fell upon the village like a plague.

But Khu remembered Ankhtifi.

Every detail of Ankhtifi's lupine face had been seared into Khu's soul before it was buried and forgotten with the amnesia he had suffered. Every single nuance, from his predatory sneer, to his dark sunken eyes, and even to the tic that made one side of Ankhtifi's jaw twitch. Khu shuddered once again as he faced the malevolent beast with the blackened soul who had butchered his family and village.

Ankhtifi sneered and turned to flee with Khety, but not before Khu ran after him once more. Khu dove at Ankhtifi, lunging low at his legs, driving his dagger deep into the back of Ankhtifi's left thigh.

Ankhtifi shouted angrily in pain as he twisted free of the blade, kicking Khu hard with his good leg.

Khu rolled on the ground, putting distance between him and Ankhtifi, but two of his ribs had broken from the force of the kick. Khu winced as he got up, wobbling a little from the pain, wrapping a protective arm about his ribcage. He was bent over with his eyes fixed on Ankhtifi, panting with the effort of breathing through the stabbing sensation in his side.

Then a glowering Ankhtifi swung his mace, twirling it high in the air as he edged closer to Khu, who was backing away from the wounded wolf-man.

"KHU!!!" Nakhti yelled.

But the warning was wasted, for Khu had been watching Ankhtifi all along. He was unable to tear his gaze away as he stared, transfixed, at the man who moved with the calculated precision of a predator readying to pounce.

Khu ducked but not fast enough. The mace glanced hard off the side of his head. He stumbled and fell as the men fled, and Nakhti ran to his side.

The blow did not kill Khu, but it stunned him badly, and blood ran freely from the jagged cut in his smooth-shaven scalp, spilling down his face and neck.

Nakhti kneeled down on the ground, placing a supportive arm under Khu's bleeding head, and another under his back, holding his brother closely as a violent trembling assailed Khu's body.

"It's alright Khu," Nakhti whispered worriedly. "They have fled. It's alright."

"No," Khu uttered between breaths, "he... he k-killed them..."

Nakhti watched his brother intently, not sure who he was referring to. "They fled," he repeated in a calming voice. "They are gone. It is safe now. You are safe."

"He k-killed my f-family."

"Who?" Nakhti asked, utterly confused.

"Ankhtifi."

And then Khu closed his eyes.

Khu's last thoughts before succumbing to the darkness enveloping him were with his father, his mother, and his little sister who waited for him in the Afterlife—in the Field of Reeds. He saw their beautiful faces smiling to him, as they stood together, holding hands, side by side, in an open field, under a limpid sky, warmed by a golden sun.

Hot tears rolled slowly down from the outer corners of Khu's reddened eyes. Hot, bitter tears that bled from the raw, biting wound in his soul, whose thick protective scar had been savagely ripped open after all these years. His tears mingled with the blood and dirt staining his skin, and then dripped, one by one, to the ground, as he finally lost consciousness in Nakhti's arms.

TWELVE

A smoky haze hung over Abdju. It was deathly quiet, and the eerie hush stifled the city that had been ravaged by King Khety's insurrection. The sun shone through a mass of clouds that stretched thin over the large settlement.

The last of the revolt had been quickly crushed, though it took days to drive away the crowds, and clear out the last of the pilgrims, who had arrived on foot or by boat. But Abdju had suffered extensive ruin. Mentuhotep left troops stationed at the ancient cult center, placing the city under guard to keep away looters from descending upon the settlement, whose many temples, shrines, and vast necropolis had been charred and partially crumbled in the fires.

The Temple of Osiris was among those structures which remained standing. It was as though the blood drenching the floor of the sanctuary had deflected the ravenous flames from consuming it. The price of peace is innocent blood spilled on the altar of death. But the Avenue of Sphinxes and the pylon of the great temple had not been entirely spared. Many of the human-headed monsters were blackened by the fires, and now resembled something fiendish out of the Netherworld, like hulking, soot-smeared, crouching beasts ready to pounce on passersby, and drag them to the depths of their fiery dens.

Khu lay on a bed inside the lower hall in the home of an official who had remained loyal to King Mentuhotep. Although the ground floors of the upper class homes were usually reserved for the household servants, Khu had been placed there so he would not have to walk up and down the stairs leading to the family's living quarters, on the second floor of the home. The gash on his head had been stitched and bandaged, but nothing much could be done about his broken ribs, other than wrapping a linen cloth around his torso to help immobilize him, and provide a small measure of comfort. He lay still, keeping his breathing even so as not to exacerbate the pain in his side. Several days had passed since his fight with Ankhtifi and his head still throbbed from the pounding gash he had received.

"I want to go with you Father," he told King Mentuhotep, after a moment of silence.

Qeb and Nakhti were pacing in the hall of the house where Khu's bed had been laid, but they stopped their pacing to look at Khu, and frowned.

Mentuhotep sighed, shaking his head as he released a long, frustrated breath. He had gotten very little sleep in the last days, and it showed. Stubble had grown over his smooth scalp and face, shadowing his features with fatigue, while the black *kohl* lining his eyes was smudged, making the circles underneath his eyes appear darker.

Yesterday he had assembled a large group of his men to devise a plan to defeat Khety and Ankhtifi once and for all. He knew that the northern king had a powerful influence which commanded people's respect. But it was a grudging respect, for many people did Khety's bidding out of fear rather than faithfulness. And those who rule through intimidation end up commanding a legion of cowards, who are quick to turn and scatter like the sands of the desert when facing a shift in the wind.

Mentuhotep had met with an assortment of advisors, warlords, generals, and other officials and leaders from various regional settlements, in the pavilion of one of the noble's homes, near the temple complex of the city. With the help of Qeb, he had delineated his plans and instructed the men to gather more troops for the assault that was planned to happen as soon as possible. They wanted to strike the iron while it was hot, and use the momentum from their victory in Abdju to continue pushing north after Khety and Ankhtifi.

Ankhtifi was a fugitive now. The chieftain of Nekhen had no choice but to abandon his settlement after their defeat. He would not dare show himself near Thebes for fear of retribution. It was well that he hid, for Mentuhotep had already sent spies all along the Nile as far south as Kush, and up north by the Nile Delta.

After options were discussed, details ironed out, and questions were answered, the king had dismissed the men so that they could make their preparations and raise more troops. Men and boys of fighting age would be conscripted into Mentuhotep's growing army, alongside the household troops of the various chieftains who were loyal to the Theban king. With proper planning and training, they would move forward in hopes of defeating all remaining obstacles including Khety, before capturing the throne of Lower Egypt once and for all.

A deep vertical line etched Mentuhotep's forehead as he drew his brows together. He was staring at Khu with a look of worry. "If something had happened to you..." the king cast a disapproving look at Nakhti and Khu. "You attacked three men—"

"Five," Nakhti corrected, as he walked over to the king's side.

"Five," Mentuhotep nodded with a snort. "Five seasoned warriors!" He had gone to sit by Khu's side, but got up suddenly, upset. He closed his eyes and pinched the bridge of his nose in an attempt to alleviate the strain he felt. Part of him admired the courage of his sons. They had gone after King Khety and Ankhtifi without a second thought for their own welfare. But the other part of him was furious at their impulsiveness.

"You are too impulsive Nakhti," the king scolded his other son. "How many times have I told you to think first before acting? How many times has Qeb said the same?" Mentuhotep knew that the boys could have been killed. "Whatever gave you the idea that you could possibly attack Khety and Ankhtifi and survive?"

"They do not know of Ankhtifi's reputation," Qeb added in their defense. He too looked worried, and the lines on his dark skin were more pronounced. But Mentuhotep disregarded him.

"I wish it had been my idea, Father," Nakhti said regretfully, ignoring the rebuke.

"It was my idea, Father," Khu spoke up. "But it could not be avoided."

"Your idea," Mentuhotep repeated, raising a single eyebrow. Khu never ceased to amaze him.

"Yes," Khu said simply, without any trace of defensiveness.

"And what would I have told your mothers if something had happened to you both?" the king admonished them with a shake of his head.

"That is the risk of battle, Father," Nakhti answered after a solemn moment.

"No," the king argued.

"What else could they have done?" Qeb asked, crossing his arms over his chest. He had been standing by and watching the king chiding his sons. He understood Mentuhotep's concern. When Qeb had first heard of Khu's injury he felt a molten blend of rage and fear surge through him. Fear for the boys he loved as sons, and rage for the men who could have killed them.

Mentuhotep's fatherly instinct was the first to rear its head where his sons were concerned. But the boys had proved themselves as young warriors. They had survived their first real battle, and it would serve them well in the uncertain times lying ahead. After all, iron is forged in fire. And there is nothing like battle to forge a warrior.

Mentuhotep shot Qeb a censorious look, but said nothing. He knew that Qeb was right. "They could have gone for help," he finally said after a moment, but his words lacked conviction. He realized that he would have done the same in their place.

A servant girl brought in a tray of food, and laid it on the wide table standing between two painted columns supporting the spacious room's high ceiling. No reed mats covered the three windows set high up in two of the walls facing each other, and light poured into the room, illuminating the vast space. The walls were covered in painted vines and flowers, as were the columns. Incense burned from a corner of the room, sending delicate tendrils curling through the still air. Amulets encircled Khu's bed for protection. Two more amulets were tucked within the bandages of his head and his ribcage, to speed up the healing process. He had been given warm infusions to sip that were made with special curative herbs. But they tasted awful, and he winced every time he drank, forcing himself to swallow the bitter liquid.

"Father..." Khu got Mentuhotep's attention, and the king turned back to his son.

Mentuhotep sat down at Khu's side once again. He placed a fatherly hand over Khu's hand that was now larger than his own. Khu was still growing, and the king knew he would soon surpass him in height.

"It's alright, Father," Khu whispered as he gave his father's hand a gentle squeeze. He sensed the king's distress.

Mentuhotep could not stop thinking about how his sons could have been killed. It would have destroyed him if anything had happened to them. Utterly destroyed him. For a moment, the idea of losing his sons made him think of Khety, and how the northern ruler had lost his wives and children; he had lost everyone that mattered to him. The thought was unbearable, and Mentuhotep frowned, quickly shaking it away.

Mentuhotep's gaze turned to one of the high windows and he stared at the light. Tiny speckles of dust moved in lazy patterns through the brilliant streak. He thought about the terrible massacre from which Khu had escaped as a child. Although the king was well aware of those things happening in the villages north of Thebes, Khu's story made it more real—and far more personal.

Once he had regained consciousness in the presence of Nakhti, Mentuhotep and Qeb, Khu had recounted everything that had happened to him on that grisly night in his village when he was a child. His encounter with Ankhtifi had triggered every sordid detail of those long repressed memories, and he told them the story with a grim and faraway expression. Only a slight trembling of his hand, and a silent tear marking a glistening path on his cheek, betrayed the emotions roiling within him.

The king turned back to Khu. He regarded his son with a quizzical eye, as he pondered the bloody pillaging Khu had witnessed and escaped. What if Khu had died alongside his family that night when he was a boy? What if he had arrived to another settlement after his narrow escape, instead of coming to Thebes? What if someone else, other than the palace servants, had discovered the sick child hiding in the reeds? So many questions ran through his mind.

Mentuhotep thought of the Seven Hathors and what fate they must have decreed for Khu upon his birth. It was believed that these seven mistresses of fate were responsible for the destiny of a person's life. They were present at the moment of birth, pronouncing the child's fate in all things, including the lifespan, key events, and manner of death. How they must have smiled upon the infant Khu when he was born. They must have kissed his eyes, imbuing them with the special gift he possessed. Whatever bleak future he had held in that humble village, must have been promptly exchanged for something brighter. The short and dark thread of his destiny had been replaced by a golden strand that would lead him to the Theban palace on his seventh year. It was full of portent, and the king felt a strange thrill prickle his skin as he pondered the fate of the boy who became his son.

"Father…" Khu sensed the turmoil within his father. But Mentuhotep closed his eyes and shook his head.

"You cannot come. You must rest and heal. You can barely move as it is. Look at you," Mentuhotep gestured with a hand over Khu to indicate his debilitated state.

"I injured Ankhtifi, Father," Khu said.

"How do you know this?" Mentuhotep narrowed his eyes.

"I felt the blade hit bone. He will have a limp at the very least, if he does not lose the leg to infection."

Khu had indeed injured the chieftain when he had lunged and driven the blade into his leg. The wound in Ankhtifi's thigh had been cleaned, sutured, and bound tightly afterwards. No infection ensued. But the dagger had inflicted nerve damage, and would leave Ankhtifi with an obvious, permanent limp. It would hinder him, making it difficult to walk for long. It would also affect his posture, so that he would grow more stooped over time, from the efforts of favoring the weakened leg.

"An animal is far more dangerous when wounded," Qeb muttered aloud as he thought of Ankhtifi's feral instincts. The man seemed more animal than human.

"Sudi left yesterday for Nen-nesu with a few men," Mentuhotep changed the subject with a wave of his hand. "He will find and keep close watch over Khety and Ankhtifi's whereabouts while we prepare our forces."

"What if Ankhtifi sees him?" Khu asked.

"He won't recognize him. I spoke with Sudi before he left, and he never got close enough to Ankhtifi before or during the revolt. Besides, they have never met, so Sudi's identity is quite safe."

"I do not know about that," Khu said.

"What do you mean?" the king asked.

"Ankhtifi can sense an enemy as a predator senses his prey. He is all instinct." Khu closed his eyes a moment as he recalled the way Ankhtifi moved when they walked in the shadows of the street. The wolf-man seemed to be sniffing the air like a dog. "He got to Pili," Khu reminded them.

"That is what I have been saying," Qeb added.

"Sudi will be alright," the king insisted.

"And then what, Father?" Nakhti asked.

Like Khu, Nakhti was also eager to hunt down Khety and Ankhtifi. He wanted to kill Ankhtifi himself, after the chieftain nearly took his brother's life. He glanced at Khu, tightening his fists and setting his jaw against the anger he felt for the man who almost killed Khu—twice: years back when Khu was a child in a small village, and again several days ago.

Khu sensed Nakhti's emotions and looked at his brother. He had always admired Nakhti's courage. But there was more to him than that. Nakhti had a fiercely protective spirit, one which was backed by a boundless generosity for those whom he loved. He never stopped to think of himself when the welfare of others was at stake.

"We will go north." Mentuhotep got up and wandered over to the table where several dishes of food waited. He helped himself to a handful of grapes. "If we do nothing, Khety will make another attempt to take the Upper Kingdom," Mentuhotep said around a mouthful of food. "That is what I would do if I were in his place," he nodded. "He knows his time has run out. And desperation makes men fearless."

"And impulsive," added Qeb.

"We should hurry, Father," Nakhti pressed eagerly. "He'll get away."

"And go where?" the king said flatly. "He has nowhere to go. He is most welcome to leave Egypt if he so desires. It will make things easier for us."

"He will not leave," Khu said, and all eyes turned to him. "He wants to take Upper Egypt. You heard him," Khu looked at his father. "We all heard him in the speech he gave in front of the Temple of Osiris," he was speaking to Qeb and Nakhti as well, who nodded slowly in assent.

"No, he won't leave. You are right," the king replied, chewing thoughtfully.

Nakhti went and helped himself to some bread and cheese. He brought a cup of heqet for Khu, winking at his brother conspiratorially, as he placed it on a small table next to his mat, so he could have something more palatable than the bitter infusions he had been sipping.

"This will taste better than those vile potions they've been making you drink, brother."

Khu thanked his brother but remained lost in his thoughts. His eyes were roaming about the spacious room as his mind reviewed his father's campaign plans to capture Lower Egypt. Mentuhotep's men had advised him to go north as soon as possible and take the throne by force. They had cautioned the king against waiting. Any delay would only allow the northern king to amass more men, artillery, and support for his cause. But Khu was not so sure that they should proceed so openly. He knew that Khety and Ankhtifi were shrewd as weasels. And to catch a weasel, one must think like a fox.

Mentuhotep saw Khu's mind working. He knew his son was thinking. He could see those golden eyes moving about the room. His son had been a beautiful child, and now he was growing into a very handsome young man. But it was the honor and integrity within him that shone most brightly. "What do you have in mind, Khu?" he asked him.

Khu's eyes finally came to rest on one of the painted walls on the other side of the room, where ducks and geese were poised in sudden flight from the marshes where they had been foraging for food only moments before. Something had startled the fowl, flushing them from the dense vegetation. Khu tilted his head to one side, narrowing his eyes as an idea took shape in his mind.

"We'll lure them out of their hiding," he spoke up after a moment.

Mentuhotep followed his son's gaze to the mural of the frightened waterfowl. The birds were rising in a bustle of flapping feathers as they tried to escape a trap set by two hunters with nets, crouching in the reeds. "How?" he asked Khu.

"Why should we chase after them when we can lure them to us instead?" Khu paused a moment to let the question sink into their minds. He tried to sit up a little, flinching at the stab of pain in his side. Nakhti walked over to prop a few cushions behind Khu's back so that he could be more comfortable. He handed the cup of heqet to Khu, who nodded gratefully to Nakhti for his help, before sipping it slowly and looking back at the painted wall.

Qeb and Mentuhotep had neared Khu's bedside as he spoke, wondering how Khu intended to lure them. "We'll set a trap to bait them," Khu said, as though reading their minds. He reached out to put the cup on the table, and then very carefully lay back on the cushions, holding his breath against the pain until he could relax once again.

"Bait them?" Qeb asked with interest.

"Does he not have allies elsewhere? In several of the settlements north of here?" Khu asked.

"He does," Mentuhotep nodded.

"In Zawty," Qeb said. "They have supported him for a long time."

"In other settlements too," Mentuhotep said.

"Yes, but Zawty especially," Qeb continued. "They are a wealthy province whose power has always sided with the kings of Lower Egypt."

"Then Zawty it should be," Khu nodded with a faint smile playing about his lips. "That is where we should set the trap."

"Hmm..." Mentuhotep narrowed his eyes in thought, scratching at the stubble growing along his jawline. He was wondering how he could possibly bait his arch nemesis to a province full of his own enemies. The people there would never accept anything Mentuhotep said. They would remain suspicious and guarded. And they would warn Khety against Mentuhotep's plans.

"He trusts them," Khu said quietly, looking at his father.

The king ran a hand over his scalp before letting his arm fall by his side. "Go on," he said, staring at Khu with interest.

"King Khety trusts the people of Zawty. Isn't that so, Qeb?" Khu asked.

"Yes, this is true. He does trust them," Qeb answered.

"He knows he has their support," Khu continued, "and so he will be far more inclined to believe them, and go along with whatever they say or do."

"How so?" Nakhti asked.

"Look at that wall," Khu pointed to the mural with the hunting scene. "Imagine chasing the birds out in the open. They would see you coming and fly away," he paused for a moment and had another sip of the heqet, then replaced the cup on the table before continuing. "Those hunters are luring the birds to them. They have their trap set with their nets, and are hiding in the reeds. Who do you think will catch the birds? They, or the first group chasing them out in the open?"

"Ah," the king smiled and nodded slowly. He understood what Khu had in mind. It was a better plan than that which had been worked out with his advisors the previous day. Khu had not been at the meeting because of his injuries, and Mentuhotep had felt the absence of his son. Along with Qeb, Khu's instincts and intuition were the ones he trusted most. The king was grateful that Khu was well enough to at least discuss their plans together now. "So you are proposing that we have his supporters in Zawty convince Khety to go there."

"Yes."

"By planting our own spies among them?"

"Something like that," Khu replied. "You can sort out the details. It should not be too difficult. They are all nervous, and desperate, and afraid."

"Fear makes men predictable," Qeb said in his wise way.

193

"It certainly makes them more pliable," the king added. "Desperate men are willing to take desperate measures. It will open them up to the power of suggestion, which is precisely what we will need to get them to convince Khety to go there. Khety wants to win more than anything... I know how he feels," he added quietly after a pause. The king's eyes traveled up to the dust-speckled light again, and he watched the golden streaks as they played over the walls and on the floor. "Let them lick their wounds first," Mentuhotep continued, as he mulled over the idea for himself. He stepped closer to the wall to study the beautifully painted scene. "We'll give them time to lower their guards. Khu is right," he nodded. "If we chase them now, they will only run. They are expecting to be chased. So we will wait. Then, when they think they are safe, we will bait them."

"And then what?" Nakhti asked.

"And then we spring the trap," Khu answered. He turned toward the king. "Perhaps you could have Sudi go to Zawty instead, Father. He might be able to convince them that he is betraying you. You can send word to him. He cannot have gone far yet."

Khu closed his eyes and exhaled slowly. He was tired, and his head was throbbing. His body ached from the beating he had taken. But he liked the plan. He especially liked the fact that it would buy him plenty of time for his bones to mend. All he wanted was to accompany his father. He could not stay behind. Not after having come face-to-face with the monster who murdered his family. He wanted to hunt Ankhtifi down like the animal he was, and send him to an eternal death in the pit of darkness where he would be swallowed whole by the serpent-demon Apep, before being vomited again and again, and then scorched in the goddess Sekhmet's cauldrons. There, in the Slaughtering Place, Sekhmet's butchers would torture Ankhtifi in all his senses, for all eternity, in the inextinguishable Lake of Fire.

"Yes," Mentuhotep said, pulling Khu's mind back from the Slaughtering Place. "We shall go north and spring the trap, then unite the lands once again," as though it were that simple.

The king smiled, and his optimism was infectious. It all seemed so easy. The revolt had been crushed very quickly, considering the thousands of people that had been involved. Certainly most were pilgrims, not warriors, but sometimes battles are won from sheer numbers rather than skill or strategy, though that had not been so in this case. Fear had quickly broken the mob's resolve, and scattered the pilgrims like rats from a sinking ship.

"The timing is right," Mentuhotep nodded. "Khety actually did us a favor."

"A favor?" Qeb raised a questioning eyebrow at the king.

"Yes. If he had not instigated the revolt, we would have remained complacent. And nothing would have changed."

"You have been planning this for years. Planning to reunite the kingdoms," Qeb said.

But the king shook his head. "It takes a spark to start a fire. Khety does not know what he has set into motion," Mentuhotep scratched at the stubble along his jawline again; it itched as it grew. "Or perhaps he does, and regrets it now. But whatever he thinks does not signify," he waved a hand dismissively through the air, "for the spark has ignited a fire which will sweep north all the way to where the river feeds the sea."

Khu settled back on his mat, pleased that he would be accompanying his father's troops north soon. He kept thinking about Ankhtifi, recalling every detail of the chieftain's bearing, manner and form, as his mind searched and probed for possible weaknesses in the wolf-man, which would help him take down the lupine warrior. Just a while longer, Khu thought to himself with resolve. A little while longer and he would finally avenge his father, mother and sister, and all those in his village who had died on that blood-misted night, long ago.

King Mentuhotep went back to the table of food as he pondered their plans and all that was said. He was imagining a new and unified Egypt, purged of the vermin that had been plaguing it for years; purged of thugs like Ankhtifi who inflicted death, destruction and despair wherever they went. He was already planning his assault to take the lands of the north.

But the Seven Hathors had other plans for Egypt.

The Mistresses of Fate shook their heads at the folly of men trying to impose their own will above that of the gods, for they had long ago chartered a course of their own. And for all Mentuhotep's soldiers, strategies and strength, it would be years before Khu would finally face Ankhtifi once again. Years—not days, nor even several courses of the moon—stretched between Lower Egypt and Mentuhotep's dream of unification.

"Yes," said Mentuhotep, oblivious to the decrees of Fate, as he drank some of the heqet waiting on the table alongside the food, "it is time to restore Egypt to her former glory."

And he raised his cup high.

THIRTEEN

Odji panicked when he got word of what had happened in Abdju. What would he do now? Every detail of the uprising plunged him deeper into despair.

His friend in Abdju was dead. Many of Khety's supporters who had been there were dead. And Khety himself had fled.

All the gatekeeper could see in his bleak future was a colossal wall rising before him. In his mind's eye, it stood between him and his sadistic dreams. He felt as though a door had been shut, trapping him inside a tomb—alive.

Odji stared at the boatman, but looked right through the older man. They were sitting inside Odji's house, which stood on a far corner of the palace grounds, near the quarters where many of the servants were housed.

"How could things have gone so wrong?" Odji asked in disbelief. He kept uncrossing and re-crossing his legs, then standing up to pace about and sit back down.

"You tell me. You had said that King Mentuhotep would be in Kush." The boatman wrinkled his brow in accusation. His face was a map of lines etched by time and the sun. He was thin and stooped through the upper back, as though the effort of straightening his posture would cause his bones to break.

"I must leave," Odji said, as he stood up to move about the room again. "I cannot stay here any longer." His guilt, greed, and ruthless ambitions had infected his mind with paranoia. He was convinced that Mentuhotep would somehow know of his treachery when he laid eyes on him, the same way young Khu had stared at him with a knowing look, all those years before. "It is too dangerous for me to remain," he shook his head quickly. "No, I do not wish to stay another day."

"Then come with me," the boatman said.

"Where will you go?"

"To Zawty. It is rumored that Khety may be staying there. They support him. You can come and find work there, or at a nearby settlement," he paused a moment to think. "They might be interested in you once they know you were working for the king. You could be useful to them."

Odji fidgeted with an empty cup he had picked up from a small table. He turned it around in his hands, studying the simple earthen vessel as he pondered the boatman's words, before blowing out a long sigh.

The boatman narrowed his eyes at the gatekeeper, shaking his head in disapproval.

"What?" Odji asked, defensively. "What is it? Why are you looking at me that way?"

"You are a fool, I think," the man reproached. "A fool to be so miserable here. It is a good life, yet you are miserable," the boatman shook his head again.

"You don't know what you are saying," Odji argued as he sat back down. He knew that the man sitting across from him was a simple man with simple ambitions. He did not care for power or wealth beyond the pittance he earned from his life on the Nile, and relaying clandestine messages. He was content with his life on the river.

"Calm yourself."

"No," Odji went on, "you do not understand." He put the cup back on the table with a clatter. "I *cannot* stay. I cannot stay even if I wanted to. It is too late for me. Once they know of my involvement, and the extent of my deception over the years, I will be condemned. Yes," he insisted with an emphatic nod, when he saw doubt in the boatman's eyes, "condemned to death!" he threw his hands up into the air, and stood up suddenly.

The boatman flinched, blinking nervously.

"It is not your head that is at stake," he said.

But the boatman looked away, pondering Odji's words as he scratched at a scab on his bony elbow.

"We better leave now," Odji uttered, after composing himself, "as soon as possible. Mentuhotep will be returning any day now. Unless he goes north."

"I heard his son was injured."

"Oh?" Odji's thin eyebrows shot up. "Which one?" he asked with sudden interest, sitting back down slowly, his eyes fixed on the boatman.

"I do not know. But it has detained the king."

Odji exhaled loudly through his mouth. He was frustrated. The boatman was not being very helpful, and his news, while interesting, was sketchy at best. Odji didn't have time to sit around. He stood up and began packing a few of his belongings. He wanted to leave before King Mentuhotep returned.

When he was ready, they stepped out of his small house and shut the door behind them.

Odji hoped it was the last time he would see Thebes.

Mentuhotep, Khu, Nakhti and Qeb were on a ship heading back to Thebes. It was their third day traveling south on the river that twisted and turned east before looping around and heading south again. A thick fog swathed the river in the early morning, but then thinned and disappeared as the sun rose higher. Date and doum palms grew in a thick mass just beyond the muddy bank, and their long, outstretched branches seemed to welcome the sailing ship with open arms. Several plover birds were pecking at the insects on a sandbar with their short beaks, oblivious to the fleet floating past them. Dragonflies flitted through the reeds and bulrushes where they hunted for smaller insects in the marshes.

They had spent the first two days traveling without stopping, except when they had docked by the riverbank during the darkest hours of night, when the moon ceased to illuminate their way. Mentuhotep was eager to return home, now that Khu was mending. They had delayed their voyage for more than half a moon's course so that Khu would be well enough to travel. But all of them had been restless in Abdju, pacing about like caged animals, except for Khu. He remained immobile as much as possible so he could heal properly. The pounding in his head had subsided, but nothing could soften the memories that had been revived with ferocious clarity. Not a day passed where he did not think of his murdered family, and of the monster who had taken their lives.

The five-day journey back to Thebes was going smoothly, and if all went as planned, they would arrive in another two days. They were heading to the settlement of Gebtu on the east bank of the Nile, where they planned to spend the night to refresh themselves and their supplies. It was there that a major trade route marked a caravan path along a dry riverbed, which cut across the eastern desert from Gebtu to the Sea of Reeds. The dry riverbed would eventually be known as the *Wadi Hammamat* in the subsequent millennia. It was the shortest route from the River Nile to the Sea of Reeds on Egypt's eastern border at Quseer. The outpost at Quseer served as a port from which expeditions to the mystical Land of Punt, and other remote places, were launched to trade and acquire exotic goods like incense, spices, ivory and pearls, as well as some of the unusual animals that were housed in menageries of the nobility. The region along the dry riverbed was also rich with quarries from where sandstone, basalts, quartz and other resources were mined.

Gebtu was the cult center of Min—god of the eastern desert and fertility. Most of the province of Gebtu was exempt from paying taxes to the king. The protective decrees had been passed down since the early dynastic kings of the Old Kingdom, and the edicts also excluded its people from having to participate in the mandated labor and military duties required of citizens conscripted into service during war campaigns and special building projects that took place when the Nile's flood kept people from working in the fields during the Season of Inundation.

But what Mentuhotep did not collect in taxes, he mined in some of the prized stone used to build monuments, temples and tombs, from the many quarries found in the eastern desert along the ancient caravan route. And while no tolls were imposed on the nomadic traders following the dry riverbed to the Sea of Reeds, the traveling merchants usually donated a portion of their imported goods to the Temple of Min, to honor and thank the god for his protection as they ventured through the eastern desert. It was these unofficial payments that made Gebtu a prosperous settlement.

The king was seated under the large canopy amidships, facing the prow, when Khu joined him from inside the cabin, lying behind a linen curtain. He and Nakhti passed the time on the river by playing endless rounds of the board game *senet*.

"How are you feeling?" the king asked, as Khu sat beside him under the canopy.

"He is feeling very well, undoubtedly," Nakhti answered on his behalf, as he followed Khu out of the cabin to stand by his father's other side. "And he should feel well, for he has beaten me every time!" Nakhti laughed.

"You told me not to let you win, brother," Khu raised an eyebrow Nakhti's way as he cast him a sidelong glance, a half smile playing about his lips.

"So I did," Nakhti admitted with a nod, crossing his arms over his bare chest. "Yes, well, I did not mean for you to be merciless!"

"It is just a game of luck," Mentuhotep waved his hand dismissively. He turned his gaze back to the river, feeling the ship sluice through the water as they moved steadily south. Two men stood on the steering platform of the helm at the stern behind them, where they manned the tillers guiding the ship, keeping it on course.

"If that were indeed true, Father, I would be doomed," Nakhti said. "It is more than luck. Much more."

"You are doomed anyway!" Khu laughed, but then caught himself so as not to strain his ribs. "You take too long to move your pieces off the board."

"That is because you trap them!"

"You should not overthink things," Khu cautioned. "You make your intentions obvious that way."

"Only to you, brother, only to you. You see things which others do not," Nakhti said in a tone of admiration that was devoid of any envy.

"All the squares on the board look the same," Mentuhotep interrupted, in one of his philosophical moods, stroking the smooth line of his jaw. "The trick is knowing which are safe, and which are dangerous. Things are not always what they seem. You never know what danger lurks around the corner."

The side curtains on the canopy were tied back, and Mentuhotep was watching the wildlife near the riverbank. A float of crocodiles sunned themselves near the marches where a great egret waded through the shallower waters of the riverbank, searching for food. The bird's white plumage shone brilliant in the sun, as it moved around a green-mossed boulder jutting out of the water. It paused to eye the crocodiles calmly before jabbing its yellow bill into the water to catch a fish.

But there was an odd stillness to the air.

The northerly winds that usually filled the sails, pushing the vessels south on the great river, did not blow today, so that the ship's sail remained furled and stowed away, while oarsmen propelled the ship onward in shifts. And although the morning had dawned cool and moist with fog, it was warm and dry now.

"Look!" someone shouted, pointing to a dark, ominous cloud clinging to the southeastern horizon.

Some of the oarsmen stopped rowing to take a better look. Mentuhotep, Nakhti and Khu stood up, as Qeb joined them from the ship's stern, to watch the growing

cloud obscure the rocky hills of the desert. It was engulfing the blue sky, as it spread in an upward and outward
motion.

"Sandstorm approaching!" Khu said in alarm, turning to look at his father. "Father, it's a sandstorm!"

"By Seth and all his minions," Mentuhotep cursed
under his breath, touching the amulet hanging around his
neck. "Of all times and places," he blew out his breath in
a long sigh.

"We should have waited longer in Abdju, Father,"
Nakhti said, a hint of fear in his voice.

"Or left sooner," Khu added.

But no one replied.

Khu had not been fit to travel anywhere, and
his bones were only beginning to mend. There was no
way they could have foreseen this. It was completely
unpredictable.

Nakhti cast a sidelong glance at his brother, but remained tightlipped. Khu looked at him and saw his own
anxiety reflected in Nakhti's dark eyes.

"It always appears without warning," Qeb said. His
face betrayed nothing, but Khu could tell that he too was
upset. Although his eyes appeared aloof, Khu felt the tension within him.

"How far are we from Gebtu?" the king asked. But
even as the question was uttered, he already knew the
answer.

Qeb shook his head. "Too far. The storm will be here
long before then. We will not make it in time. It is too late
for that."

Other men touched their amulets, as the magnitude
of the danger they faced grew more apparent. Some were
shouting between the ships, to warn the others in the
fleet of the approaching storm. But everyone had seen it
by now.

The great, billowing cloud crept steadily their
way. More men stopped whatever they had been doing,
to shield their eyes from the sun's glare on the river, and

stare at the approaching storm. It scoured the land over which it blew, like a tsunami of sand, gathering more sand and dust into its fierce embrace.

Mentuhotep glanced around at the empty land beyond the riverbank. No settlements waited nearby. The land here was barren, dry and deserted, except for the wild trees, plants and shrubbery growing just beyond the marshes. There was no place to dock their ships or pull them ashore, and if they remained on the river, their lives would be at risk, and the fleet would be heavily damaged or even destroyed.

The king knew that the storm would delay their journey. He knew that this thwarted all his plans regarding Gebtu and Thebes, but that did not matter now. All that mattered was their safety. They had to find a place to shelter themselves and their ships.

"There is an inlet beyond the next turn, isn't there?" Mentuhotep pointed. "Just past the bend, on the west bank of the river. An inlet that leads to a cove."

"Can we make it in time, Father?" Nakhti asked.

"We must try. We have no choice. We cannot stay here in the open. It's too exposed, too dangerous," the king replied.

"Yes, we should be better off there," Qeb agreed. He left the king's side to go speak with the ship's head coxswain.

"It is Seth, you know," Nakhti spoke softly to Khu, keeping his gaze focused on the southern sky. "Some say it is his way of punishing the people." His voice was low, as if he instinctively wanted to keep the god of darkness, chaos and storms from hearing his blasphemous words.

"Then he does it often," Khu said, knowing sandstorms were a common phenomenon to the region. "What better way to smite us than through the power of the elements?"

"They are inescapable," Nakhti agreed.

Khu raised a hand to the onyx, winged scarab beetle hanging around his neck, and his thoughts turned to his mother Tem. "I hope they are alright," he mumbled.

"Who?"

"Our mothers, in Thebes. The storm must have hit them already."

"They will be fine," Nakhti assured him. "At least they have shelter. We are the ones in trouble."

"Ready to row!" the coxswain shouted, after he and Qeb quickly discussed their plans.

The oarsmen had already positioned themselves to propel the ship ahead. The fleet behind them was doing the same, as instructions were shouted and directions were given over the water between the ships.

"Power on!" the coxswain yelled, encouraging the men to muster all their strength.

They squared their blades and began rowing on command, pulling on the oars with all their might. They were maneuvering the flat-bottomed ship toward the western bank, keeping a safe distance from the boulders rising prominently by the river's marshes, and the rocks hiding just below the water's surface, whose light gray color glinted in the sun. The rest of the ships in the fleet followed behind, their oars biting through the river, as they attempted to find safety.

The dust cloud crept closer, hugging the ground menacingly, as it approached from the southeastern desert region. It looked like a wall moving in slow motion. It was jaundiced, the color of a pale yellowish brown.

"Pull! Harder, pull!" the coxswain urged.

Then the wind began to blow.

It moaned softly at first as a beguiling breeze, gently ruffling the branches of trees. It was pleasant enough, but very warm. Everyone knew it was a deceiving breeze, for they had experienced these storms in previous years, and knew that it would get stronger and more forceful as the dark cloud neared, growing to threatening proportions and engulfing everything in its path.

"I think Seth wishes to remind us of his power," Nakhti told Khu above the wind, turning the conversation back to the feared god who was associated with the desert and storms.

The boys stood on deck, watching the events with wide eyes, adrenaline spiking their blood.

"Perhaps it is his way of exacting revenge on a people who shun him," Khu said, almost pitying the hated god in his lonesome existence.

Nakhti shot a glance at his brother. "He should be shunned. He is enemy to all the gods. Look," Nakhti swept a hand indicating the storm, "he is responsible for this. All he does is wreak havoc and destruction wherever he goes."

Seth's penchant for chaos and destruction earned him the title of Red God—like the red, harsh, unforgiving desert that was his domain. His peculiar animal-headed human form was intimidating, with a downward-curving snout, long donkey-like ears, large elongated eyes, and a forked tail. Jealousy and envy possessed and drove him to an all-consuming rage that seemed to stop at nothing. But Khu still regarded the god with a trace of pity, for hate engenders loneliness and despair.

"Faster! Pull! Pull!" the coxswain yelled.

"May Amun and Mut help us!" someone shouted, at which most of the men, excluding the rowers, touched nervous hands to their amulets once again.

"Father..." Khu placed a hand on the king's taut shoulder. "It's getting closer..." Khu wished he could do something to help. He felt useless with his torso bandaged up. But even if he had not been injured, there was nothing he could have done anyway.

The king did not move. He stared at the approaching sandstorm with his eyes narrowed against the rising winds, willing it to slow down.

They were directly in the storm's path. There was no avoiding it. No getting away from the sand cloud that would tumble over them like a giant wave.

"We will make it," the king replied through clenched teeth, the lines between his brows deepening. "With Amun's help we will make it."

"Pull ahead!" the coxswain shouted. "We are nearing the bend!"

Mentuhotep barely breathed as he stood at the ship's prow. A small muscle in his neck twitched as his body tensed from anxiety. He kept glancing between the dust cloud and the river ahead of them. He looked at the oarsmen rowing with all their might. Sweat poured down their faces, chests and backs, but they kept rowing. They knew their lives depended on it. They knew their sovereign relied on their unfailing efforts. And they knew that if something were to happen—something disastrous—that the very fate of Upper Egypt would be at stake.

It was a race against time.

"Nearing the bend!" shouted the coxswain. "Easy on the turn!"

The starboard rowers checked their blades momentarily as the ship curved around the western bend.

Little more than a few thorny trees, scraggly doum palms, and thin grasses grew beyond the shoreline by the river.

"Pick it up again! Pull!" the coxswain encouraged as the ship followed the river's curve near the western bank.

"Over there," the king pointed ahead. "The inlet should be there, just beyond that outcrop." He had joined Qeb and the coxswain on the steering platform, where the tillers were manned.

"Yes, we are almost there," Qeb nodded.

The rowers pulled hard on the oars. Their muscles burned and their eyes stung as sweat ran down their faces and into their eyes. But they did not falter, not for a moment. Adrenaline flooded their veins, and kept them going strong.

"Almost there!" the coxswain shouted. "Pull! Pull!"

The moving wall crept closer and closer, and the sky turned a pinkish-red. Some of the men were shouting to make themselves heard above the wind that was blowing stronger now. The coxswain kept guiding the rowers, and the men steeled themselves against the approaching tempest.

There was no place to hide.

"Harder! Pull!"

They had to get off the river. They had to dock their ships to keep them from being destroyed by the whirling gales which would sandblast everything in sight. And they had to shelter themselves from the onslaught which would skin them alive, cutting their hands and faces, blinding their eyes, and clogging their noses and mouths.

The temperature was rising still, as though the god Seth himself were blowing his hot breath over Egypt. Soon it would be intolerable.

The wind rumbled louder as a reddish haze thickened the air.

They were nearing the mouth of the inlet.

"Nearing the turn! Slow it down! Easy on the turn!"

The starboard rowers checked their blades, as the port rowers managed a tight turn around a sandbank edging the mouth of the inlet's narrow opening.

Mentuhotep closed his eyes momentarily in relief, after his ship made the dangerous turn without harm. He had been praying silently to Amun to guide them to safety. He turned around to check on the rest of his fleet, and saw them following behind as his ship led the way.

"Take it all the way in!" Mentuhotep commanded the rowers himself from the steering platform, at the rear of the ship. "All the way in to the cove!"

One by one, the ships entered the inlet. The men pulled at the oars, taking the ships all the way to the large cove waiting inside.

"Make room for the rest," the king directed. "Align the ships tightly, or there won't be enough room!"

The men wasted no time in securing the ships together, to keep them from thrashing about in the storm. The smaller ones were dragged ashore, and bound together with reed ropes so that they would not be blown away. The sails were unfurled and draped over the decks, before being tied down like tarps, so that they would have something to shield them from the blasting assault as they huddled underneath. But it was blowing strongly already, making it difficult to tie them securely.

Anything worth saving was stowed away. Men grabbed their cloaks, pulling them over their heads and wrapping them about their faces in protection.

The temperature kept climbing as the darkness approached. Dust entered their noses, coating their throats, and stinging their sinuses with its dryness. Khu's eyes were watering and his tongue felt parched, but he did not care. He wanted his father's fleet to survive this tempest. He watched the men scrambling to get under the sails.

"Go inside the cabin!" the king told Khu and Nakhti. "You will be better protected there, go! And cover yourselves well!"

The boys left to do as their father told them. And while the cabin was small, there was plenty of room for them and several more men. The king and Qeb would join them after they saw to the safety of their men.

Mentuhotep and Qeb stood by the head coxswain, guiding the men to safety. Those who did not fit under the sail huddled together, hiding within the thin layers of their own cloaks.

The reddish haze thickened into a dark brown, as the monstrous cloud engulfed the sky. The wind thundered as though the gates of the Netherworld had been thrown open, releasing all manner of ills to ravage the land.

In an instant, day turned to night as the land was plunged into darkness, and the cloud blocked the sun.

Palm trees beyond the cove and riverbank were caught up in the storm, bending low with the force of the wind that ravaged the land like a hurricane. Their branches blew about wildly, many of which were torn right off their trunks, and scattered about by the driving wind.

The men braced themselves for what would be several hours of suffocating wind. They hunkered down, bowing their heads against the wind, shutting their eyes tightly and clasping the fabric of headdresses about themselves. They grabbed onto their amulets, praying to the gods for mercy and protection.

There was nothing they could do; nothing anyone in the sandstorm's path could do but ride it out, bearing the brunt of the storm with patience and courage. They were caught in a battle of the elements—a battle they attributed to the gods—and they prayed silently as they waited, closing their eyes and listening with forbearance to the howling gale as it thrashed about like an unruly child throwing a tantrum, leaving a trail of wreckage behind.

When people in the various settlements and villages lying in the storm's path first noticed it approaching, they immediately abandoned their work to hurry home. Young children were pulled inside their mud-brick homes, and the doors shut behind them before cloth was wedged tightly through the gaps. The children's faces looked bewildered, unaware of the danger heading their way.

The wall of dust came without warning. Villages looked as though they had been deserted after people rushed through the narrow streets to find shelter from the assault. Even the wild animals disappeared to burrow in dens, hide in holes or shallow caves, creep inside abandoned ruins, or take cover among the monuments and temples providing shelter from the tempest.

Some people sheltered their pets and animals before the oppressive winds arrived to blind and suffocate them. Shepherds led their herds of sheep or goats back to stables in the villages, tapping some of the beasts on the rump with a stick to get them to move faster. Oxen and donkeys were safely corralled in stalls along with domesticated fowl and pigs.

People closed doors, covered amphorae and jars with coarsely spun linen cloth and tarps, and pulled reed mats over the windows to keep out the sand that would still find a way inside, even within the smallest crevices.

Those nomadic traders who were treading the long desert route from Gebtu to the Sea of Reeds, scrambled off the ancient riverbed to hide in caves and quarries, pulling cloaks over their heads, or wrapping long headdresses about their faces so that they would not inhale the stifling dust.

After the storm had subsided, villages everywhere were strewn with all sorts of debris once the winds had finally died down. Broken pottery was scattered like pebbles; linen clothing that had been hung out to dry in the morning, and then forgotten in the mayhem, had flown about in the wind like leaves. Some of the reed mats covering the windows were torn away by the wind, and had soared through the air like kites during the storm. Branches ripped off trees, littering the streets, rooftops and fields.

The sandstorm posed a greater risk than the obvious damages to property; much greater than the scattered debris and painful scraping and stinging of skin and faces.

The dust cloud was an unhealthy and dangerous blend of sand and soil, containing mold and fungal spores, some of which were lethal. Pollen, germs and all sorts of bacteria that was hazardous to inhale, were also thrown into the toxic mix. Many people got very sick after the storm, some of whom eventually died in the ensuing infection from the illness following the inhalation of the deadly airborne concoction.

Hours passed before the winds stopped raging. Hours of blinding, suffocating dust, sand and wind that swept across the land, painting everything in dark fuzzy shades. The silt-like matter penetrated every crevice, coating every surface including floors, walls, furniture, linens, jars, amphorae, dishes, food and drink. It adhered to people's skin, sticking to their pores, stinging their eyes, nasal and sinus cavities, and was even encrusted under their fingernails. There was no getting rid of it.

The wind eventually slowed down to a rumble, and then to a sighing breeze before it ceased to blow.

As soon as things quieted down Mentuhotep prepared to assess the damages. The sails were unfastened and removed from the decks of the ships before being furled and stowed away. Men emerged with their heads and faces covered in linen which had turned a filthy brown. They kept their faces—noses and mouths especially—well shielded from the thick dust coating the air.

Khu and Nakhti withdrew from the cabin where they had remained during the storm. The boys stepped out into the late afternoon, their faces covered with cloth as they surveyed the strange ominous world around them. The wind had completely died down, and a leprous light bled through the dust hanging in the air like fog.

An eerie hush blanketed the land and river, stifling the usual bustling sounds of nature. No birds were seen in the sky or stalking through the marshes. Even the insects buzzing and swarming in the heat of the day remained unseen.

The world was painted in sepia tones from soft browns and yellows, to a grayish orange. But what struck them most was the sun. It hung low in the sky like a huge reddish sphere from which light seeped like blood. It was striking eerie and very beautiful.

"Re..." Nakhti uttered with his eyes on the sun. The boys felt a sense of reverence and awe as they stared at the heavy sun in the sky, their thoughts following the sun-god

Re who appeared to have put an end to Seth's raging sandstorm, if only for the time being.

There was something haunting about the landscape beyond the cove, whose desert hills were obscured by the orange dust. Trees drooped with limp branches hanging dejectedly like defeated soldiers after battle. The stillness was palpable ominous and heavy, and seemed to cast everything under a spell where time had simply ceased.

It was a world suspended in a haze.

Men appeared on the deck with their faces wrapped against the dust that was everywhere, as they went to assess the damages on their ships. It was no use cleaning anything, for all it would do is stir up more of the dust which coated the air like mist.

"It is always this way after the winds cease," Nakhti said, recalling sandstorms of previous years. The headdress covering his face filtered out the dust. But he coughed a little despite the protection it afforded.

The boys took in everything around them. It had all been completely transformed in the course of a few hours. Despite the dirt and debris, it was strangely beautiful.

Khu's thoughts turned to his mother Tem again, but he knew she was alright. He would have felt her distress if something had happened, even from this distance.

Most of the ships in Mentuhotep's fleet had survived the storm, but a couple had not. The winds had torn apart two of the older vessels, and the debris had been scattered or swept away by the winds. No one was hurt fortunately, at least not beyond the expected scrapes, dryness, and inevitable coughing resulting from the contamination they breathed. The men who were on the older ships had disembarked at the first sign of trouble. They grabbed a few supplies and climbed aboard other ships in the cove where there was room.

Mentuhotep's army was forced to spend that first night in the cove before leaving in the morning for Gebtu.

Visibility had been drastically reduced, with the dense haze making it impossible to see much beyond ten paces.

Once they had arrived in Gebtu, efforts to repair any damages to the fleet were undertaken immediately. The ships were pulled onto the low bank of the port, and the ropes lashing the thick planks together were retied or replaced. Seams between the planks were recaulked with reeds where necessary. The men had also refreshed themselves and their provisions, readying to depart again as soon as safely possible.

"And it is just beginning," Mentuhotep later said once they were settled in the lavish home of an official in Gebtu, who was a relative of the king. "Yes, the sandstorm is only beginning," the king repeated with a note of irritation, of the oppressive winds that would blow for several hours every few days, over the course of about fifty days.

The storm would later—in subsequent millennia—be known in Egypt as the *khamaseen*. But Mentuhotep had no intention of waiting fifty days in Gebtu for it to run its course. He wanted to return home soon.

"If we do not depart between the gales, we will be stuck here for a long while," Mentuhotep continued. "Gebtu is not that far from home. We should be able to arrive safely before the winds start blowing again," he touched a hand to the amulet around his neck to avert the evil eye. "If the gods will it," he added hastily.

"Will it be safe to travel the river?" Nakhti asked, after finishing an infusion he had been given to help sooth his dry throat.

"Safe enough," Qeb answered on the king's behalf. "We got here safely from the cove, did we not?" The Kushite warrior was standing off to one side of the room with his arms crossed over his chest. He was not pleased with the delay either, and felt tense and agitated. "Thebes is not that much farther. We should be able to leave soon since it does not blow every day," he reminded them.

"But sometimes it does," Nakhti insisted.

"No, rarely," Qeb shook his head. "And usually not more than once every five or six days. We will have plenty of time."

"We should be alright if we plan accordingly," the king added with a determined nod.

A few days later after all needed repairs had been completed in Gebtu, the winds rose up as before. Although it blew for several hours again, there were no damages and they were finally able to depart the day after that.

The fleet headed for Thebes through the dust-misted air, traveling south along the Nile whose murky waters swirled and sloshed around the hulls. Like the rest of the landscape, the river had turned a dingy brown. The ships remained by the eastern riverbank as they sailed up the great river against the Nile's northern-flowing current. The sails were raised, catching the northerly breeze which kept them moving steadily south.

All along the shoreline were signs of life again. Herons waded through the muddy shallows to feed on small fish swimming in schools by the reeds. Snipes pecked their long slender bills in the soft mud where they searched for insects and worms. A kingfisher was perched on the slender branch of a young sycamore tree growing next to a small grove of palms. The bird surveyed the river before diving into the water to snatch a fish with its long beak.

The river curved sharply east and looped around a bend where the land jutted out into the Nile like a peninsula. A small herd of hippopotamuses was submerged in the water near the bank, with all but their eyes and ears showing above the surface. One of the bulls was climbing out of the water to graze on the lush grasses covering part of the plain, and some of the men touched their amulets instinctively when they saw the large male that was believed to be one of the many forms of the evil god Seth.

By the time they arrived in Thebes it was dusk. The sun-god Re had already made his voyage across the hazy sky in his *Mandjet* solar boat before descending into the realm of the Otherworld. They had watched the red sun setting a little while before from their ship on the Nile, where it loomed larger than life against an orange sky. Its crimson light gilded the western desert in shades of coral and amber, and its heat cast a mirage of shallow pools rippling across the distant dunes.

Tem was there to greet them when their ship finally reached the main river port of the major settlement. She was accompanied by an entourage of officials and some of the other noble women and children in the family. It was a joyful reunion though tinged with anxiety for the events that had happened, and the uncertain times lying ahead.

The news of Khu's injuries had reached Tem several days before the sandstorm, and she had gotten little sleep since then from worrying about her son. Khu saw the lines etched between her brows as she stood on the bank of the river among the shadows darkening the land. She looked fragile and small as she darted a searching glance across the deck before her eyes landed on Khu with relief, and his heart went out to her.

At the first opportunity he told Tem what had happened in Abdju, and how it was Ankhtifi who had led the massacre on his village years before. Tem listened quietly, pondering Khu's story with a sense of dread. She had always suspected that *that* was what had happened to Khu when he was found hiding in the reeds with his clothing bloodied. She assumed that his was one of the many unfortunate villages to have been raided along the Nile. She thought that he had escaped death and found his way to Thebes by the grace of the Seven Hathors who had decreed other plans for his fate. Yes she had believed this, but hearing his story was overwhelming nevertheless, and she shuddered involuntarily at the cold-blooded malice that claimed some people's souls.

Tem knew that Khu might have to face Ankhtifi once again, and she feared for her son's life. She embraced Khu after he finished recounting the details of his ordeal, and she wept with him for the terrible loss he had suffered, and the deaths of his parents and little sister.

Later Tem made special offerings at the Temple of Mut and at the shrine of Isis, in gratitude for the protection bestowed on Khu throughout his life, and also in supplication for the strength and help they would need in the times ahead.

The hot dry winds continued to rise up at regular intervals every five or six days, over the course of about fifty days, usually lasting a few hours at a time. But they were all well prepared for it, and remained safely ensconced within the palace compound each time it blew.

The winds presaged a coming change in the divided lands: a change that would rise up from the south to blow all the way to the northern settlements lying beyond Mentuhotep's reach, where it would expose the wicked to burn like chaff under a blazing sun. It was a good omen, filling people with cautious optimism despite the growing uneasiness brewing like the thick heqet fermenting in large vats. And as an orange sun claimed the stillness of the late afternoon sky on the storm's final day, people touched their amulets in a silent plea for courage, guidance and protection in the times to come.

FOURTEEN

It was on the thirteenth day of the Festival of the Inundation, on Khu's fifteenth year, that Odji's death was discovered.

The annual holiday marked the Opening of the Year—*Wp Rnpt*—with the Season of Inundation—*Akhet*—which was celebrated with festivities usually lasting about fifteen days. The star *Sopdet* had appeared to brighten the night sky shortly before the flooding commenced, as it did every year to herald the inundation at the New Year. As the astral goddess of Egypt, Sopdet's appearance was greeted with joy for the renewal of the land that was announced by her celestial rising. She was known as "Bringer of the New Year and Nile Flood."

The very first rains of the season arrived timid and trembling as they fell in scattered drops which ran red over the land from the dust still coating the air, and clinging to the settlements for almost two courses of the moon after the sandstorm had passed. It was a gentle rain which quickly gained confidence, shedding its demure pretense to bare its assertive power before proceeding to boldly beat the ground.

The people welcomed the rains gratefully, making reverent offerings to the gods in temples and shrines, especially Hapi, Amun and Isis. It was believed that the annual rains were caused by the weeping of the lovely goddess Isis whose sorrowful tears fell over the land as she grieved for her deceased husband Osiris. And as the river's many tributaries were engorged by the water which fell most heavily in the south of Egypt and Kush, the Nile swelled as it pushed its way north on its ancient course, rising above the muddy banks and rocks which jutted out of the river, until it flooded the plains, depositing a rich layer of black silt that would fertilize and renew the land once again.

The flooding of the world's longest river was attributed to the god Hapi who was considered to be the god of the Nile's inundation, and who oversaw the river's annual flooding. Hapi was a large-breasted male god depicted with long hair, a false beard, a loincloth and a fat belly, all of which symbolized his fertility. He gathered and transformed the sorrowful tears of Isis into a fertile blessing that poured out its life-giving bounty over the land. Although no temples were built in his honor, statues and reliefs of Hapi were found within the temples of other gods throughout the land, where he was portrayed as bearing offerings of foodstuffs in the forms of crops like wheat, barley, vegetables and flax.

The flooding of the Nile was a time of great rejoicing and jubilee. Everywhere people joined in the festivities now that all work in the fields had been suspended due to the rising waters and subsequent flooding of the river. Animals were herded onto higher ground by the peasants, where they would remain until after the waters had deposited a rich layer of silt onto the fields. People participated in sporting competitions including rowing, archery, fishing, hunting for waterfowl, wrestling and swimming. Others demonstrated their gymnastic agility, played musical instruments, or danced in groups.

A large procession of priests with animal skins draped across their chests exited the Temple of Amun and walked down the Avenue of Sphinxes bearing two sets of portable shrines resting upon their shoulders. The first shrine contained Amun's golden statue which was paraded on most of the major festivals on a gilded barque. The patron god of Thebes wore the *Shuti* two-feathered crown on his head, symbolizing divine law. He carried the *ankh* key of life in one hand, a scepter in the other, and stood with his right foot slightly before the left in a posture of readiness to command and aid his subjects.

The second shrine bore a smaller statue of Hapi carrying an offering tray of vegetables and fish on his lap. The god of the Nile's inundation was depicted in kneeling position in deference to Amun. This particular statue was kept in a niche lining the wall of the hypostyle hall within the Temple of Amun. It was one of several statues of deities which were subservient to Amun, yet held important roles in the overall balance and order of life.

The procession of priests fell in step behind a tambourine player who led the way through a path flanked by musicians sounding trumpets, beating drums, and playing the sweet notes of flutes, whose inspiring melody lent an emotive note to the reverent proceedings. A few priests carried incense in burners, while others fanned the fragrant smoke over the shrines in homage to their divine occupants.

Because it was a time of merrymaking and indulgence, when the people lost themselves in the elation of the occasion, a group of soldiers followed the procession, while others lined the streets carrying their shields and spears. The soldiers looked like statues themselves as they stood tall with their ox-hide shields held proudly at their sides. Although their presence was largely ceremonial and ritualistic, Mentuhotep had instructed them beforehand to be vigilant after what had happened in Abdju.

People danced, sang and waved palm branches joyfully as they saluted Amun—who was king of gods and creation—with joyful hymns of gratitude. The god was carried through the streets before being reverently set upon a royal barge that would travel slowly up the Nile to northern Thebes and back, so people everywhere in the district could worship and glorify the patron of Thebes. Many prostrated themselves as the priests carried Amun's statue along the processional route, while others burst into acclamations of adoration and delight.

Peddlers lined the roads of the procession route selling fruit, vegetables and salted meats, while others sold flower wreaths and incense cones. Hundreds of measures of heqet were consumed, as was the red wine that was stored in amphorae. Thousands of bread loaves had been baked for the occasion, as well as sweet cakes and

confections made from dates and honey, which were reserved for such festivals.

Mentuhotep and Tem accompanied the procession in the royal barge in honor of the festival, and to
offer salutations to the people of the surrounding settlements. The king and queen were dressed in all their regalia and looked stunning from where they were seated on
the barge. King Mentuhotep wore Upper Egypt's *Hedjet*
White Crown, while carrying the crook in his right hand,
and the flail in his left. Tem was seated beside him, shaking sistra ceremonial rattles which she clutched in each
of her hands, while tapping her foot to the beat of a drum.
She wore the royal vulture headdress of Amun's wife Mut,
under which her ceremonial wig was braided with strands
of golden thread, and woven with beads carved from
precious gems. Her *kohl*-elongated eyes were shadowed
with green powdered malachite. Around her neck hung
the beautiful yellow topaz and malachite collar necklace
which Khu had given her in honor of his fifteenth Season
of Inundation. It was made from the stones he had chosen himself when they had stopped in Nekhen on their
way to Swentet, just before the revolt in Abdju. The necklace shone beautifully under the clear, blue sky which had
been washed clean by the rains, and Tem smiled when she
caught Khu's eye before climbing into the barque. He was
pleased to have made his mother happy, and he admired
the necklace which only enhanced her lovely face.

Khu had presented the necklace to Tem at the very
beginning of the festival, honoring his mother with gratitude in a private ceremony at the palace which had been
attended by the royal family, other nobility and officials.
Tem had given Khu a golden arm band in return. It was
encrusted with gems among which a single black onyx
gleamed. Tem had included the black stone after Khu returned from Abdju and told her the story about how he
had escaped death as a child, when his village was raided.
The dark gem was a symbol of the loss he had suffered
as a small boy, and the grief that had forged him into the

man he had become. She had listened to every detail of that cursed night with tears in her eyes as he recounted the dark memories which had been deeply buried and forgotten until he came face-to-face with the detestable man who had taken all but his life from him.

Tem saw a change in her son after he had returned from Abdju. It was a subtle change that only a mother who is well attuned to the imperceptible nuances of her own child would notice. Gone was the boy who had first come to her, shriveled and frail years back when he was found hiding in the reeds by the river. Any last traces of boyhood had completely vanished from his handsome face. The son who knelt before her, to present her with the collar necklace, was a man now; a man who possessed patience under suffering, and power under control. And since his fateful meeting with Ankhtifi in Abdju, he had become a man with a purpose, waiting for the day he knew would come when he would avenge the deaths of his slain family, and send Ankhtifi's soul to the Slaughtering Place for all eternity.

The royal barge floated along the river, passing a large parade of revelers dancing in the open fields, where they had smeared mud over their skin in honor of Hapi's muddy life-giving waters. From head to toe, they covered themselves with the rich black silt saturating the land. It was this silt which fertilized the land with rich minerals that would help the new crops to grow.

All the priests in the surrounding Theban settlements had spent the first half of the festival in long elaborate ceremonies offering choice sacrifices of slaughtered oxen, goats, and river fowl in honor of the Arrival of Hapi, and in supplication that the god would bring a good flood—neither too low nor too high.

The mood was hopeful, for the flooding was the foundation upon which all life in Egypt flourished. Those years where the Nile had not risen high enough, were followed by drought and famine. There had been much suffering without the water required to make the fields produce a healthy crop. Likewise, too much water caused great destruction as it swept over the mud-brick villages lying beyond the protective dykes and canals, washing away their homes and leaving behind a useless heap of mud and devastation. But this year the water level was perfect, inspiring the people with much confidence for the uncertain times ahead.

People everywhere danced and chanted hymns to Hapi in veneration and thanksgiving, as they rejoiced in the annual holiday that brought the gods and the people together during this time of hope and renewal.

Rejoice and exaltation!
For the life-giving waters have come
Reinvigorating the lands
Feeding the herds
Nourishing the multitudes
O Hapi, Lord of the Fishes, Lord of the Birds of the Marshes
We extol your virtues!
O Hapi, Sustainer of Life, Quencher of Fields,
We hail your generosity!
Rejoice and exaltation!

It was well after most of the chanting, sacrificial burnt offerings, and ceremonial pageantry of the festival had taken place, that the gruesome discovery of Odji's death was made. Amun had already been returned to the somber depths of the naos in the sanctuary of his great temple, while Hapi had been placed back in his niche within the hypostyle hall, after which the priests lit a huge pyre in an open courtyard beyond the Avenue of Sphinxes. A column of white smoke rose from the fire like a spiraling staircase winding its way to the heavens. As the blaze burned brightly, the priests lit more incense which they carried through the crowds to drive out evil spirits lurking among the people, while imbuing the festivities with its sweet and sultry fragrance. People ate, drank, and continued celebrating as they danced among the acrobats and musicians playing lively tunes on their instruments.

A man stood quietly among the cheering crowds as the celebrations went on. He wore a linen cloak over a simple tunic and sandals, and had draped the cloth over his head to hide his features. The man carried with him a brown sack which he clutched protectively. He said nothing as the beating of drums and blaring of trumpets rang out over the people who were elated from the festivities that had been going on for many days.

King Mentuhotep watched the grand procession and ceremonies from an open pavilion on an elevated section of ground so that his view of the proceedings was unobstructed. The royal family and noble entourage were seated behind him. It was during this time that Mentuhotep prepared to meet with the heads of the settlements in the district. This was the time of year when he granted special requests to them in honor of the festival and the Opening of the Year.

One by one, each of the heads of the settlements renewed their allegiance to the Theban king, while presenting him with small tokens of their loyalty in the form of gifts, including foodstuffs and crafts produced by artisans in their villages.

The last one to approach the king was the cloaked man carrying a brown sack. He looked a little out of place with his serious demeanor, and Khu's hackles were raised at once. Khu knew that this man was not from Thebes, and that whatever was in that mysterious sack did not bode well for his father.

"Lord King," the man said in a sardonic tone without bowing as the others had done. "I am sent from the north with a gift."

Mentuhotep narrowed his eyes at the man's insolence. Khu stepped closer to his father's side in a protective gesture, his body tense with anxiety. He exchanged a glance with the king, shaking his head slightly in a warning. Several of Mentuhotep's advisors were in attendance, and they stared at the sack, wondering about its contents.

"Who are you?" the king asked him, but the man did not reply. He loosened the drawstring of the sack, bent down to the ground, and emptied its contents.

The crowd gasped.

A head rolled out of the sack—the head of Odji the gatekeeper. Mentuhotep clenched his jaw, and a small muscle twitched on the side of his neck. He stared at the face of his former gatekeeper, whose vacant eyes were glazed over in death.

In that instant Khu understood what had happened. He had never trusted the gatekeeper after the attempted robbery incident years earlier. Although Khu had not been sure of Odji's involvement in the crime, his instincts had told him otherwise. But with other matters to keep the child occupied, and with Odji having kept carefully clear from the boy's presence in the years since then, Khu had forgotten about the gatekeeper and his suspicious behavior.

Khu took a deep breath and held it momentarily as he laid a hand on his father's tense shoulder. The gatekeeper had gotten what he deserved. Whatever fate he had met, had been carefully cultivated by his own wickedness, so that he reaped what he had sown. It was all according to the principles of *maat* that dictated the serving of justice according to one's deeds. Khu winced as he thought of the dead man's *ka* burning in the unquenchable fire of eternal death, and he turned his golden gaze away from the dead man's vacuous stare.

The king's guards immediately seized the messenger who made no attempt to escape. The man held his head high, his expression smug and fearless now that he had accomplished his task. His impudence spoke of the enemy who sent him, and of their hatred for the Theban king. But Mentuhotep knew that the guards were wasting their time with this man, for he was just an emissary.

The one behind all of this was Khety.

Odji's appearance in Zawty had not been well received. They believed him to be a spy for the Theban king. Officials had questioned him when he was brought before them at a fortified compound off the western bank of the Nile belonging to a distant relative of King Khety.

"You still have not answered the question," one official said. He was growing impatient with the Theban gatekeeper. None of Odji's responses made sense. There just did not seem to be enough motive for him to defect from Mentuhotep's service. Every one of his responses had been without resolve.

It was not as though Odji had been mistreated, or disrespected, or suffered a grave injustice at the hands of the Theban king. None of his answers seemed to have warranted defection, especially since the economic and socio-political situation under Mentuhotep had been more stable and prosperous than in the north. No, his responses did not make sense, and the official stared suspiciously at the gatekeeper with narrowed eyes. He had to be a spy.

Several people had come forward to testify that Odji was indeed in the Theban king's service, and that he had worked for Mentuhotep for many years. But when asked about Odji's position, they said that he made a comfortable living, and the position he held was respectable. No one really liked Odji, but that could be because he exuded a haughty superiority which made him intolerable to others. Whether it was his position that made him seem this way, or whether it was the man himself who was deeply flawed, they could not say. But they had never heard nor witnessed anything that would have incurred the wrath of Mentuhotep against Odji, or turned Odji against the king.

"F-Forgive me sir," Odji stuttered when he answered the official, "I was working with Mdjai—one of the officials near Abdju." Odji named the man with whom he had been trading clandestine messages before the revolt. "He had promised me a small township in return for information leading to the overthrow of King Mentuhotep."

"Really?" the man said, feigning interest, "a small township of your own? How nice for you." He crossed his arms over his chest, tilting his head as he eyed the gatekeeper in mock-admiration. "Mdjai is dead. Or did you not know that?"

Odji said nothing, turning his gaze to the ground, his stooped shoulders sinking lower as he cowered from fear.

"Are you a liar?" the official asked Odji with no real expectation of an answer. "Tsk tsk tsk..." he clicked his tongue, shaking his head in disapproval. "A deceitful tongue poisons itself as it strikes another."

But Odji still said nothing. He felt panicked and befuddled, not knowing where to even begin to defend himself against these allegations. He was tired from the long and arduous journey he had undertaken with the boatman. He was tired to the point of exhaustion—mentally, physically and emotionally.

Odji and the boatman had been heading north on the Nile when the sandstorm struck, forcing them to find shelter in Nubt. Nubt was a necropolis on the western bank of the Nile, with a few scattered monuments, one of which was dedicated to the feared god Seth. The irony of this was not lost on the men. It was as if Seth himself were leading them to perdition, if for no other reason than perdition itself.

The men had arrived after the winds were already blowing forcefully, and their boat had broken free from its hastily tied post. The sand cloud sweeping over the sky had obliterated the sun, plunging the land into sudden darkness. Day had quickly turned into night, while dust devils whipped across the dry land.

The men had moved as quickly as they could, wrapping their cloaks about their faces to protect themselves from the thick dust and sand. And arriving to an old temple-tomb of Seth, which dated back to the third dynasty, they scuttled inside like rats seeking shelter from the storm outside. It was dark and dusty inside the old temple, and Odji and the boatman crawled inside on hands and knees to feel their way through the darkness. They made it as far as the hypostyle hall, before curling up on the floor next to the towering columns, where they tried to sleep as the howling winds scourged the land.

Once the winds had abated, they crept back out of the temple and searched for the boat along the river's bank, whose visibility had been drastically reduced. An eerie stillness choked the air like a leaden blanket. But the boat was gone. All they found was a torn strip of the rope they had used to secure it to a thick post. Even if they were to find the boat, it was probably destroyed.

"You are bad luck," the boatman grumbled as they made their way north on foot with nothing but a few meager provisions and the cloaks they wore. They stopped often to rest, subsisting on the wild fruit they found from trees scattered along the dusty plain. Both men had inhaled much of the dust which made them sick from the spores it carried, and they were forced to pass many days in one of the caves they found at the edge of the necropolis. It was the remnants of an old tomb dating back to the Predynastic period.

The sandstorm's winds rose and fell two more times before they were able to continue north on foot. From there they had stolen a small reed boat from a village which appeared deserted. They drifted north on the boat for a few days until the treacherous winds forced them to find shelter once again. It had been a grueling journey.

"Bad luck," repeated the boatman as he cast sidelong glances at the bedraggled Odji.

"Shut up," Odji said flatly. But he reached up to touch the amulet hanging from his neck when the boatman was not looking, in hopes to break the evil spell that had ruined his plans.

More than once Odji regretted leaving Thebes. Nothing but trouble had followed him since his departure, and he was starting to believe the boatman's accusations.

It was too late to turn back now. Too late to go back and face the Theban ruler who would surely know how he had betrayed him by abandoning his post to flee to the king's archenemy; too late to reclaim his old life of tranquility.

But he did not miss it.

Even in the thick of the storm, with its blinding and suffocating walls of dust, which sent the branches of the palm trees flailing like the arms of drowning men in the river, he still would not have returned to Thebes, if he had been given the choice. Only once when the winds were howling like Seth himself, and he was shivering on the floor of a cave with a fever despite the choking heat, did a terrible despair assail him. But it was short-lived, as he closed his eyes burning from the fever, to let his mind re-play one of his sadistic fantasies that would never come to pass.

By the time they arrived in Zawty, the sandstorm had blown through its course, and was now behind them. The boatman himself had disappeared shortly before Odji had been detained, on a pretext of having work to do. He wanted to put as much distance between himself and the ill-fated gatekeeper so that his bad luck would no longer infect him. Being on territory that was sympathetic to the Nen-nesian ruler, the boatman also feared for his own life and did not wish to be associated with anything, nor anyone, from Thebes. As far as he was concerned, their part-nership had ended once Odji left Thebes.

This was only the beginning of Odji's demise. What made matters worse for him was that the two thieves who had been caught during the failed robbery attempt in Thebes years back had since been residing in Zawty, and had immediately recognized Odji. When they saw the gatekeeper's cold and haughty gaze, they had gone to report him at once to the authorities in Zawty, claiming he was a spy for Mentuhotep. They had never forgotten the pain and humiliation of being caught and publically flogged at the pillar. And they wanted revenge.

There was nothing cold and haughty in Odji's eyes now.

Just fear.

Fear shone in his gaze as he stared, wide-eyed, at the small assembly of officials whose features were devoid of any warmth or compassion. Fear sent the tiny hairs on the back of his neck standing on end as he tried to keep his bound hands from trembling. Fear made his heart pound hard against his ribcage, and his breathing labored as he stuttered and stumbled over his words that sounded hollow and deceptive even to himself. It was ill luck to be caught now, shortly after Khety's disastrous uprising had disgraced and humiliated the Nen-nesian king and all his supporters.

After several days of interrogation by the officials in Zawty, the ruler of Lower Egypt had come forth to question the gatekeeper himself. Khety was in a foul temper which seemed to sully the very air around him. All his personal failings, all the bitter grief from his past, and all the deficiencies in his dynasty were under tremendous public scrutiny, and the strain of this pressure deepened the fissures that weakened his kingdom.

"Speak up when you are spoken to!" Khety shouted at Odji, rising from his seat to pace in front of the smaller disheveled man who was mumbling inaudible responses.

Odji had not shaved during his journey, and he was filthy. The stubble growing on his head and face was peppered with thinning white hair. He looked and smelled like a vagabond, and the king wrinkled his nose in disgust.

"So this is what Thebes dispatches to pursue us?" he questioned derisively, waving an imperious hand through the air at Odji. "This is your king's best weapon?" He clenched his jaw, stopping suddenly in his tracks to turn and face the gatekeeper. "A cockroach," he hissed, pointing at the cowering man. "You are nothing but a cockroach!"

"I am not a spy for King Mentuhotep," Odji defended himself in a feeble voice, keeping his gaze lowered in deference to the king.

"Shut up!" Khety spat. "You are not a spy?" he narrowed his eyes in irritation. "Then you must be a traitor. You are a miserable excuse for a man, and these two men have sworn by the gods that you are indeed a spy. You are Theban, and you work for Mentuhotep!" He said Mentuhotep's name with a scowl, as though the very word made him ill.

Khety stopped his pacing to close his eyes and take a deep breath in an attempt to regain his composure. He rubbed his jaw and the back of his neck in irritation. He thought of everything Odji had said in his own defense, including his claim to have been secretly communicating with Mdjai—a low-ranking official—who died in the insurrection at Abdju. He thought of the accusations leveled against the bedraggled man; accusations that he was a spy for the Theban king, which Odji continued to deny. But no matter how much Khety weighed the evidence, studying it from every angle, it did not bode well for the gatekeeper. Every which way he looked at the testimony, it pointed to Odji's guilt.

Khety turned his icy gaze back to the gatekeeper, exhaling before he spoke. "It would be better for you to be a spy, than a dog who betrayed his master," he spoke slowly, lowering his tone in emphasis, and pointing a finger at the smaller man. "There is nothing more despicable and loathsome than an unfaithful, traitorous dog. He is a dishonorable, vile creature, and cannot be trusted." Khety waited a moment for the words to sink in. "Did you hear me?" he asked, narrowing his eyes. "There is no honor in betrayal."

Odji kept his gaze lowered as his mind raced in a panic. He feared for his life. He feared the men who accused him, and he feared the ruler of Lower Egypt whose hardened heart bore no patience for that which was contemptible, even where his enemies were concerned. And as a thousand afflictions assailed Odji from within his tortured mind, Ankhtifi stepped silently forward to join the tribunal before him. Odji did not see Khety's enforcer at first. He was too wrapped up in the darkness of his own agony to notice him.

"You will go back to Thebes," Khety said, after a moment of deliberation. The king had turned to convene with the officials and Ankhtifi in private, speaking with them in hushed tones before facing the accused once again.

Odji did not know what to think. Had he heard correctly? Would he actually be set free? He dared to raise his eyes and glance at the King who stared back at him with loathing.

"L-Lord K-King?" Odji asked in a shaky voice.

Khety blinked hard before speaking again, his jaw set. "Yes, you will go back," he repeated. "You will go back to Thebes where you belong," he nodded slowly as his eyes filled with a cold malevolence which made Odji shudder. "It will be a gift," he said in a show of mock-benevolence as he looked down his nose at the defendant. "A gift from me to your ruler."

But Odji said nothing in his confusion. His eyes darted from Khety, to the officials surrounding him, and finally to Ankhtifi.

Ankhtifi took a step closer to Odji, regarding the smaller man with dark sunken eyes. The tic in his jaw made one side of his mouth twitch upwards involuntarily, as though he were trying to suppress a snarl. The limp from his leg wound did little to alter his menacing appearance, even making him seem less human than before. He still moved with a lethal grace, stooping and swaying in a sinuous arch as he neared the gatekeeper. Odji stared at the taller man with hope and puzzlement as he wondered if he was about to be set free. But then Ankhtifi's hand shifted to grip the hilt of a weapon hanging discretely under his kilt.

That was when Odji knew he was doomed.

Odji fell to his knees as the certainty of his impending death plunged him into desolation and despair. He was so choked up with fear and anguish, he could not even speak. He only uttered a low and pathetic cry before Ankhtifi withdrew his weapon to separate Odji's soul from his body, sending him to the Hall of Two Truths and eternal death and damnation where the gaping jaws of the demon Ammit waited with salivating relish to devour the blackened heart of Odji's spirit, which far outweighed the feather of *maat* on the scales of justice. His blackened heart—despite being shriveled with decay—weighed heavier than all the immense stone blocks used to build the Great Pyramid of Khufu on the west bank of the Nile in Lower Egypt.

FIFTEEN

About seven years passed since the revolt in Abdju and the events following it; seven long years of battles and skirmishes that thwarted Mentuhotep's dream of unification. The Kushites had gotten wind of King Khety's attack, and jumped on the opportunity to stake their own claim on Upper Egypt's throne. Like the hyenas scavenging the plains, they smelled blood. They saw an opening in Mentuhotep's tightly held reign, and they took advantage of the prospect for themselves.

The ensuing skirmishes kept the Theban king occupied in the following years, so that his plans to push his forces north and defeat Khety once and for all had been delayed. Just when he had squelched one of the Kushites' sly attacks, another battle would follow.

Khu and Nakhti had fully grown by that time. Khu stood almost a head taller than Mentuhotep, and his sinewy frame had filled out into a solid mass of lean muscle. Although Nakhti was shorter than Khu, he was thickset and strong. The boys had become the men that the Seven Hathors had decreed for them at birth, and they made their father proud. Each was assigned to a battalion where they led men into battle against the Kushites and other enemies which tried to undermine Mentuhotep's authority. The numerous battles they faced stole the last remnants of their boyish looks, earning them a few more scars in the process.

Mentuhotep's army grew into a formidable war machine during this time. Armories produced mass amounts of weapons to arm the warriors: from bows and arrows, spears and shields, to scimitars, axes and daggers used in close combat by the troops that were drafted from settlements and villages across the land. Those soldiers in reserve were called to duty, while officers of the army prepared their men—from the toughest disciplined troops, to the lowliest peasants and field hands—to mobilize for battle.

As battles were fought and won, the spoils of war were dedicated to Amun in gratitude for his assistance, and in supplication for his continued protection. Captive soldiers were conscripted into Mentuhotep's army, swelling the ranks of his forces, while their women, children and cattle were likewise confiscated as spoils of war, and assimilated into life within Upper Egypt.

King Khety had his hands full with problems of his own. Asiatic nomads had infiltrated Lower Egypt through the Nile Delta, where they had arrived battle-ready and menacing with plunder on their minds. His forces were stretched thin by these sporadic assaults which left the already weakened lands in further ruin. But what Khety lacked in manpower, he made up for in his ability to gain support and convince others of his cause. With persistence and unrelenting tenacity, he managed to replace many of the men he had lost in the battle at Abdju, strengthening his army once again.

It was Khety who had sent word to the Kushites, encouraging them to attack the Theban king shortly after the insurrection at Abdju. He promised them land in Upper Egypt if they helped him to overthrow Mentuhotep. And while the attacks had thwarted Mentuhotep's immediate plans, they did not really weaken him. His army still managed to grow stronger, his forces multiplied, and his resolve to reunify the divided kingdoms was as unwavering as ever.

It was after the last of the Kushite forces had been defeated, and a grudging peace treaty had been established, that Mentuhotep assembled his vast army and headed north on the Nile. His fleet of ships had more than doubled in the years since the revolt at Abdju. Sudi and a host of other spies had been keeping him abreast of Khety's whereabouts so that he always knew of the Nennesian ruler's activities.

Mentuhotep stared out over the water's surface that shone brilliant and blue under the sun. It was the Season of Growth—*Peret*—long after the annual flood waters had receded, and the crops had all been planted in the fields. Although this was the coldest of the year's three seasons, the weather was still clear and pleasant during the day, with temperatures dipping more sharply at night.

Mentuhotep was on the lead ship of his fleet, standing by the prow which rose in a graceful line before jutting out straight over the water, where the bronze sculpted head of a lion crushing a human skull had been mounted. The ship's single mast stood bare as its sail remained tightly furled while oarsmen gripped the oar handles and pulled on their shafts so the wooden blades sliced through the water in unison. They had left Thebes nine days before, and made a brief stop at Gebtu, and then sojourned in Abdju and again in Ipu where they waited another day for the rest of the ships in his fleet to join them before finally heading for Nen-nesu, where he believed Khety was staying with his army. Khu and Nakhti accompanied Mentuhotep, Qeb and several other generals in leading the fleet of warships north. Their own men followed behind in several ships under the guidance of the officers who served them.

The very air seemed charged with excitement as the fleet glided steadily northwards by oarsmen maneuvering the flat-bottomed ships with ease. Crocodiles eyed them warily, their sharp teeth overlapping their closed jaws in a menacing sneer. They were submerged in the water near a sandbar rising from the west side of the river where herons, cranes and storks were foraging for fish and insects. The birds waded near plants growing in a wild tangle of reeds, bulrushes and cattails that were alive with dragonflies, beetles and butterflies.

"I want to arrive while it is dark," Mentuhotep said as he glanced at his grown sons who stood by his side. "We can stop three more times on our way there—four if absolutely necessary—if we plan accordingly."

A chorus of noisy cicadas echoed across the water from the shrubs and trees along the bank where they sounded their mating calls.

"The river's current is steady, Father," Nakhti observed with a nod, "and the rowers are propelling the ships swiftly onwards. We should be able to arrive when you plan, if they continue to row in shifts."

"Khety will know we are coming," Khu changed the subject. His face was serious and his eyes had a faraway look to them.

"He will indeed," Qeb echoed as he joined them on top of a lookout platform which sat in front of the prow of the ship. "But that will not matter. Either way he will have to face us." Qeb was rubbing his left arm which bothered him when the weather cooled. "Khety has had his spies lurking among us," he slowly exhaled a deep breath, "just as we have had ours among them."

"It is the way of war," Mentuhotep explained. Deep lines were etched on his forehead. "Khety will be told we are coming once we pass Zawty."

"Unless we get to Nen-nesu before his spies," Qeb added.

With every day that took them farther north on the Nile, Khu's apprehension increased. Perhaps it was because they were leaving the safety of their own lands; perhaps it was because they were entering unfriendly waters. Either way, Khu's uneasiness grew stronger.

"Most of our sources claim that his army is smaller, despite the mercenaries he has hired. We have many more men than he," Mentuhotep said.

Qeb looked at the king. He had fought alongside his sovereign and friend for many years, and his respect for King Mentuhotep had only grown stronger after seeing the Theban ruler consistently lead his men with unwavering valor into battle. Mentuhotep could always be found at the forefront of combat. And he never asked anyone to do anything he himself did not do. He was a bold and fearless leader, having been born and bred for this role which he fulfilled well.

"I am not overly concerned," Mentuhotep stated with forced confidence. But his demeanor said otherwise.

Khu could feel the tension within his father without even looking at him. Mentuhotep was like the taut string of a bow pulled before discharging an arrow. Khu felt the same way. He had spent so much time pondering the strange circumstances and tragic events which steered the course of his life, that little else mattered to him other than his loved ones and avenging the deaths of his family.

Nakhti, on the other hand, was smiling. He looked forward to the battle with eagerness and enthusiasm, almost as one entering a great competition whose prize was beyond measure despite the risk of life it entailed. He had married a few years before, and already was a father to a little girl with another child on the way. With all that had been going on, the wedding contract had been a short and simple affair arranged on the Theban palace grounds.

Nakhti's wife was a cousin whom he had known since childhood. She waited for him at their home in Nekhen where they had been living for the past three years, since Nakhti had become chieftain of Nekhen to replace Ankhtifi. Nakhti began to be groomed for this position a couple years after Ankhtifi had fled north with King Khety, and he had done a fine job in overseeing the trade center, its mines, and its skilled craftsmen. With his own son at this important post, Mentuhotep felt more confident in the stability and security of his kingdom.

Khu had not married, and remained in Thebes where he had been serving his father as chief counselor and military chancellor, replacing Qeb in the illustrious position after Qeb had sustained a debilitating injury that had crippled his left arm. Qeb had been serving in an advisory position to Mentuhotep and Khu in the last three years since receiving the injury. Khu looked over at Qeb with admiration for the man who was like a second father to him. He saw Qeb rubbing his maimed arm when his thoughts were preoccupied elsewhere. It pained Khu to see the man he admired—and thought invincible—in any kind of discomfort.

Khu turned away to watch a hawk gliding over the floodplains near the river. He could not help the anger and frustration that surfaced every time he pondered the circumstances of the battle where Qeb had been hurt. It was a particularly treacherous battle with the Kushites; a treachery prompted from within Mentuhotep's own ranks, by the men who had betrayed him. Khu tensed, taking a deep breath, exhaling slowly.

That was more than three years ago.

Khu glanced back at Qeb, fixing the Kushite warrior with his piercing gaze. Qeb was staring out over the water's shimmering surface, his usually smooth impassive brow, drawn in concentration. The injury had done nothing to detract from Qeb's intimidating appearance. The Kushite warrior stood tall and proud despite missing part of his left arm. The attacks in that battle were meant to have assassinated the Theban king.

They nearly killed Qeb instead.

It was during a supposed respite between battles that Qeb was seriously injured. Khu was away in Gebtu at the time. He had gone north with an army of men, while Nakhti stayed in Nekhen, stationed at his home settlement with a small army of his own. Mentuhotep and Qeb remained in the garrison town of Swentet where more mercenaries were being trained.

The Kushites hatched a particularly wicked plot to assassinate Mentuhotep and capture the Theban throne. A small army of them entered Egypt through one of the Nile's minor tributaries in the land of Kush, whereby they traveled north on the river, disembarking their vessels before the Nile's first cataract, and continuing on foot over the land. They had disassembled their boats and hidden the evidence among the reeds and shrubbery growing on the eastern bank of the river. Journeying by night, they made their way under cover of darkness to avoid being seen.

It was treachery from within the ranks of Mentuhotep's garrison that instigated the revolt. But the treachery was devised by Ankhtifi who wanted revenge for the leg wound he had sustained in Abdju three years earlier, and who wanted repayment for having lost the prosperous settlement of Nekhen. The former chieftain had not forgotten the humiliation he had suffered, and he blamed Mentuhotep for everything he had lost. He blamed the Theban king for his ungainly limp, for the forfeiture of his settlement, and for his wounded pride that rankled more than anything else.

Ankhtifi had decided to send a few of his own men like wolves among a flock, with bribes to induce the Theban forces to treason. Khety had been occupied with skirmishes in the north, and was unaware of Ankhtifi's plan. While it was true that Khety had wanted Ankhtifi to help him spy on the Theban king, he had not been aware of the assassination plot until after it had already been set into motion. Khety knew that Ankhtifi was acquainted with some of the men working for Mentuhotep, from the years he had lived in Nekhen, south of Thebes, and that these old ties would prove useful in acquiring information.

"Once their loyalty is bought, the rest will fall into place," Ankhtifi told Khety after he had sent his men to infiltrate the Theban army.

Khety stared at Ankhtifi without saying anything at first. He was surprised that the former chieftain would go behind his back on such a delicate matter.

"So their loyalty has already been bought?"

"Yes it has."

"And you believe it will work?" Khety asked warily. He felt uncomfortable with the idea, and especially with the man who proposed it.

Khety rubbed the smooth line of his jaw as he examined his own feelings on the matter, and considered the implications of Ankhtifi's actions. It bothered him that

Ankhtifi had not consulted with him first. It also bothered his pride that the man he had trusted had gone around him and acted alone. What did this say of Ankhtifi's opinion of him, or of his respect and loyalty? Perhaps he was reading too deeply into the matter. But it still bothered him. Ankhtifi should have approached him first.

"Why wouldn't it work?" Ankhtifi asked the Nennesian king. "One of his own men betrayed him already, and we did nothing to encourage it," he reminded Khety of Odji.

But Khety said nothing. The lines between his eyes deepened as he regarded his enforcer with ambivalence. Khety's own ruthlessness had been tempered by a lifetime of deep superstition and a grudging respect for the gods, including the principles of *maat*. And while he possessed a trace of civility, he knew that Ankhtifi had no such scruples himself. Khety despised treachery, even where his enemies were concerned. And he was suspicious of any man inclined to such malicious behavior, or who condoned it himself. What was to prevent such a man from turning around and betraying his own loyalties? And what would stop him from usurping the throne of the very king to whom he had sworn his allegiance?

Ankhtifi glanced at Khety, and the king felt something cold pass between them. There was something disturbing about Ankhtifi's black eyes, which reminded Khety of death. It was probably just his imagination. Perhaps he imagined the contempt he thought he saw in Ankhtifi's lifeless eyes. Perhaps he imagined a hint of defiance in the man's lupine face and posture. Khety had been encumbered with skirmishes by the Nile Delta, and the strain was getting to him. Ankhtifi might have done him a favor, after all. But it bothered him nevertheless. He felt as though his own authority had been undermined by Ankhtifi's actions. He felt as though his position had been challenged, growing more vulnerable and threatened from within, regardless of the purpose of Ankhtifi's plot.

"Then do as you see fit," Khety finally answered with a wave of his hand, as he tried to mask his discomfort with indifference. "Just keep me informed of Mentuhotep's whereabouts." He doubted Ankhtifi's plan would work, and he wanted to dismiss his enforcer and the strange suspicions that left him uneasy and cold.

Ankhtifi's plan did work, to a degree. Three men who had served Mentuhotep for many years, had accepted bribes from Ankhtifi's spies, and turned against the Theban king. Despite their loyalty and service, they fell prey to the lure of greed. For even a single tainted seed can sprout and overtake a field, if its soil is fertile enough. And the soil of those three men's hearts was a fertile breeding ground to the seeds of treachery sown by Ankhtifi's spies. Promises of riches, land, and power can prove too great a temptation for even the most stouthearted of men; promises which assured them prosperity once the kingdoms were reunited under King Khety's rule. So the three men turned against Mentuhotep, giving in to the temptation that overwhelmed them like an insidious vine strangling a tree.

A small force of mercenaries had joined Mentuhotep's army the previous year under the pretense of serving the Theban king. They were a diverse group of men including Kushites from the southernmost regions of Kush, and nomadic tribes which had been assimilated from settlements bordering the Sea of Reeds. The three traitors oversaw the training of these mercenaries who had been promised much wealth and riches upon the successful completion of their mission to assassinate the king—a mission that seemed almost impossible to Mentuhotep's enemies, until now.

The mercenaries trained hard, proving themselves in battle, and gaining the confidence and recommendation of Qeb himself. And with the passing of time, the poison within the Theban ranks spread as a disease, polluting more of the men, and turning them against the king.

No one was aware of the contagion brewing from within. No one knew of the secret communication passing between the Kushites and the traitors in Swentet, as the Kushites prepared to send a small army to ambush the king. The enemy was patient, biding their time and keeping their intentions well hidden as they continued to fight and train diligently.

Khu had not been around for much for the men's training, and was stationed north in order to secure those settlements lying between Ipu and Gebtu; something he would later regret upon learning of the attack.

The vicious attack came in the earliest hours of dawn, when a spectral light steeped the camp in ghoulish shades. The sickle moon hanging low over the sand dunes beyond the floodplain had disappeared from sight, as though the moon-god Khonsu had turned his face away in shame. Most of Mentuhotep's troops were fast asleep in the mud-brick barracks of the camp, as well as in tents spreading out beyond the floodplain. More than two seasons—about nine courses of the moon—had passed since their last skirmish, and the men had been lulled into a false sense of security. One by one, under a somber sky, the Kushite warriors that had infiltrated Egypt from the south, tread like hyenas on the prowl. With their bows and arrows in hand, they advanced quickly and methodically, surrounding Mentuhotep's camp, as they lay in ambush waiting for the signal to attack.

The traitors slipped out of their tents to join the Kushite ambush, and once the signal was given, the attack was unleashed. A storm of arrows rained down over the camp, piercing through the coarse linen fabric of the tents, and injuring or killing those men who were trapped inside.

"We are under attack!" someone shouted, waking Mentuhotep and Qeb at once. One of Mentuhotep's men had gone to relieve himself when he spotted some of the strange, unfamiliar Kushite forces just before their arrows flew. He did not recognize any of the men. They were not part of Mentuhotep's army, nor with any of the newly hired mercenaries.

They had to be enemies.

The camp was thrown into chaos as troops scrambled for their weapons and headed outside. Bewildered bleary-eyed soldiers rushed with daggers, while others grabbed spears and shields. But the element of surprise had thrown Mentuhotep's army off guard, stunning them into confusion as they watched many of their own troops turning against them in a stabbing frenzy that resulted in much bloodshed.

It did not take long for Qeb and Mentuhotep to realize what had happened. Together with a group of their most trustworthy fighters, they defended themselves and their camp from the treacherous onslaught that grew more bloody and vicious with every moment. The camp's stillness had been shattered by shrieks, pain and blood that told of treachery and treason fouling the air.

Although the enemy forces were fewer in number, the confusion set off by the surprise attack gave them the advantage in the beginning of the battle. One moment, men fought the ambushing Kushites side-by-side next to their allies, and the next, those allies bared their treachery, turning against them and killing them in a shocking and deplorable counterattack.

It was a brilliant assault, hatched in malice, nurtured by greed, and reared in deception.

Qeb stayed by Mentuhotep's side throughout the fighting. Although the battle did not last for more than a few hours in its entirety, it was bloody, barbaric and brutal. As confusion gave way to clarity, the division between the traitors and defenders grew more apparent, making it easier to distinguish between friend and foe. But lives had already been lost in the turmoil, some of which were slain mistakenly, so that each side inadvertently killed some of their own men. It was a chaotic rampage of death and destruction.

The attack on Qeb came after sunrise as Re's *Mandjet* Barque of a Million Years rose higher, transforming the sand dunes into stunning hills of gold, their radiance spilling over the plains. Qeb had just killed two foes when he saw a furtive movement from the corner of his eye, coming from somewhere behind Mentuhotep.

Two of the traitors were already dead along with many of the mercenaries who had trained under them. But the third traitor had guarded his identity, leading the king into believing he was an ally. Suddenly, the man whistled and turned on the unwary king when the opportunity presented itself. His signal prompted an enemy archer to loosen an arrow aimed at Mentuhotep.

Qeb saw the arrow, and he threw himself in front of the king, blocking the assault with his own body. The arrow struck Qeb in the upper left part of his chest, close to his shoulder. In that same moment he was also stabbed by the traitor in the left forearm as he attempted to parry the attack. Qeb fell from the impact of the double assault, as Mentuhotep killed the rebel with a powerful thrust of his dagger, catching the man under the jaw with the blade.

"Qeb!" Mentuhotep yelled, his eyes wide with worry when he saw his faithful friend fall to the ground. But Qeb just shook his head, waving the king away with his good arm so that he would not be distracted from the danger.

Qeb backed away slowly on the ground, gritting his teeth against the pain as he tried to find cover by one of the barracks. He found refuge in the shadows of one of the mud-brick buildings, and he rested his back against the wall, his legs stretched out before him. He looked down at his wounds, trying to ascertain the extent of the damage. The arrow was still lodged in his chest, and his left arm hung limply as he attempted to cradle it on his lap. The traitor's dagger had sliced right through his forearm, snapping a bone, and both wounds bled profusely.

Qeb took a shaky breath and leaned his head back on the wall, resisting the urge to close his eyes. He had seen the king stab and kill the traitor, and he knew that most of the rebels were dead already. But he could not fathom how the revolt had taken place. He searched his memory for any telltale signs that might have pointed to the deception in their midst. He tried to recall any clues or hints carelessly left by the traitors over the last year, but could find none.

It was mystifying.

He felt guilty, knowing that he should have seen it coming, should have somehow known of the treachery brewing within their ranks. He berated himself silently, shaking his head at his own failure to prevent the attack; an attack that had put his esteemed sovereign and friend's life in danger. Mentuhotep could have been *killed*. What if he had not seen the furtive movement coming from somewhere behind the king in that instant? What then?

Qeb's eyelids grew heavy as the pain from his wounds throbbed, and his whole body ached. All it takes is an instant to change the course of a life—or to end it, Qeb thought grimly. A single, careless instant that would have invariably altered the fate of Upper Egypt's Kingdom.

He closed his eyes for a moment, just for a brief moment, then forced them open once again. His breathing was shallow, and his skin slick with blood and perspiration. He could hear men yelling throughout the camp, and somewhere in the distance dogs were barking. He felt cold—very cold—and a spasm made him shudder involuntarily, sending a stabbing pain through his left shoulder and chest, and he winced, clenching his jaw in pain.

He couldn't see Mentuhotep from the shadows where he lay propped against the wall, and he hoped the king was alright. He thought of the traitor who had almost killed the king, and he felt angry once again—an anger tempered by exhaustion and an increasing drowsiness. He had trusted that man, and had even congratulated him on the progress he had made with the mercenaries. He felt like a fool now.

Qeb steadied his breathing to keep the pain in check. His gaze drifted upwards toward the sky, and he thought he glimpsed something flying. It was a dark shape with wings gliding over the camp, and Qeb squinted, wondering what it might be. He closed his eyes again, reaching a tentative hand—his good hand—up to the amulet hanging around his neck.

It was gone.

The amulet must have been ripped off in the battle. He wondered where it was and if he would find it again. Then he wondered at himself for the inconsequential thoughts darting through his head. He grew colder still, and weary, so weary with fatigue. He longed to sleep, but fought the urge with what was left of the strength draining fast from his body. He closed his eyes again, keeping them shut a little longer this time as the noises grew more distant.

By the time Mentuhotep and his loyal troops subverted the enemy and regained control of the camp, Qeb was unconscious. Two surgeons worked on Qeb for hours, trying to save his life and his arm. They managed to remove the arrow after opening up the flesh where its tip had been lodged. And although they tried to reset his broken bone, mend the severed muscle and sinew in his forearm, the surgery caused more blood loss, putting Qeb's life in further danger. They finally sutured and bandaged the wounds, and then left to treat more of the injured men in Mentuhotep's ranks.

No mercy was shown to the pinioned enemy who were still alive after the battle. They were promptly beheaded for treason after swift sentencing. Following their executions, their right hands were severed and their remains scattered in the desert for the wild animals to ravage.

Qeb battled for his life for more than a full course of the moon after that. No amount of herbal infusions, compresses, medicinal unctions, spells, chants and amulets could counter the foul infection that overtook his left arm. While the chest wound seemed to be healing properly, the wound in his arm had putrefied, and the rank odor was enough to make one dizzy. Nevertheless, Mentuhotep remained at the side of his military chancellor, his own face pale and drawn from the anxiety within him. He watched his friend who was gripped by a tortuous fever. He watched him closely, his own brows furrowed, willing him to get well.

Qeb's skin burned from the temperature that left him weak and delirious. The arm wound was red and inflamed, and a vile liquid seeped from the opening beneath the sutures. At times he thrashed about and mumbled incoherently in his native tongue, perspiration coating his skin, and drenching the sheet on which he lay. Other times he lay still like a cadaver, a mask of death upon his face.

More than once, Mentuhotep placed an apprehensive hand upon Qeb's chest to ascertain the beating of his heart. The king held his breath as he laid a hand over Qeb's heart, and bent down to lean closely by Qeb's face, making sure his friend was still breathing. Qeb's heart continued to beat—slow yet unfailing—much to the relief of the king who exhaled noisily each time.

Qeb's arm was finally amputated just above the elbow, and the remaining stump cauterized in the open flame of a fire to keep the poison which was blackening his hand and forearm from spreading any further. It took six men to hold him down while the two doctors performed the ghastly operation; six strong men to keep the Kushite warrior from thrashing about wildly, despite the trauma and weakness from his wounds, and the infection tormenting his body. He had cried out loudly during the procedure, roaring like a lion in terrible agony.

The king had stepped aside to get out of the men's way, but he did not leave the room. Mentuhotep stood watching from a corner of the room, his shoulders squared and his face stoic. He watched in silence, his eyes shining with unshed tears. And when he finally blinked, those tears left a glistening trail on his cheeks, which he did not bother to wipe away.

Hours after the amputation, Mentuhotep sat at Qeb's bedside, reflecting on the battle while his loyal friend lay pale and sleeping. Although that battle had been won, it was a costly victory due to the good men who had perished, and especially Qeb's incapacitating injury that had nearly cost him his life—a life worthy of a whole battalion of men, as far as the king was concerned.

The Kushite warrior had thrown himself in harm's way without hesitation, to save the king. Mentuhotep knew that Qeb had shielded him with his own body. He knew that Qeb had taken the arrow and dagger that were meant to have taken his own life. And as Mentuhotep kept vigil over the man who had saved his life, he gave a long heavy sigh, slumping his shoulders as he closed his eyes and bowed his head in grief.

Qeb later—much later—continued his duties as trainer to the young boys at the palace, as well as to those men who were conscripted into battle from the surrounding settlements; men who were vetted with great scrutiny after the treachery had infiltrated their ranks and nearly cost Qeb his life.

The road to recovery had been long and arduous, but Qeb refused to give up or to give in to the temptation of wallowing in self-pity—a disease in itself that can infect a man's soul when he is debilitated and his guard is down, incapacitating him far beyond the physical limitations of his wounds. No, he did not succumb to the self-indulgence and misery that defeats a weaker man's spirit.

Qeb remained stouthearted, and the strength of his will grew stronger along with the scars forming a protective barrier over his wounds. He recovered slowly, regaining his strength and training himself to fight with his one good arm. He knew he was fortunate to be alive. He knew this and he was grateful for it, accepting his fate with the poise and dignity of those rare and exceptional heroic men, who rise above their tragic circumstances with un-wavering integrity and honor.

Khu blamed himself after he found out what had hap-pened, and he wept for the man whom he loved as a second father. If he had remained in Swentet, the revolt would not have occurred.

At least that is what he told himself.

He might have sensed something was amiss; sensed the presence of something wicked conspiring against them, and perhaps been able to warn his father and Qeb before the danger had erupted. Perhaps he could have done something about it long before the conspiracy had formed and taken shape; long before the deceit had spread like a contagion. Perhaps he could have flushed out the traitors right from the start, and the men they infected with their treachery. Then perhaps the rebellion would not have happened. Perhaps.

There was no way to tell by hindsight. The damage was done. It was over. It was too late now. Khu felt guilty nevertheless. He felt conflicted and resentful and angry at the Kushites, the traitors, Ankhtifi and Khety, whom he blamed most of all. He thought of the Kushites who were like opportunistic hunters pouncing on any chance they spied. He thought of Ankhtifi and Khety whom he believed would stop at nothing to take Upper Egypt's throne from his father. And he thought of the traitors who had forfeited their honor and loyalty for the promise of riches—a promise that unleashed havoc, bloodshed, death and disgrace instead. He wondered if he could have ex-posed them, if he could have thwarted their plans, if only he had been there. If.

But he had not been there. He was far away at the time—about a seven-day journey from Swentet; much too far removed from the disastrous events. He shook his head, clenching his jaw, exasperated with himself, his guilt, and the senseless thoughts gnawing at him inside.

His father had needed him up north to protect those settlements that were most vulnerable to attacks from Khety's forces; or from Kushites circumventing the Nile and infiltrating Mentuhotep's territory from another route. And Khu had prevented them. He had prevented more than one attack, thwarting several schemes that another man in his place might not have detected. Mentuhotep had done well to send him there. Khu knew this, and yet he felt frustrated and angry despite it all. The battle at Swentet had been something totally unforeseen. It had taken them completely by surprise. He could not have prevented it because he had not been there. No, there was nothing he could have done. He had to let it go.

Lessons had been learned, at least; hard lessons which would only strengthen Mentuhotep's army in the long run. Sometimes a snake's bite—if it does not kill its victim—makes it stronger, immunizing it against the poison. But the bite would leave a scar nevertheless.

A painful scar.

After Qeb's injury, Khu replaced Qeb as military chancellor, and he oversaw the extensive battalion of warriors assembled from settlements stretching as far north as Ipu, Tjeny, Abdju and Gebtu. He remained with his father throughout the years, fighting alongside the king who always led the soldiers into battle.

Mentuhotep relied on Khu's ability to command with ease, and especially on his intuition and perceptiveness that had been honed over the years. Khu had developed an uncanny ability to anticipate the enemy's move, and thus learned to defeat them. It had been Khu's gift that had played a critical role in winning the numerous battles against the Kushites. Because he was attuned to their intentions, Khu was able to advise Mentuhotep in the best strategies for victory, especially after that devastating battle in Swentet—something Khu would always regret missing, and which sat like a boulder in the river of his conscience.

More than three years passed since that treacherous battle at Swentet, and about seven since the one in Abdju. Time was marked by battles, bloodshed and a driving ambition of reunification. The Kushites had finally been defeated after a long series of skirmishes that ended with a peace treaty. The disgraced enemy had suffered great losses—far more than Mentuhotep—and they had no choice but to back down and bow out, and so they abandoned their ambition to overtake the Theban throne. After all that had happened, they just wanted to retain a hold on their own lands and kingdom, lest the Theban king take it away from them.

Mentuhotep trusted Khu with his life and kingdom, and he wanted his son close by, especially when the time would come to fight Khety and Ankhtifi. He wanted Khu by his side when the time came to go north and face the Nen-nesian ruler once and for all.

That time had finally arrived.

SIXTEEN

Mentuhotep's fleet was approaching Zawty. Oarsmen worked in shifts, plowing through the waters of the river whose current flows northward from the south. A pallid moon remained suspended over a mountain range rising in a craggy line in the distance beyond the floodplain. It hung in a violet sky glittering with the fading stars, until the first hints of dawn cast an ashen patina over the land.

The king had not been able to sleep. He was alone with his thoughts, standing on deck as he listened to the rhythm of the water sloshing around the ship's hull. He was wearing his blue *Khepresh* royal war crown, and had a dagger and short sword strapped to his legs. Almost everyone else was still asleep with their weapons next to them in case they should run into trouble. Mentuhotep felt apprehensive, and when Khu refused to sleep either, the king's uneasiness grew.

Mentuhotep hoped to sail quietly past the province that supported the northern king. He had instructed his oarsmen to push quickly along the river, so that their journey would be swift. The river curved westward, nearing a sharp narrow bend where the eastern bank formed a rocky escarpment above the water. Zawty lay on the western bank, just beyond the bend that protected the inlet leading to its natural harbor. It was an ideally situated province, naturally fortified by the limited accessibility to its port, and protected by the rocky land formations along the river as well as the mountain range beyond the floodplain.

Although Mentuhotep had received reports that Khety left Zawty to go back to his palace in Nen-nesu the previous season, Mentuhotep's guard was up, and he had stationed his best warriors on the ships at the front of the fleet as a precautionary measure.

Khu was pacing back and forth on deck like a restless cheetah pent up in a cage, when he stopped suddenly to probe the fading darkness with his golden eyes. He stood immobile on the port side of the ship, staring with narrowed eyes into the gloom. He sensed something odd and it made him nervous. A hostile presence lurked on the river, waiting for them.

Someone was out there.

Khu instinctively held his breath as they veered west by the rising escarpment. And just as he turned to look for the vessels following behind them, an arrow struck the ship's head coxswain, killing him at once. The man was standing on the steering platform at the stern of the ship, manning the tillers that guided the vessel, when the arrow struck him in the chest, piercing his heart. He slumped forward and then fell with a thud, tumbling off the platform and onto the deck.

"An ambush!" Khu shouted, waking the men. "It's an ambush! We are under attack!"

A barrage of long-shafted fiery arrows was discharged by the enemy, and rose in a high trajectory over the water before raining down on the fleet.

"Shields!" Mentuhotep ordered before the carnage began. "Get your shields!" He squinted, trying to see precisely where the attack had come from. He felt vulnerable defending his fleet from an invisible enemy.

Some of his men had ducked for cover under their ox-hide shields, easily deflecting the onslaught that came from above, while others screamed in pain and anger as the missiles found their mark. Many of the arrows struck the water around them harmlessly, hissing and fizzling out as they disappeared beneath its dark surface.

It did not take long for all the ships in Mentuhotep's fleet to be alerted to the danger. Men stood ready with their spears and shields in hand, while the archers had their bows strung, and quivers brimming with goose-fledged arrows, slung across their backs. The oarsmen continued to pull and heave, sweeping the oars in one smooth motion to keep the ships moving so they would not sit in the open like ducks. Every moment drew them deeper into enemy waters, deeper into the powerful province that supported the northern ruler. And just as the ships rounded the bend below the escarpment, another barrage of arrows flew from above, their tips ablaze in fire.

Khety's best archers were crouched among the reeds that grew thick and tall next to the marshes west of the river and along the steep escarpment on the east, beyond which sycamores, acacias and date palms spread out over the higher plain. The ranks of his army had swelled with Kushites and other mercenaries including Ankhtifi and his men, during the past few years. He had positioned his men along both banks of the Nile, which ran narrower in these parts by the province, to try and ambush Mentuhotep as his fleet passed the settlement of Zawty. His soldiers loosed their arrows just as the ships veered blindly around the sharp bend which had hidden the enemy from sight.

Farther down the Nile a blockade of ships stretched across the narrowest part of the river, just before the mouth of the inlet leading to Zawty's harbor. The ships had been tied together from prow to stern, barricading the Theban fleet from going north, and from accessing Zawty's inlet. Soldiers and archers waited to attack the Theban fleet from the blockading ships as well.

Although Khety had gone to Nen-nesu the previous season, he had recently returned in secret after being warned of Mentuhotep's intentions to sail to Nen-nesu.

"He will be coming north soon," one of Khety's advisors had cautioned him during the previous season at his palace in Nen-nesu, when they were meeting in his pavilion.

"Coming with his entire fleet," another added grimly.

Khety had turned away to ponder the news as his gaze swept the lands of his settlement, from the crop fields near the Nile's western bank, to the village lying south of the palace, to the sand plains, desert ridges, and rocky plateaus in the distance. The news was not surprising. He had been expecting this. He knew Mentuhotep would eventually come after him, but he did not want to put his own province at risk.

"We would be better off facing him in Zawty then," Khety said, turning back around to look at his advisors and warlords. "Nen-nesu is not fortified enough to withstand an attack."

"Not an attack of that magnitude," one of them acknowledged.

"Assuming the reports are true," another argued. "The reports are not always reliable. We cannot be sure of the size of his army."

Khety heaved a great breath, raising and lowering his shoulders as the lines between his brows deepened. "It is better to assume the reports are correct. We cannot take that risk. Not here anyway."

His men did not reply. They did not need to say anything. They knew he was right. A few of them nodded before looking away.

Khety preferred to face Mentuhotep in Zawty where his chances for victory were better, instead of remaining north where he would have been less secure.

"What did you have in mind?" someone asked him.

"An ambush. We will block his fleet and attack them where they will be most vulnerable as they sail down the Nile by Zawty," Khety ran a finger along a map on a scroll. "Over here," he pointed, "where the river curves sharply along the bend by the escarpment. That is one of the narrowest sections of the river, is it not?"

"Yes, Lord King," one of his warlords replied. "They would not see our men waiting for them."

"We will place our men along both sides of the river, and then attack his fleet as they near the escarpment."

"It is a treacherous bend," one of the men said, approving of the idea. "They will be trapped."

So Khety had gone back to Zawty from Nen-nesu to fight Mentuhotep on his own terms. The offensive strategy was a wise move on Khety's part, for it provided him with a more fortified battleground in which to ambush the Theban fleet using a kind of pincer maneuver to attack them simultaneously on both flanks where they were most defenseless and exposed.

"Shields! Shields!" Mentuhotep shouted, as a second assault of arrows flew toward Mentuhotep's ships. "Guard the flanks!"

This time more of the men were struck. Some were killed instantly, while others shrieked in pain from the sharp fiery tips penetrating their flesh.

The oarsmen stopped rowing to duck beneath their shields, then grabbed the oars again to pull the ships out of danger.

Qeb stood on the steering platform, replacing the coxswain after he died. "Pull!" he prompted, guiding the oarsmen along the sharp bend.

"Archers ready!" Mentuhotep ordered.

But there was nothing they could do for the moment. They had to clear the escarpment.

"Pull! Pull!" Qeb urged in his deep voice, willing them to clear past the danger.

And just as the first ships cleared the narrow bend, Khu spotted the blockade.

"Shields!" Khu shouted before the third attack. "Up ahead!" he pointed when he saw Mentuhotep glancing around.

This time arrows flew from three directions, attacking their flanks and head-on as they cleared the bend and neared the blockade where more of the enemy waited. Khu heard the ominous sound of the bowstrings being released, and then the rush of air as the arrows hissed overhead, a dark and sinister streak against the early dawn.

Three of Mentuhotep's ships had caught fire, one of which was put out soon enough. But the other two were destroyed as the ropes and reed caulking burned, and the planks quickly fell apart.

Men fell or jumped into the water in a panic of confusion and turmoil, as the ships were destroyed and sank beneath the river. Those who had not been struck and injured or killed by the arrows, scrambled aboard other ships from the water where they tried to swim to safety.

"There!" the king pointed at the blockade of ships barring their way, "up ahead! Archers!" When Mentuhotep gave the signal, they released the bronze-tipped arrows, killing some of the enemy, and injuring others.

"Attack them!" Mentuhotep shouted as they reached the blockade. "To their ships! To their ships!"

Mentuhotep worried about the reports he had received regarding Khety and his forces. If his spies had been wrong in their information that the northern ruler was in Nen-nesu, it could well be possible that they were wrong in their estimate of the number of men in Khety's army as well. Once again, the enemy had the advantage of surprise. Their ambush reminded the Theban king of the battle at Swentet three years before, and Mentuhotep nearly cringed from the memory of that treacherous attack.

"Qeb!" Mentuhotep shouted above the noise, turning to look for his former military chancellor, as a cold fear shrouded the memories of the battle where Qeb had almost died. "Qeb," Mentuhotep repeated, relieved to find the Kushite warrior nearby. The king placed a protective hand on Qeb's left shoulder, above the scarred stump of his arm. "You are to remain with the fleet. Guard the ships with the other men."

Qeb said nothing, letting a moment of silence hang between them. He knew the king meant well, and he regarded Mentuhotep with an unreadable expression, before casting a meaningful glance at his left shoulder, where Mentuhotep's hand remained. Qeb raised a single eyebrow as he looked at the king's hand on his left arm. The king followed Qeb's eyes and let his hand drop to his side.

"Very well," the king conceded with an exasperated breath, as though reading Qeb's thoughts.

Qeb gave the king a half-smile in reply.

Mentuhotep set his jaw, drawing his brows together, as he thought again of the reports he had received from his spies. Regardless of their accuracy, this battle was long overdue. It was an unsettled score that demanded payment—the final payment that would determine the fate of Egypt and its divided kingdoms.

Nakhti was among the first of the men to attack the enemy, as they struck their hulls with their fleet. Together with Khu and some of their men, they charged ahead, climbing aboard their ships, where they were met by a savage defense of spears, axes, daggers and swords. Hand-to-hand combat ensued as more men joined in the fighting when they clambered aboard the enemy vessels. Men heaved, howled, wrestled and roared as they chopped and drove their weapons into flesh.

Mentuhotep's men swarmed the enemy like an army of ants on a raid. The king fought to break through the blockade with his fleet and his forces, in order to reach land where he knew Khety waited.

"Father!" Nakhti waved Mentuhotep over to a boat he secured after slaying the men aboard.

The king joined him and Khu with Qeb and a few other soldiers, and the boats were poled to Zawty's shore. Men rushed at them with spears and daggers before they had disembarked. But Mentuhotep and two of his warriors deflected the blows, as the rest of the men hopped onto the ground while striking back. And although the king had wanted Qeb to stay back out of danger, Qeb remained at Mentuhotep's side, fighting with his favorite scimitar, which he continued to wield expertly, one-handed, despite his handicap.

Several hours passed as the men fought in the chill of the early morning. Fire was set to some of Khety's ships, so that those vessels consumed by the flames, spat and sizzled as they sank beneath the water, opening the barrier that had previously barred the inlet. The rest of Mentuhotep's army eventually broke through the enemy ranks and entered the harbor.

Khu and Nakhti stayed close to their father's side in the beginning of the fighting, but were then all separated in the maelstrom. Some of Khu's own men caught up to him and they ventured through the town, scouring the streets and narrow avenues, hunting down and killing many of the enemy, while rounding up the wounded and those who surrendered.

It was difficult to tell how many men they were up against at first, and neither Khu nor Mentuhotep felt comfortable believing the reports they had received. Although they had heard countless rumors that Khety's army was smaller than the Theban forces, the ambush on the river had overwhelmed them, making the opposite seem true. Mentuhotep preferred to err on the side of caution, and assume that they were the ones who were outnumbered.

The Theban king had scrutinized, examined and studied the various battle scenarios over the last years, carefully weighing all prospects each time he reviewed the reports he had garnered from his informants.

"They will have the advantage of fighting on familiar ground—in their own territory," Mentuhotep had warned his men in the preceding season, during one of the many strategic planning sessions with his warlords and generals who would, in turn, pass on the information to their respective battalions. "Because they will not come to us," he shook his head. "No. They will not come to Upper Egypt."

"They tried that already," one of the warlords said, speaking of Swentet.

"They did," Mentuhotep agreed with a nod, "and they failed. But they will not try that again. The chances of that happening are highly unlikely. We will go to them."

"Where they will lay traps to ambush us in their town," Khu had added grimly.

"Will it be in Zawty as you originally believed?" someone had asked.

The king had looked at Khu and Qeb, but refrained from answering. Khu shrugged, and Qeb did not reply.

"It may," Mentuhotep finally said, "or it may not. We will only know when the time comes. Some things cannot be predicted, no matter how much planning is done in advance."

So Mentuhotep had led his army north to fight his enemy on their own soil.

They had not known it would be in Zawty, especially since Khety had been fighting his own battles in several of the northern provinces, many of which lay along the branches of the Nile Delta. Once Mentuhotep's informers had confirmed that Khety had returned to Nen-nesu, the Theban king believed he and his army would follow Khety there. But the Seven Hathors devised their own schemes, thwarting the best laid plans, and outwitting men's orderly objectives. And the Mistresses of Fate led them to Zawty.

The Theban army did not go with the confidence of men knowing they cannot be defeated. That sort of brashness made one imprudent and careless. They went watchful and wary, with their hackles raised, their eyes open, and their ears perked to the very air around them. No, they were not foolhardy, especially after the sobering battle of Swentet.

Once Mentuhotep's army had broken through the blockade, and pushed into the harbor, many of the enemy forces retreated into the town, and most of the fighting occurred in pockets dispersed throughout the settlement, where a deadly match of hide and seek ensued between the opposing forces. Groups of the enemy lay in ambush, waiting for Mentuhotep's men to approach unsuspectingly, before rushing at them in a frenzy of sharpened blades, spiked maces, spears and battle axes. Others were crouched on the rooftops of mud-brick buildings, their arrows ready to besiege the infiltrating men.

But those men who were with Khu had the advantage of benefiting from his intuition. He would slow down, raise a hand for his men to stop, then point out the location where the ambush awaited them, all without saying a word. And when he gave the signal, they would charge into the startled enemy who had not expected the counterattack.

At one point Khu was up against ten men as he and his soldiers were busy fending off a much larger group of attackers. They grinned and grunted as they rushed at him with sharpened blades and savage strikes. With a dagger in one hand and a short sword in another, Khu alternately parried and lunged at his foes. Men bellowed and roared as they speared, chopped and hacked at the air where Khu had stood only an instant before. But each time, he stepped aside and deflected their blows as easily as though their attacks had been nothing but a pantomime of child's play.

One by one Khu slayed his opponents until a much larger man lunged at him from behind. He was a hulking beast of fighter who was almost three times the size and weight of Khu. His thick skull bore a twisted rendering of frightening scars, yellowed teeth, and bulging eyes that reminded Khu of an angry hippopotamus bull.

His first attack came just as Khu killed an opponent, and he slashed at Khu's arm, cutting him with an ax. It was a shallow wound that looked much worse than it was. Like a predator whose hunger for the kill is sharpened by the drawing of first blood, the beast bellowed as he swung and hammered his rage at Khu with a surprising agility and speed that were unexpected for one of his bulk.

Khu parried the jarring blows, but his short sword broke cleanly in half from the strength of the impact, and he threw the useless weapon to the ground. He ducked and sidestepped quickly away as the beast advanced howling. And as the man charged, angrily swinging his ax towards Khu's neck, Khu dove for his beefy legs, slashing through his left knee, instantly maiming him. The beast shrieked in pain, falling to the ground as Khu drove his dagger into the back of his neck, silencing him for good.

Khu's men were in awe of their leader, and they followed closely behind him as he left the bloody scene and led his men deeper into the town, fighting off adversaries at every turn. It was about two hundred paces away that they ran into Nakhti and a large group of his own men. Khu sensed the presence of his brother as though Nakhti had stepped out in front of his path. He felt Nakhti's excitement and the adrenaline flooding his veins.

"Nakhti!" he called out as they neared a blind corner where his brother had laid a trap for unsuspecting foes.

"Khu!" Nakhti said happily, stepping around a wall to clap his brother on the back. "It is well that you announced yourself or we would have made a bloody offering of your flesh." He laughed at his own exaggeration, knowing full well that the opposite was true.

Nakhti loved and admired his brother, and there was no one he would have preferred to have by his side during battle than he. Khu was a formidable warrior with the knack for finding concealed enemy like an eagle spying a hare from a great distance. Nakhti was naturally daring, but he felt invincible by Khu's side, and they stayed together for much of the battle until one of Nakhti's best fighters and closest friends was badly injured.

The man had sustained a stabbing wound to his lower back, and needed immediate medical attention. Nakhti insisted on accompanying his friend back to the shore himself, by which many of Mentuhotep's men were stationed, including doctors trained in surgery and the treating of wounds. He left with his men after wishing his brother good fortune and the favor of the gods.

Khu continued combing the town until he arrived to a temple complex dedicated to the jackal-headed god Anubis and the war god Wepwawet who was depicted as a wolf. Wepwawet's name meant Opener of the Ways, for he was believed to ensure safe passage through life and the Underworld. Khu stopped when he arrived at the Temple of Anubis, where a large bronze brazier had been lit during the night, and still burned in front of the pylon. Some of his men touched the amulets hanging from their necks, as they beheld the colossal figure of Anubis carved in relief onto the pylon. The jackal-headed god of the dead was shown standing upright with a human body, and he was holding the *Was* scepter in his right hand, and the *ankh* key of life in his left.

Directly over the pylon's center rested a statue of Anubis in full animal form of a jackal. The oversized stone depiction of the god was facing forward with his front legs stretched out before him, as he guarded the temple's entrance. And as the smoke of the brazier rose in a grayish cloud, it tricked the eye into thinking that the jackal-god was truly alive. The huge statue seemed to breathe as the air quivered around him, and Khu's men were momentarily filled with fear. Then Khu waved his men around the temple to prevent anyone who might be hiding within its holy grounds from escaping.

But no one was inside.

"No one is here," Khu said, after looking around some more. "Let's go." He was going to lead his men toward the town's wealthier homes where more officials might be lying in ambush, but then stopped to sweep the area one more time before leaving.

Something was not right.

Khu felt the tiny hairs on the back of his neck stand on end. And although he could not see anyone, he felt the presence of something evil. He stepped cautiously down a narrow street, slowing down as he approached a corner. His heart thumped loudly in his chest, and the same sense of dread he had felt in Abdju years before was back. It was

a vague and generalized fear that went beyond the immediate moment. It was a kind of preternatural instinct cautioning every nerve in his body to be on heightened alert.

Khu moved farther away from the temple complex
and headed deeper into the town where his men had gone
before him. The sounds of screams and shouting rose
above the settlement, as did the smoke from the remaining ships in Khety's blockade, which continued to burn
beyond the harbor. He walked slowly, pausing now and
again to listen and feel the air around him with that sixth
sense he possessed. Every step seemed to take him farther from the evil that had rattled him. He retraced some
of his steps in an attempt to near its villainous source, but
his efforts were futile. Like the black smoke blown away
by the northerly winds, the evil lurking nearby had simply
vanished.

For now.

The fighting continued long after dawn brightened the
sky in glowing shades of persimmon and plum, illuminating the wealthy province that was the cult center of the
funerary gods Anubis and Wepwawet. Zawty had been
largely independent during the time following the disintegration of the Old Kingdom, but then it sided with Khety
against Mentuhotep in the struggle for control between
the opposing kingdoms. It supported the Nen-nesian ruler with its troops and its treasury, knowing that it would
be rewarded well once Khety defeated Mentuhotep.

Khety's spies had kept him abreast of Mentuhotep's
wins and losses over the years, and he knew that his nemesis's army had grown stronger, even with the setback
at Swentet. But the price of the information had been
steep—costing him the lives of three of his most cunning
emissaries, after they were discovered by several of the
Theban generals. And like Odji, whose head was sent back
to Mentuhotep in Thebes, Khety had received a mysterious package wrapped in coarse linen, with the heads of
those three emissaries.

Included in the package was a small scroll with a simple message: "Thrice over has the gift been repaid."

The Nen-nesian king had turned his face away when the package was opened, and the message was read. The lines between his brows had deepened as he turned away and shut his eyes.

Khety sent fewer spies after that; at least he was more careful about where he sent them, so that their lives were not at risk. Unlike Ankhtifi who had not shown any remorse or emotion whatsoever after losing some of his own men in battle, Khety valued the lives of the men who served him. But Ankhtifi's only concern was with the inconvenience their deaths had cost him.

Khety had since focused on hiring new mercenaries, conscripting more men into his army, and on quashing any revolts or attacks from the nomadic invaders infiltrating Lower Egypt from the Nile Delta. And while his army had grown stronger, Khety knew that Mentuhotep's had as well.

"He has hired and trained many more men," one of his generals had reported two years before.

"But he has lost men too," another countered, referring to the battle at Swentet. "He has lost men, including his military chancellor who nearly died. The man lost an arm, and has since been replaced."

"By whom?" Khety had asked. He had never met Qeb, but he had heard of the exceptional Kushite warrior.

"One of his own sons," the man answered, shrugging as though it meant nothing.

Khety did not know whether or not to believe the reports he had heard regarding the number of Theban troops, and he listened with a measure of skepticism. Either way, he knew that he would have to face those troops again. And if Mentuhotep's army was indeed larger than his own, he would have to rely on more than brute strength.

He would have to somehow outwit his archenemy.

Outwitting the enemy is precisely what both sides attempted to do now, as they grappled for control over Zawty. Men fought along the riverbank and harbor, throughout the town's narrow roads, near the orderly blocks of mud-brick homes, inside structures or on rooftops where some of the enemy waited in ambush, through the open marketplaces that were presently deserted, and by the shrines, temples and monuments dominating the wealthy province.

Men shrieked and shouted to mask their own fear, as they swung, stabbed and slashed at each other in a welter of rage and destruction. Others jeered, throwing insults and challenges as they alternately parried and thrust at their opponents. They spit curses at each other, invoking their gods to strike them down, blight their crops, disease their livestock, and sicken their families.

Mentuhotep's men fought knowing that everything they cherished and believed in was at stake with this battle, while Khety's men fought hard to protect the Nennesian king, and to keep the Theban forces from capturing the town.

Qeb remained by Mentuhotep's side, fighting like a demon each time they confronted the enemy. The king was strong and skilled with his weapons, but Qeb possessed a certain grace that made him swift and nimble despite his disability and his larger size. As men attacked the Kushite warrior, mistaking him for easy prey, Qeb would sidestep or leap backwards, letting some of the blows go unparried as his opponents lunged more savagely each time, trying to break his rhythm. He would suddenly catch them off guard as he edged unexpectedly closer before delivering a roundhouse kick to the head, or a front kick to the groin, finishing with a death stroke of his scimitar to the belly or throat.

The former military chancellor remained a force to be reckoned with. He was adept at fighting with his legs as he was with his good arm. Those men who were foolish enough to underestimate and attack him, were defeated like a troop of unwary baboons confronting a fearless leopard.

The Theban army steadily gained the upper hand in the battle, leading some of Khety's men to panic and flee. Although Mentuhotep had sustained losses in the fighting, most of which were in the early part of the battle and during the ambush on the Nile, the heaviest losses were suffered by Khety's army, which was indeed smaller than that of the Theban king, despite the backing of Zawty's forces. Morale among Khety's men quickly plummeted as more and more of his supporters were caught, subdued, and pinioned with their arms behind their backs, many of whom were treated like traitors, and killed with a swift fatal blow to the head. While others who surrendered promptly were given quarter and their lives were spared.

King Khety fought hard despite the odds against him. This was not like the previous battle years before in Abdju. There was nowhere for him to go from here; nowhere to recoup his losses, no pilgrims to sway to his cause, no more settlements to conquer, and no army to lead after the last of his men were defeated. He was getting older and had also grown embittered and demoralized as the glorious vision of a kingdom under his rule faded with the years.

Although it did not take long for Khety to suspect that defeat was inevitable and his cause was lost, he was too proud to flee. He refused to run away like a coward and abandon the men who had remained faithful to his cause. He refused to betray their trust and their loyalty. They had fought for him and a dream that had all but vanished. And so he remained, fighting like a victor defending the men who had sworn their lives to him. He fought with every fiber of his being.

But Ankhtifi had no such intention.

At first the former chieftain of Nekhen fought determinedly by Khety's side, despite his limp from the leg wound he had suffered from Khu in Abdju years before. The strongest of Ankhtifi's soldiers accompanied them as they used their daggers, axes and maces to kill as many of Mentuhotep's men as possible. They hammered and hacked at their opponents, killing or driving away those men who dared to attack them. But as the fighting grew fiercer, and their army dwindled in the slaughter, Ankhtifi finally left Khety's side.

Like the wolves and jackals that are opportunistic hunters, preying on what is convenient and available, Ankhtifi saw no opportunity nor benefit in sacrificing himself for Khety's dying cause. He did not believe in self-sacrifice.

The only cause he truly believed in was his very own.

If there was nothing to be gained for himself, he would waste no time, nor put forth any effort which would not be of benefit to him. So he extracted himself from the chaos, and quietly slipped away in the midst of the fighting, to try and flee the settlement. He loped silently away like a low-ranking, cowardly wolf.

Leaving Khety and the others to fend for themselves alone.

Ankhtifi headed for Zawty's harbor after deserting Khety. He left alone, not wanting to be bothered or hindered by anyone else. But when he saw Mentuhotep's men guarding the port, he backed away again into the town.

He thought of his escape options.

The best and easiest route on the Nile was no longer available to him. The Theban fleet had secured the river north and south of Zawty's harbor, with explicit instructions to keep anyone other than Mentuhotep's forces, from entering or leaving the province. Absconding on foot through the desert beyond the floodplain was not feasible either, especially with his lame leg that made it difficult to walk for any distance or length of time. He thought of hiding in one of the temples where he could wait until nightfall, but dismissed the idea before long since he would only be trapping himself inside.

Ankhtifi had seen the Theban soldiers searching the perimeter of the temple complex, and had left the area promptly to avoid being caught. Although he did not recognize Khu and his men when they had neared the Temple of Anubis, he instinctively knew they were enemies. And he slunk away to avoid them.

The lupine warrior had shrunk over the years since his leg injury. It was mostly due to the stoop in his posture which he had acquired from his awkward gait. He was eerily calm despite his circumstances, and believed he would escape easily as he had always gotten away with things in the past. But he blamed others for his own failures, including Khety who had only made him lose his settlement in Nekhen after the revolt in Abdju. While supporting Khety had made him prosperous over the years, it had eventually led to the forfeiture of his settlement.

Ankhtifi kept to the shadows by the mud-brick buildings as he hobbled through the town. He moved slowly, scanning the streets with his dark eyes, and ducking out of sight whenever he heard or saw someone coming his way. After exploring his limited options, an idea began to take shape in his mind. If he could not escape through obvious means, he would do so another way. Sometimes hiding in plain sight is the best way to elude capture. He knew he was smarter than everyone else, and he knew how to manipulate even the direst circumstances to his best advantage. So he glanced behind him once again, drawing his cloak over his head, as he skulked through the streets in silence.

It was toward the end of the fighting that Mentuhotep and Khety finally came face-to-face.

The sun-god Re had already journeyed halfway across the sky in his Mandjet solar boat, from where he watched Khety's entire fleet burn to ashes before being swallowed up by the Nile as it sank beneath its murky surface. The great smoke cloud smeared across the clear sky, drifting south as the winds scattered the dark fumes over the river.

Little damage was done to the town in the swiftness of the battle, and most of its buildings were left untouched. Even Anubis remained seated over the pylon's entrance, where he continued to gaze out over the grounds that had been witness to the fighting. The jackal-god of the dead watched in silence, his expression unreadable, as the enemy's soldiers were apprehended and led away, including the temple priests who had remained sequestered within their mud-brick homes during much of the fighting. They too were led away with their heads bowed under the linen cloaks they had drawn protectively about themselves.

King Khety ran into Mentuhotep in an open area that had been used as a marketplace previously. It was deserted now. Empty tables and overturned reed baskets lying on the dirt ground are all that remained in the forgotten stalls.

Mentuhotep was with a group of his men, while Khety was alone with only two soldiers who had stayed faithfully by his side. Everyone else had been killed, wounded, or captured in battle or when they had tried to flee.

The two monarchs said nothing at first. They stopped and stared at each other silently, as one appraises a foe for his strengths and weaknesses. The air was charged with a current of apprehension, as though the very gods themselves were watching the events unfold.

Khety's shaven head was bare, and he was armed with only a dagger. Although he was cut and bruised with minor injuries and lacerations, and his kilt was torn, dirty and stained with blood, his bearing was as regal as always.

Mentuhotep wore his blue war crown over his shaven head, and had an aura of authority radiating from him. The difference in their ages was made more obvious now that the two rulers stood several paces across from each other. The strain of the last decade had taken its toll on Khety, and he looked worn and tired. But he remained poised like an aged lion whose glorious mane has thinned and faded with time. An aged lion facing a younger foe in his prime, during a territorial claim.

"So it has come to this," Khety finally spoke after he neared Mentuhotep's group. He took a deep breath and let it out slowly through his nose.

Mentuhotep just watched the Nen-nesian king, his expression guarded. Even now Khety still possessed an undeniable aura that commanded respect, and Mentuhotep could not help feeling momentarily awed by his presence.

"You are a formidable adversary," Khety said, a note of admiration in his tone.

A moment of silence passed between them before Mentuhotep cautiously acknowledged, "As are you."

Mentuhotep's men were restless and watchful as they stood near their regent. The encounter left them tense, and they stared at the northern king with a kind of uneasy regard.

A hawk screeched from somewhere high above the province, and Khety glanced thoughtfully at the sky. He closed his eyes briefly before looking at Mentuhotep once again. There was a look of determination in his piercing gaze, as though he had arrived at a decision.

"Do not harm them," Khety said about the two men at his side.

No one replied as his men looked at him in confusion, frowning as they glanced around uncertainly, wondering why their sovereign would say such a thing. They tightened the grips on their weapons, as they stood tense and alert to the danger they faced.

Khety had done his best to ward off all the attacks up until now. He had fought long and hard to protect his troops and defeat the men who attacked them. He had witnessed many of his men die, including a man who was killed by one of Mentuhotep's warriors only moments earlier before entering the abandoned marketplace, as they fought on the dirt roads that were now stained with blood.

"Wait," Mentuhotep raised a hand for his men to stop as two of them made to approach the Nen-nesian king. He watched Khety with a kind of suspicion mingled with a grudging respect. And although he couldn't help his feelings of curiosity, wariness and awe, he knew that the Seven Hathors sided with him rather than the northern ruler, and he knew that it was time for the Prophecy of Neferti to be fulfilled. "What do you mean?" Mentuhotep asked, narrowing his eyes.

"Let them go," Khety said in a calm yet authoritative tone. He glanced at his two men who were looking perplexed and anxious. "There is no need to slay them. They are good and loyal men, and will serve you well." He ordered the two men at his side to put down their weapons and surrender.

One of them looked at the other in confusion, unwilling to leave Khety's side. He opened his mouth, but then said nothing, closing it again and swallowing hard. After a moment's hesitation he squared his shoulders and nodded, as he resigned himself to Khety's intentions. Then both men bowed solemnly to their regent one last time before leaving his side. They gave themselves up to Mentuhotep's men, and were treated respectfully for surrendering with courage.

Khety remained standing with his dagger in hand. A strange calm befell him as he waited for Mentuhotep to speak. He had been a deeply superstitious man long ago, and believed that this moment was a fitting end to the wretched life he had been dealt. A life of heartache, pain, and misery.

He thought of his father who had died in his own bed in what seemed like so many lifetimes ago. His father had been surrounded by loved ones.

He was surrounded by enemies.

He thought of his first two wives who had died many years ago, when he was a young ruler. He thought of his third and dearest wife Shani who had been snatched from him by death, and the terrible grief over the loss of their precious children.

He was no stranger to death. No stranger to the profound ache, misery and loneliness it bequeathed upon survivors. Death had followed him like a dark shadow throughout his cursed life, and the pain and sorrow it inflicted had hardened his heart.

But at this moment that changed a little.

Something softened within him. Something inside him yielded so that he felt no resistance to his fate.

"The Seven Hathors have been kind to you," Khety said, his gray eyes glittering in the light of the sun. "You know this, do you not?"

"Yes," Mentuhotep said.

"You are like your father," Khety continued, remembering King Intef III whom he had met with so many years before when they had forged a transitory peace. "Even as a young boy in your father's court," Khety nodded as he stared at the memory from long ago, "you were like him. Even then."

Mentuhotep said nothing. He was surprised that Khety had noticed him at all at that time, and was somehow touched by his archenemy's words. He regarded him quietly with a kind of sympathetic admiration.

"You are courageous," Mentuhotep told the northern king.

"Then send me to the Field of Reeds," Khety spoke softly, "where my loved ones await."

Before Mentuhotep could say anything, Khety advanced swiftly, raising his dagger high, its blade flashing in the sun. Several of Mentuhotep's men made to step forward and defend the Theban king against Khety, but Mentuhotep shouted, "NO!"

There was no real threat in Khety's attack. No true danger in the assault. It was just a ruse to get Mentuhotep to do what he had to do. Khety admired Mentuhotep despite his own ambitions for the Theban throne. And

274

at that moment, all the hate within him dissolved. All resistance to fate and its cruel twists and turns vanished, as he let go of the last traces of pride that made him cling with a fierce tenacity to this strange, fleeting life. He knew the battle had been lost. He knew it after Mentuhotep's men had broken through the blockade, rushed into the harbor, and flooded the streets of the town. And he had fought all the harder for it. But that did not matter now. Only universal order as dictated by the principles of *maat* mattered now, despite the apparent unfairness of it all. And as Khety neared the Theban king, opening himself to Mentuhotep's assault, Mentuhotep thrust with a quick uppercut strike, burying his own dagger in Khety's belly.

Khety dropped his dagger, sinking to his knees as he gripped the hilt of Mentuhotep's weapon. He pulled it out from his body, then fell to his side and rolled onto his back. He was perspiring heavily, and he grit his teeth from the pain as his wound bled freely onto the ground. His breathing was labored and quickly grew shallow as he tried to catch his breath. His abdominal aorta had been severed, and he only had moments to live.

Mentuhotep knelt down by Khety's side. He felt a combination of deep relief and a strange sadness for the fallen king; a strange, profound sadness for the ruler who had lost everything but what was left of his honor. It could have been *him*, Mentuhotep thought for an instant, but then thanked the gods that it wasn't.

"Go to the Field of Reeds," he told the dying man as he took one of Khety's hands into his own. He reached for Khety's dagger, placed Khety's hands over its hilt, and let it rest upon his chest respectfully, so that he would die with honor. "Go to your family."

Khety nodded and closed his eyes for the last time.

King Wakhare Khety III, from the lineage of Akhtoy, Ruler of Lower Egypt, was dead.

Zawty was finally captured and secured shortly after that. Word of Khety's death spread over the settlement like the winds of a sandstorm, and any last traces of rebellion were quickly snuffed out. Many of the surviving forces who had supported the Nen-nesian ruler surrendered, begging for mercy, and pledging their loyalty to Mentuhotep. Women and children of the settlement, who had remained hidden within their mud-brick homes throughout the fighting, were placed under guard of the Theban-controlled province for their own protection. Prisoners of war were bound and restrained, while the enemy's dead were scattered in the desert for the wild animals to ravage. Their right hands had been severed before their corpses were heaped on the parched ground to keep a careful accounting of their numbers, and to take their strength from them in the Afterlife—strength that would be useless to them in the Slaughtering Place.

The Theban king was sitting on a raised platform in an expansive outside court which was customarily used to accommodate the large number of people attending the annual festivals, ceremonial feasts, and ritual celebrations held in the province. He was passing judgment on the prisoners assembled there, condemning some to die, and flogging or beating others. Those who were not executed or punished for any form of gross misconduct, would later be assimilated into his army, before which they would undergo rigorous training to prove their loyalty and worth.

Khu was not with Mentuhotep, but was on his way to join his father with a group of his own men. He had seen Khety's lifeless body for himself, where the northern ruler had been laid before he would be properly embalmed and buried as his rank and station befitted, thanks to Mentuhotep's benevolence and compassion towards his former enemy.

It was not until Khu neared the court where his father was occupied that the sense of alarm returned. He slowed his steps as the feeling awakened his primordial instincts.

"What is it?" one of his men asked him.

But Khu shook his head and did not reply. They turned a corner and then walked down another street before it opened up into the large court where Mentuhotep was seated. Qeb and Nakhti were by the king's side, along with a handful of advisors and generals. Nakhti looked very pleased, and had a new scar to show for his fighting. It was a shallow cut that ran the length of a hand, on the upper right portion of his chest. His injured friend was receiving the medical care he needed, and the prospects for surviving his wounds were good.

"Brother!" he called out above the noise, but Khu did not hear him. Every one of his senses was on alert for the danger in their midst.

The king had just pardoned some men when Khu neared the platform at the court's center. Khu swept his gaze over the many men gathered in various clusters around the court, until his eyes came to rest on a group of priests standing off to one side. They were dressed in their simple linen garments worn for daily, non-ceremonial work in the temples, with little difference between them and the other men, including the soldiers gathered about. And while many of the soldiers wore their hair cropped in regimental fashion, the higher ranking officers and officials shaved their heads like the temple priests. The most distinguishing difference between the priests and the rest of the men was their cloaks, which the priests had drawn over their shaven heads.

But there was something strange about one of the men.

From outward appearances he looked no different than the others, drawing no attention to himself as he blended seamlessly with the group. No one even glanced his way as he stood quietly among the cloaked men, his posture stooped and his head bowed and covered. Nevertheless,

Khu sensed a wickedness radiating from him like the heat of the desert, and he recognized him at once.

It was Ankhtifi.

The cunning reprobate had disguised himself as one of the temple priests. He had carefully hidden his features so that he would not be recognized by anyone. With all the fighting and chaos, the other priests had been too afraid for themselves—too wrapped up in their own fear—to even notice him. No one had noticed him.

Ankhtifi might easily have gotten away with the ruse if it had not been for Khu. He might have easily escaped attention and eluded capture for good. But Khu saw through the disguise plainly enough. And he saw into Ankhtifi's blackened soul, as though the stench of all his deeds rose like fetid vapors from an unembalmed corpse.

Khu froze for an uncertain moment as his eyes landed on Ankhtifi's form. Although Ankhtifi had aged since he last saw him, the savage within him remained as feral and calloused as ever. But Khu had grown in the ensuing years, and he was stronger than his blood enemy.

Khu glanced at the guards stationed all around the courtyard who were oblivious of the threat, and they seemed relaxed now that the apparent danger was behind them. Ankhtifi's hands were tied in front of him, though the bindings were loose. He and the priests had not posed any real threat to Mentuhotep's army, so he was left alone.

Ankhtifi wasn't worried. He knew that no one recognized him as he waited with the other priests. He remained very calm knowing he had no choice but to be patient for now. He was a very patient man after all. Cold, calculating and composed. He was biding his time to make an escape after nightfall.

"Ankhtifi is here," Khu finally whispered in Mentuhotep's ear, after reaching the platform where the king was seated.

Mentuhotep frowned. He had not given any thought to Ankhtifi since Khety's death. He had simply assumed that the former chieftain of Nekhen was dead as well.

"Where?" the king asked.

Khu gave a slight nod to where Ankhtifi was standing on one side of the court.

"One of the priests."

At that moment the vicious killer raised his eyes, locking gazes with Khu. He pulled off the loose bonds from his wrists and snatched a dagger that had been strapped to his thigh, hidden beneath his kilt. He grabbed one of the priests, locking his arm around the startled man's neck, and dragging him backwards as he stepped away with the dagger poised at the helpless man's throat.

Ankhtifi was edging farther away from the court with no intention of letting his hostage free. His eyes grew wild when he saw that he had been discovered, and he panicked in his rage. His plan had been foolproof. It had been going so well, and he was certain he would have gotten away with it all, until now. His eerily calm composure had snapped, and he darted furtive glances about him, looking as though he were about to pounce and kill anyone hindering his path.

Mentuhotep stood up at once, the blue war crown still on his head. "Seize him!" he shouted, pointing to Ankhtifi while stepping down from the platform.

Two guards immediately moved to grab Ankhtifi but he kicked them away, using the priest as a shield.

Khu ran across the courtyard and tackled Ankhtifi just before the wolf-man would have slit the priest's throat.

Ankhtifi dropped his dagger, and it fell to the ground before another guard kicked it away. When Khu saw that Ankhtifi was no longer armed, he left his own dagger sheathed by his thigh. Then he punched Ankhtifi hard, squarely in the face, breaking his long nose, and the priest scrambled away free.

"That's for my father," Khu said before Ankhtifi fell and rolled on the ground.

Ankhtifi scowled, wiping the blood from his nose with the back of his hand. He had no idea what Khu was talking about, nor did he care. His plans had been thwarted, and he was enraged. He was crouched on the ground with his black eyes fixed on Khu.

"No, not yet!" Mentuhotep shouted, raising a hand to stop some men who were readying to help Khu by attacking Ankhtifi. "Let them fight."

Mentuhotep was well aware of Ankhtifi's many crimes, especially of the massacring of Khu's family and entire village so many years before. Every time he looked at his son and saw the jagged scar on his head he was reminded of the monster that almost took Khu's life.

"Do not interfere. Let them be," the king ordered again.

He wanted Khu to avenge the deaths of his family. He wanted vengeance for his beloved son. And although the retribution could never right the wrongs of the past, nor bring back the loved ones he had lost, it would be a reckoning of all Ankhtifi's deeds according to the divine principles of *maat*, so that the serving of justice would last for all eternity in the inextinguishable Lake of Fire that waited in the Slaughtering Place.

The Theban king furrowed his brow and set his jaw as he ascended the platform once more, so that nothing would block the view of his son, and of his son's mortal enemy.

The army crowding the courtyard closed in, forming a circle around the two fighting men. They watched with eyes riveted to the scene, murmuring nervously amongst themselves.

Mentuhotep knew that fortune favored his son, and that Khu needed to face and defeat this demon by himself once and for all.

Khu gripped Ankhtifi by the shoulders, lifting him up to his feet, before thrusting his knee into the man's groin. "That's for my mother and my little sister," he hissed.

Ankhtifi doubled over, wheezing from the assault.

Khu paced around him, giving Ankhtifi a moment to catch his breath. But in an unexpected instant, Ankhtifi lunged for the dagger belonging to one of the men standing nearby. He pulled it from its sheath, and then whipped back around on Khu. And as he sprung toward Khu with the blade, Khu parried and snatched the weapon away, gripping Ankhtifi's arm and breaking it with a brutal twist, before ramming the blade in his belly, just above the groin.

Ankhtifi's mouth twisted into a rictus of savagery, camouflaging his pain beneath a fiendish mask. But his black eyes showed nothing. No emotion, no remorse, no life in their fathomless depths that reached as two pits into an abyss.

As the wolf-man sank to the ground, Khu ripped the blade upwards, slitting his belly as he whispered, "And that's for every innocent life you ever took," his gold eyes were shining brightly. "Burn in the slayers' cauldrons," he added just before Ankhtifi died, "burn in the Slaughtering Place."

An execration ritual was performed on the spot where Ankhtifi had died, and where his blood pooled on the ground at the court. It was a spell recited to ensure the eternal damnation of his blackened soul, and to keep the evil that had possessed him from defiling anything else.

A scribe was commissioned to write Ankhtifi's name on a clay bowl before it was placed in the congealing blood drawing flies over the ground where it had spilled. Then three priests recited the incantation from an ancient text to condemn Ankhtifi's *ka* spirit to the Slaughtering Place. It invoked the help of Anubis himself to see that the weighing of Ankhtifi's heart would prove him unworthy beyond any doubt, so that Osiris could pass the final judgment upon him before he plummeted into the jaws of the crocodile-headed, soul-eating demon Ammit. From there he would be led into the Temple of Anguish and Despair where the demon Apep ruled, torturing wicked souls in all their senses for eternity.

After the powerful spell had been cast, the blood-stained clay bowl was smashed into tiny bits, and the whole lot of it—including the sand that had been sullied by Ankhtifi's blood—was spat upon three times and then thrown into a blazing fire, the ashes of which were buried in the desert. Incense was then burned over the court to ward away evil and to cleanse the very air from iniquity. It was a solemn moment as many of Mentuhotep's men gathered in the large, open space. A moment filled with relief for the battle that had been won, and with cautious optimism for what it all meant for their revered monarch.

Khu was not present at the execration ritual, and had left the court as preparations were undertaken to cast the powerful spell. The sun-god Re was beginning his fiery descent into the realm of the shadows, igniting the sky in shades of red and gold, and its beauty filled Khu with a certain nostalgia. While he would never have traded the life he had led for the one which might have been—if the Seven Hathors had decreed differently—he still felt an ache for the family he once had. Nevertheless, he was hopeful for the future of his father's kingdom, and relieved that some of the evil plaguing the land had been purged through the death of his mortal enemy.

Khu slipped quietly away from the court to the lavish home of an official where Khety had been staying in the town, and he found the Deshret Red Crown of Lower Egypt that had belonged to the northern king. Although the formal coronation ceremony and feast would be held much later in Thebes, after the remaining northern settlements had been rightly secured under Mentuhotep's control, and after most of the bureaucratic matters and final arrangements regarding the unification of the kingdoms had been settled, Khu wanted to honor his father for the great victory he had won. So he got the Deshret Red Crown and returned to the court carrying it in his hands.

Men drew back to part a way for Khu's path as he walked to where his father was seated. Qeb saw Khu first, and nodded his acknowledgement and approval, as he stepped down from Mentuhotep's side to join Khu. Then Nakhti joined his brother as well, and all three of them stood before the king. An expectant hush fell over the large gathering; a hush charged with excitement and triumph. It was the moment all had been waiting for with great eagerness; the moment Mentuhotep himself had dreamed about since he was a small child.

"Hail to you, Lord of the White Crown, Ruler of Upper Egypt," Khu said in a loud and clear voice.

"HAIL LORD KING," shouted the men in reply, "LORD OF THE WHITE CROWN, RULER OF UPPER EGYPT."

Mentuhotep's face was solemn and dignified. The emotions within him were evident, but his bearing was regal.

"Hail to you, He Who Gives Heart to the Two Lands," Khu continued.

"HAIL LORD KING," the men echoed, "HE WHO GIVES HEART TO THE TWO LANDS."

Khu ascended the platform where Mentuhotep was seated, and he gently removed the blue war crown from his father's shaven head, and handed it to Nakhti. Qeb gave him the Hedjet White Crown of Upper Egypt, and Khu placed it reverently on Mentuhotep's head, followed by the Deshret Red Crown of Lower Egypt, so that it formed the *Pschent* Double Crown symbolizing the unification of the kingdoms. Then Khu stepped back down between Qeb and Nakhti, and everyone present got down on their knees and bowed low to the ground before the king.

"Hail to you, King of Egypt, Unifier of the Two Lands!" Khu shouted.

"HAIL KING OF EGYPT," the men thundered, "UNIFER OF THE TWO LANDS. HAIL!"

And the men howled their joy and exhilaration, cheering wildly as they had never done before, for their elation was too great to contain. One by one, they each proclaimed their loyalty to King Nebhepetre Mentuhotep

II, prostrating themselves once again before their brave monarch who had led them to victory. The mood was euphoric, for the great rift that had divided the kingdoms for so long, had finally been closed. The division that had long afflicted the lands had been mended and made whole.

Egypt was finally united.

A new era of peace and prosperity had begun.

HISTORICAL NOTE

K ing Nebhepetre Mentuhotep II of the Eleventh Dynasty is credited with having reunified the divided kingdoms of Upper and Lower Egypt at the end of the First Intermediate Period, giving rise to the Middle Kingdom, of which he is the first ruler. Although the exact dates of his reign have been debated by historians, he had a long and prosperous rule of about fifty years from around 2050 BC to 2000 BC.

While the early part of King Mentuhotep's reign was peaceful, that changed about the fourteenth year of his rule, for the First Intermediate Period was a time of much civil disorder and political unrest during which the split powers of the north and south competed for dynastic dominance of Egypt. Famine and hardship were rampant, as were raids from domestic and foreign nomads.

Mentuhotep led numerous military campaigns to crush opposition from northern-led revolts, and from Kush. Two momentous events in Mentuhotep's military history were his success in quashing a revolt in Abdju, and in surmounting a blockade in Zawty, after which he succeeded in overcoming remaining hostile forces on a path which ultimately led to the reunification of the divided lands.

Once Mentuhotep had control of the Upper and Lower Kingdoms of Egypt, he further expanded Egypt's territories through additional military conquests in Kush. He also conducted foreign trade by land and sea, as far as the Phoenician coast and the Land of Punt, while organizing numerous mining expeditions. Mentuhotep strengthened the kingdom through numerous repairs to irrigation systems including canals, dykes, and catch basins, so that the Nile's floodwaters could be harnessed and utilized efficiently, thus ending the widespread famine which had plagued the people before. He also undertook the restoration of many temples that had been left in ruin, particularly those in Abdju, Dendera, Swentet and Tod.

The Theban ruler had several wives and lesser consorts including his chief wife Tem, Neferu, and Henhenet who is believed to have died in childbirth, and he was succeeded to the throne by his son Sankhkare Mentuhotep III. He possessed numerous titles including *Lord of the White Crown*, *Ruler of Upper Egypt*, *He Who Gives Heart to the Two Lands*, and finally *Unifier of the Two Lands*, after having reunited the kingdoms.

Mentuhotep's grand mortuary temple complex in the western desert across from Thebes at Deir el-Bahari now lay in ruins. But one can almost imagine its magnificent splendor when it was first built with ascending terraces, sandstone colonnades, pillared halls, tree-lined courts with shimmering pools, and a pyramid and temple that included a ramp, gallery, peristyle court, chapel, and a hypostyle hall with corridors and chambers hewn right into the rocky limestone cliffs that gleam brilliantly under the desert sun. The walls were decorated with hieroglyphic texts and numerous battle scenes which were fought in reuniting the kingdoms. The valley of Deir el-Bahari was called *Djeseret* meaning "Holy Place" by the ancient Egyptians, for here was the gateway leading to the Afterlife.

Two photographic reproductions of the best preserved remnants of what is left of Mentuhotep's extensively damaged funerary temple at Deir el-Bahari are included at the end of this book. The first one is a painted limestone relief fragment depicting Mentuhotep wearing Upper Egypt's conical Hedjet White Crown. The second is the massive seated sandstone statue of the king looking regal and dignified, wearing the white Heb-Sed dress, the Deshret Red Crown of Lower Egypt, and the false beard of Osiris.

The Prophesy of Neferti dates back to the fourth dynasty of the Old Kingdom. It foretold a time of chaos and the breakdown of the power structure of Egypt, and how a king would rise from the southern lands in Upper Egypt to subdue and slay enemies, rebels and traitors. He would then reestablish unity and order by rejoining the lands and wearing both the White and Red Crowns of Upper and Lower Egypt. The author has taken creative license by embellishing the Prophesy of Neferti with Khu's role as the golden-eyed boy who would assist Mentuhotep in reunifying the lands, and by naming King Mentuhotep II as the king foretold in the prophesy.

Excavations near Mentuhotep's mortuary temple at Deir el-Bahari have unearthed the tombs of noblemen and princes, as well as a mass grave of about sixty soldiers who died in battle, an indication that the men were highly respected, and the battles they fought were significant. Included among the graves, at least one tomb was discovered of a particularly revered warrior-prince whose tomb was very close to Mentuhotep's tomb, and who was buried with weapons and Egyptian soldier clay models. And while Khu's character in this tale is entirely fictional, having sprung from some obscure region in the imagination of the author, whose own ancestors hail from the ever-mysterious and fascinating land of Egypt, the author would like to believe that the prince in the tomb could well have been someone like our beloved Khu: whose quiet strength, courage, and intriguing gift helped his king to claim a resounding victory.

King Nebhepetre Mentuhotep II

Wall relief fragment depicting King Nebhepetre Mentuhotep II with hieroglyphics taken from his mortuary temple at Deir el-Bahari

Eleventh Dynasty, c. 2020 BC
painted limestone

King Nebhepetre Mentuhotep II

Massive seated statue of the king found in his mortuary
temple at Deir el-Bahari

Eleventh Dynasty, c. 2020 BC
painted sandstone
(face and body were painted black after Anubis,
god of the dead)

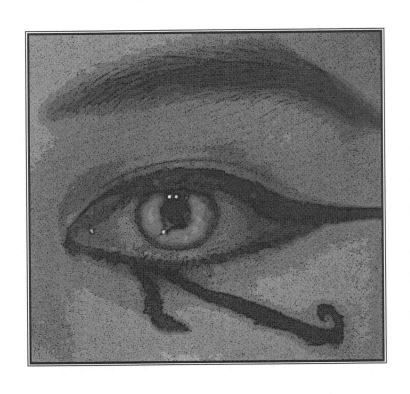

37674500R00164

Made in the USA
Lexington, KY
10 December 2014